The Wing
A Romance of the New Age

The Wing
A Romance of the New Age

by
Jean Richepin

translated, annotated and introduced by
Brian Stableford

A Black Coat Press Book

ISBN 978-1-61227-053-1. First Printing. November 2011. Published by Black Coat Press, an imprint of Hollywood Comics.com, LLC, P.O. Box 17270, Encino, CA 91416. All rights reserved.

Introduction

L'Aile, roman des temps nouveaux, here translated as *The Wing: A Romance of the New Age*, was first published in Paris by Pierre Lafitte in 1911. It was the last novel written by Jean Richepin, who was better known as a poet and lyricist, and then as a dramatist, and then as a short story writer, his novels generally being held to be the least impressive sector of his *oeuvre*. *L'Aile* was published more than ten years after his previous novel, so it may be regarded as an exceptional break from an abandonment that otherwise extended over a quarter of a century—the final third of his life, Given that circumstance, it perhaps is not surprising that that *L'Aile* is a very eccentric book, even by the standards of a markedly eccentric writer—but that is more of a recommendation than a defect nowadays, and the text warrants more interested attention than it received at the time.

In particular, *L'Aile* can now be seen as a significant text in the history of French scientific romance, being one of several—but perhaps surprisingly few—immediate literary responses to a uniquely exciting moment in the history of science and technology, which embraced the development of wireless telegraphy, the discovery of radioactivity and the first adventures in aviation, the heady combination of which was, indeed, suggestive of the dawning of a "new age." *L'Aile* cannot count as a well-informed response to those developments, Richepin having little understanding of science, but the quality of his naivety in struggling to comprehend the essence of the theoretical and technological revolution opens an interesting window into the general consciousness of the era.

The author of *L'Aile*, Jean Richepin was born in Medea (now Lemdiyya) in Algeria in 1849. He was the son of a military surgeon, and lived a somewhat peripatetic existence in his early years, before the family settled in northern France, where

Richepin went to school at Douai before going to Paris in 1868 to study at the École Normale Supérieure. According to the accounts he gave when he became an habitué of the "Bohemian" cafés of Montmartre, he had been a brilliant student who graduated from the École in 1870 with flying colors, but with a severe dose of disenchantment; other accounts suggested that he left without taking a degree. Either way, he made no attempt to obtain the teaching post for which students at the college generally aimed, and later claimed to have embarked on a career of adventure instead, serving with distinction during the Franco-Prussian War as a sharpshooter.

Although not directly involved in the Paris Commune, Richepin appears to have been infected with revolutionary ideas at around that time by the Communard propagandist Jules Vallès, of whom he subsequently wrote a biography. He left Paris shortly thereafter, but not to return home; he seems to have split permanently with his parents, who were then living in Nancy. When he reappeared in Montmartre again in the mid-1870s, where he rapidly became well-known for his flamboyant style of dress and behavior—he evidently cut a fine figure, being tall and robust, with a bushy black beard—he explained that he had been wandering and adventuring in the interim, having gone to sea for a while and, more crucially, having undertaken a kind of pilgrimage in search of his roots by traveling with a band of Romani to Italy.

The latter claim reflects the fact that Richepin, unlike most of the *poseurs* in Montmartre, was not content to have a colorful personal history, however exaggerated; always determined to go the extra mile, he wanted a colorful prehistory too. In his reckoning, he was a descendant of a nomadic tribe that had arrived in Gaul in pre-Roman times from Central Asia (the Romani, who probably came from northern India, did not reach France until the 15th century), and the atavistic echoes of that distant ancestry were still rumbling away within him, unconsciously at least. He sometimes referred to the hypothetical tribe in question as "Turanian"—a term borrowed from contemporary anthropology, referring to hypothetical ancestors of the Turks—but he referred to their French offshoot as "Thiérachian."

Geographically, Thiérache is a region in the foothills of the Ardennes massif overlapping the border between France and Belgium. Like most of the one-independent provinces gradually gathered into the nation of France, it still retained its own dialect and culture in the late 19th century. How much time Richepin spent there, and to what extent his ancestry was really rooted there, are unclear, while the notion that it had been invaded 2000 years earlier by mysterious nomads from Central Asia is almost certainly false—but the myth became a significant element of Richepin's self-representation, and it had a powerful effect on the sympathies and loyalties expressed in his literary work. No more needs to be said about the detail of the fantasy here, because it is described and developed in considerable detail in the text of *L'Aile*—which is, in a sense, its ultimate elaboration.

Although he was acquainted with the literary club known as the Hydropathes, and frequented *Le Chat Noir*, which eventually became their base—where he made a contribution to the retrospectively-famous *Album Zutique* put together by the café's regulars—Richepin was never really seen as a member of the club. Indeed, Frédéric Champsaur once remarked that Richepin was the club's most important precursor and inspiration, far too important to be merely one of its crowd, although Champsaur was probably being a trifle sarcastic. Richepin certainly wanted to remain distinct from any group, having the same mania for standing out from the crowd as his principal literary idols, Charles Baudelaire and Petrus Borel, *alias* "the werewolf." Thus, although Richepin developed his writing career in the context of a perceived contrast between the Decadent/Symbolist Movement on the one hand and Naturalism on the other, he made every effort never to belong to either camp, but to plough his own furrow. He could not avoid being categorized as a latter-day Romantic, but he never wanted to be *a* Romantic—he wanted to be *the* Romantic, taking over where Victor Hugo eventually let off as a literary helmsman.

Few people acquainted with Richepin or his work ever thought that he came anywhere near to living up to his own self-billing, but he certainly tried, and he got off to a flying start when his first collection of poems, *La Chanson des gueux* [The Song of the Vagabonds] (1876) was successfully prosecuted for obscenity, just as Baudelaire's *Les Fleurs du mal* had been two decades earlier—a punitive oppression that gleaned angry protests from Victor Hugo and Gustave Flaubert, among others. The gain in notoriety was, however, balanced out by the financial penalty of a heavy fine of 500 francs, on top of a month's imprisonment, which left Richepin in dire straits for some while.

The censored passages of *La Chanson des gueux* were not to be restored to the affected poems until 1964, long after Richepin's death in 1926. Not unnaturally, however, the author's reaction to their excision was resentfully combative, and the themes and language of his poetry became increasingly extreme in the years that followed, from the erotically-charged *Les Caresses* [Caresses] (1877) to the aptly titled *Les Blasphèmes* [Blasphemies] (1884). Having reached that offensive apex, however, he had little alternative but to retreat to deeper and more thoughtful consideration of his concerns. *La Mer* [The Sea] (1886) is by no means as nostalgic as many collections on that theme, but is mild by Richepin's standards. He gave freer vent to his bile, however, in *Mes Paradis* [My Paradises] (1895), and took his celebration of the life of contemporary nomads further in *La Bombarde* [The Bombard] (1899).

Richepin published his first short story collection, the provocatively-titled *Les Morts bizarres* [Bizarre Deaths] in 1877, and his first novel, *Madame André* in 1878, although he had a much greater success in 1881 with a second novel based on one of his poems, *La Glu* [Birdlime—here used metaphorically to refer to the adhesive capacity of a *femme fatale*]. The longer version of *La Glu* was adapted for the stage in 1883, further adapted as an opera, with music by Gabriel Dupont, in 1910, and it was filmed several times, while the poem was adapted as a song by more than one composer—one of many of Richepin's verses to be so adapted (including, of course, "La Chanson des gueux"). He liked singing them himself, often regaling the clients of *Le Chat Noir* with them, and many still survive on CD in versions by Eric Mie, Remo Gary and others.

Richepin's short fiction tended to the Decadent, especially his *contes cruels*; those in *Les Morts bizarres* include the delightfully extreme "La Machine à métaphysique"[1], but the later ones in *Cauchemars* [Nightmares] (1892) are mostly sharper, and those in *Contes de la décadence romaine* [Tales of the Roman Decadence] (1898) more colorful. Although *La Glu* has a cruel thrust too, its novelistic method had more in common with the psychologically-analytical "neo-Naturalism" that Richepin's friend Paul Bourget practiced with great success, and Richepin retained that interest in psychological analysis through all his novels, even when they dealt with such exotic subject-matter as that featured in the gypsy romance *Miarka, la fille de l'ourse* [Miarka, the She-Bear's Daughter] (1883).

Perhaps inevitably, Richepin's interest in contemporary psychological science was always subject to a marked temptation toward the offbeat and the unorthodox—as is very obvious in *L'Aile*. The effects of that temptation on his treatment of his various themes meant that the novels that found the most immediately sympathetic reaction from critics and the public alike were those in which it was muted—as, for instance, in *Braves gens* [Brave Men] (1886), a quasi-autobiographical account of Bohemian life in Paris. From a modern viewpoint, however—especially that of literary archeologists interested in the development of imaginative fiction, it is the more extraordinary effects that are the most interesting.

---

[1] Translated as "The Metaphysical Machine" in the Black Coat Press anthology *News from the Moon,* ISBN 978-1-932983-89-0.

It is safe to say that those effects were never more extraordinary than they are in *L'Aile*.

Although he had collaborated with the Hydropathe caricaturist André Gill on a dramatic piece in 1873 it was not until 1883 that Richepin's big breakthrough as a dramatist came, when the stage adaptation of *La Glu* was rapidly followed by *Nana-Sahib*, in which the central role was played by Sarah Bernhardt. When the actor playing opposite Bernhardt fell ill, Richepin insisted on taking over the role himself—to enormous public acclaim, at least in his version of the anecdote. Bernhardt did, however, pay him the immeasurable compliment of saying that he was "even odder and hammier than I am—that's why I love him." He continued to produce work for the stage in greater profusion than volumes of poetry or prose, some of it for musical accompaniment. His greatest popular success in the theater was *Le Chemineau* [The Vagabond, in a slightly less insulting sense than *gueux*, but not much] (1897), which was the first of his works to be adapted for the cinema, in 1906; three further versions followed. He did not take the central role in any of those films, but did appear as a screen actor along with Sarah Bernhardt in *Mères Françaises* [French Mothers] (1919), and played one of the key roles in the film version of *Miarka* (1920).

Richepin was a very prolific writer between 1880 and 1901—the two years in which the first and last of his numerous children were born—but he also found abundant time to travel, often subsidizing his excursions by giving lectures, and invariably reported on his travels in articles for the Parisian newspapers. After the turn of the century, however, he slowed down somewhat, in more ways than one. His fame had been primarily based on the violence of his themes and the colorfulness of his language, including his very extensive use of *argot*—not merely the popular *argot* of the Parisian streets but the *argots* of provincial peasants and nomadic gypsies. Over time, however, the effects of melodramatic inflation increased the popularity of violent themes, and many other writers began to use *argot* more freely, so the mere fact became less interesting—and other users of argot employed a careful restraint that allowed them to remain easily readable, whereas Richepin's multiform *argot* began to seem stubbornly esoteric. That tendency to difficulty was further increased by his frequently-convoluted syntax, his lavish use of metaphor, his often-bombastic rhetoric and a marked fondness for making up new words, often by means of twisting existing ones into new derivatives. The vitriolic quality of his writing eased, as his politics shifted from the extreme left toward the middle-ground, and that probably lost him the support of many of his admirers, while not winning many new ones, and certainly reduced his opportunities to indulge in critical diatribes.

Ironically enough, this relative decline in Richepin's reputation as a heroic rebel against authority and orthodoxy reached a kind of peak in 1909, when the great individualist not only took it into his head to put himself forward as a candidate for election to the Académie Française, but actually won (beating Edmond Haraucort and Henri de Régnier), and thus joined the literary Establishment in no uncertain terms— after which his views and opinions became evenly more conservative, especially during the Great War, when his name was often coupled with that of Maurice Barrès, whose "treason" against his earlier radical views was considered so extreme that he was the subject of a mock trial by the Dadaists. Richepin did not change his spots entirely—he continued to turn out such *contes cruels* as those in *Le Coin des fous: histoires horribles* [The Lunatic Asylum: Horrible Stories] (1921), which contains most of his other exercises in proto-science fiction— but he was a shadow of the determined outsider he had been in the 1870s by the time the war ended in 1918; the final poetry collection he published during his lifetime, *Interludes* (1923), tended far more toward nostalgic sentimentality than his early work.

Within this context, *L'Aile*'s publication-date—eleven years after his previous novel, *Lagibasse* (1900)—places it firmly in the "Academic" phase of the author's career, if only

11

in its early days, but it is not obvious that it really belongs there. Although the internal chronology of the novel is sufficiently evasive to be a trifle difficult to pin down, the best inference that can be taken from the clues it offers (as detailed in the footnotes) is that the "imminent future" in which it is set might be as early as 1904 and is unlikely to be any later than 1907—implying that it was at least begun, if perhaps not completed, before the fatal election. It is, in fact, possible that it had languished unpublished for several years, and that it was the author's elevation to the Académie that prompted the publisher to take a chance on it.

In any case, and however paradoxical the fact may seem in a "romance of the new age," *L'Aile* is a rather backward-looking book, in which a murky imaginary prehistory plays a much larger and better-defined part than the bright future that is perpetually promised by the narrative. Indeed, that future is subjected to an exercise in procrastination so determined and seemingly perverse as to make the book unique, not only in its insistence on avoiding its own plot—an avoidance that it eventually begins to celebrate boastfully—but in the torturing of tenses required by the artifice of consigning most of the narrative to a flashback and then refusing to move forward in time even when the text appears to have caught up with itself.

There might be several explanations for these eccentricities, more than one of which probably had a role to play. Richepin apparently made the narrative up as he went along, and does not appear to know, for long sections of the text, exactly where it is going; eventually, he seems to have abandoned any attempt at real progress and to have torn up whatever vague plan he had made before starting. This uncertainty is partly based in the circumstance that he had very little knowledge of and no understanding at all of contemporary science—a severe handicap when one is supposedly producing a psychological analysis of scientific genius and its potential results. Another, not unrelated, factor is his reluctance actually to bite the bullet and take his story beyond the tacit present into the hypothetical future into which the narrative is yearning hopelessly to leap.

By way of compensation, the problems that Richepin set himself did produce some literary effects that are interesting in their sheer perversity, and the story does provide considerable insight into his own eccentric psychology while it is treading water. The most remarkable aspect of that insight is perhaps to be found in the characterization of Blaise Yvernaux—surely one of the most bitterly unsympathetic partial self-portraits ever attempted by an author, astonishing on the part of one who never publicly lapsed into doubting his own genius, and who certainly produced far more real evidence of creative flair than the impotent Yvernaux. Equally interesting, however, is the characterization of Aunt Aline, a surpassingly strange hand of destiny gifted with highly idiosyncratic psychic powers.

Together with the ultra-disciplined but emotionally-challenged Thibaud Gasguin, those two characters form a highly distinctive triangle of influences around the heroine whose strange genius the narrative sets out to describe and analyze, instituting a unique literary geometry that maintains its fascination in spite of the occasional laboriousness of its development. As for the climactic scene, in which the heroine gathers the triangle around her for protection when fate insists on her reunion with the predestined hero of her personal narrative, suffice it to say that there is nothing else like it anywhere in the annals of literature, and that it definitely warrants reading, if only to gain a better appreciation of where the highly elastic limits of literary eccentricity lie.

It is worth noting that, as well as its own peculiar merits, *L'Aile* was not an uninfluential book, in that it very probably prompted Frédéric Champsaur—who had known Richepin since they used to hang out together in the cafés of Bohemia in general and *Le Chat Noir* in particular—to write his own account of an impending advent in aviation technology in *Les*

Ailes de l'homme,[2] which was written before August 1914 although not published until 1917, and then in a distorted form. Champsaur's novel, surely not by coincidence, sets out to do exactly what *L'Aile* conspicuously fails to do, in specifying the nature of the new aircraft and actually putting it into operation within the plot, while also providing a very different account of the supposedly essential, but evidently problematic, relationship between Eros and scientific creativity.

Before closing this introduction to the novel, it is appropriate to add a note about the title. In English, metaphorical, poetic and symbolic wings invariably come in pairs, just as real ones do, but in French that is not always the case, especially with reference to one oft-used poetic metaphor: *"l'aile du rêve"* [the wing of dream]. Many French readers encountering Richepin's novel would have mentally added the implicit *"du rêve"* to the title and read the text in that light—and they would not have been wrong to do so, even though the first chapter includes a tacit promise of a more literal wing, and the text eventually adds several further layers of complication to that initial double meaning.

This translation is taken from the version of the first edition reproduced on the Bibliothèque Nationale's *gallica* website. The translation was difficult, not merely because of the habitual convolution and extravagance of Richepin's literary style, but because of his extensive use of *argot*, particularly his use of an eye-dialect to represent "Thiérachian"—a language-variant for which, unlike Parisian *argot*, no dictionary is available. I have no idea how much of Richepin's "Thiérachian" phraseology would actually be recognizable in Thiérache, but I suspect that many contemporary French readers might have had difficulty in making sense of the *argot* in question had the author not included explanations of the more esoteric terms. In any case, some of what I have done in at-

---

[2] Translated in a Black Coat Press edition as *The Human Arrow*, ISBN 9781612270456.

tempting to represent that element of the text in translation is improvisation and guesswork. Where I was able to find English slang roughly equivalent to the text's *argot*, I have usually made a substitution, but some of the terms, including those most vital to the story, had to be left in the original, with appropriate footnoting where feasible. Some, but not all, of Richepin's neologisms could be straightforwardly transposed into equivalent English neologisms, but a few resisted easy translocation; again, I have added footnotes where I thought it necessary. Given the author's cavalier attitude to matters of scientific fact, I am sure that he would forgive me for any mistakes I have made in my improvisations; I hope that readers will do likewise.

Brian Stableford

THE WING

To Madame Francis de Croisset,
née Marie-Thérèse de Chevigné, in homage
to a very great and respectful affection,
I dedicate this new book.[3]
J.R.

---

[3] The Belgian playwright and librettist Francis de Croisset, born Franz Wiener, married Marie-Thérèse, the widow of the banking heir Maurice Bischoffsheim, in 1910.

I

"Yes, my lads, it's me, Père Yvernaux, who is telling you this! And not ironically, as a straight-faced joker, a boreal humorist—nor, as you might think, because, from time to time, I've drunk a good half-dozen too many, thanks to which, that supplementary drop of liquid activating my word-mill..."

But the speech was cut off in mid-sentence, its continuation shredded in advance by a fusillade of violent interruptions, which burst forth from all sides at once—cheerful rather than malicious, though, turning the matter into a joke, as was natural toward a loquacious sexagenarian drunkard in a gathering of young friends. There was a crossfire of:

"Enough! Enough! Shut him up!"

"To Hell with this palaver!"

"One last half in his beard!"

"And send the beard to bed!"

"To bed, Père Yvernaux!"

"Sit down, eternal Père."

And many other more-or-less witty interjections, before which the interrupted gentleman did, in fact, end up sitting down, he too gaily taking things with a broad smile, and even another half, with his nose in his glass and beer in his beard.

But what, then, had annoyed the brave and worthy Père Yvernaux, among his chosen companions, in that environment he liked so much, where he was understood and often even admired by all—and to some he was a sort of god? The true milieu, he said, required by a twentieth-century thinker.

Now, this thinker—and, until further notice, *the* thinker of the new century, as Père Yvernaux rated himself—was a failed doctor of philosophy, but a doctor of letters nevertheless, and was the doyen of the students, since, even now, he was attending Metchnikoff's lectures,[4] and had just, at the age of 62, registered for an open course. He was proud of that, moreover, and rightly so, glorying in still learning—and was singularly cherished because of his "discipular deanship," as he put it, in that special milieu for which he had such a strong affection.

In fact, the environment was exciting and impassioned, genuinely new and very much of the 20th century, of a kind that had been sought in vain for fifteen years, before the final years of the present millennium. It was, however, simply a brasserie in the Latin Quarter, nothing more, situated within the confines of the student realm on the frontier of Montrouge; and it seemed that an amalgam was in the process of taking place there between two worlds so long opposed, the bourgeoisie and the people.

Here, in fact, in the evening, *intellectuals* of the traditional sort—students, medical students, people of the legal fraternity and the fine arts, painters and apprentice writers—gathered and fraternized, communicating in amicable discussion with the *intellectuals* of today, almost of tomorrow: technologists, electricians, chemists, people from the Arts et Métiers, readers of vulgarized sciences and cut-price masterpieces. The latter were taking an interest in the others' old established "humanities", while the former, in return, were initiating themselves in the ardent hopes of the modern conquistadors of Nature.

Entering there by hazard, an habitué of the cafés that had flourished in the Boulevard du Montparnasse 25 years before, would not have relished, or perhaps even understood, the new conversations. The doyen of the students, the student in his fortieth year, perpetually rejuvenated by incessant study, Père Yvernaux, drunk on conversation as much as on beer, was on one of his favorite subjects: *the propeller of images and the triggering of ideas.*

---

[4] The Russian biologist Élie Metchnikoff, who joined the Pasteur Institute in 1888; he won the Nobel Prize in 1908.

It was with pleasure that they listened to him, and it was often profitable, even when he multiplied baroque images and the dance of his ideas became excessively jerky, turning into St. Vitus' Dance. Even when that happened, he still kept his listeners—or rather, followers—who never ceased taking his words as Gospel. And rarely, save for evenings of dead-drunkenness when he lapsed into nonsense, was silence imposed on him, as had just occurred.

This time, however, he was not in what he called the *displaced state*—meaning that of the total abolition of self—but still in the preceding phase of full and high excitement, which always abounded in paradoxes, original observations, lyrical outbursts and suggestive hypotheses. To be interrupted in that fashion, he must have uttered some blasphemy against the true faith that one of his priests had in him, and thus suddenly broken the charm that ordinarily bound his disciples to him.

That is what he had done. The "Yes, my lads, it's me who is telling you this" and so on had fallen into the silence of a general bewilderment, caused by the simple brief affirmation that he had proffered beforehand, in a dogmatic and imperious tone:

"The airplane was stillborn."

Now, a few days before, on the subject of a flight at an altitude on 2700 meters, he had taken flight himself, in one of his fine fits of enthusiasm, relative to the conquest of the air by twentieth-century humankind. And here he was today, without even having the excuse of the *displaced state*, burning what he had adored the day before, and burning it in that summary and scornful fashion, as if setting fire to a crumpled a piece of paper. Was it an aberration? Senility? Treason, perhaps? Two or three people thought so, secretly, without daring to say so. And doubtless they—for there were those who were envious of him—would have made some sharp remark if he had not been sitting there so feebly, with his nose in his glass and beer spilling into his beard.

Suddenly, all the sympathy reverted to him, with the patent evidence of his joke—excellent, in sum, since they had let themselves be taken in by it. One of his friends—an admirer devoid of respect—translated everyone's final sentiment by tapping him on the belly and treating him as a sublime fraud. To which Blaise Yvernaux—speaking almost to himself, without gaiety now, but, on the contrary, with a sad gravity—replied:

"What good would it do to explain? They don't understand. They're still in the twentieth century—as I was, forty-eight hours ago. But today, after what Geneviève said the day before yesterday, oh no, by no means! Finished, buried, their twentieth, my twentieth! I've leap-frogged them, and others, and I'm far away, far away, far way...at the antipodes, damn it!"

And he chewed a few shreds of phrases vaguer still, which he submerged beneath another half, the inarticulate words and the swallowed mouthfuls mingling in the glugs of a drowning man. That was his rational consciousness drowning, already plunged into the *displaced state*, advertising the total abolition of the voluntary self. After which, the poor fellow was no more than a limp and gentle drunkard, abandoning himself without resistance to the arms of two friends, faithful unto the future apoplectic fit, who were accustomed to carrying him home when he happened—once or twice a week—to surpass the measure of the *displaced state*.

These two venerated him even in that abdication of self, perhaps savoring what there was still to admire in him, claiming that the semi-darkness in question was particularly propitious to the most fulgurant flashes of his genius—for they found that in him.

It ought to be added that one was a Comtois,[5] with a mystical turn of mind, a former Fourierist well-acquainted with the occult sciences, and that the other was a Scandinavian steeped in Ibsen, Max Stirner and Nietzsche—and that each of them gladly contemplated Blaise Yvernaux's drunken visions through the prism of his own imagination, discerning therein

---

[5] i.e., a native of Franche-Comté, a province in eastern France.

symbols, figures and meanings with double or triple locks, to which he alone had the pass-key. In consequence, the more drunk, babbling, lit-up and goggle-eyed the fellow was, the more chance he had of being reckoned fecund in marvels.

It is only fair to admit, by way of compensation, that his worst divagations, amid tiresome drivel, sometimes did, indeed, illuminate abrupt images, opening like phosphorescent portals on gulf whose depths one seemed to plumb. And often, too, even for rational minds, some of his affirmations then had a sort of magnetic power that hypnotized you into an absolute need to have faith in him: a rigorous, mathematical, convinced faith.

So it was this evening, in particular—and his two companions were enjoying, more than ever, having him to themselves. Beneath the night swarming with stars, the brain of the old monologuing philosopher appeared to them to be even more splendid, like a scintillating firework-display. And yet, what he was saying, which was dazzling them, bore no resemblance, at least for someone judging with mere common sense, to a harmoniously-organized sky. It was incoherent verbiage, the very image of chaos; things like this, for example, cast into and snatched from the wind:

"Monoplane! Biplane! First, please, not biplane but diplane, if you know Greek. I do. Then again, diplane or biplane, it's all on the same plane, and even ranplaneplane![6] For sure. Yes, obsolete. De profundis! An old game, what! Stillborn, I tell you, the airplane. Stillborn! For what Geneviève says shatters it all. It blows up all the blades of all the propellers, so there! Centrifugal force, isn't it? But centrifugal is only centripetal exasperated. Or if not, make use of it! She's right, of course. Diffusion, then? Yes—without which, confusion. Per-

---

[6] In French, biplane is *biplan*, which permits the wordplay on *rataplan* [an onomatopoeic representation of a drum roll] and other improvised portmanteau words involving the syllable *plan*, which become awkward when switching languages, even though one double meaning of "plane" survives.

fectly? Better still? Fusion—since opposites are identical. You think it's Hegel who said that? Ha ha ha! Bunch of ignoramuses! Did he speak Greek, Hegel? No, eh? Now, the formula is Greek. And here it is."

A pause, not in speech but in motion—and the orator, posing magisterially and gravely, although unsteady on his feet, proclaimed, with an exaggerated articulation: "*T'enantia tafton.*"

Then he laughed scornfully, like the crackle of a frying-pan, and went on: "*Tafton,* yes! Pronounced in the modern Greek fashion, that goes without saying. Not in your stupid Erasamian style. Geneviève cried with joy when I told her it was Heraclitus. Hats off and on your knees before that one! And a rataplan, rataplan for him! Not a ranplaneplane like your planeless monoplanes or biplanes. He, the Napoléon of Cosmogonists, that author of the *Pata rei* and the *O polemos pater panton.* And they called him *o skotinos,* the Gloomy One! Long live the Emperor!"[7]

He had lurched with enthusiasm, lost equilibrium, almost fallen. The Scandinavian having caught him in his arms, Yvernaux had pushed him away, crying:

"No! Enough! Shut up, with your Nietzsche and his eternal return. No going and coming back! Always going! And it's my Gloomy One, again, who said that you can't bathe twice in the same water. And one doesn't drink the same beer twice. And when they lay me down in mine—the bier—the place where it'll be buried is the soul of the world, the *To*, by a big Tau,[8] neuter, like me..."

---

[7] The only bits of Yvernaux's Greek of which I can make sense are the Heraclitean maxim *Panta rei* [everything flows] and the nickname *o skotinos,* although its usual renderings as "the Obscure" or "the Dark One" are a trifle ambiguous; I have preferred "the Gloomy One" because it fits better with his other famous nickname, "the Weeping Philosopher."

[8] A T-shaped walking-stick or shepherd's crook, with a slightly curved handle, is sometimes known in France as a tau

He blithered on like that for half an hour, without pausing for breath, without resting except to lean, sometimes on one, sometimes the other, of his companions and sometimes on both at once—whose four arms were nevertheless not too many to prevent him from collapsing to the ground—by night, beneath a sky less constellated than his brain: Blaise Yvernaux, sexagenarian, failed doctor of philosophy, doctor of letters, inveterate drunkard; a poor alcoholic condemned to the worst catastrophes of atherosclerosis, but, in the meantime, and in spite of his two sessions of *displaced state* a week, a walking encyclopedia; the admired, cherished protagonist, almost the prophet, of the embryonic new religion of the Brasserie of the 20th century!

And when his two apostles had carried him up to his furnished room in the Rue Montmartre and had piously laid him on his iron-framed bed, where he went to sleep like a baby, on finding themselves back in the street, they both said, in unison: "Well, all the same, he's a genius!"

That was the affirmation that recurred as a refrain at the end of all their conversations with and about Blaise Yvernaux—which astonished them and enchanted them every time, with the awareness that they were the intimates of that genius. But they only pronounced the affirmation between themselves and the friends at the Brasserie who shared their faith in Yvernaux. To say it in front of Yvernaux in person would have been the worst insult they could offer him. He proclaimed, in fact, there was only one genius in the world at present—and, for that matter, in all the centuries yet elapsed—and one alone, to whom he would not admit that anyone could be compared, not even himself; *especially* not himself, since that unique being was his own godchild, Geneviève.

(masculine gender), by analogy with the Greek letter, and the word can be applied to a person by analogy with the stick. I have retained Richepin's *To*, although that Oriental syllable is nowadays more often rendered as Tao.

Geneviève who? That was what no one knew, even among his most intimate friends, for he never referred to her except by that forename and the description of her as his godchild. It had even been suggested that he strove to make sure that no one knew any more about her. His two faithful followers, curious about every detail concerning him, had not been able to get any precise information regarding this mysterious being, of whom his thoughts were nevertheless always full and by which they were haunted. He spread her word, with such violent effusions and cries of enthusiasm, in formulae of mad admiration—adoration, rather—as if he rendered her an interior worship, incessantly ready to express it aloud in *Magnificats*, punctuating ejaculatory prayers by telling rosary beads. And the mystic occultist had even, at length, reconstituted an entire bouquet of strange litanies with which he loved to decorate his meditations.

Here are a few of these verses, chosen from among the least incomprehensible:

"The renovatrice of all forms is Her."

"The revolution, from top to bottom, is Her."

"Newton's laws are contained in a petty corollary of one of hers."

"She's Pascal cubed."

"She's the Euclid of n-dimensional geometry."

"To multiply zero by infinity; that's her function.

"The Archimedean screw without the necessity of a fulcrum, that's her mind."[9]

"The Egg of Everything in the Chaos of Nothing, that's her word."

---

[9] Yvernaux is confusing two of the items of Archimedes' fame: the Archimedean screw, which was a device for pumping water, and the philosopher's remark about being able to move the world if he had a lever long enough, a fulcrum and a place to stand. The "error" is repeated, and is evidently deliberate.

"The blink of an eye or the *fiat lux* or the *fiat nox*, that's her gesture."

"The consciousness of the Unconscious, that's Her—and *vice versa*."

"The Self of Selflessness, that's Her—and *vice versa*."

"If God exists, he's Her."

"If he doesn't, his negation is Her."

These sayings, the peremptory absurdity of which was such that there was something almost parodic about them, the Comtois occultist understood fully, and the Scandinavian too; as for Père Yvernaux himself, he gargled them more easily than his beer. But the least bizarre of these formulae, said to Geneviève in person, made her laugh as if it were pure stupidity, like a drunkard's nonsense. She was not even embarrassed by them, so impossible did it seem to take them seriously. When, very timidly, from time to time, her godfather risked addressing one of them to her, he was certain to find himself snubbed, albeit politely, with a: "Shut up, you idiot!" Unless, entirely in fun, he was scolded for his vice by being told: "So you're still in the *displaced state*, since yesterday? Watch out, will you? That's twice in three days. You're overdoing it somewhat, aren't you?"

For she gladly bantered, Geneviève, that *Consciousness of the Unconscious,* that *Self of Selflessness*—and her sense of humor was rather joyful, in spite of the powerful reasons she had for being severe, and even morose.

The main one of these reasons was, alas, that she had arrived at the difficult age that designated her as an old spinster, since she was already seven years past 25 and unmarried. Without regrets, however—without even a hint of bitterness. She was the first to joke—like a good sport, she said—about that sad heptad, at the end of which one sees one's 33rd birthday looming.

"The fateful turning," she sighed, making fun of herself. "Not for one who has flourished in love and is, at that age, still a young woman, but for one who, having known no flowers,

27

runs to seed, and to bad seed, bitter and poisonous to others and to herself."

And something else that might have prevented Geneviève from being cheerful was the gravity of her life, entirely devoted to the more demanding and most absorbing studies, with her mind narrowly focused to the lofty speculations of modern science, which simultaneously embrace all the problems, linked in an indissoluble chain, of mathematics, physics, chemistry and biology. Even in her work and her meditation, though, her smile undoubtedly found its place, for Geneviève took to it like a good swimmer abandoning herself delightedly to deep water.

So there was nothing of the female scientist, in the bad sense, about her—any more than there was of the old spinster, in fact, in spite of the famous heptad added to the 25 years, and one could not divine on her forehead either the head-dress of Saint Catherine[10] or the mortar-board of the doctor that she could have been in all the sciences.

"Yes, all of them!" Yvernaux often proclaimed. "All of them, and more." For it only remained for her to pass some exam or other, or to win some diploma. And it was not merely a doctor of sciences that she could have been, if she had wanted to, but a fully-qualified professor of mathematics, physics, chemistry, and she could taken those qualifications in any order, at the whim of her examiners.

Sometimes he reproached her—it was his only reproach—for having scorned these official qualifications.

"Because, at the end of the day," he said, "that would give you the right to wear the professorial toga, with the red or yellow rabbit-fur border, and at a stroke, you'd amount to something."

---

[10] A woman who reached the age of 25 without finding a husband was long said, in France, to have *coiffé Sainte-Catherine* [coiffed Saint Catherine], the phrase deriving from an obsolete custom by which unmarried women made head-dresses with which to adorn statues of the saint in churches.

"Don't I amount to anything, then?"

"Not very much, damn it! To be my godchild isn't enough."

"It's enough for me." And she embraced her godfather, whom she loved with all her heart. And he, muttering in his beard, his heart bowled over with joy: "To be sure, when one is a genius..."

And into his beard, whose whiteness was yellowed by beer, rolled tears that were pearls of delight and pride. That emotion might have been that of an old crackpot, a drunkard with the trembling lips of an alcoholic, and that opinion might have manifested itself in the absurd verses of ludicrously-formulated prayers, but in spite of everything, the old drunken crackpot was telling the truth. Geneviève really was a genius!

II

"Ah! There's the crazy old English pastor with his little miss housekeeper! One can set one's clocks! No error there! Twelve forty-five! Or, to put it another way, a quarter to one!"

Toward the couple designated in this fashion, an irreverent fork was brandished, charged with a large mouthful of beef wrapped in a parcel of multicolored vegetables—and a loud laugh emphasized the phrases spoken, for the instruction or amusement of the neighbors, by one of the fat cab-drivers at table on the terrace of the Cocher Fidèle. Every morning it was the same, or very nearly, among the diners at the establishment, whose red shop-front, between the Rue Bréa and the Rue de la Grande-Chaumière, brightened up the Boulevard du Montparnasse, presently rather dismal and deserted.

Almost immediately, on the parallel sidewalk on the other side of the Rue Bréa, the modern-style curtain in the new Esthétic Bar was lifted, and one of its American clients, a male or female painter, or some escapee from the École des Beaux-Arts serving them as assistant and guide, announced the couple, with respect to whom young Yankee humorists exercised an apprenticeship in Parisian wit. There was something akin to a "tennis match" of jokes, in which the majority of the pitifully misdirected balls were called "out," the best of them having never consisted of anything but pedantic appellations furnished by vague Biblical or Classical memories:

"Oedipus and Antigone!"

"Ruth and Boaz!"

At which only the waiter in the establishment playing host to these "Mark Twains manqué"—as he called them— laughed, as a means of flattery.

Meanwhile, the couple, who were now going along the Rue Bréa toward the Rue Notre-Dame-des-Champs, were being pointed at from afar by fingers forming horns, at the ends of fists extended by a group of Italian models waiting to pose in the sunniest corner of the Boulevard. And words were whispered by the women, hiding the faces of their *fanciullini*, and by the old men with the heads of apostles or martyrs— words to ward off the *jettatura*, formulae against the evil eye of the accursed pair. It was said, in fact, in the group, that the couple comprised a renegade priest and a nun damned for him and by him—who was, moreover, his daughter.

The couple paid no attention to the gestures of exorcism, which were nevertheless glimpsed when one of them turned round, solicited by the magnetism of the fingers forming the horns. Nor did they see the coarsely mocking faces between the hands lifting the curtain of the Esthétic Bar, and they did not even hear the sonorous laughter of the paunchy cabbies splitting their sides on the terrace of the Cocher Fidèle.

And to what, indeed, would those two individuals have been able to pay heed in their surroundings, since they did not even seem to be paying any heed to one another? What exterior incident could have distracted them from the intimate distraction in which each was absorbed? One might have thought that they were two strangers marching side by side, two dreams dreamed in parallel, which would never meet.

Those two dreams, nevertheless, were but one, and those two strangers were father and daughter—but they seemed to have forgotten that. Or, rather, one single thought animated them, outside of which nothing existed; but each of them was following that single thought with a passion so intense as to be walled up in a corridor insolating them from everything around them: even the nearest, dearest and most closely-related person of all.

So, were the comparisons of the wags, which had the pretension of characterizing them, stupid and inexact? They were certainly not Ruth and Boaz, although the old man had the long hair, the wrinkled visage and the venerable air of a patriarch, while his daughter had the ingenuous, almost child-like gaze and pre-pubescent body of the young Moabite. No more were they Oedipus and Antigone, for they had nothing tragic or ancient in their bearing, and if their eyes were blind to the ambient reality—both Oedipuses, alas—they were illuminated by their dream, a dream of joy and pride. As for any resemblance to an English pastor and his little miss housekeeper, they did not offer the shadow of a shadow of it.

There remains the gestures of the Italians, and their words explaining the gestures, which approached plausibility a little more closely. The old man was probably not a renegade priest, in fact, but there was something mysteriously sacerdotal about him, that was obvious. And damned or not, for him and by him or not, the girl certainly had the face of a nun, gentle, modest and colorless, suggestive of the frontal band and the shadow of a cornette.

Finally, the silent couple passing people and things without allowing themselves any distraction, the two individuals walking together as if separately, sharing in a single thought that enveloped them in a halo of ecstasy, gave off a sort of effluvium, clearly perceptible to delicate sense. Some people turned round as they went past—not to laugh or to form horns, but with a vague disquiet, retaining the impression of a strange breath that had caused a frisson to run over their flesh.

That impression, already felt by them several times before, and which they had just felt again at that very moment, was what two young men of letters, stillborn poets in the chrysalis of journalism freshly disembarked from their province—in the Midi, of course—to conquer Paris, were talking about in a pathway in the Luxembourg. Although the new literary generations do not read Balzac much, they were talking about their desires and sensations with the imagination of their era, which is Balzacian without being aware of it. And this is what one of them was saying:

"We ought to follow that couple, you know, to spy on them. We'd learn something extraordinary, perhaps with which to reconstitute a romance of blackmail. Damn it! One needs no more in Paris, to make it."

To which the other, less ambitious, replied: "We'd only get an interesting item of reportage out of it—but that would be something."

And each of them caressed his idea while watching the couple, who had probably come into the gardens by the gate in the Rue Vavin, take the main path leading toward the central flower-beds and from there toward the Panthéon.

During the month that our two seekers of good opportunities had been coming, quite inconsiderately, to seek one while hanging around in the Luxembourg after a meager breakfast at the creamery, they had already exchanged reflections of this sort almost every day, but they had never made the least effort to act on them. Mouths open, arms dangling, their eyes like Roman candles but their feet nailed to the ground, they contented themselves with dreaming about blackmail, or even fruitful reportage, doubtless waiting for the lark to fall into their mouths ready-roasted.

And lo! That was exactly, in those express terms, what their friend Sextius Costecalde exclaimed in their ears, making them jump. Their friend, or rather their master: already a reporter in good standing—he said—with a great boulevard paper, where he was already placing 150 or 200 lines time, at two *sous* per three lines.

"So," he said, harshly, "you still imagine that it will write itself, your article? What more do you know about your characters than you knew yesterday? Nothing, I'll wager. And what will you do to make them sing, smart fellow? And with what stories will you cram your lines, curiosity-seeker? Can you even tell me where they're coming from, at this hour, the famous couple who give you a frisson, and where they're going, as they do every day? For you've seen them pass this spot every time you've been here at ten to one, but you haven't taken the trouble to wonder if that happens by chance or regularly, have you? Well, it's every day—and I know that. And I know where they come from, and through what streets. And I'll give you a spinning-lesson if you want. I'll tell you how to find out for yourselves the names that I've already half-discovered by myself. Something ending in *ov*—you'll see."

The two apprentices were dazed with admiration, and stunned by Costecalde's eloquence, and they would have been more firmly rooted to the spot than ever if he had not shaken them, pointing at the couple who were drawing away, and saying to them authoritatively: "Well, get going! Shadow the prey! Quickly! Oh, it's not difficult! They're hardly defending themselves—or rather, they're doing it expressly by seeming inoffensive. No one suspects them—and yet, if you knew...get moving!"

And, while marching in the tracks of the couple—who, indeed continued to pay no heed to anyone or anything around them—the prodigious Costecalde imparted what he had discovered to his ecstatic novices. "What a mine of lines! What a dairy-cow of reportage, perhaps also of blackmail! For all tastes! Oh, my lads!"

Every day, at daybreak, the couple left their domicile, not to return until one o'clock in the afternoon, and spent the entire morning at the far end of Vaugirard, in a sort of large wooden cabin situated in the middle of a patch of waste ground. What did they do there? Chemistry. Under what name? That, no one in the neighborhood knew. But here, at the home, into which they would go in a few minutes, that could doubtless be learned, for in the middle of Paris, thanks to concierges...

"There it is! We're here! They live in that house. Yes, exactly, that honest old house in the Rue Malebranche, near the Panthéon, yes, a hundred paces from the police station, yes, there, those nihilists. Haven't you guessed yet that that's what they are? Now, it's up to you to ask the name. Something ending in *ov*, I tell you. We'll see how clever you are."

When the two novices came out of the lodge they were dismayed—and with reason! Even Costecalde nearly fell over in amazement. The couple comprised, the concierge had said, reverently, Monsieur Thibaud Gasguin, "the scientist," and his daughter, Mademoiselle Geneviève.

III

The sole cause of the two apprentice reporters' dismay was the unexpectedness of the revelation. The nihilist couple with the names ending in *ov* had become an honest universitarian and his daughter. But the near-collapse of Sextius Costecalde proved, at least, that he was a journalist in the know with regard to celebrities, for the name of Thibaud Gasguin had immediately reminded him of a press campaign mounted nine years before with regard to a petty provincial professor, utterly unknown until then, suddenly acquiring reputation, almost glory, by virtue of several curious discoveries published one after another over six months.

True, since then, silence had fallen over the name—but not long ago, what a racket there had been in a few papers, polemicizing for or against the government on the back of Thibaud Gasguin! Some had attributed a crime to Official Science, to the offices of Public Instruction, and to its successive ministers, for having so long "hidden such a light, the honor of the fatherland, under a bushel." Others had inveighed, with bitterness and irony, against "the muffled and tortuous intrigues of clericalism, which nipped in the bud the flight of a free spirit once deflected by the teaching of the seminary, who had escaped therefrom."

On these two sides, tendentious biographies had been fabricated, in support of the theses sustained, to which the poor and innocent Gasguin gave appearances of veracity by falling into all the traps set for him by ingenious interviewers. Unfortunately, although the time in question was recent, Sextius Costecalde had not yet been a reporter in good standing with any newspaper. But for that...! He had, however, retained the memory of some of the "information obtained from the best sources"—but contradictory nevertheless—on which the legend of Thibaud Gasguin had been built. And today, all those stories coming back to mind pell-mell, he composed a peacock's tail from them, which enabled him to strut like a great reporter before his two wonderstruck pupils.

"Of course," he said, as he went with them toward the Odéon, where he was supposed to meet Antoine, "I only know him, that Thibaud Gasguin! He must have let his hair grow and no longer wears a beard"—which was a false assumption, Gasguin never having changed his appearance—"otherwise I'd have remembered his face. It was in all the papers at the time. A funny story, though, his. I have it in my files. I could write a pamphlet about it, if I wanted. Perhaps I shall—who can tell? I only need an opportunity—and I'm looking!"

On which, as a generous fellow is not miserly with his *sources*, but at a gallop—for it is a long way from the Rue Malebranche to the Odéon—he spewed out a Thibaud Gasguin of fantasy, based for the most part, even so, on accurate details. At any rate, the portrait resembled what Paris imagined, in accordance with the newspapers.

It was that of a minor provincial teacher—a professor of physics, in fact, at a college in Brittany, doomed to molder away there until his retirement, although he had graduated with a good degree, because he was known to be a former seminarian and as the younger brother of a certain Abbé Denis Gasguin, who had been compromised by some reactionary scandal. Abruptly, that obscure professor had published a paper illuminating the problem of wireless telegraphy. To begin with, the Académie des Sciences had not attached to it the importance of which it was worthy, but an English journal, and then a German one, having devoted studies to the French physicist's solution, his name had been mingled with those of Branly and Marconi, the inventor who had put the new discovery on a practical footing. At a stroke, the worth of Thibaud Gasguin was appreciated.

A second communication—on something like the transmission of force by telluric currents, Costecalde affirmed, without guaranteeing the terminology—and then a third, had set Gasguin at odds with illustrious contradictors, over whom he had triumphed. Then the polemics in the press, politics entering into play, the petty provincial professor called to Paris, appointed to a famous chair—Costecalde could not remember exactly which one—and, finally, the unknown of the previous day being hailed as an imminent candidate for the Institut.

They arrived at the Odéon. The two novices would have liked to know more—especially, why Thibaud Gasguin had suddenly stopped making such good progress, and why he was going to do chemistry incognito at the end of the Vaugirard, and various other things. Entirely intent on his rendezvous with Antoine however, the self-important Costecalde left them in suspense with these rapid final items of gossip:

"Gasguin was given an ox on his tongue, as Sophocles says,[11] by virtue of his palm being greased, as Racine says"— Costecalde was not without a certain erudition—"and he was given a cheese, in the form of a laboratory at the École Normale. Then the fellow ruminated, and didn't produce anything else. That's it."

"But why this chemistry at the far end of Vaugirard?" persisted one of the novices.

"Yes, and why on a patch of waste ground?" supplied the other, breathlessly.

"To make imbeciles talk." Such was the peremptory response of Sextius Costecalde, who knew no more in any case, and who planted them there, under the arcades, haring off into the Odéon, where he had only to meet up with his girl-friend, a second duenna, already an old laureate of the Conversatoire.

Reduced to their own feeble light, the two pupil reporters agreed in concluding that Gasguin was doubtless carrying out mysterious research in a private laboratory, situated on the far side of Vaugirard specifically in order that no one should know of its existence, on a patch of waste ground in order to cater for the danger of possible explosions.

---

[11] The expression "to have an ox on one's tongue"—meaning to be speechless—is found in the work of several Greek writers, and was probably a common expression in Athens. Sophocles uses it in *Oedipus rex*.

And the conclusions of the two apprentice journalists happened to be accurate.

The experiments, not in chemistry but in physics, that Gasguin and his daughter were carrying out there, might, in fact, have proved very dangerous. On the other hand, at the École Normale or the Sorbonne, with the laboratory assistants and students of his official laboratory, or even the laboratories of those of his colleagues who would gladly have opened them up to him and solicited his collaboration, Gasguin feared awakening curiosity and "leaks"—thefts, in sum. If he had maintained a strict and grim silence since his third paper, it was not because that silence had been bought and obtained for favors rendered; it was to keep the secrets he had already conquered, and those whose conquest he sensed to be imminent, under wraps and inaccessible.

Straight away, on arriving in Parisian society after leaving his native province, he had scented beasts of prey lying in ambush everywhere, including some under the cover of the most noble professions. Seduced by the initial caresses made to his glory, all the softer because the sometimes came from the manifestly envious, he had resisted the subtle temptation to surrender his secrets. His ancient peasant ancestry, of Thiérachian caution, had put him on his guard against those who, according to the old Thiérachian saying, knew how to tickle a goose's belly in order to steal its down more easily.

Immediately sobered from the fumes of success, he had resumed the modest air of a provincial professional, attributing his discoveries to the fortunate hazards of chance, finding himself overwhelmed by the rewards that had been their fruit—and he willingly declared that his destiny was now complete.

Faith was easily lent to these affirmations, firstly because they calmed the anxious envy of rivals, and secondly because the former seminarian that Gasguin, in fact, was, had conserved from his preparatory exercises for the priesthood a persuasive unction and all the meek appearances of Christian humility.

People had, therefore, soon got used to seeing the fellow he now seemed to be as a person who ought not to inspire any ambitious dread, a wise friend of mediocrity, whose blissfully satisfied physiognomy he displayed. And it was without hypocrisy, moreover, that he played that character; deep down, by nature, that was what he was.

And yet, a real and ardent ambitious thirst devoured him, born of the unexpected kiss that glory had given him. Put on the track of formidable results rendered possible by discoveries already made, and especially by future conclusions already in view and experiments in progress, his hopes were incubating monstrous eggs. He was sometimes disturbed and bowled over by them himself, like a hen with the presentiment, even the prescience, of chicks destined to become lightning-bearing eagles.

That accuracy of that comparison, due to Blaise Yvernaux, by which Gasguin was haunted, could not have been grasped, nor its profundity comprehended, by anyone except Yvernaux, everyone except the two of them being ignorant of the role played by Geneviève in her father's life, and especially his work. But it was also because Gasguin knew it himself, and on the advice of Yvernaux, and according to the formal and absolute desire of Geneviève, that the work consecutive to Gasguin's first three memoirs was being carried out in the private laboratory at the far end of Vaugirard.

In sum, Thibaud Gasguin really was a petty professor of physics, an excellent teacher, a perfect assimilator and propagator of knowledge received from others and communicated to others—and he was, in addition, a skillful experimenter, with a strictly logical mind, patient, orderly and methodical. Left to himself, though, he would indeed have merited languishing in an obscure chair until his retirement. And Blaise Yvernaux was right when he melted in ecstasy and cries of admiration before Geneviève's genius, because the three papers that Thibaud Gasguin had written and published were Geneviève's ideas.

Nevertheless, genius is like madness, essentially contagious, in the nervous sense of the word, if it can have such a sense. Thus, Gasguin alone would have remained an honest physicist and nothing more, but, illuminated by his daughter, he had become her reflection—the moon of that sun, as Yvernaux put it. In consequence, the halo of that splendor also ringed his head.

Whence came, when the couple passed by, the wake of effluvia that made the hair of sensitive individuals bristle.

IV

It was in perfectly good faith that Geneviève refused the homages of her godfather and politely accused him of stupidity when he caused offense with one of his formularistic litanies. And it was in all sincerity, too, that she was astonished by the seemingly-startled expressions of admiration that her father sometimes assumed—like an imperial mantle, Yvernaux said.

Then, she exclaimed: "Well, what? What's the matter with you, Father, looking at me devotedly like that, as if I were the holy sacrament?"

"It's because you are, to me, at the moment," he replied.

"Why, and for what reason?" she demanded.

And when Thibaud Gasguin questioned her about some hypothesis she had just formulated, about some extravagant association of ideas, about the absolutely unexpected and paradoxical conclusion drawn from an experiment, she started to laugh, understanding that the trivial item in question, thrown out almost at hazard, had triggered such a profound surge of ecstasy in her father's ever-religious soul.

"Truly," she said, one day, "it wouldn't take much for you to become once again the priest that you once nearly..."

"That I still am," Gasguin interrupted, swiftly, "and that I shall never cease to be before miracles as astounding as that."

That day, Geneviève had simply said to him, with regard to a problem of gravitational attraction that he had found it difficult to solve, translated into equivalents of motive force. "Isn't it funny? Scarcely had you pronounced your number than I saw it transposed to another planet—or to the Earth turning on its axis seventeen times more rapidly—and then it became false at the equator, the centrifugal force suddenly equaling the centripetal, and weight no longer existing."

At which he had smiled at first, having been familiar with that *pons asinorum* of astronomical physics for a long time—but after which he smile had frozen in amazement, Geneviève having continued thus:

"I repeat that I can see the figure transposed—alive and active, you understand—and that I can *see*"—she emphasized the word forcefully—"driven thereby, the engine we've been seeking to equilibrate the..."

And she had fallen silent abruptly before her father's face, rapt with adoration, and had laughed, breaking the charm, in order to remind him of the "failed" priest that he was.

And again, on Gasguin's interruption, reiterating his act of devotional faith and talking about miracles such as that one, she had been unable to turning her nose up mockingly and saying: "What miracle, then, has knocked the breath right out of you?"

The silliness of the Thiérachien expression did not succeed in clearing Gasguin's hallucinated face. His bloodless lips were muttering, as if in prayer: "The miracle is that I too have see either figure transposed, alive, active, driving the engine. I saw it when you saw it. And if you had not suddenly burst out laughing, you would have fixed that figure within me. There's the miracle! And you often work miracles of that magnitude. And when they take effect in my brain, that when I draw out the light of which our glory, of which your glory, which people believe to be mine..."

"But it's absolutely yours, Father dear—yours, undoubtedly yours—never doubt that!" And the violence of her protest concluded with a big and tender hug, in which she expressed all her loyal and sincere abnegation relative to him, without any jealousy, without the shadow of an afterthought reserving anything whatsoever for herself. For it was in good faith, more than ever, that she attributed the preponderant and the essential part of their discoveries to her father.

To be sure, she took good account of the unexpected, rare and quasi-divinatory element that she brought to it, and she appreciated the full range of these strange godsends, which Blaise Yvernaux called—bizarrely, but quite accurately—"hypothetical flashes, serving as point of support in the void for the screw of rationality, whose spiral ends in a new law". That Thibaud Gasguin had often profited from these flashes to travel by their light alongside-roads leading to unexplored regions of science she gladly admitted, and thus took a legitimate pride in saying that she had sometimes shortened, or even signposted, the route. Nevertheless, she remained convinced that he could have got there without her help, that he did not have any absolute need for her, that she had simply rendered his work more original and more amusing, and that, in the final analysis, he would have achieved, albeit more slowly, results that were just as good without her, whereas she would never have got anywhere without him. And that, she believed, fully and firmly.

The reason for such utterly sincere modesty was the observation of the scant effort that these so-called miracles cost her, especially when she compared that ease to the hard labor of Thibaud Gasguin, and that which she had undertaken in order to assimilate the present-day scientific encyclopedia.

Contrary to Yvernaux's opinion, she would not have conquered all the diplomas at the drop of a hat or passed the doctoral examinations with the certainty of first place. It had required a great deal of time and difficulty, and long nights, and recommencements after failed attempts, and the employment of all her energy, all her capacity for work and all her most fervent zeal "simply to store in her brain," as her godfather put it, some of the innumerable sheaves harvested by so many geniuses in the vast domain of science. Merely in holding and arranging there, in that feminine brain, the substance of various diplomas and doctorates in mathematics, physics and chemistry, she had used up her adolescence, then her youth, and then the first spring of her womanhood—and thus had coiffed Saint Catherine without being aware of it.

All of that, moreover, she had learned from her father, an excellent teacher whose reliable information had been made even more careful, attentive and penetrating for her than for his other pupils. Thus, she had retained an affectionate gratitude, and also an admiring respect, for the facility he showed in teaching that which she had sometimes found so hard to learn.

By way of compensation, in the species of scientific vision for which her father, her former master, suddenly astonished, and then admired her—those hypothetical flashes with regard to which her godfather did not spare lyrical images—Geneviève took no pride, finding no difficulty at all in producing them, and hence not the slightest merit. It was in vain that Blaise Yvernaux tried to make her sense their extraordinary value; she would not consent to see anything extraordinary in them, but only the foliage of swarming metaphors that he plucked.

"What!" he cried. "You mistake for bottle-ends those lenses of rotating lighthouses, whose jets of multicolored fire set the four corners of the horizon in flower in a matter of seconds! And you don't detect something akin to an intellectual seismic shock in the depths of your being when you release those words, whose hectowatt power makes an entire field of physics tremble! And you don't even blink in launching the spark of a gaze that plunges into the deepest darkness of what the navigators of old called coal-sacks in the sky? And you want us to believe that you're not even conscious of..."

"Of course," she often interjected, "I'm not conscious of this, or that, and especially of all the beautiful rhetoric with which you dazzle me, godfather! Since I've told you a thousand times that the sole discoverer of these lighthouse beams, these electrical discharges, these plumb-lines cast into infinity—or, at least, what you baptize with these wondrous names—is my unconscious, my subconscious."

"Yes, yes, understood," Yvernaux replied. "You've pinned back my ears enough with your pretension on to have genius in your polygonal centers, as Grasset puts it.[12] But I

---

[12] Joseph Grasset (1849-1918) was one of several contemporaries of Sigmund Freud to develop an alternative theory of the unconscious. As the present text observes, he characterized the

contend that your O centre is perfectly up-to-date with what's happening in your polygon, and I affirm, moreover, that true genius consists precisely in that conscious exploitation of the unconscious, which means that..."

"Oh, Godfather, no!" she generally concluded. "Mercy! Psychology and me, you know...!"

And she pretended irreverently to take her head in her two hands in order not to hear any more. All the same, she was not unaware of that famous and interesting theory of the superior and inferior psychic centers, to which the great vitalist doctor of Montpellier has given the original schema of the polygon and the O point. None of the significance of that symbolic schema escaped her. She distinguished quite clearly within herself between her conscious, voluntaristic self and her pologyonal—which is to say, atavistic, instinctive, passionate and automatic—self. She had even drawn some special practices from the theory, which might perhaps have caused Dr. Grasset some surprise, but she did not let their secret filter out, especially to her godfather, confident of her more extravagant fantasies.

For she had sometimes had fantasies, and sometimes truly extravagant ones, that *x*-head, apparently so wise, that old-young woman with the colorless face, whose nun-like appearance called for a frontal band and the shadow of a cornette. Yvernaux could not think of those fantasies without shivering, still in the retrospective fear of the singular parentheses opened thereby in the life of that lay saint.

---

unconscious as "polygonal" (i.e., multifaceted) while supposing that the conscious mind has smoothed out its problematic angles, becoming a "circular" O self. Grasset was very interested in "psychic research," and attempted to extrapolate the theory of the polygonal unconscious to account for the various phenomena associated with mediumistic performances—an endeavour that inevitably led to his permanent exile from the historical record of scientific psychology.

Had he not been obliged, one day, to bring his goddaughter an apparatus for smoking opium, with the "instructions for use," for which he had asked one of his comrades, a naval officer returned from Tonkin? Otherwise—she had affirmed in a certain authoritarian tone that she occasionally adopted, and why admitted no reply—she would set out herself in search of an opium-den, which she knew to exist in the vicinity of the Arc de Triomphe, and would go into it without further ado. For fear of that worse alternative, he had yielded to her evil desire, and with his complicity, therefore, she had smoked opium for nearly three months.

Another time, it was hashish that she wanted to try, and he had similarly obeyed—not without trying to scare her, however, with the possible and terrible consequences of those stimulants, which quickly became narcotics.

To which she had replied, with a mocking wink and an enigmatic smile: "Do you imagine, then, that my brain needs stimulants? On the contrary!"

And some time after that, when he recalled that bizarre reply, of which he had not yet grasped the "on the contrary," she said to him point-blank: "Well, yes, so what? What my brain thirsts for, on occasion, is stupefaction. That's how I interpret Pascal's advice to 'brutalize yourself!'"[13] Then, with all the seriousness in the world, with her expression of childlike ingenuousness, she added: "Didn't he drink, Pascal?"

He laughed out loud, hands on hips, at the idea of Pascal as a drunkard. "You're crazy!"

"I'll give you the proof that I'm not," she said, coldly. "Once, you called me Pascal cubed, didn't you? We'll square that cube, if you like—and if even if you don't."

He listened, bewildered and uncomprehending. He thought she was ill, irrational. Still very serious and no less

---

[13] The question of what Pascal actually meant by the advice "abêtissez-vous" ["brutalize yourself," "be stupid" or perhaps "stop thinking"] remains controversial, all the more so because it was advice that he certainly did not seem to take himself.

ingenuous, she continued: "You don't follow? It's quite simple, though. I intend to show you Pascal cubed and drunk."

And she had demanded that he enable her to drink those famous aperitifs of which he had so often and so bravely lauded the charms—for he was not ashamed of his vice and gave the only excuses for it that he thought worthwhile, of knowing the joys, comforts and hopes to be found therein. Today, more prudent because he was over fifty—having passed that landmark ten or twelve years before—he limited himself to beer and wine to put himself in the *displaced state*, and no longer used, except in miserly and widely-spaced sessions, the divine openers of paradise, as he called them. Once, he had owed his most beautiful flights to chimerical Eldorados to them.

"It's true," he said "that it finishes up by spoiling them for you, by virtue of having seen them in dreams—but what dreams!"

"I want to know, therefore, those that a drunken Pascal would have had."

Thus had she decreed, still with the same sort of threat, swearing that if her godfather did not procure her the famous bitters, angostura and Pernod at home, she would go to drink them elsewhere, cynically, in some café in the Latin Quarter, where she would make a spectacle of her drunkenness—too bad!

With the result that poor Yvernaux had successively enabled her to taste, methodically graduating the doses and the effects, first light vermouth, in which the innocence of distilled white wine is tainted with a perverse dose of the subtle pharmacopeia of angostura; then bitters, whose poisonous blackness corrodes the metal of counters and also that of the will, but volatilizes your soul among light dancing vapors; and finally the magical absinthe, flowering with all the herbs of the Sabbat, the breath of aniseed and star anise: the absinthe that water, dribbled in pearls or poured in a cataract, decomposes prismatically, and then becomes a molten opal, liquid, cool and burning, like a mouth that blossoms and vanishes in a kiss

47

of frozen fire; the miraculous absinthe, both slave and tyrant, that causes you to see works yet to be attempted completed, and prevents you from starting them, which suppresses effort toward goals by placing them at the end of a barely-sketched gesture; that leads you the worst discomforts with a smile of triumphant pride, provided that you no longer cease to regard the word as rose-tinted through its green eyes; the absinthe that has for its final phase, after the repositories of glory and apotheosis, the total annihilation of all sentiment, and even of all sensation, in the unconscious bliss of paralysis.

That Geneviève should never allow herself to go so far, Yverdon was quite certain, since he had been able to stop on the slippery slope in time, before arriving at the final gulf. He had been no less terrified for her, of seeing her, for nearly a month, acquire a taste for twice-daily absinthism, albeit without overmuch abuse: for the habitual smiling and happy semi-daze that it provides, idle in deed, active in speech and super-saturated with projects, dreams ready to be realized, hopes that one can almost hold in one's hand, like a picked fruit.

Thibaud Gasguin having been away that month, on a scientific mission to the United States, Yvernaux had been able to conceal from him Geneviève's complete idleness during those four weeks in which she had abandoned all work— but it was a close-run thing! On the very eve of the day when her father was due to return, Geneviève had said: "This time, I think I've found the true cerebral motor. Yours, at any rate, Godfather, for I perceive that the *displaced state* is really your state of inspiration."

But the next day, on meeting her father at the Gare Saint-Lazare, she had taken full possession of herself again, and mocked poor Yvernaux thus: "Were you really afraid, then? Reassure yourself, Godfather! It's not that motor—yours— that I need. It's over! I shan't drink any more. I understand why Pascal was sober. Your flowers of rhetoric might benefit from that watering, but not our flowers of science. They have, as you put it, stems of steel and petal of..."

She hesitated, as the image fled.

"Don't look for it," her godfather said to her, cheerfully. "You won't find anything, since you haven't had an aperitif this morning. Besides which, you're right; it's not with those stimulants that you ought to wind up your head—your head adrift in the nebula of suns in formation. Leave the *displaced state* to old clowns like me, who merely prance around outside the tent in which you do your turns. Those who walk the high wire need their muscles, their equilibrium and their self-composure—so always keep clear, imperious and obedient that which represents your muscles, coordinating the regulatory movements and equilibrium of your brain—I mean your consciousness."

That day, once and never again, she had allowed her confidant to glimpse a tiny corner of her secret, by suddenly making him this confession: "The consciousness of my unconscious, then!" And she had added, in a low voice, between her teeth, a few inarticulate words, almost thought rather than spoken, that he had been unable to hear distinctly, but whose meaning he had guessed, and which he had translated, in his own language, as: "Because the genius, if there is any in this noggin, isn't in the self of the O center but the polygonal self; except that, to collect the flowers of atavism and instinct therefrom, it requires the fingers of the expert flower-picker that is the voluntary intelligence—and even the flower-picker needs to be a conjurer."

On reflection, Yvernaux convinced himself that he had translated in the fashion of those translators who embellish a text, putting something of themselves into it. Indeed, Geneviève, interrogated on that interpretation of her thought, had become annoyed, accusing her godfather of exasperated—and exasperating—lyricism.

"Oh, you always see otherworldly things in everything one says."

In reality, he had understood perfectly to begin with, and it was on reflection that he had made the mistake—or, rather, had been deceived.

Why had Geneviève judged it appropriate to induce an error in this way? Doubtless driven automatically by an old ferment of "Romany" blood she had in her, as some of the people of Thiérache—a land of Bohemian alluvia—do. It is well known that members of that nomadic race, probably a survival of the most ancient humankind,[14] are the most tenacious keepers of secrets in the world. Geneviève, who was distantly related to them, proved the dictum on this occasion.

What she had wanted to achieve, in sum, through these fantasies, these trials, was an artificial means of capturing, with her conscious reason, the precious sources, rich in atavistic and instinctive treasures, that she sensed bubbling in the subterranean reservoirs of her most profound subconscious memory. But the example of her godfather had led her to mistrust herself with regard to the possible exploitation of these occult thaumaturgies. And since then, without ever letting her intimate preoccupations in that regard be suspected, she had searched in isolation, and had ended up finding specific practical applications of Professor Grasset's theory of the superior and inferior psychic centers that were capable to bear fruit to her profit—or, rather, the profit of her father and his science.

As she put gaiety into the most serious things, she sometimes thought: "Poor old Godfather! All the same, it's not very nice of me to keep my polygonal self secret like this."

---

[14] Although we now know that *Homo sapiens* originated in Africa, many 19th century anthropologists placed the origin of the species in Central Asia.

V

Someone who could have said a great deal—perhaps more than anyone else in the world—about Geneviève and her strange gifts, and also about her ancestry, mingling that of Gasguin with the bizarre blood of the Hescheboix, *ferlampiers* and *merlifiches*,[15] and about Thiérache in general and certain Thiérachian families in particular, and about many other things—of which no one, however, suspected that she had the least notion—was Aunt Aline.

Although she did not have anything of the female scientist about her, seeming to be a good but humble and ignorant woman—which she was, in the strict sense of the word, since she did not even know how to read and write—Aunt Aline would have been instructive for more than one scientist, of the highest order. Professor Grasset, for one, could have obtained curious information from her, very precise observations and memories handed down from immemorial generations, relating to the inferiors psychic centers. It is not that she knew what those grand words signified, but of what lay beneath them, nothing of the substance escaped her—and of the most hermetic mysteries of atavism and instinct, she possessed, precisely by virtue of instinct and atavism, the shibboleth.

Alas, to get to her to say anything, no matter how little, about all that she knew so fully and deeply, with such bright enlightenment, about these obscure matters, several unrealizable conditions would have had to be met.

First of all, Aunt Aline the silent, when she took it into her head to talk, only spoke in short sentences uttered at distant intervals, as if surreptitiously. She mumbled these rare

---

[15] The family name Hescheboix is suggestive of "woodcutters." The two argot terms used to describe them are approximately similar to such English appellations as "vagabonds," "gypsies" or "tramps," routinely used with similar contempt.

words, emitted avariciously, with seeming regret, as if desirous of taking them back as soon as they were uttered. And if one tried, having not quite heard them, to get her to repeat them, she shook her head in a sign of negation, and emphasized her refusal with a malign glance demonstrating that she was quite satisfied not to have been understood.

It would have been necessary, too, for Aunt Aline actually to have thought what she had said. Now, she "felt" more that she thought, confusedly, but also in an intense fashion. That was visible, moreover, in the sudden pallor of her cheeks, in the furrowing of her perpendicularly-wrinkled forehead, in the bushy bar of her eyebrows, in the sealing of her lips like a purse closed over her toothless gums, and especially in her gaze, both flamboyant and heavy with meaning, in which sensation and thought were amalgamated with the incandescence of dense and ardent lava from the very center of inner being in eruption.

It goes without saying that this explanatory image had Yvernaux for its author—who, at other times, also compared Aunt Aline's eyes to very distant fires perceived in the mist—bivouac fires left by some fugitive *merlifiche*. Then he claimed to see there the last guttering sparks of fires by which the soul, many centuries ago, had been illuminated by some tribe wandering over the high plateaux of central Asia—which the old lady ought not to have understood, apparently, but to the story of which she nevertheless listened with delectation.

"Well," he said, "she's an octogenarian! She's entering a second childhood. The fairy tales with which she was rocked in the cradle, with which she has passed on, are coming back to mind. She thinks that story is one of them. Perhaps she imagines having known it exactly, and thus has the sensation of remembering it."

She had known it, in fact; that was what Yvernaux did not know. She really did remember them—the vagabonds' fires on the high plateaux—without being precise as to whether or not they were in central Asia. And her memories, irreducible to photographic negatives from which prints might be obtained, but synthetically vivacious although incapable of expression in words, went back to an era far more remote than that of her childhood. She did not have, however—it is necessary to insist on this point—a *perception* of them, but a *sensation*, all the stronger for its very unconsciousness.

Most of all, she did not analyze herself, never thinking of doing so, and would have been dead against the idea of anyone doing it for her. Even Geneviève, who adored her and was adored by her, had never had the vaguest inclination to do so. And yet, she was well aware of the prodigious heritage accumulated in the state of "uncommunicable knowledge" in Aunt Aline's atavistic memory.

For everyone else but Geneviève—for Gasguin especially, and often even for the penetrative and visionary Yvernaux—Aunt Aline was just a little old woman, still active and alert, although, for two years now, an octogenarian. Neat and mousy, always occupied with some piece of needlework, uniformly clad in tight black garment, with nothing white about her but the protrusions of linen at her collar and the ends of her sleeves, and the hair beneath her mourning-dress bonnet, she had the gleam, the clarity, the color and also the mannerisms of a scarab beetle. She also seemed to have the dryness and the argumentative humor of one, and would gladly, as we have seen, practiced its verbal mutism, contenting herself with communicating in gestures, since, even when rare brief sentences escaped her, she crushed them between her gums—expressly, one might have thought, to render the unrecognizable and unintelligible.

In any case, the things she expressed in that fashion were doubtless of no great interest; and that is why, attaching no importance to them, she did not require anyone to pay any heed to them. Such was, at least, the reason furnished by Thibaud Gasguin to explain Aunt Aline's habitual silences and premeditated mumbling. For—without a trace of malice—he considered her as a creature of a very ordinary intellectual category, almost a simpleton, endowed with all the honest mediocre qualities that make a perfect housekeeper: not so much a good housewife as a model servant, in his estimation.

To tell the truth, he had never known her, and certainly not studied her, in any other appearance, and in the more than sixty years she had lived in the same house—save for rare intervals, the longest of which had been his time in the seminary—he had never had occasion to taken the trouble to look into her. For as long as he could remember, she had always seemed the same, just as simple and just as enclosed in her black scarab carapace, uniquely made for the work of a Cinderella, never emerging therefrom and not suffering in consequence. It took him an instant of reflection to observe that she had grown old. Although he did not think of computing the time elapsed since his childhood, it seemed to him that could still find her there, in the process of caring for him, he being a child and she already a woman. He needed to make an effort to remember her young rather than imagine her in that fashion, when he had been very small and she had already been nearing thirty. The extra half-century and more that she had aged today, he had always put on her forehead, where he would have sworn that he had never seen any but white hairs. In reality, for him, she had no age at all.

It was in exactly the same way that he attributed a personality to her. She was an integral part of him, difficult to distinguish from his own self. Aline was like an indispensable limb—and he showed her no more gratitude than one testifies to one's arm or one's leg, or any other organ. She was his housekeeping organ.

He had only been a few hours old when she had become that, exclusively, having replaced, with respect to the orphaned Thibaud, the mother stolen by a attack of eclampsia after having delivered him into the world. One could even say that her caring for Thibaud had begun before he was born, for it was Aline who had been the nurse—how attentive and zealous!—of her sister Idalie, whose pregnancy, which was her second, had developed in particularly bad conditions.

If one had been able to read what was in the utmost and most secret depths of Aunt Aline, one would have learned one thing there that she scarcely admitted to herself, without being wholly certain of it: that she had already watched over Thibaud for a very long time, before the pregnancy, when he had still been—as the philosopher Yvernaux put it—among "future contingencies" for Aline, that bizarre and abnormal creature possessed a gift of obscure prescience, of which several proofs had already been given in the history of the Gasguin family.

Thus, it was in prevision of the Thibaud to come, and especially of Geneviève to be born of him—all without exact names or clear designations, of course—that Aline had acted, under automatic pressure and instinctive suggestion, to marry her younger sister, Idalie Hescheboix, to François Gasguin. For it was really her, simple Aline, the quasi-mute, the humble servant—one of those who, in Thiérache, are said to "overdo things"—of the Gasguin family, who had made the marriage by her manipulations.

And the task had not progressed of its own accord; it had required cunning and eloquence, if not in the words with which Aline was scarcely skilled, at least in her actions, in which she had shown an innate experience that one might have thought—and which really had been—accumulated by innumerable generations of horse-traders. How many steps to take and overtures to make, traps to set and others to avoid, hazards to render favorable and obstacles to change into supports, it had required to succeed, as Aline had done in two assiduous years of patience and science, in marrying Idalie, the poor *merligaudière* (*merligodgière*, in Thiérachian) of Pré-Pourri,[16] to the only son of the Gasguins, the richest farmers of the richest land in Buire!

---

[16] Even the non-dialect form of this argot term is absent from the dictionary, but it relationship with *merlifiches*, and the fact that the Latin *gaude* signifies delight, probably allow its mean-

Undoubtedly, there was one trump card in Aline's hand—her sister's resplendent beauty. That was, however, only a winning card in appearance, for it was mistrusted and could not be led. Prudent families know only too well what the beauty of a *merligodgière* represents: an inclination to idleness; an appetite for fast living and costly frippery; ruinous expenses; and eventual bankruptcy. On the other hand, for gallants who are smitten regardless, there is the notoriety that the commodity in question does not ordinarily pay in the currency of marital bliss.

The supposed high card of Idalie's beauty was, therefore, perhaps a false high card, and in any case, how many low cards there were alongside it in Aline's hand! Firstly, the poverty, or, to put it better—meaning worse—the disastrous pennilessness of the Hescheboix. Disastrous without giving rise to pity, alas! For Père and Mère Hescheboix, once not-unprosperous sellers of farm produce, then petty general traders and still good earners, had fallen by their own fault—their idleness, their slovenliness, their drunkenness—into the quasi-beggardom to which they had now been reduced, living in a half-demolished building, the remains of the old collapsed mill of Pré-Pourri. What work did they do there? The question was asked but unanswered. So-called second-hand dealers, rabbit-skin merchants, basket-weavers, mole-catchers, rat-poisoners and informers, they lived primarily by poaching and smuggling, less as bold operators to their own account as vile receivers and intermediaries.

No one, even among the most modest "sod-busters" had any desire to get involved with such people, to the extent of marriage. One can imagine what the Gasguins, honorable among the "swells" of the region and proud of a fortune that would not be shared out, reverting to their only son, would have thought. The idea never even crossed their minds. It would have passed for a sudden fit of madness, at which they

---

ing to be inferred. The literal significance of the hypothetical place-name is "Rotten Pasture."

would have laughed wholeheartedly, as they laughed at hoaxes, absurdities and the fashionable couplets, in the mode of the strolling players of old, hawked around by Père Hescheboix—whom they would rather not have made up a song based on an old Thiérachian saying about their land of Buire, the mocking refrain which he would come to squawk at them when he was drunk, in the guise of an appeal for alms, in the old Picard patois:

The people of Buire are red-faced folk
With fiery eyes who live in hovels.
Buire in France, fifty leagues from Paris:
Twelve houses, thirteen wells, fifteen thieves![17]

Certainly, they were amused by them, the rich and all-powerful Gasguins, perched so high and far above those paupers, whom they did not even do the honor of fearing, or even holding them in scorn—the scorn of a Gasguin being too precious an ammunition to waste on poor sparrows like those *merligodgiers, merlifiches* and *ferlampiers*. It is relevant that, pitying the Hescheboix because they had once known joyful prosperity, and pitying them in spite of their vices and their merited discomfort, the Gasguins had no hesitation in giving the miserable family the hospitality of the building in Pré-Pourri, which they had bought for almost nothing along with the abandoned mill-pond. They had done even more, taking into service with them the elder daughter Aline—who, by an extraordinary contradiction with her environment of sloth and excess, turned out to be the silent and active being we know.

Oh yes, active! Better than that, and more so than the Gasguins were able to observe in the "overdoing" of her vulgar tasks. That Cinderella was as active in mind as she was

[17] I have not attempted to simulate the eye-dialect employed in the representation of this lyric, but have simply reproduced its approximate meaning. If Buire were a common noun, it would refer to an antique drinking-vessel.

with her hands, and more so, even though she appeared to be as mindless as she was poor—as poor as her unfortunate parents were in everything, especially in virtue. Active she was for two full years, dreaming, wanting, preparing, manipulating and finally accomplishing that unexpected marriage between the rich François Gasguin, whom she coaxed on her sister's behalf, and her sister Idalie, whom she adored!

And all that, once again, without a plan fixed in advance, without any expressed idea, but with an unconscious meditation and the prescience—there is no other word for it—of an instinct working toward a birth in which an entire race had to end and flower.

Thus proceed certain insects of the family of digger wasps, such as those of the genera *Sphex* and *Cerceris*, whose perfect anatomical knowledge and impeccable surgical dexterity have been brought to light by the brilliant observations of the great naturalist Henri Fabre, the hermit of Sérignan. These sharp operators deliberately paralyze the living prey on which their larvae will nourish themselves. They, who live on the nectar of flowers, prepare the pasture of lethargic flesh, and dose that lethargy according to the needs of the growth that their larvae must undertake. These fabricators of the species to come, different from themselves, commit no sin in the complicated and difficult preparation of that mysterious genesis, for which they work in complete darkness, without any other knowledge of their certain progeniture but the impulsion of their maternal instinct, blind and automatic, rich in secrets accumulated by an immemorial heredity.

Thus, blindly but surely, Aline had proceeded, first in marrying her sister Idalie to François Gasguin, then in raising Thibaud Gasguin after Idalie's death, and finally in becoming Gasguin's servant throughout his entire life, all in order that the larva might be born, and find appropriate pasture, that would one day be her beloved Geneviève.

VI

Aunt Aline had, in fact, been more fortunate than the *Sphex* and the *Cerceris*, working, as Fabre says somewhere, "for the future children that their compound eyes will never see." For a long time, as for them, according to another expression regarding insects by Balzac "the ultimate goal of her work" had remained "occult." If she had been obliged to cease to live only ten years before, she would have died like them, like so many other beings in the chain of generations, without having knowing the meaning of her seemingly-absurd enigmatic labor. But today, thanks to her divinatory gift, which was one of her automatically-acquired virtues, and thanks also to her great longevity, which had given her reference-points in the past with which to triangulate the future, she had a very clear notion of having done for Geneviève alone all that she had done for such a long time without knowing why, and the perception, still vague but already stirring, of something great that Geneviève would soon do.

Who could have told poor simple Aunt Aline that, long ago when she had hired herself out as a little "overdoer" in the old Gasguin household, to the great discontent of Père and Mère Hescheboix, who were making such good use of her in begging by the roadside? Who could have told her that she had entered into that household to work there mysteriously for the birth of Geneviève's genius? And was it not the same when she had subsequently worked so hard negotiating Idalie's marriage to François Gasguin? And also when, after the birth of the elder son, Denis, she had installed herself beside the young mother who had become pregnant again almost immediately with Thibaud, and fallen ill? Why, in spite of the devotion that she professed for her idol, Idalie, had she then thought so often and so forcefully about the imminent and certain death of the poor beauty, adored so much, as "necessary"? Why, if not because it was necessary that Idalie should die in order that she should pass entirely into her younger son: into the Thibaud destined to be the obscure transmitter of the torch that would finally burn resplendently in Geneviève?

But for that, she would have been horrified by Thibaud, her Idalie's murderer. On the contrary, she had cherished him, cared for him, pampered him, doted on him, as no prince had ever been doted on. And she had stood guard over him, preventing François Gasguin from marrying again, so that, she thought—for she had no fixed plan then—Denis' and Thibaud's inheritance would be assured. How had she been able to put so many spokes in the wheels—breaking all the wheels—of all the marriage plans aimed determinedly at the widower, still young and "fertile"? She did not know how she had been able to do it, but she must have done it well, since François had, in fact, never remarried.

It is true that, in preventing that remarriage, she did not attain the envisaged goal of protecting her Thibaud's inheritance; but another goal, and the only important one, had thus been achieved, as we shall see—and in order that the bull's-eye of the other target might be hit, it was first necessary that the Gasguin fortune be squandered. That was the hidden purpose of the marriage and the subsequent widowhood, as we shall be able to judge.

Already, after the two brief years that Idalie had lived, expenditure had made considerable inroads at the farm, which had become a meeting-place for hunting and revelry, as if in perpetual festivity. In spite of old Mère Gasguin reprimanding her coquettish "embarrassment" of a daughter-in-law, and going so far as to box the ears of her big booby of a son for his captive amorous weakness and always giving in to the beauty's caprices, and whatever the doughty old bird had done in trying to manage the farm as her worthy late husband had done, the farm had rapidly come into jeopardy. The work was left undone, the profits disappeared and the land suffered, far from the master's eyes. And the mother, dying of despair and rage, joined Père Gasguin in the cemetery, where the solid plow-pushers of old were sleeping.

With François a widower and an orphan, the flight of the wealth not only continued but accelerated. After the two years of spendthrift honeymoon, things might yet have been put back on to a sound footing, with energetic effort. Aline had plenty to do maintaining the house, more or less, and bringing up the two sons as best she could, paying particular attention to pampering her angelic Thibaud, and above all to making sure that no one marriageable succeeded Idalie; with her energy devoted to these various tasks, she had none to spare to look after the fortune itself, of the management of which she knew nothing. Her father, the old mountebank, having convinced her that he was an expert, she introduced him to François as an adviser—and straight away, after lavish hunting lunches and fine revelry, there was dirty and crapulous debauchery, heavy drinking, gluttony, womanizing and interminable card games: a dance in which everyone joined.

A dance at Gasguin's expense, moreover, with no profit for Père Hescheboix, now also a widower, and brought his filthy retinue of drunks, guzzlers, card-sharps and prostitutes, who stole from him to begin with, and then assisted him to strip bare more rapidly, and especially to ruin physically, the handsome and sanguine young fellow that Francis Gasguin had once been, soon turning him into a fat, rubicund—almost purple-faced—stupid wreck in danger of a stroke. Ruined financially too, the unfortunate farmer died before the age of forty-five, leaving his affairs in disarray, with lawsuits in progress and others in prospect, and large debts—and, to face up to the men of law and the creditors, the simple Aunt Aline, flanked by her two sons, Denis and Thibaud, seminarians.

About that fortune, however, so keenly coveted for Thibaud when he was very small, and now lost when he might really have needed it, Aline did not care. No remorse troubled her then with regard to that ruination, for which she might have judged herself slightly culpable. She was not even visited by regret. Her obscure awareness of things and her sense of the future had revealed to her, doubtless in confidence, that this poverty was henceforth necessary in order that Thibaud's destiny should work itself out fully—which destiny was not for him to remain a seminarian, to become a rich curé, on the way to climbing up to the episcopate and dying plump without posterity.

The true and fateful destiny of Idalie's son—Aline had not known it then, but she knew it now—was that, being too poor to continue to be a future ecclesiastic, he would renounce the priesthood, while Denis alone entered holy orders, and that he should turn to a new vocation, leading him to marriage, in order that Geneviève should come into the world and eventually do what she had to do there.

VII

Although he was the son of Idalie the *merligodgière*, and was to serve as Geneviève's channel for the blood of the Hescheboix, so richly mineralized with strange and powerful atavisms, Thibaud Gasguin was primarily, very strongly and almost essentially marked with the seal of the Gasguins.

Established since time immemorial in the northern corner of Thiérache, of the old autochthonous race, prehistoric in origin, their stereotype was both serious and refined, tenacious by nature, positive in mind and inclined toward serious things. Cultivators for the most part, for many generations, they hardly ever departed from that profession, in general, except to become priests, notaries or schoolmasters, François Gasguin had followed a family tradition in sending his two sons to the seminary at Notre-Dame-de-Liesse,[18] the elder to have a good bourgeois education before returning to take over the paternal farm and the younger to retain the soutane and raise himself, eventually, to some good position in the church.

Now, it had happened that the elder, Denis, had conceived a particular taste for theology, classical culture and letters, and even developed therein a sort of intellectual elegance uncommon in a Gasguin. By contrast, Thibaud proved resistant, not only to a veritable priestly vocation but to the humanities in general. By way of compensation, he got his teeth into the sciences, education in which was neither in much favor nor much provided for in the seminary's courses, only extending to what was strictly necessary for the paltry scientific component of the baccalaureate in letters.

Thibaud got his teeth so firmly into what had previously been regarded as a refuge of dunces that he suddenly mani-

---

[18] As with the other fictitious place names in the text, Liesse has a meaning as a common noun, roughly equivalent to "merriment."

fested first-rate aptitudes therein, which astonished his professor, Abbé Dujars, the only X-head in the seminary—a former Polytechnique man[19], no less! In announcing the fact to the director, the latter could not help making a humorous remark.

"One imagines that all the positivist and serious members of the Gasguin ancestry will finally be able to celebrate this enthusiasm of their descendant for geometry, algebra, physics and chemistry!"

The director smiled at the remark, and, as he was a Jesuit with a flexible mind, knowing how to take advantage of the most unexpected circumstances, he immediately, and most ingeniously, addressed the question of the fate of the two brothers. The news was then quite fresh of the definitive ruination affecting the sons of the late François Gasguin. If Thibaud had been a rich heir, the debility of his ecclesiastical vocation could easily have been passed over and his preparation as a potential bishop continued, without renouncing the probability that Denis, no less rich an heir, would quite naturally become one of the most distinguished and useful members of the Company. In the present state of things, the director very wisely judged it preferable to "invert the order of priorities"— as he said to himself privately, no less humorously, on this occasion, than Abbé Dujars, but without letting it show—and he decided that Denis Gasguin would henceforth be allowed to follow, simply as a humble priest, his comfortable path to some rural parish, while Thibaud would be directed into a career as a scientist—in which, priest or not, having been raised by and for the Company, he would later bring it profit and honor.

Here, once again, the occult work of the *Sphex* that Aunt Aline was pursuing by instinct to prepare for the advent of the larva intervened. Without that, in fact, none of what had to come to pass would have done so, even after all that she had already done in that obscure hope. Happy to remain at the seminary as the favorite, unique pupil of Abbé Dujars, Thibaud

---

[19] The students of the École Polytechnique are known as X's.

had thousand and three chances, against the thousandth part of one, of letting himself be confined there, and finally taking the soutane anyway, while satisfying his frenetic passion for the sciences. And it seemed that in that regard, loving him as much as she did, Aunt Aline should have encouraged him.

It was the opposite that she had done, scornful of all reason and all prudence, even to the apparent detriment of the immediate and distant interests of her dear Thibaud.

For two and a half years, without saying a word, she had at first tolerated the fact that he was living away from her, indoctrinated by his brother Denis, flattered by the director and seduced by Abbé Dujars, who was opening all the Eldorados of science to him. Thus, she gave the appearance of accepting that her Thibaud had escaped her. Certainly, no one suspected the extent of her grim determination to get him back. Neither the brother, nor the professor, nor the director himself, had the slightest suspicion of it. The entire seminary, including the stones in its walls and the desks in its classrooms, would have protested in indignation if anyone had said, or even thought, that Notre-Dame-de-Liesse would not have, as the supreme ornament in its diadem, the glory of the future Abbé Thibaud Gasguin.

And such was, in fact, the prospect imagined in honor of Gasguin by his best friend, his comrade in all their classes, the "brilliant" Blaise Yvernaux, the person who had, until then, been nicknamed at Notre-Dame-de-Liesse, exactly as Bossuet had been at the Collège de Navarre "the Angel of the School." Abdicating his title to the embellishment of the former dunce of letters, who had so rapidly become the Pico della Mirandola of the science, The famous Yvernaux had composed to that end, in praise of his friend and conqueror, an admirable epistle in hexameters parodying Horace's *centos*, the delight of the good Fathers, who had inserted a copy of it in the book of honor, in Gothic calligraphy, with initial indented letters illuminated in blue, red and gold.

Now, it was precisely by the intermediary of this Yvernaux, however far removed from her he was in his glory as a *latinum elegantiarum magister*,[20] that Aunt Aline had contrived the repossession of her Thibaud, necessary to the mysterious germination from which the supreme flower of the Hescheboix was to emerge.

Blaie Yvernaux too did not feel an ecclesiastic vocation, but in his case, it was by virtue of infatuation with his triumphs in rhetoric and philosophy, and because he felt that, although poor, he was called to play a role in life different from that of, as he put it, a "fieldmouse of a curé" or a "schoolmaster force-feeding geese to fatten them on Latin cuisine." And *bang!*—a joyful *bang*—one fine day, as he was mourning not having a foot in the stirrup of some career appropriate to his stature, he received, out of the blue, it seemed, a request to serve as tutor to the family of the Walloon Vicomte Pyckelsberghe de Lumay. In consequence of which he resolved, having first accepted it provisionally, to take advantage of it to "throw his soutane into the nettles" in due course—a gesture that the mere contagion of the dream soon suggested to Gasguin that he should do the same.

For that request had not come out of the blue, as had seemed to be the case; it had been contrived over time by the manipulations—ever tenacious and without any fixed plan—of Aunt Aline, who was then living, or rather vegetating, separated from her favorite, as an exile in Belgium, placed in the capacity of a nurse in the presence the old Comtesse de Pyckelsberghe. Placed there how and by whom? At a distance of forty years, Aline could hardly remember that. But placed there why? After having not known for more than thirty years, today she knew. Placed there, of course, in order that she might unshackle Thibaud's fate, which threatened to settle at Notre-Dame-de-Liesse, interring Geneviève's there.

---

[20] This phrase does not appear to be a standard Latin expression, although the two latter terms crop up frequently in other contexts, referring to elegant mastery of other subjects than Latin.

On Yvernaux's advice, solicited thanks to Aunt Aline, Thibaud too had been summoned, to share the work of tuition. The director of the seminar had willingly let him go—for a year, he told himself—in the expectation that the two pupils of Liesse, especially Thibaud Gasguin, so grateful, so submissive, would not be wasting too much time out there, except perhaps on their own account, certainly not that of the company, in gaining a voice and a foothold in the opulent and powerful Lumay family, one of the fortresses of the Belgian clerical party,

But once Thibaud was under her influence, all the more pervasive because it was more covert, Aunt Aline had had him to herself, as when he was very young. She said nothing too him, still being taciturn and so simple—but his friend Yvernaux spoke for her, doubtless inspired by her, without he or she ever getting wind of it. He spoke about the great joy, the fine and legitimate pride that there would be, since the ecclesiastical vocation had refused them, in finding a niche elsewhere, in the lay world, honestly, by virtue of their talent. What a fine future they saw opening before them, one as a philosopher, a professor of letters, perhaps a writer, certainly an orator, the other at the École Polytechnique, to begin with, or the École Normale, also a professor, an engineer perhaps an inventor, certainly a scientist!

Aunt Aline gave her assent, nodding her mourning-bonnet—but not in mourning for her hopes, for she only unsealed the purse, already tight, of her lips over her gums to allow golden prophetic phrases to spring forth, such as these:

"Yvernaux's right, far-sighted and clear-sighted."

"You were born with a caul—a lucky sign!"

"Messieurs the priests know your worth.

"The younger sons of *Cattelinettes* are magicians."[21]

---

[21] Again, this *argot* term is unknown to available dictionaries, but it probably derives either from a diminutive of *chat* [cat] or a variant of the *chatouiller* [to tickle]. A more intriguing possibility, however, is that it might derive from *Catalauni*, a

"Two and three make five and you make six."

"If you want your future, open your hands."

"On the eve of your birth, your mother dreamed about an eagle."

"Poor Idalie! She's waiting to live again."

"One only has oneself—so much the worse for me, where you're concerned."

In little formulae of this sort, sometimes more singular still, she unburdened her heart from time to time, half-stifling them between her teeth, amid sobs that were also stifle-not sobs of grief but of impatience, at not being better able to make herself understood, and, at the end of the day, not wishing to do so. Thus, at least was the interpretation of Yvernaux, a lover of more verbose rhetoric, more lavishly spiced with metaphors.

Gasguin allowed himself to be touched more fully, often deeply penetrated, by these "sayings" reminiscent of childhood memories, proverbs, riddles or mottoes, which gripped him and made his fibers resonate. He resented being so sensitive to words denuded of sense—he affirmed—and to ancient and troubled things trailing in the old *cafourniaux*[22] of his memory. Nevertheless, he was prey to them without admitting it, and it was by virtue of them, even more that Yvernaux's impetuous declamations, that he was definitively extracted from the seminary, and conquered his liberty.

Latin name applied to a Gallic tribe from a region adjacent to Thiérache. Attila's Huns were defeated in that region in a battle that turned the horde away from Gaul, perhaps lending some credence to the notion of an earlier invasion of a similar kind.

[22] At a later point in the text this word will be identified as a plural version of a dialect equivalent of "capharnaüm"; in literal terms, a capharnaüm was a kind of toll-booth in the Ottoman empire, but the term was used metaphorically in France as an approximate equivalent of the English "glory-hole."

That did not prevent him from denigrating those lyrical declamations. They alone still gave him something like the frisson of the mysterious chains by means of which the clock of destiny works. And to translate entirely the period in which Gasguin's liberty emerged, necessary to Geneviève's birth, nothing is better, in sum, than a prose poem that Yvernaux composed at a later date.

In the starch of the heavy solidity that had made all his Gasguin peasant ancestors before and including him into notaries, curés and schoolmasters, and the dough that the eloquence of Yvernaux was now rolling repeatedly, kneading and baking, those little sibylline phrases uttered by Aunt Aline were pellets of yeast that were about to make the bread rise. And that bread—Aunt Aline did not know why, but the blood of the Hescheboix knew it on her behalf—had first to be cooked, in order that the surplus of flour could be made into a disk of unleavened bread, of holy bread, of synthetic and symbolic bread: the host by means of which an entire race would express itself and offer itself to the adoration of the world, in the sublime and resplendent monstrance of genius.

VIII

Ah! That faith, that exaltation of pride, so lyrically expressed, later, by Blaise Yvernaux, how far away they were from it, forty years before, when the sad reckoning was made of the first battle fought against Paris and so completely lost! Only Aunt Aline was not disappointed, doubtless not understanding very well, the poor ignorant woman—in the estimation of Thibaud, and even Blaise—the total lack of success. But the two superb peacocks, who had set off displaying their tails in a fan flourishing with all their illusions—what lamentable, pitiful jackdaws they were when stripped of their hopes, with their self-confidence in tatters![23]

In the beginning, things had gone well for some time, in spite of the bad omens that marked their debut. The tutorship having ended abruptly in a dismissal due to their exasperated and exasperating vanity, they had put a fury of stubborn self-respect in refusing an apology, if not to Pyckelsberghe, at least to the newly-appointed director of Notre-Dame-de-Liesse, who had no reason to cherish and protect those "favorites" of the old regime. Abbé Dujars, also having changed residence, was no longer there either to intervene on behalf of the disciple who had done him honor. Egged on by Yvernaux, and even, mutedly, by Aunt Aline, Thibaud had argued with his elder brother, who had advised him to submit and solicit his reintegration into the seminary. That had led to his falling out with Denis. In spite of everything, the two escapees were not without resources for throwing themselves into the water, and that is why they had, in the beginning, been relatively cheerful.

---

[23] This reference—echoed subsequently—recalls Aesop's fable of the jackdaw who donned peacock's plumage in order to show off but was undone when it came unstuck.

To begin with, the matter of his inheritance having been settled, Thibaud had 12,000 francs to come, to which was added about 2000 francs saved from the salaries of their tutorship, which they had pooled. Basic but inexpensive accommodation organized by Aunt Aline permitted them to live without too much anxiety, while working on the preparation of their prodigious future, before which they had to pass their examinations—for they had wisely resolved to "go through the necessary channels" to reach the desired honors. That was according to the formal desire of Thibaud, who was only half Thiérachian—and "not a Gasguin for nothing," as Aunt Aline observed. And Yvernaux had conceded—a trifle regretfully, being more of a fantastic, but congratulating himself almost immediately, since their two baccalaureates had been obtained with ease, Blaise's in letters and Thibaud's in sciences and both with white balls, the expenses of the examination reimbursed.

Nevertheless, disillusionment had set in as soon the preparation for the *bachot* had been replaced by that for entrance to the great Écoles, Normale or Polytechnique. *Latinarum elegantiarum magister* as he had been at Notre-Dame-de-Liesse, Yvernaux was incapable of competing victoriously with the candidates aimed at the Rue d'Ulm by the Lycées de Louis-le-Grand and Charlemagne, strengthened by the expertise of their ancient institutions. And Abbé Dujars had scarcely guided his "prodigy disciple" Gasguin—a prodigy primarily from the viewpoint of the seminary, where the *Jardin des racines grecques*[24] was cultivated rather than the less flowery one of square roots—to the threshold of "special mathematics." The result was that the local Pico della Mirandola now found himself an average pupil of "elementary mathematics"

---

[24] *Le Jardin des racines grecques* [The Garden of Greek Roots] was a popular educational aid whose original version was compiled in the 17th century, a list of linguistic roots compiled by Claude Lancelot being integrated into verses by Louis Isaac le Maistre de Say.

and no more—which is to say, in need of at least two years' "swotting" to be able to compete with the "solid candidates," accomplished veterans aspiring to the honor of choosing between the "leather crown" of Normalian sciences and the "tangent" of the Poly.

Each of them having failed twice to obtain privileged entrance, it was necessary to renounce the vanity of being there, and fall back on the humble and not very comfortable diploma, which only requires a patient labor of assimilation, and which thus offers near-certain admission, albeit without the conceit of competition, and to resign themselves to marking time, shining "gregariously," as Yvernaux put it.

They had, indeed, marked time, the overly brilliant Yvernaux for longer than Gasguin of the solid bovine effort. The latter at his first attempt and the former only at his third— because of his intemperate lyricism and frightening the Sorbonnards, he said—had got their hands on the donkey-skin that permits beating the retreat from special lessons at to enlist in the famished regiment of liberal education.

In the meantime, their war-chest was exhausted, in spite of the savant parsimony of Aunt Aline in eking out their provisions. Merely the expenses of enrollments, books to be bought, and clothes to be bought, in order to be properly presentable on the premises of private tutors, along with a few follies and petty fantasies risked by Yvernaux, had quickly put an end to the 12,000 francs. By the third year of their sojourn in Paris the dolorous farce had been played out, and the mad ambitions were vanishing into thin air—fizzling out, Blaise said, trying to meet ill-luck with a brave heart.

But both of them did, indeed, have stout hearts, and it was then that the fundamentally-modest Thibaud had had the cruel remembrance of his humanities, and of the jackdaw ornamented with a peacock's plumage. Upon which, brave and tenacious, braced rather than depressed by the bitterness of his disappointment, and revealing himself more Thiérachian— which is to say cautious—than ever, he had said to Yvernaux:

"Since the University doesn't want me through its main door, I'll get in by the back one, but I will get in."

And he had applied for a way-station, a position as a teacher of general science at a wretched college in a distant province, where he might, by force of solitary and harshly assiduous "slogging," prepare for the second diploma—that of physics after that of mathematics—and later for his doctorate. Still encouraged by Aunt Aline—who had mumbled a furtive and heartening "To Gasguins, patience brings profit"—he did not despair.

They had not even discussed—neither him not Aunt Aline—the cruel choice that had been made for them of a wild and remote corner in Basse-Bretagne, of a town of which they had not even known the name a week before.

Yvernaux had tried to put them off in advance, but in vain. They had, moreover, separated from him a trifle coldly, without too many regrets, especially on Aunt Aline's part. She had always judged him rather scatterbrained, but for some time, she thought, he had gone too far. Certainly, he had had his usefulness, when needed, with regard to Gasguin, and perhaps he would again someday. For the time being, however, he risked becoming harmful to him with his ideas of taking things in his stride, saying a great deal but doing nothing, with his vanity of thinking no end of himself without knowing whether there was anything to be admired, with his spendthrift tendencies in general and, most of all, with his new inclination, already very marked, to feel more often than was reasonable that his "tongue was dried by the salt of too much talk" and his "throat was in need of washing."

It is certain that, about this time, Yvernaux took certain side-roads that risked leading him where Aunt Aline would have been scared to see Gasguin go, and where Gasguin himself would have been horrified to set foot. Sometimes a junior teacher in "*bachot* ovens" of equivocal reputation, sometimes a tutor of young foreigners procured for him by shady agencies, one day a plagiarist in the service of some bankrupt Encyclopedia, the next secretary to a defrocked monk exploiting a sort of Buddhism for mature ladies, Blaise Yvernaux, the ex-angel of the school at Notre-Dame-de-Liesse became bogged down in Bohemia, rolling from one low dive to the next, and heading straight for a renown in the Latin Quarter that scarcely resembled the one formerly imagined for him by the good Jesuit Fathers, lovers of his intimate epistles parodying Horace's *centos*.

Undoubtedly, he clung to the pretension of soon passing his doctorate in letters, and also his doctorate in philosophy, but his habit of preparing for them by holding forth at tables over aperitifs and nocturnal drinking dens—without ever obtaining any advantage—was not to the liking of the bourgeois that Gasguin remained and always would remain or Aunt Aline, who had never been a Hescheboix in that regard.

"All right! All right!" Yvernaux had declared, not without scorn. "Go to the provinces to recover the snail's life for which you were born and brought up, and show me the horns as you go. Me, I'll stay in Paris, where glory awaits me. I have it already in the Quarter. Tomorrow, or the day after, I'll have it on the great boulevards as well as on the Boul'Mich. And I'll see you in thirty years, perhaps in twenty—or even before, who can tell?—when you'll be my old Thibaud, a petty functionary of the University, sucking the sour milk of your approaching retirement from the meager breast of the *Alma mater*, while I..."

For once, by an extraordinary exception, Aunt Aline had had no need for a half-strangled phrase be wrenched from her gums; she had interrupted of her own accord, aloud, no longer as a quasi-mute reluctant to speak but, on the contrary, almost as a chatterbox delighting in being loquacious.

"Shut up, shut up, fake *ferlampier!*" she had screeched, forcefully. "If you ever become a doctor and falsifier"—that was how she pronounced *philosopher*—"you'll be a doctor of stupidity and a falsifier of silly ditties. Unlike the son of Idalie Hecheboix, who will be someone and something, since she will flourish again in him—yes, yes, I tell you, me who is saying this, since I see it, I see it, I see it!"

Never had she expressed herself at such length in one breath.

Yvernaux had fled, thinking that she had gone mad, after cocking a snook at her as he ran away. And once outside, he really thought that he had left them forever. He did not hold anything against them—even Aunt Aline—retaining good and curious memories, among the sweetest and dearest in the depths of his heart, of Thibaud, his childhood friend. He had pitied him, saying to himself: *Poor fellow! Perhaps he does have something in his noggin! If he'd continued living with me, it would have borne seed in the sunlight of my words!*

Aunt Aline sensed that thought from afar, telepathically. And, mutely—having fallen back into her habitual silence—while packing the meager trunks for the departure into exile, she ruminated as if by way of reply, less in articulate sentences than in troubled and ambiguous sibylline terms of which Thibaud understood nothing, although he grasped fragments in passing: the only distinct phrases amid obscure mutterings, like—as Yvernaux would have said if he had heard them—nuggets in a matrix of crumbling flint.

"No, no, not by you, that seed..."

"The other seed, the true, yes, a little..."

"But first, the fine Breton sun..."

"When Idalie's blood has been filtered..."

"In the sand, the sand, the sand..."

"We'll meet again, anyway, we'll see..."

"Almost an entire week and a half of years without seeing one another..."

"We'll meet again, I tell you: we'll see one another..."

Thibaud, who had long since given up paying any heed to her absurd outbursts of oracular gibberish—which were widely spaced in any case—had not been able to prevent himself, this time, as on certain past occasions, being impressed, shaken by the frisson of mystery. To defend himself against it, he had taken her firmly by the wrists and said: "Indeed! I think Yvernaux wasn't entirely wrong just now, slamming the door in your face as on a madwoman, Aunt Aline! Your head's a little upside-down today, eh? What's that you're muttering? Is there any rhyme or reason to it? What are you thinking about? Of whom?"

Suddenly, she had calmed down, and had replied softly, in a childish voice "Nothing, nothing, my son. I wasn't thinking about anything or anyone."

And a dialogue was established between them, abrupt on his part, vague in her mouth.

"But what do you see, then, looking into God knows where, with a fixed and seemingly interior gaze? What do you see?"

"Things, things."

"What things?"

"The one that are out there."

"Where, out there?"

"Out there and in me."

"Explain yourself better."

"I don't see them anymore, now."

After which, with a slight foam at the corners of her lips, her face very pale, her eyes dull, the purse of her speech sealed over her gums and determined not to open again, Aunt Aline resumed packing the trunks. Absorbed by her meticulous work and concentrating all her voluntary self therein, she had become once again what she had always been, and what she would continue to be for the 25 years of their provincial existence, and what was, in sum, in the ordinary state of her nature, outside of her rare divinatory crises—which is to say, the worthy little woman, neat and mousy, in the black uniform, with the appearance and humor of a shiny scarab beetle, active, grim and silent.

Thibaud, in spite of the kind of fit that he had just witnessed, found her once again to be as he defined her, so exactly, in the everyday routine: his housekeeping organ, no more. It would have required what he had never had—a strange delicacy of telepathic touch—to perceive that the pretended housekeeping organ, of vulgar utility, was also, and especially, an organ of magnetization, directing his entire life toward an unknown pole, which only that humble insect could detect.

IX

During his first ten years of provincial teaching, the story of Gasguin, flanked by Aunt Aline, was that of happy people who have no story. Their monotonous happiness had been woven on a weft without snags, but also devoid of embroideries, or nearly so. Very conscientiously, Aunt Aline had looked after Gasguin's modest home, while he, also very conscientiously, had looked after his classes—which had not prevented him from preparing privately, still very conscientiously, for his second diploma, in physical sciences, and for his future but distant doctorate, henceforth the supreme goal of his university ambitions.

They were both able to count the major events of those ten years, the rare embroideries embellishing the bleak desert of their day-to-day uniformity with bouquets of flowers, and they took pleasure in them, in fact, like misers adding up their treasure.

First and foremost, there was a journey to Rennes, the seat of the academy to which Gasguin had gone to pass his famous diploma and from which he returned with a further diploma, which gave him three more than the principal of his colleague, a mere baccalaureate-holder. Now in possession of four parchments, the teacher of general sciences could hope for advancement, and he had obtained it, in spite of the malevolent envy of his superior. Distinguished by a scrupulous inspector, Gasguin had been promoted to a less miserable position—and that had given him and Aunt Aline their second notable joy.

That change of residence, soon followed by another—the excellent and highly-qualified master rose quite quickly—caused them scant excitement, however. The pay was slightly better, it's true, but one small town in Brittany is very similar to another, even if one is in Basse-Bretagne and the other in

Haute-Bretagne, so Gasguin and Aunt Aline scarcely noticed any difference.

Also, they never made any friends anywhere; the teacher never had any horizon other than his classes and the doctoral program to come, not amusing himself even in a few special lessons of which he had no need, thanks to Aunt Aline's skillful economies. The augmentation of salary had permitted him to indulge himself in the only distractions he appreciated, since they consisted of the acquisition of books and journals, all instruments of labor—not to mention the actual instruments that gradually made up a small laboratory of sorts.

And that too—more than anything else—had embellished and colored his grey existence, and that of Aunt Aline in parallel. When he rubbed his hands after some successful experiment in the vacant cupboard pompously designated as his "physics laboratory," Aunt Alice was gladdened by seeing him content, and doubled that contentment with some remark such as: "You'll get there, I tell you, you'll get there"—unless she limited herself to clicking her tongue and imparting a: "Well! You've found the bird on its nest, then?" She had no idea at all what Gasguin had done or what had happened, or what bird and what nest were involved; his delighted expression was sufficient proof of how perfect their present collective felicity was, although made of so little.

Another joy—very vivid, this one, and perhaps the richest ornament adding a protrusion of silk and gold to the flat tapestry of their happiness—had been a complete reconciliation with the elder brother, Denis. After having been without news of him for nearly seven years, they had suddenly received a letter announcing that he was coming to visit Saint-Brieuc, with the express intention of making up with those he loved. And that, truly, had been a great celebration for all of them. To begin with, Denis had brought a genuine affection to the reconciliation, Then he had give them some important good news. Ordained as a priest, he had stopped off at Saint-Brieuc before leaving for the Channel Islands, where he was to spend a phase of his novitiate with the Jesuit Fathers established on an island between Herm and Sark. Thus, he too was prospering in his chosen path.

What he did not say, being too sincerely modest to take any vanity therefrom, was how and why he had effected the conquest of this destiny, which had been temporarily refused to him. For, as you will remember, having become poor after his father's death, Denis had been classed among the pupils destined to obscure priesthood in the minor clergy, no longer among the elect that the Company reserved for itself. And yet, by dint of gentle and smiling determination, Denis has overcome that obstacle. His very rare distinction, his real, natural and ever-increasing mental elegance, the flexibility of his character, and also the seriousness of his religious vocation, which had nothing crude or sad about it—quite the contrary!—had finally reckoned with the limitations imposed on the former director by the total ruin of the Gasguins. The new and more refined director, doing justice to Denis, had finally declared: "As a spiritual resource, no fortune is worth as much as the seductiveness of that young abbé."

Aunt Aline, of course, had not heard that pronouncement, and Abbé Denis was unaware of it himself—but Aunt Aline made an occult allusion to it even so, when she congratulated the elder brother on his success and said to him, more chattily than usual: "You owe it your mother, you know, Monsieur l'Abbé. It's a renewal of her charm, and a second crop of her seductiveness."

For everything that was good, precious, powerful, gentle and strong in the present or future descendants of the family, Aunt Aline invariable attributed to her former idol, the flower of the blood of the Hescheboix, to the one from whom the flower of the flower of that blood would one day be born, to her Idalie, whom she had called during their childhood and youth, until the hour preceding her death "my Idalie, my lovely sister, my little God!"

And, chancing to be in a vein of slightly less brief utterances, she reminded the new priest of that—and Abbé Denis proved, moreover, that he would soon be the fine recruit anticipated by his director, for the idolatrous, quasi-sacrilegious expression did not scandalize him at all. Thibaud had frowned anxiously, on behalf of the Abbé freshly emerged from the mold of ordination, but the future Jesuit Father had smiled indulgently, and the two brothers and Aunt Aline had savored a collective delight, the first two in having heard again and the last-named in repeating, as if in ecstasy: "My Idalie, my lovely sister, my little God!"

Less profane than that day's joy, but almost more agreeable still, and undoubtedly the second best, had been the reappearance in Thibaud's life, in which he had previously played such an important role: Blaise Yvernaux, another dead man suddenly returned to life.

Even Aunt Aline, who had separated from him on a sour note, did not see him again without a sentiment of pleasure— quite simply, at first, because she retained, beneath the layer of the final memories, a substratum of older and more favorable memories. Was he not the one who had contrived to remove Thibaud's soutane? And who, with his eloquence, had brought him to white heat in order that Aline might forge him according to the new shape demanded by destiny? And who else but him could have professed that perennial fine faith in Thibaud's future, that faith from which the good seminarian, the prudent Thiérachian, had extracted the audacity necessary to hurl himself into the adventure?

In memory of and in loyal gratitude for all that, Aunt Aline had therefore taken satisfaction from the knowledge of a possible imminent return into their lives—but what she rejoiced in especially was the idea, or rather the sensation, that the event of his return would be the forerunner of other, more important events to the advantage of something obscure for which she was waiting. What that thing was, she could not have said, any more today than on the day of the separation; that the thing in question was nevertheless *en route* toward them, she sensed.

Without adding anything more precise, she had not been able to help saying to Gasguin, when he had received the letter from Yvernaux making an appeal to their old friendship: "I was sure, my son, that we'd see one another again." And as the words of yore rose up to her teeth again, she chewed some of them over again, among them a pronouncement whose prophetic quality was manifest:

"Almost an entire week and a half of years without seeing one another..."

Which Thibaud, not having paid any heed to it before, or no longer remembering it, did not understand; otherwise, he would have been amazed, in calculating that ten years had indeed already elapsed between the departure from Paris and Yvernaux's letter. Ten years—which is to say, seven years plus three years, and not more three years and six months, but exactly three years and five months; in brief, what Aline had called, in her bizarre language, "almost an entire week and a half of years."

In any case, Gasguin was certainly in no state to notice such "Chinese puzzles of hazard," as he would not have failed to describe it if he had heard it. Yvernaux's letter gave him other interesting information, and he had reached a critical junction himself the day before, which he considered to be definitive.

He had gone, in fact, for the second time, and with the firm resolution that it would be the last, to take the examination for admission to the doctorate. Since his first failure, five years earlier, in a period of his career when he really had not had the material and intellectual means to prepare for that redoubtable contest, he had sworn not to go into battle again until he had every chance of victory. Thanks to his increased salary, the purchase of books and instruments, and the proximity of a Faculty of Sciences, where he had devoted himself, as if under pressure, to study, in order to catch up with the most recent theories and discoveries, he was as formidably armed now as it was possible to be—and if he did not end in triumph this time, it was because he was condemned to defeat without appeal. In sum, he went into it with a clear conscience—and one can imagine the state of excitement to which he was prey.

This, in addition, is what he learned from Yvernaux's long and dithyrambic letter, here filtered and summarized as briefly as possible, without entirely obliterating its bouquet:

After a further five or six years of bohemian existence in the Quarter, of furious swinishness alternating with seasons of mellow idleness, Blaise had chanced to come into an unexpected inheritance assuring him, not of a fortune, but an honest ease: the famous *aurea mediocritas*[25] of the Latin poet; for a thousand francs a year. He had taken advantage of it to "turn over a new leaf," to immerse himself once again in the healthy springs of work and ambition, and, according to the Thiérachian expression "to get hold of the horse's mane again"—on the Pegasus of Glory, he added, in parentheses. He had determined to pass his examinations and become a great thinker. He had failed the doctorate in philosophy, still "by the fault of Sorbonnards shocked by the audacity of his theories and the lyricism of his language." He was too "mythic" for those "misfits"—one can imagine him proclaiming that. All the same, they had been forced to lower their flag (an old nightshirt, he emphasized) before his (a triumphant horn, he emphasized immediately, underlining it three times) and, after a prestigious defense—before which the simulated-bronze bonzes had melted in admiration, to the applause of a "roomful of brains," if he might express it thus—Blaise Yvernaux had received his doctorate of letters, on the very eve of the day on which he was writing, and earned it with two theses "destined to last," two works "marking a crucial date in the annals of Ideas": his Latin thesis *De calignosi Heracliti ad illustrandum Enti et Nihili essentiam sicut eamdem fulguribus quibusdam*,[26] which he described as being Spinoza reviewed by Hegel and written by Seneca; and his French thesis, of which the

---

[25] Golden mean

[26] Approximately, *On the enlightening illustration by the obscure Heraclitus of the fact that being and nothingness are essentially the same thing.*

title alone, *The Metaphysics of the Absurd*, was, he affirmed, undeniably the Open Sesame of all mysteries.

What a delight it was for Thibaud thus to rediscover his "brilliant" Yvernaux of old, an honest man again, finally having assumed the rank in the world that he had occupied in the seminary—and just at the moment when he was about to set the seal on his ten years of labor by his triumph in the doctoral examination! For Blaise's success appeared to him to be an omen of his own. Together they had set out and together they would arrive.

And in that conviction of a hope suddenly ripened into a near-certainty, it was with assurance that he took the train for Paris, crowning his ten years of patient effort with that final surge of self-confidence—for which reason Aunt Aline was again sincerely grateful for Yverdon's reappearance. Had not her Thibaud, rendered lyrical with joy, said to her:

"Don't you think that his fiery letter is like a comet announcing for this year a vintage of memorable happiness?"

X

It is unfortunate that Yvernaux never found out about that extraordinary fit of lyricism on the part of his Gasguin. He would have taken it as a license to preach in favor of his beloved lyricism by saying: "You see how good it is! The one time that you were lyrical, you went as far as being a prophet."

It was not only for the present year, in fact, but for the entire series of years from then on, it seemed, that the comet had promised prosperous vintages, From then on, Gasguin's life had not ceased to be fortunate—even, as we shall see, in the few side-roads by which fate attempted to deflect him, only succeeding in further ensuring his good progress.

There was, to begin with, the famous doctoral examination—passed in the end, it goes without saying, and in honorable conditions, the competition having been particularly strong, but passed nevertheless, if much less triumphantly than Gasguin's momentary lyricism had desired. That cruel disappointment was, however, without his suspecting it, good for him.

Too brilliantly received, and immediately set above his peers thanks to the aureole of the competition, he would probably have been immediately marked down for a chair in Paris. Now, that "immediately" would have been "too soon." Only Aunt Aline suspected that, we must assume, for, on learning that Thibaud, instead of the desired first place of which he had been almost certain, had scraped into the next-to-last, she told him, when he became indignant, gazing at him vaguely but fixedly: "It's better this way, my son."

And when he ground his teeth, she added one of her favorite old sayings: "To the Gasguins, patience brings profit."

Whether she had said that blindly or not, to console her son for his quasi-defeat or with the real apprehension of a Parisian "immediately" turning out to be a "too soon," it remains the case that by that nomination—which is to say, by excessive success in the competition—the future of which she had the occult care would have been lost. That is what no one suspected, not even Gasguin, who turned his back on her resentfully that day, concluding that she really was a little too stupid sometimes.

Almost an idiot—who knows?

To which, as if he had spoken the sentence aloud, she replied: "It's in the province that you ought to marry."

Never before had she made any allusion to the idea of marriage. Nor had Gasguin. Celibacy had remained dear to him, as if he were still awaiting the priesthood. From his adolescence in the seminary he had retained an absolute appetite for chastity, and had felt it increase rather than decrease in assiduous work and carnal solitude. In reality, amorous sentiment had not even needed to be extinguished within him, nothing ever having set it alight. It was a seed within his being, atrophied and, worse still, absent. So Aunt Aline's bizarre affirmation made him burst out laughing.

He laughed again, on his own, that evening, when he related the strange occurrence to Yvernaux, in a letter in which he announced his doctorate.

"If I'd had the luck," he wrote, "to run into you in Paris, incorrigible Thiérachian that you are, I'd have invited you here to spend the rest of the vacation with us; but I don't regret it too much, for you'd have found an Aunt Aline almost fallen into infantilism, although she's only just a quinquegenarian. Can you imagine that she's now got it into her head to marry me off? No. Can you see me in the power of a woman—me, a defrocked seminarian, a failed curé, henceforth devoted to a new priesthood, more demanding than the other: that of Science? Can you see me...?"

And, perhaps hilarious for the first time in his life, he continued in that tone, almost jokingly, while laughing out loud—with the result that Aunt Aline arrived, anxiously running to his rescue, imagining that he had, as she said "swallowed his saliva the wrong way."

Three days later, he received Yvernaux's rely, and collapsed in surprise on reading it. The former bohemian of the Quarter, the maker of speeches laden with panache and the animated ironist, had retracted all the claws of his irony and all the ruffled plumage of his metaphors, and spread wise counsel like butter, advising Thibaud to allow himself to be married off by Aunt Aline.

"Just as I've turned over a new leaf," he wrote, "you need to turn over one. And for you, that consists of matrimonial calm. A scientist, a university man, needs a family. With your doctorate, and your bread on the board, and your retirement in prospect, you ought, indeed..."

And Yvernaux sermonized thus for ten pages running—not because he was much changed, as Gasguin thought, but because he knew the essential bourgeois that his friend was, and loved him as such, and wanted him to be happy, with the happiness designed for people like him. A hint of egotism was mingled with that desire, naturally; Yvernaux knew that he was destined himself for adventure, in spite of everything—at least intellectually—and he was not averse to preparing for his old age, as a philosopher still bohemian in spirit, a refuge of stable and familial tranquility.

"I shall be content," he wrote, in all naivety, "to see your children and be their godfather."

Gasguin fell off his perch. What! Everyone, then, had abandoned him. He grew sad. He experienced a sort of reversion to the distant and vague religious appetency of his youth and regretted the ecclesiastical peace in which he might have had the leisure to cultivate the sciences conjointly with his divine service. And he wrote a long letter on that subject to his brother, Abbé Denis, the only person in whom he thought he would encounter a heart sympathetic to his exclusive desire for celibacy.

The prompt response was a thunderbolt. The Abbé informed him of his imminent visit, precisely to discuss with him the subject of a marriage that he had in mind for him.

And that marriage was made, all the people dear to Thibaud wanting it. He too, finally persuaded that it was for the best, wanted it. After the objections that he had been the first, and the only one, to raise against the universal desire that was soon to become his own, his fate had been brought back to the true path by the second happiness of his life, even sweeter than the doctorate: an exquisite union.

Not that Gasguin was obliged thereby to experience and savor the joys—especially the sensualities of amour—for which he decidedly seemed not to have been made, at least until then. But he found therein what Aunt Aline, in spite of her qualities as a perfect housekeeper and the great affection of a devoted servant, could not offer him: an assiduous companion, an intelligence capable of associating itself with the work that he loved.

To tell the truth, Mademoiselle Anne-Herminie-Luce de Saint-Ylan would scarcely have seemed espousable by anyone except Gasguin, so energetically persuaded by his brother Abbé Denis, the insistent letters of Yvernaux, the silent but stubborn objurgations of Aunt Aline, and by himself, convinced now that he ought to provide himself with a household. It needed no less than that to prevent him from observing that his intended was neither pretty, nor young, nor equipped, in spite of these deficits, with anything that might excuse them under the pretext of a god bargain.

Eighteen hundred francs of income for life was not sufficient, in fact, to dazzle a professor with a doctorate, with a minimum annual income of 3600 francs, with an assured pension. And even if he had had the hypnotized eyes of a pauper, that would have been unable to make him forget that Mademoiselle Anne-Herminie-Luce de Saint-Ylan was 35 years old—five years older than Thibaud—and that she evoked the idea of a caricature rather than that of a feminine face, with her overly long nose, her overly high forehead, a mouth like the slot in a money-box, the vitreous eyes of a dead fish, and the meager vermicelli of her hair stuck to her hollow temples.

And yet, Thibaud had not found fault either with the dowry, which seemed to him magnificent, being constituted as an income, nor her age, to which he did not attach any importance, having manipulated numbers so extensively in mathematics that he always attributed an abstract and absolute character to them. As for her physiognomy, he had been quite satisfied to have noticed excitedly, during their first meeting, that her mask—he took the word literally, as we shall see—bore an extraordinary resemblance to the death-mask of Blaise Pascal.

To be sure, he entered into it complacently, his vision blinded, not by love, but by passive obedience to the suggestions to which he was prey. For Mademoiselle Saint-Ylan's visage lacked exactly that which rendered the other splendid and miraculously alive in the mould of death: it lacked thought, ready to reignite in the vitreous eyes sealed beneath the eyelids and vibrant still as a sublime arrow in the bow of the lips, vainly compressed, it seemed, by the plaster that it was about to burst asunder in an explosion of genius. But that was all that Gasguin saw, so profound was his adoration for Pascal. Thus, at the first stroke, through that admiration and his passion for science, he had loved, as much as was possible for him, the woman offered to him as a spouse.

Why did the Comtesse want to find a husband for Mademoiselle de Saint-Ylan? Firstly, by virtue of what adventures did the Comtesse have a foster-sister with a *particule*?[27] What, that is to say, had led to a gentleman—the Saint-Ylans were authentic Breton squires—espousing a nurse, a simple Pontual gamekeeper's daughter? And how exactly, in seeking a husband who might suit Anne-Herminie-Luce, had Thibaud Gasguin been sniffed out?

---

[27] In the 19th century, the children of aristocrats were routinely handed over to wet-nurses for feeding, thus acquiring "foster-siblings" with whom they sometimes maintained unequal but close friendships.

That, in truth, would be too long a story, since it would involve another whole history much thicker with confusion than the present one. Anyway, the details of it would be of purely romantic interest; those concerning the family, life and character of Thibaud Gasguin and a few others at least have the excuse for their perhaps excessive abundance of being necessary to a knowledge of Geneviève.

Without having the pretension to reconstitute here—to employ grandiose terms—the exegesis and the genesis of genius, we shall not hide the keen desire with which we were smitten and which we have obligingly satisfied, the opportunity having been offered, of digging as far as we could into the roots, the soil, the environment, the vital saps, the fertilizers, the chemistry and, above all, the souls from which issued that extraordinary, rarest of the rare, and ultimately unanalyzable, soul of a genius. We have, in our fashion, fulfilled that dream, the ambition of which has nothing ridiculous about it, we imagine, simple as it is, knowing that the best means possible, not of analysis but of partial explanation, is collecting, with patience and modesty, naively and methodically, impassioned by the slightest details, everything that a Saint-Simon curious about such a subject would have called the "ins and outs," including the "round abouts."

Still, it is necessary not to linger on those that would be too distant. And that is why a few words will suffice to state—without enquiring as to the ifs, buts, hows and whys—that the director of the Jesuit Fathers established in the Channel Islands was the Comtesse's cousin, that he had sent Abbé Denis Gasguin to tutor the Vicomte, then only just eight years old, and that by virtue of that association, evidently, he had easily been able to make Thibaud's marriage.

Aunt Aline, seeing through the most opaque veils, had not taken so long. One might have thought, when she had first been introduced to Mademoiselle de Saint-Ylan, that she was "finding her again." And on hearing her speak, overcome with emotion, she exclaimed: "It's Idalie's voice!"

She alone could know that. And why should she be mistaken? And that was one more reason why Thibaud loved his wife.

Alas, that amour, so tender and sweet, although so dissimilar to what is normally described by that name—that sweet sisterly affection in which two souls melted without having need of their bodies—poor Thibaud was not to enjoy for long. And of the few misfortunes that tried to kill his happiness, that alone had taken on the aspect of a catastrophe of terrible magnitude. A year after the wedding, his wife was dead.

"Like Idalie," Aunt Aline had remarked.

For it was also in bringing a new Gasguin scion into the world that the poor creature departed, and by virtue of the same accident: a fatal attack of eclampsia.

Thibaud almost died of grief before his shattered happiness. But it was not Aunt Aline who was able to bring him consolation at that moment. Silent, devoid of tears, she watched a sentence "come to life" inside herself, in the blackest blackness of her most profound self, and writhe like a fiery serpent, which she dared not pronounce aloud but thought with an extraordinary force:

It had to happen, and it's better thus.

Why did it have to happen, and why was it better thus?

We would be lying in even insinuating that she might know. Nevertheless, we must confess that everything happened as if someone or something knew it for her.

Suppose, in fact, that Anne-Herminie-Luce had survived. Thibaud would gradually have got a taste for the paradise of his household, and doubtless even for the fruit that he had initially considered forbidden, having only bitten into it once. And, fairly rapidly, he would have become what Yvernaux had suggested that he become, believing himself destined to it, and because he really was destined to it, in the capacity of a Gasguin—which is to say, the mediocre bourgeois, the humble universitarian following his banal career until his anticipated retirement.

That death, by way of compensation, returned him to himself, to science, and, above all, to his true fate, exceptional in this: that he was to serve as the preparer, the initiator, and later the collaborator, of a genius of which he was to be the reflection.

And that is what Aunt Aline sensed; that was what the *Sphex* of the race of Hescheboix had worked for so long in advance, and so surely, in her instinctive determination. The larva could be born now.

And, indeed, Geneviève had just been born.

XI

In a family in which Aunt Aline did not exist—which is to say, probably, any other than Thibaud Gasguin's—nothing would have seemed notable in the actions and gestures associated with the advent and early infancy of Geneviève. No one would even have thought that there were actions and gestures there. The craziest and most doting of grandmothers would not have admired that which is ordinarily admired, in the most admired of babies—which is to say, that which causes such exclamations as "My God, what a dainty creature! There's never been such a beautiful one! It's a marvel without equal in all the world!"

It was in terms less general, and with affirmations far more precise, that Aunt Aline observed and pointed out the merits that made Geneviève a miraculous individual.

"She's the spitting image of Idalie."

Such had been the welcoming greeting of the poor little wrinkled, grimacing, whimpering, blind thing, violet with congestion—and in order for Aunt Aline to have addressed it to her with such sincere devotion, she must really have seen her idol of splendid and ideal beauty resuscitated in that sort of obscure sketch promising nothing but a monster. She had said it with an accent so profound that the unfortunate Thibaud, in the anguish that was strangling him as he watched, at that very moment, his wife's death throes, had not been able to help smiling at the compliment—which was, as he was not unaware, the greatest of which Aunt Aline was capable.

And he had replied, tears of paternal pride mingling with those of his conjugal grief: "You think so, Aunt Aline? She's beautiful, then?"

"Yes, she's beautiful!" the quinquegenarian had exclaimed, clapping her hands like a girl and shuffling her feet in a desire to dance. And to the tune of a popular song, she had sung, in a very low voice—yes, sung, at the bedside of the dying woman, really sung—in an old Thiéarchian patois, whose words were assonances in themselves:

Belle! Amon! Chi teu n'crès nin l'vielle,
Woit' à chès leum'rott's, min chtiot fieu.
L'iau veet'dins l'or f'chès gluer d'solel
Qu'étot l'fond d's yux d'min p'tit bon Dieu.[28]

It is evidently through the infant's creased and as-yet-unopened eyelids that Aunt Aline was contemplating, in those dull and troubled "leumerottes" the perverse, seductive, profound, enveloping gaze of her dear Idalie—a gaze similar, indeed, to glaucous water flowing over a bed gilded by wispy rays of sunlight. It is necessary to believe, even so, that the veil of the eyelids and the vitreousness of vague pupils had not prevented the clear perception of reality, for later, when they really did open to the light, Geneviève's eyes really were, at times, just as the old woman, who could not have seen them, had described them.

It often happens that grave expressions pass over infants' faces, in which one suddenly finds resemblances to some long-dead relative. It was thus with Geneviève, but Aunt Aline was never wont to evoke resemblances of that sort on such occasions. The memories that abruptly surged forth in her were much more ancient, and sprang up like geysers, originating from the utmost profundities of the race. Thus, at least the lyrical Yvernaux characterized them, having chanced to hear

---

[28] Needless to say, there is no dictionary of Thiérachian patois that could assist in making sense of this verse, so I have transcribed it as written. The text spells out the gist of it, but it is worth noting that two of the vague terms of endearment it concerns are henceforth used repeatedly by Aunt Aline: *amon*, which is equivalent to "my love" but is also given a second meaning, spelled out when relevant, and *chtiot*, more usually rendered *ch'tiote*, which signifies something like "little darling".

some of them, on the very day when he came for his god-daughter's baptism.

As the child, after having first cried on contact with the cold water and pulling a face on spitting out the salt, unexpectedly took on a meditative expression, furrowed by austere wrinkles, Aunt Aline had murmured: "A thousand years ago she knew that thought."

And short while later, as the baby's face blossomed like a rose laughing in the sunlight when she finished feeding, and droplets of milk pearled in the corners of her mouth and dripped into her bib, the old woman had added, with a smile: "She's counting her treasures."

Almost immediately, weary of the ceremony and drunk on the rich cream crammed into her by her nurse—a brunette *galotte*[29] from Saint-Cast—the child had fallen deeply asleep. She was "blowing peas," according to the old popular expression, and trickles of "flumes"—to employ an onomatopoeic Thiérachian term—were running down her chin. As the nurse reached out to wipe them away, Aunt Aline had stopped her with an abrupt command.

"Leave it! That's sap, from the time when she was a plant."

As for the pea-blowing, she was positively ecstatic about it, the darling now continuing it in her wicker cradle, the old peasant crib in which Gasguin himself had insisted on installing her. To please the godfather, who had offered a fashionable iron bassinet, painted cream, with muslin curtains with pink silk knots, the cradle had been overhung by those veils, which were suspended from a gilded curtain-rod—but Aunt Aline parted them in order to respire the little girl's breath, and each pea blown the old woman said: "Another one! Big one! And one! And one! And this! And that! And one! Big one!"

---

[29] This appears to be a feminine form of "gallot," which the text employs several times as a slang term for a native of Britanny.

And at that moment, Gasguin would have willingly believed that she had fallen back into infancy, but not Yvernaux, whose imagination, stimulated by the formulaic game, reminded him of his distant past, and also—more especially—Aunt Aline's brief muttered soliloquies. For, in those refrains, which Gasguin supposed to be merely remembrances borrowed from fairy tales—when he consented to suppose that they were anything at all—Yvernaux heard the voices of extinct things taking form again, and dead people coming back to life. He reflected expressly on the atavisms that phrase such as these suggested, rich in meaning for those who sought it out:

"A thousand years ago she knew that thought."

"She's counting her treasures."

"That's sap, from the time when she was a plant."

To be sure, he said to himself, *that poor old woman's noggin can't and shouldn't take account of the mysterious meanings wrapped up in her words, which Yvernaux has sought and found there.* He alone, he flattered himself—to Gasguin's detriment as much as hers—embroidered those grandiose dreams on the canvas of coarse cloth. And yet, it was not him, the philosopher, and it really was her, the illiterate simpleton, who had uttered those sentences of formidable import, and who, at that moment, whispering in patois, her lips pinched so that almost nothing could be heard, had suddenly, after breathing in the baby's breath, murmured this enormous thing, so powerfully perceived by her that her teeth chattered:

"Y en d's âmes, dins ch'tiot vint-là!"[30]

It is true that Yvernaux, at that moment, was more than ever inclined to excitement, quite drunk on his godfatherhood, and also joyful at having seen the dream he had had of a family refuge whose pleasures he might have without its burdens realized so soon. From that, perhaps, came the facility at bouncing on trampolines of enthusiasm that were furnishing him—as he claimed—with Aunt Alice's elastic expressions.

---

[30] Approximately: "These are souls in that child, coming out."

It is indubitable, however, that for him to, quite apart from any godfatherly enthusiasm, his goddaughter was not a little girl like all the rest. And even Gasguin, if he had not been Geneviève's father, would not have been able to help thinking her extraordinary. Aunt Aline's tricks and nonsense aside, the child was certainly worthy of being noticed, and of being the subject of precious remarks.

Her beauty, in spite of all the admiration for her famous resemblance to the idol Idalie, was far from being indisputable. That, while hiding it from Aunt Aline, Yvernaux and even Gasguin were forced to concede. Their paternal and parrainal (Yverneux's term) indulgence went as far as the excuse of ingrate age, and would be prolonged without any interruption through all Geneviève's ages. The equity of the scientists and the esthetics of the philosopher were not, however, able to acquiesce in the imperious affirmations of the indefatigable admirer, always decreeing, as at the moment of her birth: "She's the spitting image of Idalie." Unless, they declared, secretly, Grandmama Idalie had not, after all, had the miraculous beauty with which she was credited.

If Geneviève was not that celebrated marvel, however, nor ever promised to be, she nevertheless did not give rise to any anxiety that she might turn into the ugly caricature in which the exquisite soul of her poor mother had been wrapped. All things considered, she was neither truly pretty nor the opposite.

Her eyes alone answered to the eulogies that Aunt Aline had uttered in advance, and which their gaze and countersigned. They did not always merit those eulogies, though, or, at least, not the same ones—which made them more beautiful when they did, the ingenious Yvernaux suggested. And his ingenuity was fully justified. Although Geneviève's eyes, in fact, even while she was still a child, often had a strange, attractive and almost dangerous seductiveness—the famous eyes of Idalie—they did not always have it, nor did they have it consistently. At certain times they seemed to be extinct. The wisp of gold in their depths was tarnished, losing its sunlight.

The green of their water ceased to be the same transparent liquid. Their gaze became discolored then, their glaucous quality soon turning to gray, almost neutral. By way of compensation, though, at certain times, often after these intervals of effacement, they suddenly flared up with a strange gleam, as to the nature of which there was no conceivable doubt, for it was all intelligence.

"That, Idalie didn't have."

Thus Aunt Aline, impartial to the point of refusing something to her idol, had pronounced. On another occasion, she had made her idea more precise by specifying: "The Hescheboix males, yes."

And she had added, with a significant shrug of the shoulders showing what she thought of it: "Anyway, that—*pfft*!"

But Yvernaux and Gasguin had immediately protested, and had given the phenomenon its true explanation; in unison, they almost shouted the retort, which defined the exact meaning of the famous "that," by virtue of which, for the first time, they had dared to contradict the old sentence-spouter to her face:

"It's thought!"

"Eh?" the old woman had queried. "What? Say again? What? You're making fun of me!"

"I tell you," Yvernaux had insisted, bravely, "that in Geneviève's eyes, at times, there's a *that* that Idalie didn't have, and I tell you that that *that*..."

"Yes," Gasguin had interrupted, "*that*, which the Hescheboix males couldn't have had either, *that*..."

"Well, what *that*?" the old woman had abruptly cut in, playing stupid. "What *that*?" And articulating the *that*s with an increasing hiss, she had repeated, volubly, until she could repeat no more, furiously, as if she were spitting the *pfffts* in the face:

"*That, that, that. pfft! pfft! That, that, pfft! That, pfft! pfft! pfft!*"

And then, both together, after a loud burst of laughter that she had thought stupid, they had started howling madly, with one voice, louder than hers and shutting her up:

"Thought! Thought! Thought!"

XII

From that day on, Aunt Aline's utterances of authoritative sentences had become increasing rare, and her sibylline semblance had become increasingly attenuated.

This observation was made by Yvernaux on two consecutive trips, and corroborated each time by the testimony of Gasguin, who had also noticed it. And they both found great amusement—although on the "*muchetenpot*," as they say in Thiérache—in the mortified expression that the old woman now had.

At the same time, the father told the godfather, who came every year to spend a month's holiday with them, about the incredible aptitude, increasing every day, the Geneviève manifested for the sciences.

Yvernaux would have preferred that she had had aptitudes for other things that were dearer to his heart, in the appreciation of which he was more competent. With respect to the sciences in general, especially mathematics, he had to take Gasguin at his word. That was not, in the beginning, without a sort of chagrin, which freely translated itself into irony, even at the expense of his beloved godchild. One might almost have thought, at times, that he resented it, as if she were betraying him by not liking that which was not dear to him alone.

"Oh," he said, once, "as soon as a kid, especially a girl, throws herself into the undergrowth of algebra and walks without falling over, you equation-crunchers think she's Pascal."

"Geneviève isn't content to walk," Gasguin had replied, imperturbably. "She dances."

"She's the Terpsichore of logarithms, then!" Yvernaux had jeered. And as he had a good memory for all vocabularies, even those in which he could not put a clear meaning to the words, he reeled off a series of mathematical terms, making bracelets and necklaces for them with comical gestures, and continued, with fervor: "Yes, the Terpsichore of prime numbers, whose legs are guided by extractions of cube roots, which make *points* among the alternate internal angles and *entrechats* above the asymptotes—a Terpsichore that you are proud of having for a pupil, and to whom you teach the steps of the $x^2 + px + q = 0$."

"When you've finished with your verbal buffoonery and juggling with words that you don't understand, I'll talk to you seriously about your goddaughter."

Yvernaux's broad seam of boastfulness had been abruptly cut short and emptied by Gasguin's interruption, made in a severe and serious tone, with a hint of scorn and a touch of near-mournful reproach. Fundamentally good and tender, adoring Geneviève more and more, the poor godfather had had tears in his eyes and had replied, very humbly: "Forgive me, old chap! I won't insult the child any more. What I did was out of resentment of not being able to appreciate her famous aptitude fully, and knowledgeably. Oh, if it were also for philosophy or lyricism, you'd see what I mean!"

"But the sciences lead to philosophy and lyricism," Gasguin replied, "as to everything else. Give it time! Geneviève isn't yet twelve years old. At that age, Pascal had already reinvented—there's no other word for it—the first two books of Euclid's geometry with a ruler and compasses, and he would soon produce his treatise on conic sections, but that didn't do him any harm when he eventually came to write *Les Pensées*, did it? Far from it."

That burst of eloquence, unusual for Gasguin, had completed his victory over Yvernaux—who wanted nothing better than to be beaten, anyway, and was content, since the true victor in the matter was Geneviève.

There and then, the philosopher resolved to attempt something that seemed difficult, even slightly humiliating, which he had never had the courage to undertake, even when he was preparing for his doctoral examination in philosophy. Admitting to himself that he was perhaps a little too uniquely oratorical, and malnourished with facts, he finally deemed them necessary to "the health of his ideas," as he put it. He regretted only having drunk "the strong wine of Science," as he expressed it, in "the vague prelibations in which one only tastes the foam that consists of general ideas."

Loyally and sincerely, gripped by a beautiful passion for that Science of which his goddaughter seemed bound to become an Egregore,[31] he became a student again in order to be able to follow her, no matter how far, on the route she was traveling. It was from that moment on that he gave the Latin Quarter the edifying spectacle of a doctor of letters transformed into a perpetual student.

His mind being made for generalizing rather than for observation, he did not become a better man of science in consequence, but merely a logician and orator armed with more serious arguments. Most importantly, though, if the philosopher did not gain much thereby, the godfather, in compensation, benefited greatly and entirely. His admiration for his goddaughter acquired justification and substance. He was no longer limited, as he had been pitifully obliged to do before, to talking through his hat—his dunce's cap, he said—when Gasguin credited Geneviève with some astonishing insight. Henceforth, he was able to measure the full amplitude, or very nearly, of the giant steps that she was taking in that veritable dance through the virgin forest of the sciences.

For Gasguin had found the correct expression; it really was as a dancer, with agility, grace and a smile, that the young woman—or, rather, the 12-year-old girl—moved through the impenetrable undergrowth and intertwined creepers, penetrating its depths and clearing away its tangles. She did not put any visible effort into it. She was playing.

Not entirely, for, at certain details—the simplest and often the most important—she stumbled, stupidly getting stuck. In confrontation with the higher obstacles, on the other hand,

---

[31] Yvernaux probably means "giant," construing *egregoroi* in the sense in which it is used in Greek versions of *Genesis*, in the mysterious passage referring to the *nephilim*.

and the blackest pot-holes, she often reached the objective with a single bound. Then, her ease was miraculous.

"When one thinks that she has learned something," Gasguin often said, "one perceives that she had no need of being taught, for she had a sort of memory of it. Thus, for instance, yesterday..."

And every time, there was a new story, as marvelous, in its genre, as the reinvention of Euclidean geometry by Pascal. So, at least, Yvernaux deemed it; and he had taken notes to support his admiring affirmations, which he proposed to publish in due course, in the guise of addenda to a *Treatise on the Innate Sciences*.

One of those with which he was most satisfied, and which might give some idea of the "innateness" that was sometimes truly prodigious in Geneviève, is a note relative to the "Theory of Division," and here it is:

Gasguin told me, last vacation, to study the "Theory of Division," and that I would only be certain of having a scrap of mathematical intelligence on the day when I had fully mastered that theory, one of the most difficult aspects of arithmetic. After spending a trimester in that study, I thought I had arrived at a thorough understanding, but the sort of comprehension I had did not give me any pleasure. I felt that it was still difficult, even tenebrous, with the viscous blackness of pitch, in which I found myself—as we say in Thiérache, using a word that really ought to have remained in the language— ahogué. At Christmas, I went to Gasguin's house in order to deliver a present for Geneviève. It was a little electrical machine with a big box of apparatus, for that's the sort of plaything she prefers. She thanked me, and told me that she wanted to give me a present too. And this is what it was. Her father had told her, entirely against my wishes, that the "Theory of Division" did not seem clear to me and that I was not very happy about it. Now, she became indignant about that because nothing, to her—nothing in the world, she said—seemed clearer, more beautiful and more delightful. Those were the three adjectives she used. Then she gave me an "oral exam" to see how I had got turned around—that expression is hers too. I did get turned around, spinning like a demon in holy water.

"Oh, poor godfather," she said, with affectionate pity. "I can see that you don't find that funny—but it's dismal. Where did you get all those steps from? One might think it was from an ox?"

"From the authorized course at the Polytechnique, which your father told me to take."

"Papa's playing a practical joke on you. Why didn't he tell you about the problem we did the other day, which explains everything so nicely?"

I interrogated Gasguin. He blushed. He confessed to me that he had indeed, in selfish jealousy, kept to himself the new theory that Geneviève had invented very recently, in solving a problem, to amuse herself and without attaching any importance to it, with the sole desire of delighting herself.

And Geneviève told me her theory, politely and slyly, as if she were telling me a story full of surprises—and there was a series of surprises, to be sure, and delights. One would have thought that she was, as her father put it, dancing—instinctively, without having learned it. Arithmetic? Let's go, then! To her three exact epithets—clear, beautiful, delightful—I would add "sublime," quite simply. I wept and laughed with joy at the same time. And Gasguin, for the first time, did me the honor of finding that I had a glimmer of mathematical intelligence, since I was sensitive to the elegance of such a thing.

There follows, in the notes appended to the *Treatise on the Innate Sciences*, the theory of division itself, as Geneviève had explained it to her father, and then to her godfather. For Yvernaux had been able to write it down what the little girl had said—and the most miraculous thing about the business was that, so vivid was the impression it made on him, he had retained not only the steps, but also the dancing gait, with its elegance, its agility, its grace, and its cheerfulness.

One can imagine that such sensual delights were a paradise forbidden to Aunt Aline. Had the poor creature tried in vain to penetrate it, Gasguin and Yvernaux would have prohibited access, leaving Cherubim with flaming swords posted on the threshold.

And that was exactly the attitude they had taken—Yvernaux had been unable to help being witty in observing it—the only time the uninitiate had said, timidly: "I'd like to know that she's talking about, which makes your eyes catch fire." The scornful gazes with which they had crushed her, without making any reply, had driven her back into her shell of silence and confusion, from which she never dared emerge again before the two of them.

On one other occasion, she had risked asking Gasguin a small question when he was alone. Less puffed up with pride on that occasion, he had contented himself, without any rebuke, by explaining to her gently and mournfully that there were things that a woman could not understand.

Having retreated into her shell again—a definitive retreat for the time being, Aunt Aline concentrated her puzzlement in a reflection that desiccated her: "Is she not a woman, then?" And she admired her more, in considering her as not being what she herself was, imagining her as something approaching the fairies, perhaps, or the saints, or more probably those in the times of inverted saints who had "cavorted" at Sabbats. Well, was here anything surprising in that? Had not Idalie, her grandmother, been a "Cattelinette"?

Her devotion to Geneviève was tainted henceforth with superstitious terror. Already, sine the "that" scene, it will be remembered, she had largely given up emitting her sallies in the form of oracles or aphorisms. The rebukes, and the pity regarding her ignorance, irrevocably condemned no longer to understand Geneviève, had completed her diminution. Her present fear reduced her, for a time, to no longer being anything but the "simple" wretched object of indifference that everyone believed her to be because she was no longer in communication with anyone—even Geneviève now, it seemed.

She was bitterly sad about that. She had the depressing conviction of no longer having any part to play in the great event to come. Was her role as an instinctive and occult preparer of the way over, then? She had previously played it—without spelling it out, it is true, but *sensing* it—with everything she had to give. No longer being haunted or sustained, she fell back to being the humble worthy woman uniquely absorbed in household matters.

It was for that reason that she had at length become once again, in Gasguin's mind and even Yvernaux's, the neat and mousy little old woman she gave every appearance of being. They had forgotten, or at least allowed to fade away into the obscure cellars of their memory, so much of the strangeness by which she characterized herself. And the vague effigy that they had unjustly and too frequently formed of her lot was, unjustly, that of an individual without any distinct personality, less a person than an old piece of furniture, always situated in some corner of the house.

Nevertheless, and without ever seeming to, she continued to be impassioned, in spite of everything, by anything that manifested Geneviève's grandeur. Although, in fact, she did not understand her at all now, she knew that the girl knew enough of what her father knew to fill him with joy, pride and amazement. And Yvernaux's grand metaphors, whose terminology usually seemed to her to be a foreign language, were intoxicating to her, because she got drunk on their praise of Geneviève.

Even with no other delight than that, she would soon have ended up consoling herself for no longer being the preparer and predictor of anything. Fortunately, she had one other, even more profound and unexpected, and the recompense of all her occult devotion: it was that, when she believed her idol had drawn away, she found her one day even closer, more familiar, more intimate than ever, almost more so than in the blissful times of her earliest infancy.

Geneviève, in fact, had quickly penetrated the secret of the devotion and the terror she inspired in Aunt Aline. She found them quite sweet and divinely enjoyable, all the more so because they were hidden, for she did not admit Gasguin, or anyone else, to the celebration of mutual rediscovery of their two hearts.

The celebration was exquisite, though. Alone with her Geneviève in the sealed den of their mutual confidence, Aunt Aline rediscovered her popular soul, with the mottoes and sayings handed down from the distant past, and bearing on the distant future. And if the good woman sometimes trembled before venturing them, it was a tremor that was dear to her, because Geneviève immediately calmed it with a caress, to thank her, and soothed her with childish words of reassurance.

"*Core, core*, Aunt Line," she said, affecting, to please her, to speak Thiérachian to her. "I need to be coddled, and no one but you knows how to put me at my ease."

XIII

Without her good Aunt Line's grandmotherly "coddling," without the release that Geneviève found therein, and especially without the habit that the worthy and safe guardian resumed of mounting her guard and perpetual vigilance around the treasure, the treasure would have run a considerable risk of being lost. The poor little child-prodigy, in fact, might have fallen victim to her own genius. The real "ingrate age" for her was around her thirteenth year, in an extremely violent crisis that coincided exactly with the most powerful excitement of the cerebral excesses revolutionizing the other side of her.

Quite innocently, and because she delivered herself without apparent expense to those excesses, her father had never thought about the precocious wear and tear that her feminine nerves, still in formation, must be suffering in consequence. Yvernaux, whose intelligence was less abstract, whom life had more fully steeped in humanity, would have been more likely to perceive it, but he was absent at the time and very far away, on an expeditionary voyage to Ceylon—a matter of initiating himself into the lore of Buddhism, a fantasy that he had long wanted to fulfill. Thus, the unfortunate Geneviève, prey to the critical metamorphosis that every young woman must undergo, and simultaneously put under increasing scientific pressure by her father, marveling at the gifts which he saw becoming frenetic within her, was genuinely in danger of death.

If Aunt Line had been, as she had quite recently, separated from her by her disdain for others, but her own admiration terrorizing her and by the renunciation of the role she thought unnecessary, that was what would have happened to the girl. She had no suspicion herself of the double peril she was in, of the two currents that were about to collide within her and bring about a conflagration of her entire being. Fortunately, Aunt Aline perceived the effluvia and, suddenly recovering her former authority, exclaimed one day to Gasguin: "Shall I only have lived in order to be killed?"

"Who is killing you?" Gasguin had demanded, without understanding.

"You and your sap," she had replied. And, remembering one of the words proffered some thirteen years before about "*flumes*," she had added, with her old sibylline air: You know full well that she has been a plant, in the time of times. Yes, a plant, plant, plant!"

She repeated the word, emphasizing it more every time, because Gasguin, bewildered, continued not to understand. So he replied, bitterly, under the rain of blows that the word thus repeated inflicted upon him: "I hear you, you old madwoman, I hear you—but I thought you were cured of your nonsense."

She had looked deep into his eyes—a gaze like a drill that bored into him—and, without paying any heed to the insult, had simply said, while driving in the drill-bit: "I'm trying to bore a hole into your heart, to see if you still love your daughter."

"More than ever!" he cried, stunned by sudden and real anguish. "I adore her, as you know full well—she's the only thing I adore. What, then? Is it true, that she's threatened with…?"

Her dared not go on, having read, engraved in him by the drill, words speaking of death, whose imminent reality he was afraid to render by expressing them aloud. But the worthy woman, a seeress once again, knew that he had finally understood, and she made the twisting drill into a blade, which she planted full in his heart, thus:

"She's in agony, yes, the plant." Then, grimly, like an animal defending its young: "And while the sap is eating her away from below, you're burning her from above—there!" She has seized him by the wrists, and shook him with imperious syllables. "That, you shan't do any more. That, I forbid."

Frightened, Gasguin had given her full authority to save Geneviève, to whom Aunt Line had immediately explained, while pampering her, amid cajoleries for little children and with patois expressions dear to both of them, that it was necessary to give up studying completely and not to rack her brains any more over anything, and to live like a blade of grass, which grows and has nothing to do but grow.

"Good!" Geneviève had said, joyfully, instantly subjugated. "That's very amusing. It's true that I'm a blade of grass; I can feel myself in the process of growing. You're right, you know. It's necessary to grow first, to do nothing but grow."

And she clapped her hands, kicked as if dangling from the hangman's rope, resumed an entirely childish nature, and instantly, in profound obedience to the abnormal, even monstrous being that she had constituted so long ago, leap-frogged over the exceptional being—that stranger of sorts, abolished in an instant, swallowed up in a hole that she had passed over in a great leap backwards—and rejoined the other little being of thirteen years before, the blower of peas, in whom she felt the desire to recommence her existence. Such had been the abrupt shock of her "reviviscence," as some physician of both the body and the soul might have analyzed it. There was no one with her to write that analysis—but for sure, if Aunt Line had had the talent to write down what she was doing, in reality, by mans of her instinctive power of suggestion, those are some of the things she would have said so much better.

Abbé Denis had assisted in that curious regeneration without understanding it any more than his brother. Just as the latter might, if informed and specialized, have been a good physician of the body, so the Abbé might have been a good doctor for the soul—but neither of them, dissociated as they were, was capable of combining the two therapeutics into one. In sum, even in combination, they could not have saved Geneviève. Once she was saved, though, each of them attributed the merit to himself, and wanted to supervise her convalescence.

The physician, it must be said in all fairness, retained the idea of a malady of maturation that Aunt Aline had cared for as a good lay nurse. More delicate, the Abbé, a man of refined psychology, claimed that scientific work was too arid for a young woman and that what Geneviève lacked more than anything else was ideal nourishment.

"By the way," he insinuated, "what are you doing, from the religious viewpoint? I'm quite certain that you haven't become, in spite of your renunciation of the ecclesiastic estate, either a miscreant or an indifferent. So why aren't you more anxious about her soul? The last time we saw one another—three years ago, alas—I talked to you about that scruple, and you seemed to me disposed to have her learn the catechism with a view to her first communion. You haven't told me anymore. What happened?"

Slightly confused before his elder brother, changed into a Reverend Father admonishing him as to his fate, Thibaud was obliged to admit, stammering, that he had given it no further thought. Nor had anyone else around her! He, Thibaud, had come a long way from his past—without any hostility against that that past, to be sure, but without any idea either of returning to it, since a slight crisis when people had wanted to marry him off. As for Yvernaux, the less said the better. He had never been a very fervent Catholic, even at the Seminary. And Aunt Aline had not practiced religion for a very long time. Had she ever believed? When and in what? No one knew. In that case...

"In brief," the Abbé had continued, "if you're not careful, you'll turn your daughter into an atheist."

"Oh no—impossible!" the former good seminarian had exclaimed. For the conviction had remained, at least, in default of personal faith, that religion was a good thing for women.

Why and how had that theory remained a dead letter with regard to Geneviève? He really did not know. But that was not proof that he was nourishing some preconceived aversion to having her given religious instruction. She herself, consulted, for form's sake by Aunt Aline, did not experience any reluctance in that respect, nor did Aunt Aline see anything objectionable in it.

It will amuse her, the old woman said to herself. And the girl, for her part, merely at the possible advent in her life of something new, had, like a curious child, thought the same. The mathematics and physics into which she had already made inroads, had a strong grip on her heart, in spite of her desire to be a blade of grass just growing, as her old Aunt suggested; and to help her detach herself from them, it required nothing less than the announcement of that beautiful unknown about which the Abbé had spoken as another science, the science of God: religion.

In another form, that was exactly the calculation that Aunt Aline had made, and she made use of it to indoctrinate Thibaud, who would have been desolate to lose his pupil had he not retained the secret hope—unexpressed in front of his brother—that the "diversion" provided by religion would not prevent Geneviève from being brought back to science by her genius.

For all these amalgamated reasons, and to complete the young woman's convalescence, and in order that, having become a growing blade of grass, she would be a blade of grass flowering in the poetry of the ideal (the Abbé's words) it was decided that Geneviève would spend her holidays, which were then due, with her uncle, who would catechize her—but on the formal condition that she would be accompanied by Aunt Aline.

XIV

What a unique, marvelous, almost unreal memory those two months of vacation—in the strict and proper sense of the word, for the girl's everyday life had been "vacant"—so full and so rapidly passed, left behind, one life having been totally replaced by another! What an absolute forgetfulness of everything she had forgotten, to the point of seeing herself, when she looked back on it later, as a stranger!

The forgetfulness of accustomed occupations, sensations and ideas had been reinforced by the absence of familiar faces and surroundings. Even those faces and objects that seemed to have followed her—since they were, after all, there—were, in a sense, not there, having been completely renewed. Neither the Abbé not Aunt Aline any longer resembled themselves.

It is true that Geneviève scarcely knew her Uncle Denis, having only seen him three or four times since she came into the world, at long intervals. From the conversations of her father and Aunt Aline, however, she had nevertheless built a sufficiently exact representation of him. Now, of that representation, nothing survived.

As for Aunt Aline, who was so intimately familiar to her, almost to the same extent as her own personality, perhaps more so, from the very first moment—and more so time went by—it was as if she had been transfigured. At times, she positively did not recognize her.

Given that the whole world around her had changed, as much as she had, must it not be the case that Geneviève had spent those two months, not in life, but in a dream? That was what she asked herself subsequently, very often, on reflection, never being quite certain that it had "actually" happened. It became necessary, then, for her father to affirm the reality of the memory, and for Aunt Line to authenticate the facts by repeating to her, with all her authority: "Since I was there with you, of course! Since I was there myself!"

And in spite of everything, Geneviève "never got over" having truly possessed so much happiness, having being that chosen one in that paradise, as she put it. Only to her father and Aunt Line, however—and very rarely to them—had she spoken with any abandon about that ecstasy. To Yvernaux, she had never dared. She would have been afraid that his eloquence might transform the blissful experience into a matter of rhetoric. She scarcely permitted herself to express it inwardly, without being able to do so in a satisfactory manner, always reproaching herself for excessive materialization, no matter how subtle she was, when she found, for example, such expressions as:

"It was an abyss of soft light and tender joy in my life. No, not an abyss! A summit, rather! Something less profound than an abyss, though, and not as high as a summit! A cloud of dream that enveloped me, caressed me, on which I slept, but was wide awake all the same. Yes, that's it! That description is very nearly accurate. And more! No, better, for sure. For, abyss and summit and joy and cloud and dream, it was, above all life."

And sometimes she got around to adding, in a vague smiling melancholy: "Who knows whether it was not, in my entire life, the only truly living fragment of real life?"

Thus, a long time afterwards, having thought about it in increasing distant bursts, she had retained that sort of breath, caressing her still—and notwithstanding, without her conceiving and black humor or bitterness against her ordinary life, in which that alone was a ray of sunlight and a taste of honey. We have seen with what a good and gentle resignation she accepted having coiffed Saint Catherine, and how she was the first to joke about it, without rancor.

The fact nevertheless remains that, without that two-month holiday, and the ecstasy she tasted therein, she would never even have thought of her destiny as an old maid, even with a smile. On the other hand, without the tender memory that tainted her heart—her girlish heart—forever, she would have remained more Gasguin's daughter than Idalie's granddaughter; she would have been dried up, knotted—unsexed, according to Lady Macbeth's expression—within her exclusive passion for science, and her genius might perhaps have become sterile.

Although her supreme theories were to end, in practice, with the wing that we shall see open herein, everything indicates that the plumes of that wing had for their initial down that of the dream formed during those two months of vacation. That would only become comprehensible later. No one, even those who shared or caused that dream, could have imagined that blossoming. In spite of all her divinatory instinct, even Aunt Line had no suspicion of it. That tells us how tenuous the thread was by which that down was collected in mid-air, secured in Geneviève's memory, and suspended in her heart, thus retaining the potential wing until the future, when it was transformed into plumage twenty years later.

It was Yvernaux—often a false lyricist, but more often still an illustrative thinker by means of imagery—who was to express in that rather bizarre metaphor, exactly twenty years later, a phenomenon much more bizarre than the metaphor itself. And when he fund it and said it, someone commonsensical having had the misfortune to judge it obscure, he replied:

"You're right. I've omitted to light my lantern. I'll light it, then. Well, the thread in question, that tenuous thread, which I thought I had no need to identity for you—that almost immaterial thread, which myopic gazes can't see—was quite simply, not at all stupidly, M'sieu, but entirely angelically, a *fil de Vierge*.[32] There! And I hope that you understand now—don't you?"

---

[32] The term *fil de Vierge* [literally, Virgin's thread] is normally applied in France to a floating wisp of spider-silk, but the commonsensical listener—apparently the notional author, although readers might not agree that he is conspicuously blessed with common sense—evidently suspects that Yvernaux has another, more nearly literal, significance in mind, as of course he has.

115

"Yes," said the critic, who did not want to make him a liar. "Indeed, I shall understand, but later."

It was also later that it was necessary to resign himself to finally seeing the present story clearly, about which the same Yvernaux, to whom the essential elements ate due, had no fear of saying:

"If I wrote it myself, I'd make it such a firework-display of images that that the readers would be blinded by it, and wouldn't be able to continue to read, lost in the dark."

XV

The paradise in which Geneviève had lived that delightful dream of two months did not, however, have a name promising such felicities. Nor was it situated in one of the pleasant corners of Brittany. Nor did it have for hosts people of whom the first glimpse could covey the idea that they were cheerful, and especially not tender and prepossessing.

The old manor of Kairnheûz had been called that, a long time ago, in ancient Haut Breton, compounding two grim words descended directly and without any softening of their crude syllables, one of Gaelic ancestry and the other of Cymric.[33] Now, the first, "Kairn," signified "a pile of stones," and the second, "heûz," had the meaning "terror." It was, therefore, as if it were to say, at the time of its baptism "the stone-heap—or monument—of terror," and those who had characterized it thus were not the kind of folk to be terrified easily.

One can imagine, therefore, that the manor, conserved almost intact since then, and whose ruined portion did not add any cheerfulness, maintained a surly physiognomy for the gazes of today, less familiar with horror. In fact, it seemed to exaggerate that horror and that terror, and made a décor of it, so pleased was it thereby. That, at least, is what a witty Parisian painter said, having arrived there by chance in search of the picturesque, and who had found it "more beautiful than nature," appearing to have become "ostentatious."

---

[33] In fact, both halves are Gaelic in origin, Kairn being a local variant of "cairn" and Heuz being the name of a particularly nasty Gaelic god, although the Breton and Welsh (Cymric) languages overlap the Gaelic tongues to a considerable extent, the supposed distinction between Celts and Gaels being largely a figment of the 19th century anthropological imagination.

It is certainly the case that, for the taste of a witty Parisian, there are perhaps a few too many of these architectures "fit for etchings or the backdrops of rustic theaters," as the jolly denigrator also said. "And even a romantic dramaturge," he added, "would quickly weary, by the fifth act, of machiculations, posterns and subterrains, in merely running through the detailed catalogue of all those chivalric junk, walls of cyclopean construction (if one may employ that term with respect to the Middle Ages) moats and ponds, portals with drawbridges—unusable now, but still in place, it seemed, to seal their openings—turrets, battlements, loopholes, watch-towers and other sullen defenses, a massive high tower standing up like an arm brandished menacingly in the sky, ready to bring a fist down on the countryside, recumbent or cowering in fear before it, etc., etc." For our witty Parisian's patter was well-furnished with vocabulary and erudition.

With regard to individuals less corrupted by art and literature, however, the manor had retained its horror. It had even acquired a surplus by virtue of an exceedingly ancient chapel, doubtless anterior to the tower, of which nothing survived but the ruined shell crumbled amid the rocks all the way to the muddy bed of the Kawchmôr. Nor did the Kawchmôr, or "sea of mud" make the landscape any more pleasant, being the widening of a little, half-dead stream, to which only certain high tides lent a little life, but in the form of sinister and viscous eddies. So the good people of the region only spoke the name of the manor in a whisper, without really comprehending the Gaelic and Cymric roots any longer, but as if they had divined all of their extinct significance. For them, Kairnheûz really had remained the terrible heap of stones.

The entire location, including its less horrific parts, was worthy of having for a mirror the heavy yellow sheen of the marshes into which the black rocks of the slope and the blue granite debris of the chapel crumbled. Those bright colors did not succeed, any more than the pink heather and the golden gorse, in cheering up the lugubrious frame of woods of which that corner was a sort of junction. There, in fact, the bushy oak-woods of Ponthual and the somber fir-woods of Plouër hurled themselves against one another, after a fashion, and beneath them, in caves of branches, a perpetual flux of darkness poured out and thickened, especially on the side of the firs.

The manor was bordered by that mourning-dress on its saddest face, which formed a continuation of the bleak skeleton of the chapel, leprous with lichens and scabbed with moss. The rare windows opening there took on the aspect of diseased and blinking eyes, only suffering as they gazed at the spectacle of that desolation.

The other, brighter, face—which would have been sunlit if they bay windows there had been less narrowly and meanly ogival, at least had for its nearest neighbor an uncovered plain whose pale verdure was enameled with flowers, and the sea for a distant horizon. But the flowers of the plateau were only those of wild gorse, and the verdure they enameled was only furnished by tufts of poor "*ami-castu*," a kind of grass that seemed discolored by the briny sea breezes—for that plain on a plateau was heathland. As for the sea, which might have been able to animate the background of the scene with its life, it was the glaucous and rigid strip that stands up like a wall of steel at the end of low-lying marine reaches.

The heathland of Kairnheûz is not at all similar, in fact, to that of Fréhel, for example, which is borne high up on a pavement of rocks that set it a hundred meters sheer above sea-level. Thus displayed to the open sky, like the palm of a hand presented to the sun and burning a cassolette of abundant aromatic plants beneath its kisses, the heathland of Fréhel is joyful, at least by day. Its foundations, moreover—the sheer walls it overlooks—are granite and porphyry, which set sapphire and ruby cabochons on the plaque of the fluid emerald sea. Only in the evening, when the waves can be heard breaking, does their melancholy cantilena give a certain strangeness to the solitude and mystery of the heath. And even then, one still dreams of poetic fairies, or, at the most, of lubricious Korrigans.

Even in broad daylight, the heathland of Kairnheûz must have inspired nightmares. The open space of the uncovered plain was crushed between the woods that rushed toward it in cataracts of immobile darkness, and the horizontal steel wall of the sea. One no longer had the impression of an open space there, but that of an enclosure—and that enclosure, although a level plateau, seemed hollowed out at the center in the form of a basin. It was oppressive there, in spite of the wind that swept it. The leaden sunlight fell heavily there, warming the very wind—and the dreams one dreamed there were also warm and heavy, oppressive and stifling.

Because of those nocturnal dreams, it was necessary for no one to be stay within ten leagues of the place, unless they wanted give themselves gooseflesh and other frissons. Accounts were given, moreover, of unfortunates whom mist, dusk falling unexpectedly after a storm, an exceptional blizzard of snow or a squall causing rain to fall "in curtains," had taken by surprise in the middle of the heath. The majority preferred not to speak of the abominations of which they been had been the victims—in dreams, of course, but in dreams as palpable, it appeared, as reality. The rare individuals who contented to unclench their teeth did so only that they might chatter in the terror of stories of phantoms, supernatural voices, infernal dances, shaken chains and cadavers giving you frightful smacks, or kisses more frightful still.

Not to mention that there were other tales than those, perhaps swollen by details imagined by fear. There were the authentic adventures related in Breton ballads, according to facts that had often been recorded in French newspapers. More than one old "*pillaouer*"—a wandering rag-picker—after singing one of these ballads, recalled having heard the tale not sung but narrated, in the times when it was talked about as something that "happened the other day."

Crimes—yes, true crimes—had been committed on the heath, and below the ruins too, in the mud of Kawchmôr, and even, as was said a first surreptitiously, "in the manor itself." It is true that they were rendered with an even more respectful surreptitiousness at present, their tellers hastening to add: "Oh, the crimes committed at the manor were committed many years ago, of course."

On the strength of which a certain head garnished with reading, a reject from a seminary or a young schoolmaster freshly molded by the *Normale primaire*,[34] related unthinkingly and unhesitantly, affirming that it was no more than a legend, the "historically accurate" story of a lord of Ponthual who had once entered into competition with the famous Gilles de Retz, whose château, the ruin of Guildo on the Arguenon, was not so very far away. Then he passed on, still in a bold voice, to a certain lady of Plouër, who, under the ancient kings of France, if they had had their court at Versailles, would have been a poisoner there as celebrated as Brinvilliers,[35] but had limited herself to the manor of Kairnheûz to perpetrate her misdeeds, and who had expiated them under the axe in the public square in Rennes. And from there he arrived at the era of the great Revolution and the Chouans, and that of the return of the émigrés, in which things that had happened to make one shudder, as with the Breton Brinvilliers of old, captations of inheritances, substitutions of children, pretended suicides that actually covered up murders, etc...

At that moment, the strong head took on a knowing expression, pinched his lips as if to restrain himself from saying

---

[34] The *École Normale*—the aggregation of French teacher-training schools—had gradations, the *primaire* being, of course, considerable lower in status than the *supérieure*.

[35] Marie d'Aubray, Marquise de Brinvilliers, was tortured in 1676 after being accused of having conspired with her lover to poison her father and two brothers for the sake of an inheritance, and was persuaded to produce such an extravagant account of her crimes that it sparked the so-called "affair of the poisons," in which numerous other women were arrested and charged with various nefarious practices—a panic only suppressed when the "confessions" implicated several highly-placed courtiers.

too much; but one less prudent insinuated, albeit in a low voice, between two puffs on a pipe and swallowing a mouthful of *eau-de-vie* in order to half-stifle his words: "It's been known in our time."

"Only ten years ago," risked another.

"Go on! At the manor? Impossible! Who told you that?"

Thus exclaimed some newcomer arrived the night before, a passing stranger, a merchant from the next town, an ambulant maker of knick-knacks: all fish asking nothing more than to take the bait of scandal—or slander, if there's any difference. Immediately eager to put themselves on the spit, all ears, they drew nearer to hear the most recent legend, or history, of the manor of Kairnheûz.

So, only ten years ago, on a dreary equinoctial morning—when the tides are high—the cadaver of Comte Alain-Mathias-Bertrand de Ponthual-Plouër, had been found in the marshes of Kawchmôr, directly below the ruins, where the rising tide had left it. It had not been known that he was in the locality, having left it a week before to go to Brest. Why had he come back without being seen by anyone, deliberately concealing the fact of his return, since he had not come by railway and the station at Lamballe, his usual halt? That was what no one had ever found out, and from which emerged the Pharaoh's serpent[36] of the following tale.

According to the scandal-mongers, or slanderers, the Comte had staged a fake departure for Brest, where he had no appointment, and, in reality, had gone to see his wife's cousin, who was the director of a Jesuit college in the Channel Islands. He had gone to demand a definitive explanation regarding a singular adventure that had occurred within the Comtesse's family at the moment when his future wife was born.

There might then have been a substitution of children, as a consequence of which the pretended granddaughter of a ga-

---

[36] "Pharaoh's serpent" is an effect once popular in firework displays, produced by igniting a block of mercury thiocyanate, which expands in a long, twisting streamer.

mekeeper, really of noble blood, had become a poor woman and, later, the future Comtesse's wet-nurse. And that was why the Comtesse's foster-sister, young Anne-Herminie-Luce, had been, in due course, adopted by an impoverished gentleman, the squire Melchior Yves de Saint-Ylan. And that was also why, by virtue of the intrigues of the Comtesse and her cousin and the director of the English college, that demoiselle Anne-Herminie-Luce de Saint-Ylan had been married off on the day that "someone"—no one could say who—had come to the Comtesse threatening to reveal the ancient ugly truth.

In spite of all the precautions taken against him, this "someone" had succeeded in making known to the Comte papers—a wad of old letters—proving, if not the absolute truth, at least the great probability, of the accusation blighting the family, which was scarcely respectable in any case, of the Hugons de la Goëlwec, the ancestral stock of Blanche-Hortense-Perrinaïck, the Comte's wife. If the accusation were true, the Comte would have espoused the doubly-adulterine daughter of a Goëlwec, fallen into black poverty in Paris and fished out of the rabble by a Jewess, a former high-society "woman of ill repute," presently a wealthy dealer in antiquities. It was to win this girl her mother's large fortune that the famous child-swap would have taken place, Hugon de la Goëlwec having had for accomplices his wife, who as no better than he was, and the gamekeeper, whom the prostitute had seduced.

Still unraveling the tangled thread of this skein of hallucinatory tales, this is what had happened between the departure of the so-called Comte for Brest and the discovery of his cadaver in Kawchmôr:

The director of the English college, confounded by the proofs that the revelatory letters brought, had confessed everything, or at least that of which he could not be unaware—that Mademoiselle Anne-Herminie-Luce de Saint-Ylan, the Comtesse's foster-sister, was, in fact, really the fruit of a sin committed by a Hugon de la Goëlwec, his own brother, with the wife of a simple gamekeeper. And that was the reason for the marriage, contracted subsequently by the poor squire of Saint-Ylan—for money, it cannot be denied—with the gamekeeper's widow, who had murdered him. Certainly, in the formalities that had to be arranged in order that the squire's adoption of the child could take place, there had been irregularities—frauds, even—but the priest had absolutely refused to confess anything more

Furious then, and beside himself, according to the storytellers, the Comte had returned secretly to the manor, had terrorized the Comtesse, throwing the letters in her face and boasting of having forced the priest into a full confession. The Comtesse, losing her head, had renounced the further continuation of the lie; and, in the vein of confession—the Comte having had his suspicions in that regard anyway—had revealed the worst of her secrets regarding the birth of their son, who was not the Comte's.

On which the Comte, intending to kill her, had taken up a weapon and attacked his wife, who ran away—but the son, then aged eleven, had arrived. He admired his charming and tender mother, with whom he still lived, having been brought up in the house. On the other hand, he had no great attachment to his father, the Comte being bad-tempered and almost always absent. Acting on a perfectly natural impulse, his heart riving his arm, the child had leapt to the aid of his beloved mother, against the armed enemy threatening her, and had tried to take the weapon off him. An atrocious and brief struggle had begun, in front of the mother, who had almost fallen into a swoon.

The Comte had retreated, without being aware of it, toward a low window, and had stumbled, his heels having tripped on the sill. The backward fall had been so sudden, and the disappearance of the Comte into the void so fantastic, that the Comtesse and her son had not even had time to utter a scream.

When the poor woman, fallen into complete unconsciousness after the catastrophe, came round, the son was kneeling beside his mother's bed. Without summoning anyone, he had carried her to the bed himself, loosened her clothing and bathed her with a damp cloth; then, seeing that she was breathing and that her heart was beating—almost imperceptibly, but manifesting life—he had knelt down to pray beside the woman he called his "saint."

The Comte, having fallen in the dark into the fracas of the rising tide through that long narrow window, like a loophole open over Kawchmôr, must have made a formidable leap toward the water, plunging into the mud even so, to be tossed about there, unable to extract himself because of the violent eddies, to be drawn out to sea by the ebb-tide and then brought back—a few tides later, assuredly—by a new flow. For what the narrators had forgotten to mention was that the body had been found in the state of a shipwreck-victim who had spent quite a long time in the water.

That would have been sufficient to render less acceptable the legend of the return after a week's absence. Reasonable mariners, having seen the cadaver, would not have thought for a minute that he had been tossed by the waves for only twelve hours—but the tellers of these tales were not reasonable mariners, nor, especially, men with empty stomachs. They were Bretons, with an imagination ever in love with epics, legends and fairy tales. They were of that race which once drank, from the springs of chivalric romance, the heady wine of the most beautiful chimerical adventures, and who drink today, with the same crazed avidity, the inferior wine of ballads and even the coarse befuddling wine of *romans feuilletons*. Doubtless the inventors of all those tall tales concerning the proprietors of the manor of Kairnheûz have heads thickened by that, not to mention their bowls of cider and even *eau-de-vie*.

The research being completed, the few nuggets of certain truth that it is necessary to retain from this medley of confusion are, firstly, that which concerns Mademoiselle de Saint-Ylan, secondly the aversion of the son for his father, and, very probably, the final drama whose last scene was the tragic death of the Comte.

What it would have been interesting to reconstitute, if one had the necessary documents, is the long romance from which that frightful and possible last scene of the final drama emerged. Possible, certainly, for the son was aware, in spite of still being a child, of his mother's martyrdom with respect to the Comte. Not in detail, of course, the Comtesse having been discreet regarding her suffering, especially in front of her son; but he would have to have been devoid of affection, instead of steeped in it, not to have penetrated, in spite of himself and in spite of her, the secret of the tears in which the poor and plaintive creature's youth faded away. And from that came his aversion, almost hatred—even though he did not admit it to himself—for his father, that victim's torturer.

The first years of the union had been happy, though. Both rich, handsome and young, the spouses had everything that could be desired, and their honeymoon had been almost as insolent as a triumphant sun—but it had been quickly and permanently eclipsed behind frightful clouds, only swept away momentarily by the fortunate breeze of the initial tenderness.

The Comte had two vices, frequent in men of his class, especially in the provinces, where those vices are transmitted by a long heredity: he was a drunkard and a gambler. He had quickly returned to those two emetics of gentlemanliness, in which all he had of pride and dignity was drowned and burned at the same time in drink and the candles of green baize tablecloths.

In a few years, the two fortunes had melted away and been swallowed up, even that of the Comtesse, who was initially too weak with respect to a man she adored and of whose base deceits she was unaware. For the Comte, once ruined, became one those unscrupulous knights of industry whom the aristocracy of the 18th, and even previous centuries furnished in abundance, capable of anything in order to acquire what as necessary to "take the bank." Thus, going from one moral collapse to another, he had come to demand, in scenes of violence the money of which he had need, and which he extracted from the Comtesse by force, from the little that she had been able to save from her inheritance, finally put aside.

There was, therefore, in the present-day legends of the accursed manor, some truth at least regarding the attempts at extortion made upon the Comtesse by her husband, with regard to the old story of the family of which Mademoiselle de Saint-Ylan had once been the fruit. That one of these scenes had occurred, therefore, in which blackmail had degenerated into straightforward, even physical, threats, was by no means astonishing—nor that the son, having chanced to witness it, might have intervened, in a brave impulse, to defend his threatened mother. Certain information is lacking to establish the exactitude of that version, but one can, in all justice, consider it plausible.

It is also necessary to admit the hypothesis, doubtless hazardous, of an agreement after the fact between the mother and the son, she so weak and gentle and he so young, scarcely out of childhood, to keep the terrible secret—not only never to betray it, but to invent the lie with which, according to this hypothesis, they had masked the truth. For the version confessed by the mother and confirmed by the son, in the course of the enquiry required by the circumstances, had been this: a sharp difference of opinion had arisen between the two spouses and had rapidly turned into an argument on the part of the Comte, who was drunk. When the son ran to help his mother, who had called out to him, the father had tried to flee, doubtless ashamed, and in a sort of alcoholic fit, had leapt out of the window.

That version had been believed, without the examining magistrate even trying to raise an objection. The exemplary life of the Comtesse, her character of Christian resignation, the age of the son and, on the other hand, the well-known detestable "machinations"—as the enquiry put it—of the Comte, a drunkard and gambler, having three-quarters ruined his wife after squandering his own wealth, had all concurred in rendering the family version plausible and incontestable. No one among the honest folk, and even the others, of their society had dreamed of casting the slightest shadow of suspicion upon the two, not actors but victims of the drama.

It had required the imagination of petty individuals, gossips, storytellers, scandal-mongers and unwitting slanderers—and that the imagination in question be Breton and overheated by strong cider, whipped up by the alcohol of apples and congested by the remembrance of old ballads and the reading of current *romans feuilletons*—for the story, already so tragic and somber, to become part of the black imbroglio of adventures that was called, on late evenings between puff on pipes, "the horrors of Kairnheûz."

It nevertheless remained the case that the proprietors of the manor, living in the "terrible heap of stones" amid the horrors of the surrounding woods, the heath and Kawchmôr, and especially the memories of the catastrophe, the image of which had to haunt them, could scarcely maintain a joyful and smiling attitude. One would have been surprised, almost shocked, to encounter such an attitude, so little in harmony with the location, the environment, the very name of the place, and their own history. One would have reproached them for it, instinctively, if such a sinister past had not weighed upon their present.

It seemed that it did weight upon them, and heavily. The manor had residents worthy of it, its ruins mirrored in the yellow sheen of the marshes of Kawchmôr, its two woodlands mingling heir darkness, its mysterious health that walled the steel bar of the sea, its massive tower, its bleak façades with the half-open eyes and its abandoned grounds invaded by wild plants. Those residents, in addition to the Comtesse, were an old gardener and his wife, who were reminiscent of a household of gravediggers, an even older gamekeeper, who gave the impression of mostly protecting phantoms and appeared to be one himself, and, finally, the cook and her daughter, the chambermaid, both of whom gave the impression of silent nuns muffling their footsteps as they walked.

As for the Comtesse herself, still dressed in full mourning then, almost withered, her face very pale with its two large and exceedingly soft eyes, a smile of melancholy resignation frozen on her lips and giving them a bitter twist, she was the veritable soul of the sad manor—a slightly weary, extenuated soul, ready to take flight soundlessly. She had already lost the air of the days when her beloved son had lived with her, whose presence had brought her perpetual comfort and obliged her to live. For the two years that he had been at Brest, a cadet on the *Borda*, only seeing him on rare days of leave and during vacations, she had let herself fall into total languor, and it seemed obvious that that, at the conclusion of that languor, her soul would depart as the same time as her soon departed to be a naval officer.

It was his tutor, Abbé Denis Gasguin, and her cousin, the director of the English college, who had decided the young man on that noble and beautiful profession. He, it must be admitted, in spite of his profound affection for his mother, had directed his ambitions toward it with pleasure. The adventurous ardor of his Breton blood drove him toward the sea, where so many atavistic memories sang and called to him.

All the same, this vacation being the last that he would spend here before embarking for two years, he had not brought a light heart to it, as one can imagine. His passion for the sea could not extinguish the affection and almost religious gratitude with which he loved the woman who loved him so much.

He had arrived with tears in his eyes. He had found his mother readier than ever to take flight for the eternal beyond. She had tried to smile in order that the two of them should not to weep too much right away.

"Come on," she said. "Come for a walk in the grounds, in the virgin forest of the poor 'Mourner in the Sleeping Wood';[37] she will show you a new little beast that she has had in her thickets since his morning."

---

[37] The Comtesse's *Triste au Bois dormant* plays on the title of Perrault's fairy tale "La Belle au Bois dormant," whose title is usually translated as "The Sleeping Beauty in the Wood" or abbreviated to "The Sleeping Beauty." Although it is, indeed,

And the young Comte, having seen Geneviève, who was in one of her depressed moods, could not help thinking: *My God! What an ugly little thing!*

He had not said it aloud, but Geneviève had understood what he was thinking nevertheless. She had remained still, confused, slightly humiliated, entirely steeped in vague melancholy and sudden fear, before the unbenevolent welcome of the young man with the arrogant expression and the tall woman in mourning, like an apparition.

That happened in the corner of the grounds where the two dark woods met, near the ruins, above Kawchmôr. And that was the first sensation experienced by Geneviève on her first day in her paradise.

---

the Beauty who is sleeping in Perrault's version, not the Wood, I have assumed that the Comtesse is implying, as the phrase actually suggests, that it is the wood that is dormant rather than herself.

XVI

Does one ever know exactly of what a memory is made? What analysis is subtle enough to reconstitute all the elements, even when one feels certain of possessing the essential element? How can the new imprints amalgamated on the most ancient print with the backcloth of the palimpsest be discerned? Around that initial point, how many successive acquisitions have come from wherever and whenever, before and even during the crystallization whose definitive shape they sometimes determine?

To be sure, the first sensation experienced by Geneviève on her first day in her paradise seems to have been painful, and the wound ought to have left a scar in her memory. Far from it! It was something like a perfume that it left there, a strong, sweet and penetrating perfume on which Geneviève still intoxicated herself with joy—as much today, and perhaps more, than then, for the soon-to-be-old woman of almost thirty-three as to the twenty-year old girl of yore; an intoxication as abrupt and as powerful as the day when Geneviève found herself alone with Aunt Line, after the introduction to the young Comte. For, as soon as she thought about her two months in paradise, it was on that precise moment that her dream first alighted, like a bird perching on the edge of its nest in order to take flight among the marvels of the nascent world. And the most marvelous of those marvels, the flower of that incessantly resuscitated April that nothing could wither, consisted imperturbably of a memory expressed in this form:

How we loved one another at first sight!

Geneviève, however, neither in her thirteenth year nor at any other time, had never been pretentious or coquettish, and that day she was less so than ever. But the first sensation of her first day in her paradise was engraved very clearly and very deeply in her memory, such as we have scrupulously reported it—which is to way, without anything that could authorize an interpretation similar to that of today.

What, in sum, did it amount to? This: no exchange of words between "her" and "him"; a disobliging thought read in the eyes of the arrogant young man, in the presence of the tall black-clad woman; and that in a corner of the grounds where the junction of two dark woods overlooked the muddy gulf of Kawchmôr; then immobility, confusion, humiliation, a hint of melancholy and fear—and that was all.

And those were the essential elements of which the memory was made, whose translation became that phrase in the liquor of joy, the warm, balsamic and intoxicating exhalation:

How we loved one another at first sight!

It must be said, moreover, in order to get to the heart of the matter right away, that neither twenty years ago, nor at any other time, had Geneviève given that statement the meaning that anyone else would have looked for therein—and, it goes without saying, she was incapable of seeing it there, today more than ever, even by subconsciously putting it there. In her naïve mathematical mind, there was a sort of equation in which "she" and "he" were the two terms, nothing more.

Thus, at least, was how she had explained it, many times, to Aunt Line, who, as can be imagined, would not hear of it, and always reduced that disguised avowal by the "mathegician"—as she put it—to the simplest and most human formula:

"In short, you'd like to marry him, wouldn't you? That's it, isn't it?"

"Married or not, what does it matter?" Geneviève invariably replied. "That's not what it's about at all—not at all." To which, in a nervous tone, she added: "What a pity you aren't a bit of a 'mathegician' like me, Aunt Line! You'd understand, being so intelligent—you'd understand what I mean."

"In that case," the old woman riposted, "why don't you explain it to your father or Yvernaux? They're what you're said."

132

"But it's also something other than mathematics," Geneviève always ended up confessing, with a sigh.

"What? Let's try to find it. Let's try!"

Aunt Line had often concluded in that manner. Geneviève had never wanted to try, though. She preferred to savor the intoxication of her memory without knowing to what she owed it. She dreaded losing it by trying to analyze it. At the most, one day, she had consented slightly, and had then recovered one very tiny fact, which it was infinitely sweet for her to remember, although she was not certain of it—not absolutely certain. Oh, a very tiny, very tiny fact, besides, but by which, in sum, her first sensation of her first day in her paradise had been modified almost as soon as she had experienced it.

That very tiny, very tiny, fact, that trivial fact, that almost nothing, was that the arrogant young man, as he went away with that almost scornful expression of indifference, had turned round after taking a few paces, and had darted at her—yes, at her—a furtive glance, and then a vague smile.

Only, she hastened to add, that furtive glance had been the heavens opening, and that vague smile all infinite felicity conquered.

More words in which Aunt Line, according to her Thiérachian expression *"s'empiergeait,"* or even *"s'empiergeonnait,"*[38] especially when Geneviève, in order to interpret them had further recourse to a mathematical comparison, such as, for example:

"Yes, a very tiny fact, almost nothing—let's say nothing. Except that nothing is everything, you realize, like zero multiplied by infinity. From that zero, thus multiplied, all the numbers emerged. And for me, similarly, from that glance, from that smile, from those nothings, emerged all the joys, all the Heavens, all the eternity of Heaven..."

---

[38] The significance of these dialect terms, and the play between them, can be deduced from their analogy with the French terms *piège* [trap] and *pigeonner* [swindle]. In essence, Aunt Aline fell into a trap, or deceived herself.

"La la la!" Aunt Line interrupted. "You're up to your ears in Yvernaux. Better to stick to the simple reading of my common sense, and say that you were made to be married, you and him."

"Get away! You're crazy, Aunt Line! Shut up! That's ridiculous."

Thus Geneviève, annoyed, always concluded discussions on that subject. Or, at least, she tried to conclude them thus; but one, Aunt Line would not let go so easily. In vain, Geneviève adopted a sharp tone with her; the old lady clung obstinately to her idea, delighting in blithe ripostes.

"For one thing, I was only thirteen then!"

"Well, he liked the juice of unripe grapes."

"But my uncle was preparing me for my first communion..."

"It's souls in mint condition for which the Devil is thirstiest."

"I forbid you, Aunt, to slander Monsieur le Comte's intentions..."

"Go on, go on, tell all those names like a rosary—I can see that you want to relish them."

And then, when Geneviève shut up, in order not to risk laughing, yet again, at that Breton litany that had so often amused her aunt, it was the good woman herself who declaimed, with a comical emphasis: "Monsieur le Comte Elme-Cast-Jagut-Marie-Joseph de Plouër, Seigneur des Ebihens, des Pierres-Sonnantes, des Treize-Îles—and other places, also known as Joson, also known as the Little Chouan!" For she had retained miraculously, in her memory so hospitable to formulas, that string of names and important titles, terminated by two pirouettes of soubriquets.

It was the young Comte in person who had amused the little girl with all that, one day, in the presence of Aunt Line, who had also taken great pleasure in it, like the old child that she was. He had explained, that day, that Elme, Cast and Jagut were Breton saints, and that along with those baptismal names, retained in the family, his ancestors really had left him the

134

lordships of Ebihens, Pierres-Sonnantes, Treizes-Îles and other places that sounded like fantastic domains, and that Joson was the local derivative of Joseph, and that the nickname "the little Chouan" had been given to him on the *Borda*.[39] And Geneviève, then—and Aunt Line too—had found it all delightful, nor had they changed their opinion since.

With the result that, generally, Aunt Line, who had reeled off her declamation with the intention of "winding up" Geneviève, forgot her intention *en route* and crowned her tirade of ridicule with this laudatory reflection:

"Not to mention that, even so, it would make a fine conclusion, like a peacock's tail, for a fairy tale."

And immediately, Geneviève, forgetting her annoyance, started laughing, then smiling. The laughter was of gaiety, on observing what children they both were, her and Aunt Aline, she a near-old maid of 33 and her aunt an octogenarian. The smile, which came after the laughter, was of melancholy, on remembering all the fairy tales of which she, indeed, had once dreamed among the syllables of those named, chanted by the young Comte's lips.

Fairy tales in which were reunited, in baskets of flowers, at that moment, all the beautiful and lovely new sensations experienced by the little girl during those two months of paradise. Fairy tales in which, since then, other imagined sensations had mingled, in recalling those. And from all those memories there always emerged—certainly the most durable, the most profoundly rooted, and the one in which the most odorous and intoxicating flower rose up, always and sincerely similar, so firmly believed, and thus so real—the memory of the first sensation transformed into the first sentiment:

How we loved one another at first sight!

---

[39] Had such a nickname been given to the young Comte in Paris it might have implied not more than that he was a Breton, but in Britanny itself, it would link him more specifically to the particular Bretons who fought against the Revolution of 1789, implying that he is old-fashioned in his views.

And whether or not Geneviève attached to it the only meaning that could be attached to it in Aunt Line's opinion, it scarcely mattered. The quasi-old woman of today was still hypnotized by that memory, as the little girl had once been hypnotized by that glance darted by the young Comte as he turned round. From the present crystallization the same lightning-flash sprang forth, twenty years later.

And Aunt Line, the *merlifiche*, who wanted to joke about the long litany of the young Comte's names—and who could never prevent herself from remarking, in a laudatory fashion that it would, even so, make a fine conclusion, like a pea-cock's tail, to a fairy tale—undoubtedly knew that. And it was not only for a fairy tale of old that she, the seeress of old, imagined that possible conclusion, that peacock's tail; it was for a fairy tale not yet told, a future fairy tale, of which she imagined the denouement without daring to believe that she was a seeress still.

For now, with respect to the future, she no longer had any enlightenment coming to her from the past. Of all her extraordinary treasures of prescience via presentiments, the atavistic gifts that had enabled her to find the pole determining the magnetization of the blood of the Hescheboix, she had been deprived with regard to the blood of the Ponthual-Plouërs. It was, therefore, uniquely through Geneviève's obscure desire that she dreamed of the tale's conclusion, without a shadow of certainty, even subconscious—but in all faith nevertheless, so closely was she in communion with her beloved's desire: with that unexpressed, almost inexpressible desire, all the more powerful because it was blind and mad.

It was, indeed, quite blind and beyond all reason, that desire of love that would not admit to being love, born of a furtive glace and a vague smile darted twenty years before—a desire of love nevertheless, bewildered, tenacious and intense, since even now, that girl of soon to be 33 years of age, that old girl, with a brain thoroughly burned by the sciences and a heart doubtless dried up beneath their arid cinders, sometimes said, in thinking about the arrogant young man vanished so long ago and probably separated from her forever:

How we loved one another at first sight!

XVII

In reality, if the image of the young Comte had flourished in Geneviève's memory solely under in the guise of the glance and the smile darted like alms after the initial disobliging greeting, it was because all the memories of two months of paradise had been condensed in that unique memory, by virtue of a sort of religious transubstantiation—but the paradise had been made of many other things. Although she had not been conscious of it, then or since, those things are noteworthy, since her juvenile soul was to conserve the ineffaceable imprint of them, and since, above all, her present soul must have been fashioned thereby—including, as we shall see, her genius.

To begin with, what Geneviève had loved immediately, and by which she had immediately sensed herself loved, was not the young Comte, as she believed so firmly afterwards. In truth, doubtless through him, and because he was a perfect incarnation thereof, the object of that lightning mutual love was the entire domain, the land itself: the grounds where the two dark woods met, Kawchmôr and its cove of marshland beneath the collapsed walls of the chapel, Kairnheûz and its sullen tower, the heath and the wall of its horizon, the bar of liquid steel, and the grim old château with all its inhabitants, so strange but, by virtue of that very fact, familiar in advance to that strange and grim child.

There was nothing troubling for her in the abrupt leap backward that plunged her into the heart of the Breton Middle Ages, and more profoundly still, all the way to the prehistory from which the Gaelic and Cymric roots of the name of Kairnheûz, the "terrible heap of stones" had sprung. Was she not the worthy grand-niece of Aunt Line, whose atavistic memories—in Yvernaux's paradoxical terminology— doubtless went all the way back to the plains of Central Asia? Then again, she usually did not pay much attention to the external world, absorbed as she was in the abstract world of numbers, figures, forces and their relationships—and even if had she paid more attention to it, would not the austerity of the present landscape have accorded with that of the arid scientific landscapes to which she was accustomed?

As for the residents of the château, they had what it took to please her, by virtue of their silence and their effacement.

In the couple comprising the gardener and his wife, reminiscent of insouciant gravediggers, the old gamekeeper who mostly appeared to be protecting phantoms and to be one himself, another might have seen terrible shadows therein—but not her, for all living beings seemed to her to be shadows, of which she was not afraid. They, moreover, before the little girl, so calm, so gray, so shadow-like herself, and so different from ordinary little girls, were suddenly humanized, to the point of smiling. This was a child the phantoms could understand: serious, devoid of turbulence, making no more noise than they did themselves!

Similarly, the cook and the chambermaid, both with the mannerisms of nuns, mouths sewn shut, footsteps muffled, had welcomed affectionately, albeit mutely, the silent Aunt Line, who seemed to have sprung from the same stock as themselves, and her little niece, so modest and well-behaved. And Geneviève and Aunt Line on the one hand, and the cook and her daughter on the other, had immediately been glad to find, on the other side, "very discreet individuals."

Aunt Line was of her race, and possessed to the highest degree the gift—superficial but perfect—of fitting into her surroundings. Her originality, it will be remembered, was often concealed, even from her most intimate associates—from her nephew Thibaud, her Benjamin, even from the subtle and curious Yvernaux. As one can imagine, she hid it carefully here, in order not to clash with these "discreet individuals" and to appear so convincingly to be one of them. That explains how, subsequently, in remembering Aunt Line during her sojourn at Kairnheûz, Geneviève saw her transfigured: an Aunt Line that she could hardly recognize.

In fact, that transfiguration of Aunt Line, and the complete change that Geneviève had also observed in herself in the course of that period, and the atmosphere of melancholy peace and pleasant light in which those two months in paradise had bathed, all came, without any possible doubt, from the Comtesse.

Now, naturally enough, the Comtesse had no more suspicion of that than anyone else. If anyone had thought of pointing it out to her and asking her to explain it, she would certainly have attributed the general influence to her dear Abbé Denis Gasguin and to the particular virtues of the catechism with which he perfumed Geneviève's soul, with a view to her first communion.

It is incontestable, moreover, that the habitual unction of the priest, the elegant and eloquent Jesuit, distinguished in mind, refined in culture, penetrating and conciliating in psychology, had slowly impregnated the dwelling and the behavior of everyone at Kairnheûz during the almost thirteen years that he had been Joson's tutor. Nevertheless, it would probably be more accurate to say that he had first refined himself in order to refine others, and had acquired that elegance and distinction by contact, and ever-increasing intimacy, with the Comtesse.

That was a curious and fascinating study of two souls, both beautiful, pure and noble, communicating in a very profound affection that extended as far as veritable tenderness, but without any kind of disturbance. Indeed, the unique object of that tenderness was to be found, not in mutual ardors, but rather in convergent ardor, regarding the fate of young Comte, the scion of the Ponthual-Plouërs. Such a study, unfortunately, would have too much of the present in it, more appropriate to a feminine genius; one must, therefore, limit oneself merely to noting, very hastily, that which might serve this one.

It was by virtue of a miracle of maternal love, and thanks to the patient and intelligent aid with the no-less-miraculous devotion of Abbé Denis Gasguin had sustained it, that the Comtesse had succeeded in bringing up Joson as she wished.

That had not been an easy task. Without the Abbé, perhaps she would not have succeeded.

It had required more than patience, intelligence and devotion—yes, much more: exactly that unknown element of the miraculous which only love can give, and the kind of tenderness in which the Abbé's soul and the Comtesse's had "communed." The expression was his own, in a confession written to his superior, as without the shadow of a sacrilegious illusion, as one may imagine. He acted solely, not to excuse that tenderness, since there was nothing culpable about it, but to explain it, first in his nature and then in the motives that had rendered it necessary—and, in consequence, licit, not to say meritorious.

Meritorious it was, in fact, the last scion of the Ponthual-Plouërs having a future that the Company could utilize, and that future being in peril if the Comtesse did not watch over it, and thus, if help had not been provided, everything would have gone awry. Which was exactly what Abbé Gasguin provided, without any in the affair—for even his affection for the Comtesse, tender as it might have been, had furnished him, not with a goal he wanted to attain but a means, and the only means employable, to steer Joson into the path that it was "necessary" to make him take.

Joson was only Joson with his mother, Joson being the childish diminutive, in Breton parlance, of Joseph. With everyone other than his mother he instantly reverted, even in his earliest adolescence, to a hardness that had nothing childish about it, as ill-disposed as possible to being the definitive of what was, ultimately, the haughty—from the height of all his names and titles—Emile-Cast-Jagut-Marie-Joseph de Ponthual-Plouër, Seigneur des Ebihens, des Pierres-Sonantes, des Treize-Îles and other places.

And yet, as with his mother in person, he had ended up being, with the Abbé also, the little, the gentle, the childish, the tender Joson. That testifies to exactly what point, in their love for him, the two souls of which his own had been made had communed. For his own was changed henceforth—and presumably forever. The heir of Ponthual-Plouër, the wild child in whom all the vices had momentarily threatened to grow vigorously, was today the good and well-behaved pupil emerging from the *Borda*, ready to make a fine career for himself as a naval officer. Until the day—it had been calculated over Abbé Gasguin's head—when the young man, brought up in the ideas and tastes of the past, and for that reason nicknamed "the little Chouan" by his comrades, found himself overtly at odds with the ideas and tastes of today! On that day, it was certain, the sickened Comte would renounce an impossible struggle, hand in his resignation from the navy, and come back to seek a refuge in the bosom of the Company.

The future result was "a long shot," as the popular saying has it, but there had been no means of doing better. The prudent Abbé had not wasted a moment in steering Joson immediately toward the pure religious life, firstly because the Comtesse herself had not been ready for that, good Catholic as she was, and secondly because it had been necessary to hasten to the most urgent matter, which was to subdue the little savage's most violent instincts, in which all the worst moral toxins of all the Ponthual-Plouërs in general, and his father in particular, were seething.

Fortunately, the depurative agent for cleansing that blood was to hand, evident and sure: it was the profound and quasi-religious love with which Joson adored his mother. Whether or not he had defended her against his father, as the legend said, he was indisputably capable of having desired to do it, and having done it if the opportunity arose. And he proved that, moreover, when left alone with her, by defending her against himself—because it was for her, to be agreeable to her, in order that she might smile in satisfaction, that he had allowed himself to be subdued by his tutor, amended and gentled, gradually becoming the good, submissive, childish little Joson, a true model of a noble and nobly-educated child.

All his secret revolts, all his appetites for battle, independence and adventure, all his crazed instincts under pressure, had been provided with a safety-valve by the naval career by which he would enter into life. The hope of a future explosion throwing him back, broken, to the Company, did not originate, of course, with his mother, nor even the Abbé, the latter merely being used to put the idea of that career into the Comtesse's head and to inspire an appetite for it in the adolescent.

The mother had consented, in spite of the chagrin of the separation to come, out of wise foresight with respect to a nature that would one day need expansion, and for fear of seeing it etiolated here in excessive languor. The young man had accepted joyfully, in spite of his devotion to his mother, thinking that he was, after all, a Ponthual-Plouër, that he ought to do honor to his name, and that his mother would soon be proud of him. Deep down, without being conscious of it, he was thirsty for liberty, even if it were as harsh as the ocean wind, after the excessively gentle softness of his adolescence, as reclusive as a sick-room.

In the meantime—before abandoning himself entirely to the ocean wind when he quit the *Borda*—he enjoyed, for the last time, and with delight, the lukewarm and confined air in which he had become the meek little Joson. That was the special air into which Geneviève found herself suddenly transplanted; and she also took delight in it—whence came, later, the memories of luminous paradise, in a suavely softened light, that were to remain in her heart.

It was, however, a singular paradise, which would have appeared to reflect a very extravagant Catholicism, if any attempt had been made to imagine it and pin down its images. Now, that is what made—already had made, but especially would make thereafter—in spite of her, in involuntary mystical gusts, the exceedingly mystical individual that Geneviève had always been. But what strange forms there were, indeed, in the intimate chapel where her memory celebrated its worship, taking the information she had extracted from the catechism and the beings that had been mingled with that exaltation!

Those forms, in any case, were never extremely precise, drawn with vigorous strokes and cored brightly. They floated in smoke—probably of incense—and behind veils of white mist, as if the veils of her fist communion had vaporized around her and become confused with the fumes of the incense. And it was through those clouds that she saw vaguely appearing to her the light figures with indistinct outlines and faded nuances, on very distant stained-glass windows paled by the dusk.

The angel Gabriel and the Holy Virgin were, on the window to the left, Abbé Denis and the Comtesse. He was slowly pronouncing words, sugared with unction, which, on emerging from his invariably-smiling mouth, inscribed themselves on long, sinuously folded ribbons—and those words were the questions and responses of the catechism, to which the Comtesse was opening her heart, traversed by seven blades. Those blades were not doing her any harm, however, for her mouth too, although a trifle melancholy, was invariably smiling. She did not allow any words to escape, though; only her eyes spoke, saying by means of their infinitely tender gaze:

"Love my son as I love him."

And on the window to the right, there was the same phrase of adoration that all the gazes were expressing, and the mouths too, from which a broad ribbon flew, expanding into a banner, and bearing capital letters that seemed to shout:

LOVE HER SON AS SHE LOVES HIM!

And those gazes and those mouths were the gazes and mouths of the inhabitants of Kairnheûz, all of them: the gardener and his wife, with the blissful faces of insouciant gravediggers; the phantom gamekeeper, guardian of phantoms; the cook and her daughter in nuns' head-dresses; everyone praying—and Aunt Line kneeling too, her hands joined for prayer, her upper body stiff in her bodice, black and shiny like a scarab beetle, the only silhouette in relief, colored like the others in gray.

In the center of the triptych, in the largest window, Geneviève herself was crouched at the bottom, as if crushed by ecstasy, her arms limp, her mouth open, her tearful eyes illuminated by joy, her heart bare and flaming red beneath the white ash that the veils of her first communion made—and above her, in a glory of apotheosis, blessing her with the gesture of Our Savior Jesus Christ, the One of whom the Comtesse and all the residents of Kairnheûz were saying that it was necessary that he should be loved as his mother loved him.

And it really was Christ, in fact, in terms of his gesture and his costume, and even in terms of the essential features of his traditional effigy, since he wore the double-pointed beard and the russet hair separated in the middle of the forehead and crowned with a diadem of thorns. Nevertheless, beneath the traditional effigy, Geneviève saw appearing, and becoming transparent, and sometimes resplendent, none but the face of Joson, so different from the august visage, the characteristic face of the last Ponthual-Plouër, with the forehead bulging with idealism beneath a kind of cowl of flat black hair, hollow cheeks allowing the muscles of the carnivorous jaw to stand out, lips arched like a bow, from which the word of command was about to spring, the nose of an erne and the eyes of a petrel.

For, in even sharper relief and color than Aunt Line's scarabean bodice, among the vague grays of the three windows, Joson's face, especially in certain exalted moments of memory, transported itself, as painters say, emerging from the background and coming forward—particularly those two typical details, to which Joson had drawn attention himself several times, of which he was not very proud: the erne's nose and the petrel's eyes.

With that, and his nickname on the *Borda*, the little Chouan, Geneviève and Aunt Line had been regaled by him, in intimate confidence, during excursions into the dark woods or across the heath. He had been pleased, happy to be venturing forth and feeling that he was being admired for something other than being good. He had explained to the curious Geneviève and Aunt Line, who was fond of tales, what the erne and the petrel were: the eagle of the seas and the bird of storms, and what Breton legends had sung about them, giving their souls to certain heroes.

To which Aunt Line, generous with her science, out of gratitude for what she had just learned, had observed sententiously: "It's the soul that one has in the eyes that always eats the others."

"Personally, I try to protect both," the young man had replied, bravely.

And at that moment, in fact, he really had the red eyes and soul of a petrel, driven mad with joy by a storm, intoxicated therein by peril, which cries recklessly for adventure, even if it be mortal. But he also had the curved nasal dagger and the soul of a ferocious and rapacious sea-eagle, fond of lacerating its living prey, and it was with a brusque clenching of his masseter muscles, like steel walnuts, that he had uttered bursts of laughter like the clacking of an erne's beak.

Aunt Line alone had retained the memory of that redoubtable laughter. Geneviève, no. The words had stayed with her—erne's nose, petrel's eyes—with the clear images that she contemplated in Joson's face, apotheosized in the center of the triptych, but she did not attach any terrible significance to them. Were not all her memories of paradise always bathed in the tender and gentle light suavely filtered through the Comtesse's eyelashes, the silk-fringed eyelashes, in that soothing light in which nothing could appear other than pleasant?

Although the decor could change in the three windows, their charm never changed. Whether the scenes of the catechism taught by Abbé Denis, or that of the adoration manifested by the residents of Kairnheûz, or that Joson in the ascension of apotheosis, were taking place in the grounds, or the château, or on the heath, or even in the darkness of the oak-wood hurling itself into the fir-wood, or amid the ruins of the chapel before the sinister sheen of Kawchmôr, the dear evocation always had for its magic word, the Comtesse's own words, coaxing, slow and musical, in the choice atmosphere of the pretty Louis XV boudoir in which she resided, for preference.

For, although the lugubrious "Terrible Heap of Stones" had remained the same since the Middle Ages externally, certain parts of the interior, restored and furnished in the 18th century, had taken on a very different character, which made a new habitat for a new soul. The feral den with a somber carapace thus sheltered pleasant and cheerful corners. The Comtesse's boudoir was one of them, and the most exquisite.

Her feminine elegance and maternal tenderness had flourished there and perfumed the air. Furnished in a pure style, with pastel fabrics and delightful contours, delicate wooden moldings painted gray, paneling of sober and spiritual design to which a few precious engravings added their grace, and light curtains which seemed powdered by old lace—such as the frame made according to the Comtesse's wishes, and which her memory transported everywhere, so to speak, at least in Geneviève's memory and imagination.

And so, it was as if in the mirror of those colored engravings, and among those delicate surroundings, that she was glad to review—and was incapable of doing otherwise—her entire existence at that time. The sensations experienced during those two months, she only re-experienced in the ambience of that boudoir, in the air flowered and perfumed by the Comtesse's feminine elegance and maternal tenderness—and the catechism itself, and her first communion, and the widows of her intimate chapel, remained powered by a charm of old lace. And it was the supreme surviving charm of all the charms that had enchanted Geneviève's eyes, mind and heart during her unforgettable days in paradise.

147

XVIII

"Are you thinking about your windows again, *amon*?"

That was what Aunt Line said to her when Geneviève had a certain look in her eyes, which the old woman called "the curly look."

One can imagine, in fact, that their intimacy had often been embellished by that confidence regarding the memories transformed into the strange vision of the windows. They had ended up smiling at it, a little—first Aunt Line, who gladly mocked her darling for that kind of love, simultaneously childish, religious and chimerical; then Geneviève, similarly, so bizarre did it seem to her, not so say absurd, to have been able to be something akin to a lover and a mystic.

And because of that, when she lingered on her dream in reflection, she acquired what Aunt Line described, so aptly, as her "curly look"—so aptly, that is, in her special parlance, with such singular associations of ideas! For her, the word meant that the look in question was simultaneously joyful and mocking, like certain glances darted by little boys with short curls.

And Geneviève, in fact, while delighting in her memories of her paradise, had nevertheless begun to find them, at length, slightly ridiculous. It is true, too, that the nuance of ridicule itself pleased her—and her sentiment, then, was well-translated by Aunt Line's phrase, evoking contained little outbursts of mischievous laughter and twinkling eyes, like curly hair.

"Right now, you're in the black hole."

When the good woman said that to Geneviève, it was because she saw her eyes troubled, stressed and bleak—eyes that said, like the Thiérachian song:

Dgerlindez sans derlindindins,
Pour chés yux qui pleurn't pau l'dedins.

And one could easily imagine, in fact, silent carillons *guerlindaient* within poor Geneviève, without any *drelindindin* of joy, at the times when she had those sad eyes, weeping inside while she sank into morose contemplation before what she herself had baptized "the black hole." Oh yes, the black hole into which her life had almost fallen and been interred! The black hole whose blackness always horrified her, by virtue of its absolute blackness and mystery, even today, when all that was no more than a distant and concluded nightmare.

It was not only her life that had nearly plunged into that "black hole"; it was much more, and although no one had ever told her about it, she had retained an obscure and dolorous sentiment of aftershock—a post-sentiment, one might say—all the more frightful because it remained unexplained. That which had been as if dead and buried, lost forever underground in the four-year black hole immediately succeeding the paradisal vacation, was Geneviève's genius.

Abruptly, on returning from Kairnheûz, while enjoying a physical and moral health that had never been more flourishing, the little girl—who had now become a young woman— had awakened as if with a different brain. Such, at least, but terribly exact, had been the impression made on her father, as soon as the first conversation, in which he had cried, effusively, with the great delight of a teacher meeting a favorite pupil again:

"Oh, how much fun we'll have working together! How splendid the crops will be, after two months lying fallow! You'll see, my dear."

But the unfortunate fellow had only seen a vague gaze, without any flame for Science, thinking about something else, with which he did not feel any longer in contact. Before a series of exciting problems, which he had prepared expressly to enjoy Geneviève's inventive faculties, he found her incurious, closed and closed. He had tried in vain to renew her appetite; she seemed henceforth, instead, to find it repugnant. Out of obedience and politeness, she had tried to apply her attention to it, but had not been able to find the slightest interest therein. One might have thought that he was speaking to her in a foreign language.

Gasguin had thought he was going mad, with rage and chagrin. What! Two months had sufficed to change that intelligence so utterly! For it was not only her taste for the sciences that Geneviève seemed to have forgotten; it was their meaning, even the simplest and most vulgar comprehension. She no longer loved them because she no longer understood them. That was further demonstrated by the difficulty she now had in applying herself to them, always deferentially, as a docile pupil, but always poorly, as a pupil devoid of talent.

It was then that the despairing Gasguin had had the sinister impression, terribly exact, that his daughter had woken up one day with a different brain; and he had said so to Aunt Line, who could not see it, alas, and thought that Geneviève was exactly the same, or even better—"with a woman's body"—than she had been before her departure for Kairnheûz.

He had written to Yvernaux, who had come running immediately, and had found Geneviève very healthy—grown, embellished, and even extraordinarily refined in her sensations and ideas, at least with regard to everything but the sciences. On that particular point however, incompetent as he still was, in spite of his recent studies, he had been forced to recognize, having interrogated his goddaughter, that she was no longer the child prodigy that had previously bowled her father and himself over with admiration.

"You're right," he had concluded. "That's not the same brain. Your expression is devastatingly accurate."

Then had then each sought the causes of that radical transformation, Gasguin with discouragement, certain of the catastrophe and saddened because his daughter might be prey to some incurable malady, Yvernaux with a glimmer of hope nevertheless, and not without a secret selfish desire—it must be confessed—that he might reconquer his goddaughter entirely for himself, thanks to the unexpected reorientation. Indeed, Geneviève seemed to him to be closed to the sciences, properly speaking, but not, according to his expression, to the other blooms of which the infinite compass-rose of the intellectual world was composed. Thus, as she continued to have an open and studious mind, doubtless still curious—provided that one found the new aliment appropriate to nourish that curiosity—there was no reason to complain of the abomination of desolation, because what was henceforth lost to Mesdames les Sciences might be recaptured elsewhere...

He had pronounced "Mesdames les Sciences" with a comical emphasis, and he continued, in a joking manner intended to cheer the lugubrious Gasguin up a little—which implied that Gasguin was an idiot: "Come on, old chap! Surely, Mesdames les Lettres or Madame la Philosophie are not despicable hussies."

While he joked, however, he was not very tranquil himself, deep down. Once his wretched selfish thought had died away—rapidly, let us say to his credit—his anxiety flared up again. Geneviève did indeed seem to be more refined in her sensations and ideas, and to have progressed in that regard, the general health of her mind having followed that of her body—*mens sana in corpore sana*—it was nevertheless in the fashion of any young woman, no more. And all things considered, when Geneviève had been adroitly questioned by him, and all her possible curiosities cleverly directed towards other nutriments than the sciences, it had been necessary to admit her present absolute impotence to bowl her father and godfather over, in spite of their willingness.

Ultimately, that which had been lost for Mesdames les Sciences had been lost to the same degree for Mesdames les Lettres and Madame la Philosophie. There was not even the consolation of thinking that it might be recovered for religion, by which it was briefly feared that Geneviève might have been caught, and via which Yvernaux would have hoped to lead her sooner or later to Metaphysics. No! It was with respect to any ardent intellectual activity that that average adolescent "noggin" was now reluctant, restive in confrontation with the least complicated problems, with no appetite for knowledge regarding the most elementary notions of physics and chemistry, as if it were applying itself to the Sciences for the first time.

For the strange cerebral anemia—what else can it be called?—had extended that far. Methodically, Gasguin, a good teacher experienced in the routine, had begun Geneviève's scientific education again at the very beginning, seeing her resistant to the difficult questions that had impassioned her before. And it was precisely in finding herself thus, at the very wellspring of the sciences, where her thirst, only two months earlier, had slaked itself in such deep draughts and caused new streams of water to flow, that Geneviève now had a sort of reflexive impulse of disgust, extending to a veritably horrified retreat.

How could that wellspring, in which she now tasted only bitterness, be rendered as sweet as before? How could she even be given the desire, regret for the recently-lost savor? Lost forever, alas, Gasguin soon thought, having exhausted himself in futile attempts without obtaining the slightest result. Lost forever, even Yvernaux, more easily duped, finally had to confess, who had tried more ingeniously than Gasguin, in the most various directions, without any more result.

War-weary, they had renounced all hope of seeing the Geneviève of old again, and. having come to that point of renunciation, told themselves that they had doubtless been deluded before. They tried hard to recall some typical, indisputable detail establishing the formidable promise of genius she had shown; now they imagined that they had invented, or at least exaggerated, the facts on which they had built the chimerical edifice of her promise.

And how could they not have added faith to that new explanation, which they furnished after the fact? When, to settle their conscience, they interrogated Geneviève herself on the subject, her astonished, often foolish, replies were sufficient proof that all of it had doubtless been merely a beautiful dream born of their enthusiasm and having left no shadow of a trace in her indigent memory, the silly girl!

"It was you," Gasguin had said to Yvernaux, "yes you, who put that folly in our heads, with your sacred lyricism and your verbal fireworks."

"Not at all," Yvernaux had riposted. "It was your infatuation with Pascal that worked the trick on us. You saw the genius of the great Auvergnat in your little girl, just as you had earlier seen his sublime mask in your wife's poor mug."

And they were each resentful of the other for being mutually deceived, as if it had been deliberate. The worst thing was, however, was that they blamed the unfortunate girl for their error, as if she had induced the false opinion in them by cunning, calculation or God only knew what damnable precious and malevolent feminine coquetry. Yes, it was at that degree of disenchantment in her regard that they ended up one day, suddenly both becoming misogynists.

It goes without saying that Aunt Line and Geneviève suffered in consequence, overtly held in scorn from then on. But the two friends suffered no less, without having intended it. Their friendship was corroded by it. Their love for their daughter and goddaughter had been the strongest bond of that amity. That love having faded with their admiration, the bond was soon stretched; and the amity, having ceased to make a bouquet, immediately withered into simple and banal camaraderie.

By the end of the first year after the return from Kairnheûz, Gasguin and Yvernaux no longer found pleasure in being together. They contented themselves with writing. Then the letters became rare. During the third of those four lamentable years, the correspondence between them was limited to vague epistles on New Year's Day and anniversaries. During the final year, nothing at all.

What would they have had to say to one another, in fact, except that each of them had returned to his own concerns had felt no need to introduce the other thereinto? What interest could the ambition to be a "thinker," with which Yvernaux was still intoxicated, be to the petty professor of physics and chemistry that Gauguin had always been? It would make the poor devil envious, Yvernaux told himself. And of what importance to Yvernaux could be the desire for advancement that now limited the horizons of Gasguin, the humble universitarian. No importance at all, Gasguin sagely estimated. Given that, how could they have any desire to write, since their daughter and goddaughter was decidedly no longer, to the glory of both of them, a genius?

The neglect to which Yvernaux condemned him pained Gasguin particularly, and rendered him more sensitive to the cruel disappointment caused by Geneviève. Without any malevolence or rancor, he made the child suffer for it—and thus she suffered doubly. For she sensed clearly—all too clearly—the present scorn of her godfather and father, and the abandonment of one and the resigned peevishness of the other had further envenomed her suffering, all the more so because she did not understand the reason for that peevishness and that abandonment, and thought them unjust. She was so keen to please her father! She devoted herself with so much zeal and patience to those harsh scientific studies that now pleased him so little!

It was in that era of hard and often fruitless labor, of efforts as vain as they were assiduous to be a perfect pupil, that it was necessary to overcome the aversion that she was later to feel for examinations and syllabuses, beaten pathways by which one slowly travels the entire domain of the sciences when one wishes to conquer them rationally by means of small methodical steps.

You will doubtless remember Yvernaux reproaching her frequently, ten or fifteen years later, for not having taken the trouble to obtain ore diplomas, and talking to her regretfully about the "doctoral toga" with the rabbit-fur trim, with which, he affirmed, she would have been able to deck herself had she wished. When he teased her about it, she often, you will remember, made fun of herself, laughing. Had she been less kind, and without being nasty, she would have had the right to reply to him, in all fairness: "It's the fault of the 'black hole' in which you and my father, bad friends, forgot about me for four years."

What they had always ignored, in fact—not merely the godfather but the father, unpardonably since he was living with her—was that, in feeling that she had been abandoned in that "black hole," the poor child had been at risk of the death, not merely of her genius, but her reason.

That her genius was extinct she had not perceived, not knowing that he had had it. That the affection of the people she loved was lacking, she had fearfully observed, and felt dolorously—and her heart had been deeply wounded by it. And that is no mere metaphor; it was in full and atrocious reality that she nearly went mad because of it.

Several times, the catastrophe had been close at hand: notably, during two crises of amnesia, which the physicians were obliged to treat blindly, without being able to diagnose either the why or the how; on another occasion, by virtue of an almost-epileptiform attack of nerves, of which they had even less understanding; then again, more slyly, in the course of an indeterminate fever vaguely labeled "consumption" and "languor."

And if Geneviève's brain had not, in spite of everything, turned turtle and sank to the sea-bed in those four semi-shipwrecks when her poor head was taking in water at every hole—as Yvernaux would have said, had he been present and if he had understood what was happening—but had recovered her footing, her life, her intelligence and, finally, her resuscitated genius, she owed it all to Aunt Line.

Oh, not to an Aunt Line capable of great lyrical images, although, on occasion, in her fashion...nor to a brain able to judge Geneviève's, but to the being of atavistic devotion, of occult and instinctive knowledge, still lying in ambush in the worthy woman. What is genius? Of what did Geneviève's consist? Aunt Line knew absolutely nothing about that, but she had once more been, all the same, the guardian and the rescuer, as Henri Fabre's wasp is to the larvae she will never know.

Never had she, the illiterate *merlifiche*, the one-time roadside "swindler," the former maid-of-all-work in the Gasguin household, the present housekeeper in the black scarab bodice, the simpleton, had the slightest doubt about the great individual who was to blossom in Geneviève. Not that she ever pronounced the phrase "great individual," which was too precise for her. She contented herself with designating it by the tiny and vague term "that," and commenting on it thus in her obscure thoughts:

"*That*, from Idalie, from the blood of the Hescheboix, which wants to spring forth again, having slept for such a long time."

After which, between her teeth, she added, not speaking for the others but for herself: "And I would breathe my last breath into it, *amon*, and die of it, in order that *that* might live."

But why, though? she asked herself, mutely, without pronouncing the words, although the question stood up straight in her head, like a serpent on its tail.

Because needs must.

Thus she replied, with closed lips, and without saying anything more—but her prominent eyebrows came together, and fused into a bar, so rigid was her determination.

And, more ingenious than the physicians, she had cured her Geneviève of the two crises of amnesia, the epileptiform attack and the unnamable fever. And, better still, she had saved her above all from the ferocious tortures inflicted unwittingly on the girl by the scorn and abandonment of her father and godfather. She never ceased to give her back the confidence and hope that the unfortunate girl lost after so many vain efforts to become once again the pupil who had once made the master so proud, instead of remaining the pupil of whom he was now ashamed.

"Courage!" she trumpeted, by means of her ever-enthusiastic and fervent gazes of admiration—for, if her speech was silent, the old woman's eyes knew how to cry out and sound the charge.

"Tomorrow, at six o'clock, you'll understand again!"

That also, in words this time, she often said to her. And the precision alone of that day and that hour, thus fixed, sufficed to lend fiber to Geneviève's weary and broken will-power. Toward that day and hour, so imminent, she valiantly stretched out her energy and her hope—and the next day, at the specified hour, she forgot the prediction of the day before, only to hear the same person saying the same thing, in the same terms, and prolonging the hope and energy again.

And thus, from day to day, the months had passed, and also the years, without Geneviève's reason giving way, without her being buried, entombed in the black hole.

So, with the memory of horror and mystery that she had retained, of the black hole, there had also remained in her heart a good and dear memory of Aunt Line. And that was the only luminous point in so much blackness—but the light within it was as soft as that in which her two months of paradise bathed. To such an extent that, sometimes, Aunt Line was deceived in saying so her suddenly, with her teasing smile: "Are you thinking about your windows again, *amon*?" For, at that moment, she ought to have said: "Right now, you're in the black hole." But that was when Geneviève, while being in the black hole, was not contemplating for the moment any of what had been so dismally black, but was concentrating the joyful attention of her memory on the point of soft light lit by Aunt Line's devotion.

And suddenly, flinging her arms around the old woman's neck, she embraced her with all her reckless tenderness, gratefully—with the gratitude, it seemed, of her entire race, melted in that filial caress. And it was doubtless also the gratitude of the entire race that the good woman savored—for she, so seemingly grim in her stiff black scarab bodice, started weeping large, slow, heavy tears, of which she was ashamed.

"What?" she said, rudely. "What's got into you, you old crone, to wet your cheeks with all these teardops?"

"Come on, Aunt Line," Geneviève said, gently. "Let me drink your tears, your kind tears, which aren't salty like others, but sweetened by your good heart."

And they were both laughing and crying. Aunt Line, to take her revenge, called her little faker, ferret-face, *latusée*, little devil of a *cattelinette*, like her grandmother Idalie. "Because, of course, it goes without saying, you led me astray just now, pretending you were thinking about your windows again, when you were in the black hole. Do you think I'm a ninny, *amon*?"

"But you were, and a great one," Geneviève riposted. "And you can't tell, as you boast, where I am by my eyes alone. For just now, I didn't have my eyes that were weeping *pau l'dedins*, and yet I was in the black hole. Only what was *dgerlindait* there were *drelindindins* of joy, because it was broad daylight in the black hole. Oh, not because my windows were lit up there, as you seem to believe, great ninny, I repeat, but because of a beautiful, beautiful, beautiful star, shining in the night and making sunlight there. And that star was you, Aunt Line—and that's why, even in the black hole, I had my curly look."

And the two children, the old woman and the genius, embraced one another again, with tears of happiness, truly sweetened, as that great individual Geneviève had said, who also had a tiny flower of a soul.

XIX

By what manifestations, evidently singular and characteristic, had that monstrous eclipse ended, by which Geneviève's intellectual sun remained completely veiled? That is a
story whose circumstantial details it would be interesting to
know, and whose development would be fascinating to follow
closely. It would make a fruitful contribution to the study of
physiology and psychology of genius, as yet so poorly docu-
mented.

Unfortunately, we only have randomly-accumulated
fragments of that story, conserved without order or method,
and collected and transmitted with no serious critical concern,
but rather according to a scarcely scrupulous whim. Such as
they are, they can scarcely be useful from any but the picturesque viewpoint.

It was mostly Gasguin, however, who accumulated those
fragments—oh, as well as he could! One might have expected
that he would have done better, but it was it was not be, so
little of the philosopher was there in him. The meager facts by
which Geneviève's reawakening was revealed, he did not
sense or perceive as typical, and was not at all anxious to clarify by means of their light the mechanism of that awakening. In
any case, would he not only have attached real importance to
the facts in terms of their pedagogical value, considered as
theorems to understand or problems to resolve? The conscientious professor, which he was above all, had been uniquely
enchanted by the progress made, step by step, remade by his
docile pupil, outside of which, no other consideration of any
sort had struck him.

It was thus that he had—in good faith!—absolutely neglected to note any silly questions, absurd interruptions, or reveries pushed to the point of complete "absences," through the
holes of which, so to speak, an Yvernaux would surely have

seen rays of sunlight emerge, ready to triumph over the eclipse.

Some of these curious phenomena had, however, escaped the total oblivion to which they seemed to be condemned by Gasguin's inattention: those whose singular enormity had excessively offended his common sense and exhausted his patience. When they had irritated him as quasi-voluntary stupidities, and he had reproached Geneviève for her seeming insolence, often with rudeness and scorn, it had transpired that the unfortunate girl thought such brutality in her regard unjust, and complained to Aunt Line.

"Would you believe it?" she confided. "What a swine! I'd worked so hard on my lesson"—or "my problem"—"and he treated me like an imbecile, a blockhead, because I said to him..." or "because I sat there with my nose in the air, thinking that..."

And Geneviève told her, unthinkingly, about the silly question or the absurd interruption with which, without intending to, she had "enlivened" the theorem or the problem, or the strange distraction she had had instead of following one of her father's demonstrations, and what she had "seen" or "heard" during that distraction.

It goes without saying that Aunt Line could not understand why the question or the interruption was silly or absurd. Even less could she take account, even approximately, of what Geneviève "saw" and "heard" in the course of the veritable "visual" or "auditory scientific hallucinations" that caused these "absences." But it also goes without saying that, although she did not understand any of it, Aunt Line took an interest, with all her might, in the indisputably-captivating confidences and revelations of her darling, whose slightest word was gospel to her, and consequently worthy of being heard and collected with pious care.

That is how the most interesting scraps of this story were conserved—conserved pell-mell, devoid of any order, as will be seen, in Aunt Line's memory and glory-hole with the sayings, adages, mottoes, refrains, aphorisms and personal eccentricities with which it was cluttered. It was there, much later, under the dust of six or eight years, at random, among the hand-me-down rags of that bizarre bric-à-brac, that Yvernaux was to find it, when he resumed his project of writing his famous *Treatise on the Innate Sciences*. He then had the—quite justified—certainty of being able to find "in that Ennia's dung-heap,"[40] as he jokingly put it, a few inestimable pearls.

Unfortunately, too—another sort of misfortune—he allowed himself, in collecting them without collating them, to put a little of himself into them, and sometimes more than a little. Inevitably, to be sure, and in spite of his perfect honesty! But the information furnished by Aunt Line was sometimes so shapeless, so obscure, and so difficult to interpret! Even more inevitably, and not in spite but because of her no-less-perfect honesty, she sometimes extended devoted adoration to insignificant trivia, transformed into pure relics! Upon these irrelevancies, presented if on a sort of paten, how could Yvernaux's lyrical imagination not have worked retrospectively, giving meaning to their insignificance and carving reliquaries for the pretended relics?

It was not entirely his fault that the collection and the transmission—or, rather, the translation—of these more-or-less curious details, some of them extraordinary and incredible, had been carried out without any critical intelligence. And when his *Treatise on the Innate Sciences* appears—if it ever does—in which mention of it is continually made in the Notes and Commentaries, it will be necessary not to treat him too harshly for the not-very-scrupulous but innocent—because involuntary—fantasy that presided, most of the time, over the drafting of those Notes and Commentaries. It will be best to take from them only that which a severe exegesis allows to filter through. And undoubtedly, we repeat, the physiological and psychological study of genius will profit from it far less that the merely picturesque viewpoint.

---

[40] This reference is obscure; Yvernaux is probably feminizing the name of Ennius, the "father" of Latin poetry.

At the risk of also encouraging the reproach of fantasy toward serious persons, but not to omit anything that might, even so, illuminate the mind of Geneviève, even by employing Yvernaux's magic lantern, here are a few of the imageries seen in that magic lantern.

They have not been chosen with overmuch order, nor method, and especially not with critical intelligence. To tell the whole truth, naked and ingenuous, one has to confess to being directed primarily by Yvernaux own choice, but guided—he affirmed—by that of Aunt Line in person. Like Molière reading his comedies to his simple servant Laforêt, the "thinker" Yvernaux did not disdain, in fact, to submit to humble Aunt Line the written version of the information that she had furnished him, and the passages that he has communicated here are exactly those about which the good woman said, without hesitation—even when visibly devoid of understanding:

"Yes, that's it, *amon*."

Yvernaux was, in any case, sufficiently impartial, although both judge and party, not to be afraid of recognizing that Geneviève, witnessing such readings, had fallen about laughing and had had the cheek to cry, in Aunt Line's and her godfather's faces: "But that's not true! I never uttered such an insanity! Where did you get that story, Aunt Line? And what diabolical absurdity are you extracting from it, Godfather?"

At which Aunt Line, behind her, would make desperate gestures to Yvernaux, to signify that Geneviève could not remember the incident or sentence incriminated with falsity. "Because," she explained to Yvernaux subsequently when they were alone, "when it happens, she's always absent, and doesn't know afterwards."

And Yvernaux, sagaciously, concluded that the states of hypnosis in which these actions and words were produced left no trace in the conscious memory on awakening. He could have played a trump card then by confounding Geneviève with Grasset's theory of the O and polygonal centers, but he carefully refrained, fearing that she would forbid Aunt Line to make the revelations from which she was profiting—and he preferred to let her believe that he was not, in fact, taking seriously the silly things invented by the old woman and the embroideries that he had added to them.

"All right, all right!" he said. "Let's not talk about it anymore. Aunt Line must have had a drink when she thought you'd said this or done that—as for me, when I wrote it down, I'd always had at least two drinks: one of cognac to get me going, and one of pride in thinking that you're my goddaughter. Then, you understand, there's a double dose of craziness—but what can it matter to you that I amuse myself drawing rockets of paradoxes and petards of images therefrom?"

"Oh, if it's to amuse yourself, Godfather..."

"Not just me," he interjected, "but Aunt Line as well. Look at her eyes! She too is extracting petards of joy and rockets of ecstasy."

Geneviève could not help observing that Aunt Line really did have a blissful expression, and generally concluded, with polite acquiescence: "Given that it gives the two of you so much pleasure, then, dress her blunders in your silk and gold, Godfather. Go on, continue to amuse yourselves. Don't hold back!"

And they didn't hold back, in fact, as you will finally be able to judge, from these few extracts from the Notes and Commentaries to the *Treatise on the Innate Sciences*—extracts that have been prepared so that their value can henceforth be estimated at its true worth, neither more or less.

XX

At the moment of going to press, we find ourselves under a sudden and absolute obligation to renounce the publication of the present chapter, without having had, in consequence, the time—nor the desire, moreover—to rewrite the preceding and following chapters. This is the reason, as unexpected as it is imperious, the honest explanation of which will take the place of the chapter itself, suppressed *ipso facto*.

The prodigious event whose ultimate relation will be the conclusion of this story has not been, nor will be, the object of a communication to the official scientific world. Very few people know about it as a great scientific event, even among the people who pride themselves on being up to date in such matters. In that, they are in the same situation as the general public, whom the newspapers have informed of the material "fact" and nothing more, and who have seen nothing else in it, taking it quite simply for one of the various facts, so frequent and almost ordinary nowadays, gathered under the rubric of *Aviation*.

A few more perspicacious minds, more alert in tracking the solutions reported every day to that present and exciting problem, have nevertheless scented something new here— entirely new. Among the first rank of those capable of anything in trying to "set the record" for being "collectors of original documents concerning the modern sport *par excellence*" is the representative of a celebrated American publishing house.[41] Yvernaux, whose excessive lyricism does not prevent him, as you know, from occasionally indulging in word play— often badly—even risked one, claiming that the house of "Édition," was, behind a mask, the house of "Edison."

---

[41] I have translated "maison americaine d'édition" [American publishing house] here, but have had to replace "édition" subsequently in order to recover Yvernaux's pun.

It does not matter, anyway, by whom and for whose profit that sort of monopolization is operated. The essential thing is that the coup was carried out and that it had for its specific objet, and specifically in consequence of the afore-mentioned prodigious event, everything concerning the prepa-ratory work from which Geneviève's discovery emerged. And one must believe that the famous "document collector" was on the lookout for the least immediately-detectable and, as it were, the most distant of these "luxury documents," if one might put it that way, for he has not hesitated to acquire for his house, with the exclusive right of publication in all forms, even of Blaise Yvernaux's *Treatise on the Innate Sciences*. He had undoubtedly got wind—from whom?—of the Notes and Commentaries, certain anecdotes of which had been revealed, albeit in secret and to a few intimates, not in written form but by oral citation.

We cannot hold it against the author of the "famous" *Treatise*—still incomplete, of course—if he was legitimately excited by the flattering offer and accepted it. It is appropriate to say, to his credit, that financial considerations had nothing to do with his acquiescence, for he has generously donated to his goddaughter all the authorial rights that his *Treatise on the Innate Sciences* might produce. What convinced him to make the deal, and drag Gasguin and Geneviève into the conspiracy, is the all-powerful publicity that the American house has at its disposal, and which can henceforth be placed in the service of an invention destined, in his eyes, to revolutionize the world.

In the meantime, it is nonetheless forbidden to publish, until further notice, the Notes and Commentaries to the *Trea-tise*. An exception has been made, you will have noticed, for the note, of no real practical importance, comprising the anec-dote on the theory of division you have read in chapter XII.

It is permissible, moreover, by means of that anecdote and so many phrases and metaphors, so many poetic or para-doxical effusions, directly borrowed by Yvernaux, to imagine fairly accurately what those Notes and Commentaries must be like. Their interest, ultimately—we must insist—is far more literary than scientific. Although Yvernaux's vanity might suffering somewhat, and the American's too, perhaps it is permissible to believe that the representative of the American publishing house, in buying the rights to the *Treatise on the Innate Sciences*, was not, as our forefathers would say, striking a good bargain. The majority of the Notes and Commentaries, which would seem inappropriate and bizarre in a scientific journal, might have been better placed in some lyrical *avant-garde*—or *arrière-garde*—periodical, in the form of poems in prose.

In renouncing, since it is necessary, the publication here of the advertised extracts, we are not renouncing the pleasure—all the more agreeable for being slightly forbidden—of leaving in the text of this story many of the expressions of florid imagery, previously or subsequently collected in the text of the Notes, with which Yvernaux made up the slides of his magic lantern.

XXI

Furthermore, nowhere in the Notes and Commentaries to the *Treatise on the Innate Sciences*, nor anywhere else but here—where these few supplementary pages are being added for the purposes of exception—is any mention made, or could there be any mention made, of the primordial and capital incident by which Geneviève herself had felt herself emerge from the eclipse of her genius. She alone, in fact, had been both the theater and the witness of it, and this time, for the only time in her life, she truly perceived something that was within her, and greater than her, and foreign to her, and left a double impression, either of that which she imagined as her genius, or of a delirious passenger, but ready in either case to turn into pure mental alienation.

The person to whom she was one day to make the very moving confession, at such a tragic moment—the mysterious individual that you will soon see involved in Geneviève's life, in such an intense fashion, only spoke of it himself, and very discreetly, to one person. That person was not Yvernaux, nor Gasguin, nor even Aunt Line. It was a priest, a friend of Abbé Denis Gasguin and, through him—having met him in China, where both were missionaries—of the Abbé's former pupil, the young Comte de Ponthual-Plouër.

In what circumstances did Geneviève make that strange confession, and to whom? And by what channel did the story reach these pages? The moment has not yet come to reveal that, and perhaps it never will. All that it is appropriate not to leave unsaid is that the revelation of the story is being made without Geneviève's knowledge, it is true, but not without the tacit assent of the person who received the first confession, and with the formal authorization of the person who decided—or rather who was expressly determined—to pass it on.

When the incident in question occurred, Geneviève had just begun her eighteenth year.

During the four years of the "black hole," although her intelligence had been at a low ebb, sometimes debilitated to the point of stupidity—even, as Gasguin shouted in fits of anger, to idiocy—she had enjoyed, by way of compensation, the most admirable physical health. She was never to recover, to tell the truth, the full development of the robust plant into which she then blossomed. The hard and assiduous work that her father pitilessly heaped upon her, far from hindering that strong sap, seemed rather to overexcite it. Like a boy at play, it only increased her appetite.

Aunt Line, amazed, sometimes said to her: "Even with your nose in books, you're thriving."

"Yes," Gasguin put in, "like children guzzling pap."

"Leave her alone!" Aunt Line retorted. "She's growing."

"Yes," the professor complained, furiously, "she's growing like a weed, for there's no longer anything but weeds in her brain now—weeds, weeds, filthy weeds."

And Geneviève began to cry, wounded by the injustice of the reproach—since she was working as hard as she possibly could, in vain expense—but also confused by her scandalous good health, since her poor brain seemed to be its victim. She was truly ashamed of not feeling any remorse, nor getting any headaches, in that weed-cluttered brain. But when her father had gone, she smiled through her tears at the thick slice of bread and jam made for her by Aunt Line—who, on watching her eat it avidly, rubbed her hands and muttered joyfully: "Even when she cries, she still thrives."

There was, therefore, no reason for Geneviève, in that state of stable vigor and regular growth, to experience any malaise whatsoever. So she was amazed one day, immediately after a scene of this sort, while digesting her bread and jam, at peace with her conscience as with her stomach, suddenly to feel a absolute void in her brain, ordinarily so comfortable in spite of the weeds and the labor with which it was overloaded.

It was an entirely physical sensation, and real, of emptiness—not an imagination, an idea! It was as if everything that she had in her brain, good or bad or anything else, had been removed by a single stroke of the piston of a vacuum pump.

She was familiar with the effects of that machine, by virtue of having seen it in action many times in the course of experiments: the light of combustion extinguished under the bell-jar, and life too. And in her brain, abruptly and brutally, the same effects had just been produced: no more light, save for a pale electrical spark, and no more life! There was nothing henceforth within her skull but a sort of night. Not a black night; a pale, gray night. And in that grayness and paleness, a little dead bird.

At that terrible moment, Aunt Line was beside Geneviève, and yet, nothing must have been apparent in the face or the eyes of the young woman, for the old one, looking at her directly, had not said a word not even made a gesture.

Can't you see what's happening to me?

That was what Geneviève had wanted to shout, without being able to do so. Then it seemed that she had recovered the ability to emit the cry that remained in her throat, but by that time the words to express what she wanted to say had fled her memory—and not only those words, but all words! Then, after the words, it was thought itself that escaped—and finally, sensation too.

Of all that, quite clear within the vagueness, she had retained the memory, as far as the moment of total annihilation, in which she had perceived "Absolute Nothing for an eternity."

Those first two words in combination, which she deliberately emphasized in her confession, insisting upon them, had not had the slightest significance for her then, but had had one, more precise and concrete, as sublime as absurd, during the no less sublime and absurd eternity in which she had perceived the Absolute Nothing. As for that eternity, it had certainly had a duration less than that of a lightning-flash, since while traversing it—in the fashion of a circumference—Geneviève had continued to seen in Aunt Line's eyelids, always at the same point, the lashes commencing a blink, while the infinite gulf of

169

that eternity was perpetually open before the brain that was plunging into it.

But many other things had taken place during that lightning eternity, before Geneviève had seen Aunt Line's incomplete blink. There had been so many of them that several eternities, it seemed, would not have been sufficient even to name them.

Some of those things, however, stood out as if in relief from all possible forgetfulness. Some, moreover, were ineffable, quite unevocable in words, even in that phantomatic state. There were others, on the contrary, whose translation, even into current language, happened of its own accord, almost imposing itself—for Geneviève had very often been haunted by them thereafter, to the point of obsession.

There was, above all, a myriad of constellations replacing all the extinct light in the void of her brain, and also an immense aviary of birds singing the resurrection of the little dead bird. Those constellations, furthermore, affected the form of equations with countless terms, each of which engendered a whole endless series of numbers. And the chorus of birds added "living" words to the music denoted by these terms and numbers.

And "someone"—she did not know who—said then, with regard to these "living" words:

"For algebra is only the ashes of numbers, and numbers are the souls of which things are the bodies; and everything is born from nothing."

And while the voice of that "someone" spoke thus, a gesture traced, on the blackboard of unlimited space, the "sideways eight," ∞, which is the mathematical symbol of infinity, and then the multiplication sign, x, before a zero, and then the sign for equivalence, $=$; and from the latter emerged, in an endless incessant turbulent cataract, all the numbers; after which, the sideways eight having vanished, the endless incessant cataract of numbers went back into the egg of the original zero and were lost therein; and, the voice having fallen silent, the gesture having vanished, the blackboard of unlimited space itself evaporated, bringing back total nothingness.

But the most fantastic aspect of that entire vision was that, amid the cataracts of numbers, those whirlwinds of figures, those cyclones of algebraic formulae, two equations of a new character had been expressly "dictated" to Geneviève, the memory of which remained exact. Now, they had been "dictated" not by "someone" any longer but by "something"—she had perceived—that was within her, and greater than her, and foreign to her, and which recited to her alternately, with veneration and then with mockery, and vice versa, repeating it within her to the pint of satiety, the two affirmations differing by the transposition (alternate-internate,[42] she affirmed, without being able to comprehend the why of that geometrical qualification) of the two expressions, the reverent and the mocking:

"Hello, genius! Goodbye, folly!"

When she finally emerged from all these things and an infinity of others, and after that eternity during which Aunt Line's eyelashes had not advanced the blink they had commenced one iota, Geneviève had not dared to ask the old woman anything, seeing that, for her, nothing at all had happened. The sensation of the void in her brain, like that under the globe of a vacuum pump, had returned, and then she had resumed her work in progress, in the fashion of a somnambulist, "conscious, but dead"—another two words that she emphasized without understanding them. Eventually, that evening, she had gone to bed as usual, save for the persistent sensation of a physical void in her brain.

From the next day onwards, she had gradually lost her beautiful blossoming of a robust plant, and begun to develop her definitive appearance, thinner and stiffer. In compensation,

---

[42] *Alterne-interne* [alternate-internal] is a neater item of wordplay in French than in English; I have improvised slightly in order to reproduce the symmetry in translation, as Richepin would surely have done had the boot been on the other foot.

however, as soon as she awoke, she had recovered the two characteristic equations dictated within her and to her by the "something" greater than her.

Subsequently, one of those two equations became the very formula, fundamental and generative, of her most startling discovery.

XXII

All things considered, Yvernaux's absence and complete abandonment had been a great boon to Geneviève at that time, and very probably the conclusive salvation of her genius, which was in a critical phase. Likewise for the mental denseness of her father, who was to go for some time yet without observing the end of the eclipse, and would become more impatient in the meantime, and sometimes press the harshness of hat impatience to a veritable brutality, of which the poor girl was the victim. Had Yvernaux been present, of even in continued epistolary contact with them, and Gasguin endowed with a more sensitive touch with which to take the pulse of genius, that genius might perhaps have risked resembling one of those unhealthily hasty trees which only grow leaves without producing fruit.

Who can tell, moreover, whether Aunt Line, in her habitual fashion, might not have been brushed in an occult manner by the effluvial "aura" of that double peril of the godfather's premature return and the father's premature realization? So many things she said at the time authorized the belief, their apparent simplicity concealing an underside of profound meaning relevant, if one were able to pay any heed to it, to the situation in question.

Why, in fact, did no one pay any heed, given the intonation with which the aged Sibyl was able to emphasize her words, and the sly winks or profound gazes with which she illuminated them, like zigzag lightning-flashes or sheets of flame?

One day, when her father had been particularly brutal to her, by means of the kind of brutality that horrified her more than any other—which is to say, coarse jokes and vulgar acidity—Geneviève had baulked like a racehorse, with a *pooh* of disgust, and had then come to seek consolation from Aunt Line, saying to her:

"I've had enough of swallowing his acid iniquities. I'm going to leave his house, to earn my bread somewhere else, as best I can."

"Let it be," the old woman had replied, sententiously. "It's the acids of the leaven that made the dough rise. The dough has yet to rise." Then, in a low, mysterious voice, her eyes heavy with thought, recalling a Thiérachian distich or some ancient ballad, or perhaps improvising, she sang:

Tindis qu'ti ming's tin pain noir d'hui,
Ch'bois fieume où tin bline s'ra cuit.[43]

On another occasion, all alone, Geneviève thought, bitterly, about the absence of her godfather, and all though her lips never moved or emitted a sound, she said to herself internally, uttering a profound sigh:

What a pity I can't talk to him about that "someone" who speaks inside me now, and so often tells me incomprehensible things!

For on several more occasions, in a much less intense manner, and by means of vaguer representations and expressions, she had had fits analogous to the one she called "the crisis of the two equations." These further fits were only comparable to the first by virtue of the sensation, still strong but now obscure and confused, although perceptible, of that "someone" or "something" greater than herself, foreign to her, whose haunting presence, and especially speech, almost always tenebrous, never failed to cause her embarrassment, which was sometimes difficult to bear in her solitude.

And that is why, alone at that moment, she mutely regretted not having her godfather with her, whose lyricism was always ready to translate everything into images. In the murky speech of the "someone" who came expressly to impose on Geneviève mind something akin to a helmet of darkness,

---

[43] Approximately, "While you're eating today's black bread, the fire is burning on which your pancake will be cooked."

Yvernaux's metaphorical speech, she thought, would have planted such luminous plumes! And because she was unable to light the fireworks herself and turn them into fires of joy, she expressed her chagrin and discouragement in a profound sigh.

At that very moment, Aunt Line came in, her mouse-like scurry even more urgent than usual. One might have thought that she was hastening to the rescue. Whose, if not Geneviève's? And Geneviève had so clear an impression of it that she could not help saying, point-blank: "No, I didn't call you, Aunt Line."

"Yes, yes," the old woman had replied. "I'm answering."

"I swear to you that I never opened my mouth."

"I heard you, all the same."

Then an embarrassed silence having followed those rattled-off replies, Aunt Line had said, not with a wink this time, but looking straight into Genevieve's frightened eyes: "The one you to whom called has no need to be here. Quite the reverse!"

Without being unduly astonished that her unexpressed thought had been read by Aunt Line—for she was accustomed to that frequent telepathy between the two of them—Geneviève had merely and immediately demanded the reason for that "quite the contrary," whose hostility toward her godfather was manifest. And that did astonish her.

"Yvernaux," the old woman had replied, "your Yvernaux. Ha ha ha!"

Then, abruptly, her mouth had tightened around her outburst of laughter to form an o—and, at the height of the most bizarre excitement, as if, in laughing in that fashion, she had found a pretext for dancing vocally on that vowel "o," in an explosion of assonances crowning improvised verses of a sort, she had squawked:

> *Your Yvernaux*
> *Came home too slow*
> *The fire aglow*
> *In the stove's throw*

Caused an overflow
Of milk like snow
To the fire below
A waste! O woe![44]

At first, Geneviève laughed too, like the overgrown child she still was, in spite of her seventeen completed years. After which, especially in the days that followed, on reflection, she had been more inclined to take that litany of silly lines as a serious warning—of what? no matter—on which Aunt Line had offered a grave and unexpected commentary herself, in practical prose, when she returned to the subject the next day.

"Your godfather is better where he is. Let him stay there!"

Geneviève had been annoyed, in truth, by that condemnation, but was immediately consoled, happily, on learning that the exile was not permanent—for, to her question, asked with a sincere sadness: "Shall we never see him again, my poor godfather?" Aunt Line had replied: "Yes, just as we have seen him again before."

"And when shall we see him again?" Geneviève had added.

"Oh, you're asking too much of me. That I don't know. Perhaps I shall—but not yet."

"Are you sure you don't know? Tell me, Aunt Line, are you *finally* sure?"

In the face of this wheedling insistence and the tender Thiérachian inflection of the adverb, Aunt Line smiled and muttered: "Indeed! To know, at least, that I don't know, *Chipette*...hang on. Does one ever know what one knows without knowing it? Wait! Wait!"

---

[44] I was only able to make the other seven lines of the ditty rhyme with the first, thus reproducing the "dancing" effect on the vowel "o," by treating the meaning slightly freely, but have preserved the gist of it, and its potential as a veiled warning.

A long pause, her gaze seemingly looking inward; a profound inhalation of air, followed by a long exhalation; then a pause in which there seemed no longer to be any respiratory movement of any sort—and Aunt Line, finally breathing again, very pale, the corners of her lips slightly flecked with foam, murmured: "Another not quite a week and a half of years since we saw him last."

Geneviève did not know that once before, before she was born, that it was after a similar term, of approximately ten years—a period called by Aunt Line, in the language of a *merlifiche* seeress, "not quite a week and a half of years"—that Yvernaux had made his first reentry into Gasguin's life. Ready as she was not to be astonished by anything with Aunt Line, the young woman would certainly have found in that coincidence—and in the subsequent verification of the similar prediction—grounds to profess more confidence still, if that were possible, in the old visionary's suggestions. But she had no need of that proof, in addition to so many others, to have faith in her good fairy, as she called her, and to obey her. So, from that day on, she had ceased to regret Yvernaux's absence, content to wait, with a foundation of desire, for the return now fixed or seven years hence.

Similarly, she was resigned to endure without complaint her father's unjust severity, merely taking revenge in her own fashion—which was certainly no less cruel! For that revenge consisted of the absolute ignorance to which she resolutely condemned him of the reawakening, more and more evident to her, but only to her, of that which he had once called—as she knew from Aunt Line—her "Pascalian genius."

The old woman fully approved of her acting thus, taking as much joy as the child herself put into the secret of her reawakening—but not as a result of testimony authenticating the fact, as one might think, although Geneviève could have done that fully for her father by revealing to him, for example, the two equations of her mathematical vision. Quite apart from the fact that Aunt Line would not have understood any of it, was not an affirmation without the shadow of any evidence sufficient for her? And the profound intoxication of pride that the old woman experienced therein, befuddling as it was, held no danger for Geneviève, who was used to being, a profound object of admiration for her, even in the fallow era of the black hole.

By contrast, Gasguin's enthusiasm, and that of Yvernaux's even more so, in response to the young woman's resuscitated genius, would have been deadly to her. The mathematical vision, revealed to her father, would have dazzled him, positively blinding him, and would have defected him from completing his patient professorial task, still so necessary to the full maturation of the genius, the sap of which required cultivation, fertilization, direction and perhaps grafting. The child prodigy, deprived of nourishing substance, would have risked becoming an abortion, a hydrocephalus, a monster.

The disaster would have been worse, for sure, with Yvernaux's purely metaphysical vision, open to the soaring of lyricism. He would have drawn her away with him in a frenetic flight, lending her soul to the delirium into which it had already strayed of its own accord. In the heavens of Abstraction, the Absolute, of Being and Nothingness, and Essentials, in which more solid brains have sometimes first misted over and then volatilized, Geneviève's would have been bound to melt almost instantaneously A primarily lyrical mind is capable of being drawn out there by images, in which it can, at least, slake its thirst for the Beautiful, but a primarily scientific mind, finding no pasture there for its appetite for Truth, withers away from inanition or swells up with folly to bursting point.

Reduced to the wine of admiration that Aunt Line poured out for her, to which she had been accustomed since infancy, Geneviève was never "intoxicated" by it, as the English say.[45] Her faith in herself, strong enough frequently to make her con-

---

[45] Richepin uses the English word here because its French equivalent, *enivré*, does not have the linguistic link to toxicity that he wants to extrapolate.

scious of the worth she had, and, above all, promised one day to have, in the Sciences, did not go so far as to poison her with an infatuated vanity that would have prevented her from working.

Furthermore, the revelatory vision of her genius—a vision that other rises of the same sort had corroborated—far from filling her with an inordinate pride, had made her slightly mistrustful, having frightened her. The afterthought subsisting that she might have lost her mind, and might still, if the occasion arose, tormented her like an odious nightmare. As the mathematician she was, in spades, she valued above all else the stability, rectitude, equilibrium and sane logic of her reason and was, in a manner of speaking, coquettish about it.

Thanks to the concurrence of all these circumstances, and perhaps also the obscure guard mounted over it by Aunt Line's occult clairvoyance, the slow and complete growth of Geneviève's genius could be accomplished in peace, during the seven years taken up by the incubation that had followed the eclipse.

It took Gasguin himself three full years to begin to perceive the taste gradually recovered by his pupil for subject-matter that she had first called, and often still called, the "bitterest" in the syllabus. For, with his mania for determinedly-routine method, in order to make certain, it goes without saying that the professor had never admitted any caprice into the program of study, although the pupil sometimes wished that he would. The syllabus had been strictly followed, in total. The entire domain of modern science had been covered and conquered by assiduous, progressive, scrupulous assimilation, with the products of each sector carefully classified and stored. Impossible to wander idly here or there, to more agreeable spots or less brackish springs. It had been necessary to swallow everything, and pause on the arduous and stony sites for as long as the others, or even longer, since there was less desire to possess them but they had to be mastered anyway.

Wherever she had had to make special efforts, the courageous adolescent had persisted valiantly. The difficulty that she had then, sometimes considerable, was the reason for the Gasguin's delay in observing the great awakening that filled him with such joy. He, who shone primarily by virtue of his assimilatory capability, could not admit that his daughter had not inherited that. He did not have a sufficiently spontaneous mind accurately to measure the leaps, or rather the bounds in prodigious truth by means of which she often, without saying anything, and with expressions so distracted as to appeared stunned, she replaced the slow and steady tread of patient study to which he was obstinate in constraining her.

So much patience in teaching and so much determination to learn, expended on either side and united in the result, had not, however, failed to bear fruit. The progress, too slow for her taste, obtained by Gasguin thanks to the ingurgitation of programs, and Geneviève's interior leaps, which she jealously kept hidden from him, had ended up, in combination, by putting the student in possession of everything constituting the encyclopedia of present-day science, at least for the part dependant on Mathematics—which is to say, Mathematics itself, pure and applied, Astronomy, Physics, Chemistry and Mechanics. In seven years, the pupil had absorbed that formidable intellectual "bolus," about which she was later to say, so modestly: "I learned it from my father, as from a feeding-bottle."

It is indubitable, in fact, that the meticulous, sure and perfect professor had "prepared" her, with every chance of success, not only for the two diplomas, which she could have passed hands down, but, doubtless better still, for the difficult entrance exams that form assaults upon the doors of the École Normale or the École Polytechnique, and perhaps even—as Yvernaux would one day claim—the competition for the most forcefully disputed doctorates.

All that, it is necessary to say, and repeat as necessary, without Gasguin obtaining any suspicion of her genius, first reawakened and then in full expansion, especially in the last two of the seven years; all in silence, almost in hiding, without anyone in the world caching wind of a "leak"—primarily because Geneviève herself maintained the sort of mystery in which her work was accomplished. She kept the secret of her visions tenaciously, and that of her interior leaps as well, even against the potential curiosity of her father—and what interest had he invested in giving confidence to the little that he perceived of it?

As for Geneviève's purely scholarly progress, why should he have boasted about fulfilling his professorial task so well in that regard, having always been accustomed to fulfill it thus, for his other pupils as for his daughter? And to whom would he have boasted, anyway? To envious colleagues? Not to mention that, in the provinces, an overly knowledgeable demoiselle, who might qualify for diplomas concurrently with boys, was swiftly held up to ridicule. A future student, then? Gasguin was too bourgeois to present such an eccentric appearance, even if vanity had urged him to it.

There only remained, as a possible "leak," Aunt Line. Nothing to fear, therefore. What did she know? What could she have said? And even if she had known something, was not Aunt Line the tomb of all the family secrets? And was *that* not one of them?

XXIII

On one occasion, however—but how memorable!—
Gasguin had had an almost irresistible desire to break his silence regarding Geneviève's vocation, faith in which had returned to him at a stroke. He had almost yielded to the temptation, in spite of his terror of the scandal that divulgence of the
fact that had restored his faith would certainly have caused a
scandal, not only in the provincial world of Rennes, where he
was then teaching, but, he imagined, the whole universitarial
world, and perhaps even further afield. For the fact seemed to
him to be of such a magnitude, at least in its consequences, to
create a scientific stir "the world over," as one says nowadays.

It was a matter, undoubtedly, of an idea of authentic genius—what other word could one use, in all justice?—which
had come to Geneviève, of which she had found the integral
formula with the commencement of its practical application.
She was then twenty-three years of age, in the middle of an
arid period of more preparatory studies for the most recent
syllabus in physical sciences, and had made her discovery
without interrupting the conscientiousness of her studies or
any lapse in her zeal as a disciple.

That the discovery was important, Gasguin, as we shall
see, could not be in doubt.

He was then the only person in his entourage to know
exactly what stage the question of wireless telegraphy, with
which he had occupied himself with a special and even jealous
care, had reached. In addition, he counted among the two or
three physicists, at most, in possession of the very latest work
done on the subject. It had been imparted to him, in fact, in an
absolutely confidential manner by a letter received the day
before, whose author was one of his former students at the
Collège de Dinan, a young Englishman who had remained in
scientific correspondence with him, and was now an assistant

to the knowledgeable Cambridge professor, Monsieur Lodge.[46]

This letter, locked in his desk, could not have been read by Geneviève. Even if she had read it, she would not have had time physically to write, after a summary reading, the rather long work that she submitted to her father that morning, without attaching any more importance to it than that to any other problem.

"It's quite interesting," she had said, "because of the probable applications to be drawn from it, but no more."

Now, the conclusion of that work, which Geneviève had reached by a different route than that of the English physicist, was exactly the same as that of Monsieur Lodge himself, with an identical formula. As for the commencement of its possible application, it was indicated in Geneviève's work, and there alone. The epistolary communication from the young Cambridge laboratory assistant had made no allusion to anything of the sort. And that application alone, in Gasguin's judgment, could pass for a stroke of genius.

The proof, moreover, that he was not being excessive in his judgment is that the same idea of practical application was found independently the following year, and became the parent idea of new theories due to Monsieur Bose and Monsieur

---

[46] Oliver Lodge was actually at University College, Liverpool when he made his important modifications to Édouard Branly's coherer in the late 1890s. He moved to the University of Birmingham in 1900, four years before he and his collaborator, Alexander Muirhead, sold their patents to Guglielmo Marconi. Lodge's key lecture to the British Association on "Hertzian waves" and their potential use in communication was delivered in August 1894; it provided a crucial spur for Marconi and other researchers in the field, including Jagadish Chandra Bose. This passage is the most significant clue to the internal chronology of the story, implying that this scene is set in 1894, and that the climax therefore takes place in 1904-05, and the coda in 1906, or perhaps 1907.

Lodge—and then, mostly importantly of all, became the essential element of the famous Marconi system.

It is only fair, nevertheless, to record here one important observation, which is that the idea put to work by these scientists was presented in Geneviève's work in the state of a mere hypothesis. It would be quite unjust, on the other hand, not to note that the young scientist lacked a laboratory and the material means necessary to transform her hypothesis into a reality.

Another proof, more convincing still, of the precious value that such work had in this era, was that one of its consequences, relative to the action of Hertzian waves on the metallic filings of Branly tubes, constituted the basis of the first paper published the following year by Gasguin.

People familiar with these slightly abstruse questions might recall the tenor of that paper, and especially the curious passage in which "ionization" is suggested as the probable source of those as-yet-inexplicable electrical manifestations.[47] We shall not go into purely scientific details here, which would be out of place, but we have the right at least, and even a duty, to reveal them with regard to the paper and that passage on ionization; it was to them that the obscure petty provincial professor Thibaud Gasguin owed the resounding explosion of his celebrity.

Certainly, Gasguin, in taking heed of the work that Geneviève had presented to him, had no suspicion of the magical result that was about to spring forth therefrom. One can understand, however, the very high value that he had immediately attached to it, the faith that he had recovered in his daughter's marvelous vocation, and how glad he would have been, in spite of his bourgeois pusillanimity, to be able to cry out to someone:

"She's my pupil, and she has genius!"

---

[47] The behavior of the iron filings in Branly's coherer was eventually explained in terms of ionization by Antoine Blanc in 1904.

Not to mention the afterthought that had just, for the first time, occurred to him, and which would later take root, and grow increasingly, and finally, as we shall see, invade his heart a trifle excessively—which she ought not to hold against himself too much, nevertheless, given that it was perfectly natural and naïve: the idea, in sum, that he too might perhaps have genius! Would not the as-yet-vague consciousness of that "perhaps" be changed into certainty by the divulgence of the fact glorifying the pupil, and, with the pupil, in all fairness, the master?

It was Geneviève, initially, and violently, who was opposed to that divulgence.

"It isn't worth the trouble," she had said, "and I'd be ashamed of noise made for so little. Besides, since my conclusion, you say, is that of Monsieur Lodge, would he not accuse me of having stolen it from your correspondent's letter? He and his master would be bound to do so, and appearances would be against us—against me, at least. Father, I beg you, don't mention this to anyone! If anyone were to accuse me of having stolen someone else's idea, I swear to you that I'd die of it."

And Aunt Line, grinding the teeth that she still had, without understanding what it was a matter of not doing, had muttered: "You mustn't do that, Thibaud. I forbid you to."

Then, taking her Geneviève in her arms and looking at her with the eyes of a nurse, finding the best argument to obtain Gasguin's certain obedience, she had said: "It's there, inside—but wait a little bit longer, for it to ripen fully."

And she had kissed Geneviève's forehead: a long-sustained, avid kiss, as if she were drinking the juice of all the future fruits that were seeded in the earth of that forehead. Nothing could reach the core of Gasguin's heart better than such a gesture; all the depths of Thiérachian peasantry that were in him, and the seeds of atavistic stinginess too, had suddenly revealed themselves and had shown him so many riches to be harvested at a later date in that orchard, and how wise the advice was, in fact, not to let anyone into it, and not to pluck the flowers himself, stupidly, in order to see whether the fruits were already in formation within.

At that moment, under the hypnotic gaze of Aunt Line, he had an obscure but profound presentiment of the high destiny reserved for his daughter. Oh, no longer dreamed by his paternal generosity, but glimpsed, in its imminent possible realization, seen in her competence as a scientist, that high destiny in which he would be largely involved, thanks to Geneviève's modesty and gratitude!

Meanwhile, resigned as he was to silence—and resigned with conviction, in the certain hope of the enormous gain that would soon emerge therefrom—he would not have been sorry to be able, without saying anything precise, at least to allow his delightful secret to be divined by someone. And his happiness would have been maximized had that someone been Yvernaux.

He had missed his Yvernaux so much during that final year in which the advance signs of the final explosion were rumbling. How he would have loved to impart this new confidence—merely by his attitude, but what a triumphant, superior, overwhelming attitude!—to his old friend, recovered and reentering his life for the second time, and this time definitively, he was sure, to Geneviève's godfather, and above all to the confidant of his former pride, so poor in comparison to his present pride.

"Bah!" he said, sometimes, to the two women. "To him, we might perhaps tell everything."

"Not to him or anyone else," Geneviève replied, still implacably resolved to silence. Isn't that so, Aunt Line?"

"*Amon!*" said the old woman, in the fashion of *amen*. Her gesture was as imperious and trenchant as the thrust of a saber, and her eyes aimed two pistol-muzzles at poor Gasguin, their gaze two bullets ready to be fired.

The rare times when Geneviève relaxed her grim determination to keep their secret slightly were when she thought about her two months in paradise and her stained-glass windows representing Kairnheûz, and when, alone with Aunt

186

Line, she sighed: "To the people out there—yes, to them and them alone—one might be able to say things." And immediately, it was to the Comtesse that her heart reached out. "Yes," she went on, "to the Madonna, for example, who spoke so softly, so tenderly, like music, and who must still be speaking in music in Heaven, where the good lady of Ponthual-Plouër is now, alas!"

For the Comtesse was, in fact, no more. In the year following the departure of her son for his first campaign as a naval officer she had departed herself for the death for which she had seemed to be preparing herself, smiling the while, during her beloved Joson's last vacation in the grounds of the "Mourner in the Sleeping Wood."

"Oh, that vacation!" Geneviève moaned then. "The last vacation! My paradise; her purgatory!"

When Geneviève was in her moments of "devotion in the Breton mode," as Aunt Line put it, the old woman let her languish there "like a New Year's Eve mass," as she also said, murmuring if needed the melancholy verses of the mass, with responses in the same tone. "That does her good," said the nursing mother, who knew it. "So many tears that she bottles up inside, which don't flow outside."

Then, with the prayer said—another of her sayings—in memory of the Comtesse, Aunt Line passed on to the Abbé's *memorare*. She began it herself, knowing full well where to go next, abridging the route with that extremely brief anthem, said as if thinking about something else—as priests often do during belated evening offices.

"Poor Comtesse! Yes, up there! And the poor Abbé too, of course." And she knew that they would not be any further delayed by the Abbé's disappearance.

The story of it, however, would have been interesting, not to say strange—like the entire relationship between the Comtesse and him. Oh, how pure it had been, and of such a high moral tenor—such perfect heroism, in all—at least so far as the Abbé was concerned. For the Comtesse, apparently, had never experienced in his regard what is called true love, but can one affirm that he remained insensitive toward her? In fact, yes. In thought, who can tell? At any rate, when she died, the Abbé became a missionary and departed for China, and had not survived her by more than three months.

Exciting as the story of that passion devoid of adventures might have been, though, and even if Aunt Line had been capable of knowing it telling it, or even of speculating about it with Geneviève, she was too certain that Geneviève had never dreamed of any such thing to want to talk to her about it—hence, in the manner of an insignificant anthem, abridging the route, her brief and indifferent: "And the poor Abbé too, of course."

The route to what was it a matter of abridging? To a period of meditative silence that followed Aunt Line's vague remark. Meditative, need we say, in a hypocritical vein? No. Sincerely meditative, in truth, in the pleasant memory of the Abbé teaching his catechism, and opening her soul to new, fresh breaths of piety and mysticism. Meditative in an even more profound sense, nevertheless, in the expectation of the supreme prayer, to which the evocation of the imaginary windows of Kairnheûz still tempted Geneviève, and caused her first to repeat, as if bracing herself for the leap: "To the people out there, yes, one could have said things. Yes, said things! Everything!"

After which, a final silence having led to another, very tender sigh, she added—heard devotedly by Aunt Line, herself in an effusion of devotion—words that were often childish, along the lines of: "Yes, isn't it so, Aunt Line? To tell things to the people out there would have been possible. To the Madonna, for sure. And the 'poor' Abbé, *amon*, of course. And to HIM too, eh?"

She pronounced that HIM as if it were written in capital letters. Then she continued, in a distant and almost inarticulate voice:

"To him, who could have said so many things to us, too, and who loved us a little, truly a little, I'll answer for that, and who must think about us sometimes all the same, a few little times, sweetly, like his mama, and with a musical voice like hers, in spite of his own commanding voice, and his prominent forehead, and most of all, most of all, you know, his erne's nose and his petrel's eyes."

XXIV

Crises of that sort, simultaneously puerile, religious, sentimental and even a little sensual—quite unconsciously and innocently—had been, in effect, the last vibrations, in fading echoes, of the unconfessed love that the thirteen-year-old girl had once conceived at Kairnheûz. They became increasingly rare. The very last had taken place on the occasion of the work in which the complete resurrection of Geneviève's genius was revealed.

And it had been fortunate, for that resurrection, that the chimerical objet of that love had always retained that chimerical aspect. The young Comte's reappearance, in living reality, no longer as an image in a window, might perhaps have sufficed to transfigure the ideal and mystical love and make it, quite simply—which is to say, humanly, and, in consequence, cruelly—passion, something overwhelming for a twenty-three-year-old girl like Geneviève. For, child-like as she still was, she was at the same time, in terms of her brain, a mature, strong and intense individual. What internal storms such an amour would have released in such a nature!

Cloistered—that is the right word—in the closed and severe convent of Science, and not finding it severe, since she tasted grandiose joys there at her leisure, she had ended up no longer allowing herself to be distracted by the clouds of her memories, which floated less and less frequently above the cloister. At any rate, she had accustomed herself to paying only a dreamlike attention to them, no longer that of her thoughts.

She still took pleasure, certainly—a sweet pleasure, mingled with a melancholy almost as sweet—in seeing the mirages of her paradise and the vaporous bliss of her mystical windows pass over the sky, but it was in a vague smile of her heart, not in a reflective effort of her brain that she now completed the dream of childish love so naively sketched ten years before by the soul of the first communicant. And in completing it thus, that dream of ingenuous love, she rediscovered that former soul, still pure and still candid, in a white dress and virginal veils.

She sometimes still said, when she remembered Joson and herself at Kairnheûz: "How we loved one another at first sight!" But the tone in which she said it, without her being aware of it, gave the sentence the meaning of: *And to think that, in spite of that, it's over, over, over.*

Aunt Line was often saddened by that all-too-manifest meaning. She rebelled against it, however. One might have thought that she had a presentiment of the return, in the darkness of a perhaps-distant future, but perhaps imminent—she did not know!—of that meteor, as a comet, and the necessity of such a return for Geneviève. For in those moments of total renunciation of the old dream, she never ceased muttering: "But no, no! That mustn't be. No!"

And she urged the young woman not to abdicate thus, to strive energetically not to become an old maid. She doggedly repeated: "Yes, yes, how you loved one another at first sight! Oh, at first sight!" And she added, with the most insinuating glance, the most penetrating and lightning-like: "And at first sight it will be again. Oh, at first sight!"

And as Geneviève remain cold to these promptings, even the semi-predictions that seemed to demand at least a request for explanation, the old woman persisted, replying, even though no question had been asked: "Will it happen again, you ask? Since I know it! Since I see it!"

And she repeated, as before, but without any intention of mockery now, and seemingly in the manner of an incantation, the litany of Joson's names, which she terminated with this formal prophecy: "And we'll all three tell it, that fairy tale, three, *amon*, three, one a man, who will not be your father."

But all of it, even these attempts at suggestion, had become vain—most particularly during the last of the seven years that the final incubation period of Geneviève's genius had lasted. In an increasingly grim silence, in a mental contention that was easier to release with every day that passed, the entire cycle of her preparatory studies, henceforth completely encompassed, in possession of everything that her father could teach her, her brain—which had reflourished in that first endeavor of the pupil amazing the master—now became self-absorbed, in a sense, gathering itself and concentrating itself, before blossoming into its thunderous explosion of aloes.

And it was then, more and more rapidly, and also more and more conclusively, as the terminus came closer, that the physical transformation had taken place, fundamentally no less integral, of the young woman into the old maid. For poor Geneviève had not waited, as she believed, until the age of 25 to coiff Saint Catherine. She had begun to do so at the beginning of her twenty-third year, at the moment when her intellectual sun had emerged from the eclipse in all its glory, which was also the time when she had ceased to feel her amorous heart beating, no longer paying any heed to anything but the scientific genius seething in her brain.

Farewell to that appearance of a robust plant, in full development with strong sap, that air of quasi-vegetal triumph which she had presented during her slothful fallow phase! Farewell to the avid appetites excited by the excess of work, as in boys by games! Farewell to the times when Aunt Line said, with the joy of a good woman seeing her brat prosper: "Even when she weeps, she still profits!"

Changing day by day, after having only changed month by month, Geneviève had declined, shrinking on the stem like a plant, no longer now under the pressure of copious sap, but with the vein exhausted, the stem filamentous, the juice dried up by the withering gusts of an arid wind. All the flesh of her eighteenth year, promising a woman, seemed to be "shriveling" as they say in Thiérache of fruits whose skin tightens over the "supped" flesh—another local expression. For Aunt Line perceived these changes and characterized them by means of those old, expressive terms, when she grieved over them, in private, with Gasguin.

The latter, to tell the truth, scarcely experienced any anxiety. What did that physical deterioration matter, since the intellectual being was still growing strongly? Was the one not the price of the other? Then again, didn't Geneviève continue to "enjoy perfect health," never falling ill, remaining strong and showing endurance in labor, in spite of her new slenderness? Even suffering, he would have found her as he liked her, with such a admirable brain, served by such an incredible ability to work. Was not the sovereign health that of the mind?

Not to mention that Geneviève was, after all, no uglier for having the svelte and agile thinness of a young man rather than the rounded contours of a future mother! She was destined, was she not, for something better than that paltry fate!

On which note, casually and disdainfully, misogynistic in a more refined fashion than before, and venerating his daughter all the more as he estimated her less womanly, he laughed in Aunt Line's face.

In the simplicity of her feminine heart, still sublime although that of a barren old woman, she riposted: "One always needs to be beautiful."

And she would have loved, in consequence, the flower of the blood of the Hescheboix, while developing the "something great" that she would eventually become, not to lose, even so, any of the charms bequeathed by Idalie...

"My Idalie, my lovely sister, my little God!"

So she hastened to add to Gasguin's compliments regarding his daughter's boyish elegance more serious compliments, such as: "Fortunately, she doesn't entirely resemble a boy, even so. Just look at her hair and her *leumerottes*!"

Gasguin shrugged his shoulders and only replied with a scornful "*Pfft!*"

Geneviève laughed at that, but not Aunt Line. All her womanly pride up in arms, she put on her loftiest expression to riposte to things of that sort, without any comic intent: "Provided that she keeps our hair and our eyes, all will be well. And she has them, you know!"

Needless to say, the "our," applied to the hair and eyes, was not Aunt Line's own but Idalie's, concentrating all the beauty and charm of the blood of the Hescheboix. And that hair and those eyes, in fact, you will remember, Geneviève had always had, and had them still.

That hair, fortunately so beautiful, indeed—long, silky and thick, with various rich colors ranging from chestnut-red to ash-blonde—Genevieve, unfortunately, seemed obstinately to hide from view. It was necessary, to know its real splendor, to divine it, beneath the hat, befitting a poor schoolmistress, with which she covered it, or even the dull flatness that she inflicted upon it by her fashion of arranging it in smooth bangs and a tightly-bound chignon. Even when she was bare-headed, with her mild, modest, plain face, that sort of hair-do invited, to the point of evocation, the frontal veil of a nun, and the desire to hide it in the shadow of a cornette.

As for her *leumerottes*, in which, according to Aunt Line, all the magical virtues of Idalie's eyes lived again, Geneviève did not often consent to illuminate "*l'iau vert' dins l'or d'chès gleus solel.*"

The flash of pride, which sometimes traversed them now, must also have passed, sometimes, through those of her *catte-linette* grandmother when she triumphed over some masculine will, as Geneviève did today over a problem—but where and when in the scientific genius, all in the brain, was the gaze of the *merligodgière* to be found, also possessed of genius in it fashion, anywhere but in the brain: her luminous, perverse, seductive, profound, enveloping gaze; her gaze of an amorous woman damned of her own accord; and others still, gazes in which one had the desire to drown oneself and drink fire there, prestigious gazes similar, indeed, to glaucous water running over a bed gilded by wisps of sunlight?

And yet, Aunt Line was right! Well-hidden as they were, nothing had been lost of the treasure of her eyes and those of her hair—nothing. Geneviève still possessed them. And Aunt Line knew both of them well, *amon!* One for having so often combed the hair of her darling, whom she continued to care for and always coddle as an infant; the other for having seen it scintillate fully the last time when Geneviève had said: "How we loved one another at first sight!"

And if Thibaud Gasguin had not been so myopic, opaque and impenetrable to certain lights, no doubt he too would have contemplated the gaze of the *cattelinette* in Geneviève's *leumerottes*, on the day when he had read her famous work anticipating—as was really the case—Monsieur Lodge's discovery. And again on the day when, using a fragment of that work as a base, she had constructed in its entirety, in a miraculous improvisation, the entire edifice of his first paper relating to ionization as the probable source of the phenomena manifest in Branly tubes.

For at certain moments, in profound scientific action, Idalie's granddaughter immediately recovered, without wanting to or being aware of it, the gaze her grandmother had in profound action of another sort. Now, such moments as that, Gasguin had witnessed, especially during the aforementioned improvisation, from which he had drawn all of the paper written by him but thus dictated, in reality, by her alone.

Subsequently, similar actions had been shared with other witnesses—and they, observers more clear-sighted than Gasguin, had noted the characteristic fact, doubtless unique, of that special gaze, whose flash, simultaneously proud and voluptuous, caused Yvernaux, for instance, to say: "That flash Pallas Athena had in her sea-blue eyes—but Aphrodite Kypris also had it in her violet eyes."

Of the nature of that gaze, so rare and complex, Aunt Line, in her simplicity, was not unaware, for at times, abruptly, she had said to Geneviève: "What are you busy grasping, then?"

That was because she had just seen Idalie's luminous, perverse, seductive, profound, enveloping gaze appear, while her darling was thinking. It was because she had, indeed, seen a victory being "grasped" in the *cattelinette*'s *leumerottes*. It was because she was able to recognize, with her magical virtues, *l'iau vert' dins l'or d'chès gleus solel.*

And it was with those *leumerottes*, no doubt, those eyes of an amorous amazon, attacking and taming the mystery as Idalie had once attacked and tamed another mystery, it was as a *cattelinette* that Geneviève, the old maid of twenty-five, had won her father's glory by the communication, one after another—always he as the writer, always she alone as the inventor—of two further papers, catalogued as follows in the *Bulletin des Societés Scientifiques* under the rubric *Communications à l'Académie des Sciences*:

117. "Note on the transmission of force by means of telluric currents," by M. Thibaud Gasguin, Ph.D.

117a. "Comment on the deflection of cathode rays by a magnet, in response to an experiment by and the conclusions of M. Lénard," by the same.[48]

---

[48] The Hungarian physicist Philippe Lénard had begun his extensive pioneering study of the behavior of cathode rays in 1888.

XXV

You will certainly not have forgotten the sensation that Thibaud Gasguin's three successive communications to the Académie des Science caused, a decade ago. The uproar surpassed the usual limits of the restricted and cultivated audience whose élite minds keep up to date, as one says, with the flow of scientific news. It was propagated as far as the broad lay public, which perceived its echoes and took an interest in them, as evidenced by the memories recalled at the beginning of this story, which the reporter Sextius Costecalde had retained so freshly after nine years. Like Costecalde himself, the broader public retained, at least in memory, the confused but still noisy buzz of the press coverage stirred up and alimented by the three communications.

As for the specialist society impassioned by these lofty questions, it had been, as is well-known, positively bowled over by the adventure of the petty professor, unknown the day before and famous two days later. The *Revue Anglaise*, and then the *Revue Allemande*, which had been the first to take notice of the first paper, set the spark to the powder-keg of enthusiasm by associating Gasguin's name with those of Branly, Marconi, Sir William Preece and Van Beschem,[49] but the lively debates unleashed by the second, and even more so by the third, had been decisive for the arrival of the newcomer.

---

[49] Sir Willliam Preece developed a primitive wireless telegraphy and telephony system as early as 1892, prior to the patenting of the telephone in the U.S.A., but it was never put into practical use; he subsequently—and rather selflessly—became an enthusiastic supporter of Marconi. The name of Van Beschem was bandied around at the time because of a paper on wireless telegraphy that he published in collaboration with someone named Le Royer, but has since fallen into obscurity.

You will doubtless remember, in fact, that in consequence of polemics, and thus in the full glare of publicity, Gasguin had found himself at odds with illustrious adversaries, and defended by no-less-illustrious adherents. Thanks to the irresistible arguments with which Geneviève had furnished him and a very ingenious method of exposition—which is to say, of combat—of which he was the real strategist, he had been the victor in a tourney in which the other participants, for or against, had included Dr. Gustave le Bon, the Liégeois physicist de Heen, Becquerel and a member of the Institut.[50] It was the consecration of his worth, and the formal recognition of his dazzling glory.

As one can imagine, Yvernaux, an old student—though already a doctor—still in the vicinity of the Sorbonne when he was not at the Sorbonne itself, had not been the last person alerted to the matter. As soon as the first effervescence was excited by the articles in the foreign journals with regard to the first communication, it was necessary for him to proclaim his eulogy. He had written to his dear Gasguin immediately, to congratulate him—and his letter, very sincere, began with this call to put out the flags:

"I always told you, my old brother, that you too would make your mark!"

That "too," of course, emphasized that he, Blaise Yvernaux, had had made his mark a long time ago. Even so, to be fair, the cry was emitted by a good and worthy heart, without envy. For his own mark, Yvernaux had made not merely long before, but always, in his own imagination—and no further, alas! He was still expecting—in the peasant sense of "waiting for"—the public to bow down before that mark. In Gasguin's

---

[50] The citation of Gustave le Bon's name in conjunction with those of Pierre de Heen and Henri Becquerel—the discoverer of radioactivity—is significant; Richepin probably found de Heen's relatively obscure name in Le Bon's book, *L'Évolution de la matière* (1905), which attempted to extrapolate the possible consequences of the discovery in question.

mark, by contrast, which as well and truly within his victorious grasp, the voice of the public had faith, no less than the acknowledgement of the communication—with a slightly dry but nevertheless laudatory note—by the Académie des Sciences.

And it was good of Yvernaux to have no sentiment of base jealousy, neither with regard to the enthusiasm of the pubic, nor the acquiescence of the official "bigwigs"—whom, as we know, he did not like at all. He had, one suspects, taken advantage of the slightly haughty tone of the praise to mock the arrogance of those Messieurs, and that had only rendered more sincere his surge of joyous admiration for the success of his friend, his "old brother."

The proof that the excellent fellow harbored no stingy reservations or rancor is that his joy, and his admiration too were redoubled by the second communication, and they knew no bounds during the charivari led by the third. He was even one of those who led that charivari, at a hot pace, without sparing their trouble, their zeal, their combative fury, their eloquence or—most of all—their lungs. No one else was seen and heard more frequently in the corridors, the courts and the peristyles of the Sorbonne, the Collège de France and the École de Médicine, and in the student cafés frequented by the creators of "buzz." He perorated in favor of "the unknown petty professor" to the detriment of the "green palmed bonzes" and organized student processions in which, according to traditional rites and rhythms, Thibaud Gasguin's adversaries were booed and jeered.

And how could his enthusiasm and fervor or the glorification of his friend not have been absolutely sincere? In good faith, without seeking it, and in all conscience, pure and loyal, did he not sense a certain apotheosis of his own in the apotheosis of his *old brother*? With what profound and beautiful effusions of the heart he boasted of their age-old friendship, so faithful on both sides! What authentic tears rose up from that emotional heart to eyes rapt as if in ecstasy, as he said, in a tremulous voice:

"The first time that I had the frisson, the slight clenching of the throat, the fluttering eyelids with large tears beneath, at the presentiment, delightful and frightening at the same time, of his genius..."

For he believed, with iron-hard firmness now, in Gasguin's genius. And what is even more extraordinary—and yet quite human, and perfectly natural—is that he believed that he had always believed in it, and as firmly. If someone had, at that moment, reminded him about his former opinions regarding Gasguin's manifest mediocrity, he would have been ashamed of it and indignant about it, as something foreign to him.

In reality, in his current ingenuous worship, with increasing sincerity, his good faith becoming a rolling snowball by autosuggestion, he had succeeded in confusing the present Gasguin with the past Geneviève. He attributed to the former what he would once have lent to the latter.

With regard to his abandoned goddaughter, whom he had not seen for ten years, he retained the disillusionment that she had caused him then. He did not know the present Geneviève. But as he had had the certainty that the Geneviève of yore, before the black hole, had been a genius, in order not to give the lie to that certainty, he found this explanation by way of excuse:

"Idiot that I was, but without being one! There was, indeed, genius in the house, but her father, and I, because of him, thought the genius was in Geneviève. In fact, it was Thibaud, by virtue of parental modesty, who transposed into her what was only in him. And I, incompetently, came to believe..."

Thus he duped himself, to the point that he wanted to rewrite his "Note on the Theory of Division" to make it a new argument, no longer in favor of "Innate Sciences" but to the advantage of another thesis. Thus far, however, he did not know what.

In spite of everything, and even in spite of the complete redirection of his admiration, he had not failed to conserve, deep down, nor occasionally to bring out, a memory of affection for Geneviève. He also mingled it, without any valid reason now, with a sort of pride—perhaps because she was the daughter of a man of genus; and he similarly affirmed that he was a man of genius himself, saying with an involuntary catch in his voice of whose utterly comical character he was unaware:

"Yes, the daughter of that genius...ahem!"—a little cough here, and the catch in question—"is my goddaughter."

Those were the sentiments in which Gasguin and Geneviève had found Yvernaux when they had returned to Paris, the author of the three famous communications having been summoned to a chair in the capital, then furnished with an École laboratory in the Rue Ulm. From the very first day, their mutual affection had resumed contact, their old familial intimacy resolidified.

Without any "posing" on Gasguin's part, Yvernaux had observed with a veritable joy—but not without a certain mockery in the sidelong glances of Aunt Line, he noted. And similarly, although larded in a more discreet, almost genteel fashion, he had sensed quite sharply a hint of mockery—yes, definitely mockery—in certain glances and smiles addressed to him mischievously and slyly by Geneviève.

Very quickly, being quick on the uptake, he had found they key to those equivocal subvocalizations, rather wounding in intent, which seemed to say, with a slightly angry irony on Aunt Line's part and a affectionate pity on his goddaughter's: "Not very smart, our Yvernaux!"

And, indeed, a few conversations, free philosophical flights into the open skies of science, between the father, the daughter and himself, had sufficed for him to discover the true measurement of the respective values attributable to the professor and the inventor. After two or three banal reflections by Gasguin on the soaring ideas of Geneviève, he had jumped, and then fallen flat, his entire being extended toward the surprising sheltered truth.

But it was simply too fine! He dared not believe in such a prize, at first. He had observed patiently. A few further conversations of the same sort had gradually convinced him. Piece by piece, he demolished within himself the legend he had constructed regarding the father and the daughter, following the success of the paper, with the image of Geneviève luxuriant in body but fallow in mind. On the ruins of that legend—recognized as absurd and imbecilic—the ancient picture had taken shape again, of Geneviève the child prodigy astonishing her father, the scientist, and her godfather, the "thinker," renewing the exploits of precocity of the formidable Pascal, furnishing the *Treatise on the Innate Sciences* with that extraordinary Note on the theory of division, and finally...

No, in fact, I'm not very smart, Yvernaux said to himself, pointedly. *And my goddaughter was quite right to look at me pityingly, with her genteel smile, which accused me all the same of being slightly stupid. And as for Aunt Line, for the mockery with which her whiplash gaze stings me, I'll gladly kiss her old wrinkled prune of a mug for that.*

And one day, he did exactly what he said, unthinkingly. Taking advantage of a moment alone with the old woman, he threw his arms around her, and after kissing her on both cheeks, he exclaimed: "Yes, there! I'm nothing but a birdbrain. It's over now, though. I understand. I've got it. I know everything."

After which, both having tears in their eyes, they had embraced again.

At that precise moment, Gasguin came in, his expression proud, his manner triumphant. Amiable, to be sure, at the same time, still without "posing," Yvernaux observed, but nevertheless—how could he help observing as well?—with the air of already being the bust of Thibaud Gasguin. There and then, Yvernaux had the desire to shout at him, even more in his face, if possible, almost with an intention of insult: "Yes, you hear, I know everything."

Which single little three-word phrase meant all the seething anger, protest, truth and revolt against a false god, and faith in the real divinity, that was in the presently-exasperated, volcanic soul of an Yvernaux ready to do anything to proclaim his absolute certainty regarding the nullity of Gasguin and the sublimity of Geneviève. For he did, indeed "know" now, as if he had witnessed from first to last the history of the ten secret years, that Geneviève alone had genius, and that the ideas in the papers were hers, flowers of her brain, perhaps gathered into a bouquet, at the most—and how!—by that mediocre and vulgar "scientific market-gardener" Gasguin.

And in his "I know everything" Yvernaux would have spit that out, and afterwards, what an eruption of lava in outrage! He could feel it rumbling inside him, and the ardent, sulfurous syllables were already setting fire to his lips...

But behind the father came the daughter. And between Geneviève and Aunt Line a fulgurant glance was exchanged, charged with thoughts that met in that fulguration—and from the electric and magnetic spark thus produced sprang a shock that caused Yvernaux to quiver all the way to the core of his being, paralyzing him.

All that was instantaneous. For Gasguin, without having perceived any of it, had only had time, still showing of the "good side" of his bust, but benevolent, to see the embrace that was still in train when he arrived—and it was jokingly, in that regard, that he said, gaily:

"What's this, then? Are you going to ask me for Aunt Aline's hand in marriage? God damn me! You were embracing. Just look at them, Geneviève—like cats being stroked. They were embracing, I tell you."

Yvernaux, increasingly paralyzed by Geneviève's gaze alone, now, was only paying attention to that imperious gaze commanding him to keep quiet. He understood that she had understood—and he was firmly resolved to obey. But what could he do? How could he respond to the old imbecile's joke?

Fortunately, Aunt Line got him out of the embarrassment, catching the ball on the volley. "It was me who kissed him, *amon!*" she exclaimed. "Why? Because he told me that you're a great man."

"Dear me!" said Gasguin, amiably. "If everyone kissed him to whom he said that, he wouldn't have enough cheeks to go round. It seems that in the Latin Quarter they call him my apparitor, and at the Polytechnique, my tangent."

Yvernaux stood up straight. Geneviève restored his relaxed posture with a glance, no longer harshly imperious this time, but which caused Aunt Line to mutter clandestinely between her gums: "Ah! The mongrel *cattelinette*! There's Idalie's *leumerottes*!"

And while the old woman dragged Thibaud into the next room—on the pretext that he had to change in order not to fall ill, being soaked by rain—Yvernaux trembled with profound emotion at being left alone with his goddaughter, hardly daring to look at her. Before she followed her father, he would have liked to greet her with the words that were swelling is heart to bursting point—"It's you who are the genius, you, you!"—but he could not say them, for Geneviève's gaze *willed* that he should not pronounce them, at least on this occasion. That gaze ordered him not to humiliate Gasguin, even in his absence, by the affirmation of the secret, condemned to remain a family secret between the four of them.

And when she went out, in her turn, her godfather simply said to her: "Don't worry. I'll still be his apparitor and his tangent." Then, emphasizing every syllable, albeit in a low voice, he added: "I won't say anything—that's understood."

XXVI

That first experiment having been carried out, and triumphantly, of her power to paralyze Yvernaux's will, and then to direct him hypnotically, Geneviève had had no need to give him any longer explanation regarding the mystery of the collaboration between her father and her. Another, in her place, would have left it there, her vanity being flattered by it—but Geneviève had no vanity.

Taking honest account of all that she owed, in sum, to the instruction of her master and the strategy of the translator of her ideas in the art of explaining them and defending them, she judged it equitable to inform her godfather of all that. She would have blushed with shame and remorse to leave him with the overly scornful and hence false opinion that he had of Gasguin.

The poor man's present infatuation, entirely natural in any species of *parvenu*—which he was, in reality—his naïve pride, his bust-like attitude, all were owed, at that moment, to the fuss being made in the press, trumpeting his name and his cause, with the enormous exaggerations of interviews, flatteries and, even more, to the attacks of envious colleagues, and the very intoxication of the struggles in which he had confronted public opinion alone. The sagacious Yvernaux was too good a psychologist, in spite of his lyricism, and too much a Parisian, although exclusively of the Left Bank to be unable to explain and excuse these effects, whose causes were obvious to him.

With a few clever insinuations, Geneviève, in the presence of her godfather, had put her father on guard against the dangers of success, against the traps hidden among the flowers of excessive compliments. Yvernaux, understanding immediately, without any prior agreement, had tuned his instrument in the same key. In order to awaken the suspicious Thiérachian asleep in the new drunkenness of vainglory, Aunt Line, always vibrating in harmony with her darling, had talked to him about people who, according to the local assaying, knew how to tickle the goose's belly in order to steal the down more easily. And under these various pressures, the sage Gasguin had soon become the modest Gasguin once again.

It was then that the resolution had been made, in a family council fulfilling the function of a council of war, to hide away, as it were, from the joys of triumph, only to savor them privately, without ostentation, shunning publicity.

To begin with, Yvernaux had been obliged to promise no longer to play the herald with the loud-hailer, relentlessly singing the praises of Gasguin and his genius in the student cafés. One can imagine the secret satisfaction with which he made the promise and kept it.

As for Gasguin himself, it was with a glad heart that he renounced his strutting attitude, his nature being little inclined to it, after all, and inclining instead toward the modest, unctuous and apologetic stances of his early education in Christian humility. Also humbly, and with a glad heart, without being asked, he thought it his duty to reveal to his "old brother" the secret that the latter had already deduced, but which he was pleased to receive from Gasguin himself. With a truly generous and noble effusion, which went as far as tears, the master had bowed down of his own accord before the genius of his pupil, in her presence.

Geneviève had been embarrassed by that. With no less noble generosity, she had immediately restated things, simply as she saw them, as it was necessary to see them, as Yvernaux saw them henceforth, as they might be summarized once and for all in complete impartiality, with an indulgence toward Gasguin that was only slightly exaggerated. For that was what was invariably demanded of the best of judges in the best of circumstances—which is to say, Geneviève enlightening Yvernaux's religion.

All things considered, everything having been weighed accurately in the scales of the strictest justice, it remained given, without any possible dispute, that Geneviève had moments of genius, unconscious visions in which the solutions appeared to her, as if dictated to her by another self, of problems turned over repeatedly in her meditations. But it was patent, by way of compensation, that Gasguin had the art of submitting these problems to her, or preparing those meditations for her, and, once the solution had been found, of methodically constructing its origins, its progress, its conclusions and it consequences. And no one could doubt, either, the invaluable services rendered to Geneviève's mind, even for her most spontaneous faculties of invention, by the rich provision of raw materials that Gasguin had heaped up there, with an order and clarity that multiplied their worth tenfold.

The genius farthest reaching in its bounds—and Geneviève had that at certain times—is not unable to cohabit, often in excellent accord, with the wisest common sense, and one can see that such was the case in her, by virtue of the reflections that she made one day to Yvernaux, of which he took care to make a note.

"It's the association of ideas, sometimes bizarrely produced and without perceptible reasons," she said, "that gives birth of godsends. The further apart from which ideas come together, above the abyss, unexpectedly, and outside of all plausibility, even in utter folly or absurdity, the more chance they have of being original. But it's still necessary to have the ideas in order to associate them—and thus, it's necessary to have a thoroughgoing knowledge of all the sciences. And it's also necessary that one can check out the godsends born of these quasi-demented associations. Thus, it's necessary that knows what one knows with the absolute certainty that only an integral, scrupulous, well organized, perfectly adjusted, logical education can give, with its connections always ready, its arguments always at hand, for encyclopedic and instantaneous consultation."

And that grave dissertation she had concluded with a note of humor:

"The conclusion of this long speech, my dear and very equitable godfather, you have already deduced, haven't you?

It's that, without her brave father for a professor and guide, your scatterbrain of a goddaughter, most of the time, perhaps even all the time, would be at grave risk of being a failed genius—which is to say, what you call, I believe, something like a wolf...a kind of wolf! Yes, let's see...a marine wolf. An amphibian, eh! Ah—I have it...in brief, a *loufoque*."[51]

Yvernaux had been forced to yield to arguments of this sort, whose ingenious dialectic enchanted him. And finally, he had admitted, as one had to admit in his society, that Gasguin was to some extent—and in a certain fashion, retaining a sense of proportion—Geneviève's collaborator.

The severe Yvernaux would not go so far, however, as to qualify that collaboration as indispensable. Even less did he acquiesce in the opinion—which he declared to be ridiculous—according to which Gasguin would have been capable of obtaining on his own, as surely although more slowly, the results that Geneviève had attained effortlessly. And finally, no matter how obedient he was to his goddaughter's suggestions, the godfather baulked and snorted, whinnying with indignation, when she claimed that she herself, reduced to her own means, would never have accomplished anything at all, save for the dreams of a poet.

"But geniuses," he cried, like an eagle, "in the sciences as in any other area, are nothing but poets."

"Yes," she replied, "except that in the sciences, when they stick to dreams and do not have a foundation of facts beneath their dreams—which is to say, when they have no knowledge—they are like poets without words."

"Those," said Yvernaux, "are sometimes the greatest of all." One day, carried away by his oratory flow, he had even added: "Me, for example..."

---

[51] *Loufoque* [lunatic] sounds as if it might be compounded out of *loup* [wolf] and *phoque* [seal]—hence the labored wordplay.

She had burst out laughing, then raised her arm into the air and cried: "You, Godfather? On the contrary—you're nothing but words."

And the debate had finished in gaiety with these ripostes, like children playing tennis:

"It's when I shut up that my words are most beautiful."

"You don't say, you old lyricist."

"With the respect that I owe you, my genius Goddaughter, you're another."

"Another what?"

"Lyricist, of course."

And that's the truth, amon. Aunt Line would have pronounced, as a last sally, if she had known the word and could understand all it expressed. And that is also why, everyone in the house sensing in some manner that it really was the truth, including Gasguin, and none of the Thiérachians, all tainted to a greater or lesser extent with Romany blood, including Yvernaux himself, liking to be overgenerous with the truth—a secret treasure dilapidated as soon as it is no longer secret—with a common accord, as if by tacit agreement, they had acted in conformity with an old saying from their homeland, as "word pie." They had not even said, but only thought with closed mouths, like Aunt Line:

Vérité dins ch'treu cuit son v'nin
Gayant qui la tait; qui pas, nain
Ch'ti qui sais n'sait qu's'il ne l'dit nin.[52]

For it was definitely—whether they wanted to admit it or not—out of terror of the incongruous and scandalous *lyricism* in which one soars, and in order to hide it, that they had grad-

---

[52] Approximately: "Hiding truth cooks its venom, delighting those who keep quiet; anyone but a fool knows that he should say nothing about what he knows." (Many toxins are destroyed by cooking, which therefore renders some poisonous plants edible.)

ually and religiously fallen into complete silence outside the house regarding its mystery, the family secret. Certainly, no one had ever pronounced the key to the secret even in private. They had, nevertheless, lived as if that key, that qualification of *lyricism*, designated a blemish, a deformity or a monstrosity of which nothing must be known outside.

Gasguin had, therefore, resumed the modest and humble appearance of the petty provincial professor, attributing his discoveries to the fortunate hazards of chance. He did not like to talk about them, as if he dreaded anyone overrating them. He gave every appearance of being a person henceforth devoid of ambition, whose destiny had been fulfilled in its entirety, truly complete, who would grow old in the bliss of his over-rewarded mediocrity. He had played the part without too much hypocrisy, in spite of the thirst for glory that continued burning away in him deep down, and which he hoped to slake again thanks to new marvels in embryo in the subterranean springs of Geneviève's brain. But hush! Mouth shut, in the Thiérachian fashion of Aunt Line: *Ch'ti qui sais n'sait qu's'il ne l'dit nin.*

So, in his laboratory at the École Normale, with his pupils and assistants, as in the laboratories of colleagues glad to solicit his collaboration, he revealed nothing of his endeavors or his hopes. For fear of "leaks," possible thefts of ideas, he only allowed his methodical but pedestrian mind to be seen. Soon—understandably, with respect to a "lucky" success greater that he doubtless desired—people acquired the habit of saying, without any appearance of excessive malicious severity in his regard: "Oh, Gasguin—he's finished! One lucky strike, exhausted now. Overdone anyway, eh?"

As for Yvernaux, he had long since ceased his word-of-mouth campaign, his charivaris and his attempts to have rivals booed to the profit of his "old brother." He even avoided opportunities to talk about him—which were, in any case, increasingly rare. The generations of students change quickly in the Quarter. Those of nine years before were far away now, professors, physicians, notaries or advocates in the provinces.

And those of the present day no longer knew that Yvernaux had once been—in the night of time—Gasguin's "apparitor," or, for the Poly boys, his "tangent." Most of them, save for the *X*s, probably had no idea who Gasguin was.

To be forgotten to that extent presumably gave the professor no pleasure, but Geneviève was delighted by it. The worthy but shameless Yvernaux had ended up seemingly profiting from it, resuming his professions of faith as a "lyrical thinker." At length, in fact, all prudence—even the most Thiérachian—having gradually become unnecessary, the old student in his fortieth year, doctor of letters and proud of his famous "discipulary deanship," had not been able to resist letting out a little of his secret, holding ajar the door to the mystery whose cage he was, but he did that without being aware of it, in the Thiérachian, or even the Romany mode— which is to say, for himself alone, others seeing no more than "something blue in the fire"[53] as Aunt Line would have said.

It was thus that in his brasserie, the environment propitious for the effusions of the thinker and the lyricist, he intoned hymns in honor of his goddaughter, of Geneviève, "magnifying" her and "litanizing" her genius, as we have seen. Except that it was in such a fashion that the goddaughter took on the appearance of a chimerical being, an "entelechy," as he also sometimes put it. And no one, not even his two faithful followers, the former Fourierist turned apprentice mage and the Scandinavian Nietzschean, could tell what that Geneviève, that genius, was, nor even whether she existed other than in Yvernaux's imagination when he was in the "displaced state."

In the Rue Malebranche, where their concierge spoke reverently about Monsieur Thibaud Gasguin "the scientist" and his daughter Mademoiselle Geneviève, no one knew that she too was "the scientist." And finally, in the vicinity of the private laboratory in the most distant part of Vaugirard, she was

---

[53] *Voyant que le bleu*—literally, "only seeing the blue"—is used as a metaphor for being at a complete loss, so the "Thiérachian" addition merely adds fire to the metaphor.

assumed to be something akin to the servant of the mad old chemist doing dangerous experiments in a hut in the middle of an area of waste ground. And on the way from there to their home, they passed, as we have seen—she even more than her father—for caricatures of a sort, two grotesques.

Thus, save for imbecilic jokes and the ramblings of a drunkard, Geneviève, in the eyes and mind of the public, was really "non-existent." She was dead at the precise moment when the present story began, to the extent that she had not even been given an obituary footnote by Sextius Costecalde. And yet, the strange quasi-absurd work to which that genius was frenetically applying itself and whose goal it foresaw, had what was necessary, if successfully completed, to revolution-ize the world. Alone in the world, her genius knew that the secret could be realized. The conclusion of the experiments in progress, in which Gasguin was incubating hope as in a mon-strous egg, without yet discerning what form the hatchling would take, while Yvernaux divined in that hatchling the eagle of the new age, was only possible thanks to Geneviève.

At the thought that the egg was close to hatching, how-ever, one might have thought that she was now afraid. The silence maintained for some nine years around her mysterious new research, around the very name of Gasguin, around her and by virtue of her own wishes—that silence unpenetrated thus far and doubtless impenetrable—seemed to her more pro-found and isolating as the walls of a prison. For the other day, face to face with Aunt Line, she had suddenly said to her, shi-vering from head to toe: "My father has seen too much of it. My godfather has dreamed too much of it. Sometimes, I no longer to want to be the person who will know what remains to be known."

Aunt Line, without any plausible reason for shivering except that her *ch'tiote* was shivering, also experience a fris-son in her old flesh, and had demanded: "Why is that?"

And Geneviève had immediately replied: "To be certain of *ne l'dir'nin*."

212

Then, with a shrug of self-disgust, she had added, swiftly: "No, that's a lie. That's not the reason. I would like not to be the person who will know because I'm a coward, because I have an idea that *knowing it will do me harm.*"

XXVII

The day after that critical day, she had given the excuse of not feeling well in order not to go to the Vaugirard laboratory with her father. He had been amazed, almost to the point of being indignant.

It was the first time since they had had the laboratory that she had missed a session there. Even fatigued and suffering, during attacks of neuralgia, by which she was often tortured, or the high fever of influenza, she had never done such a thing. Her absence was even less excusable today because it was necessary to finish a whole series of complicated experiments with one last, fairly simple operation, the results of which promised to be definitive and to render the entire series conclusive.

On the slightly harsh observation that he could not help making, she had become annoyed, and had replied to him in an even harsher tone, with an insolence to which he was unaccustomed: "Do it yourself, on your own, if you want. I don't want to. I don't *scent* it.[54] If you do, so much the better for you. And then, enough! I don't want to. I don't want to do it anymore."

And she had shut herself in her bedroom, slamming the door nervously. This behavior was so new to her father that he had forgotten is amazement, then his indignation, and had been gripped by a runaway anxiety, thinking that she was very ill. He talked about sending for a doctor. Aunt Line, insolent

---

[54] In French, *sentir* means both "to feel," in a general sense, and "to smell," in a specific one. Geneviève probably starts out merely suggesting that she doesn't feel up to the task in hand, but her ambiguous remark is subsequently extrapolated into a sequence of wordplay involving *argot* terms as well as commonplace ambiguities, with the result that the passage sounds rather odd, in both English and French.

in her turn, had put him off, saying in response: "She's no more ill than you or me. What she needs isn't a doctor, but to be left in peace. You're getting on our nerves! Yes, me too. You know that you don't understand 'scents' at all. Go away!"

He had gone away, crestfallen, had had not dared to go to carry out the final operation on his own, fearing that Geneviève would be offended if the work were completed without her. *If she doesn't scent it*, he thought, *best to wait.*

That was precisely what he said to her when he went back, cajoling her instead of irritating her further—to which Aunt Line had deigned to pay attention, congratulating him on not being such a bad "sniffer" when he had gone to get a little fresh air.

Geneviève, jumping on the good excuse thus furnished, had claimed that she had now ceased to "scent" not merely the operation still to be attempted, but the entire series of experiments already made.

When Gasguin objected, very timidly this time, that it was a pity "to give up on…" she had no even let him finish his sentence and had contented herself with nailing him to the spot with an authoritarian stare the instructed him peremptorily not to persist, or even to continue. And the poor man, having swallowed his words and his saliva, had shut up.

"Good," Aunt Line had approved. "That's how it ought to be between the men and us, *amon*! It's the only way—we don't talk, they don't talk back."

The old woman's condescending manner was so comically pretentious that Geneviève had smiled. Disarmed, therefore, and to offer Gasguin some consolation for his discomfort, and also to give herself a valid reason for deserting the work on the threshold of success, she had had the sudden inspiration of offering him, and herself, the bait of another task.

"What I can 'smell,'" she had said, "as if it were already complete, is our solution to the machine for electrical fertilization."

She had stressed the "our," which was more accurate in this instance than others, for that idea was "almost" Gasguin's—at least, he had furnished, a long time ago, the fist clear outline of it.

That went all the way back to the era of the second paper, the "Note on the transmission of force by telluric currents." When the Note was drafted, Geneviève had regretted a lacuna relating to the quantity of "positive ions" present in the air in placed where the earth has just been plowed on stormy days. Gasguin had then filled in the lacuna, instantly, by means of a meticulous calculation giving the probable voltage of that potential. And from that he had, as a sure logician, deduced the formula from which the idea had subsequently emerged from Geneviève's creative breath the idea of "electrical fertilization."

This is not the place to explain the idea in detail. There would be a risk of distorting it in a hasty explanation, especially without the necessary expertise. Perhaps the little that had just been said is already too much, its very brevity making it seem more obscure. It has only been mentioned in order to show why the matter ought to have been particularly dear to Gasguin.

It is necessary to add—in order that it regains all the importance that had once inflated it—that he had momentarily nourished the hope of being, with that possible invention, a serious contender for the Alexandra Prize funded by the Imperial Agronomic Institute of St. Petersburg. You will certainly be familiar with that prize,[55] less famous than the Nobel Prize but older and almost as valuable, since it is 25,000 roubles. It is designed to recompense, every five years, the author of the best work, both theoretical and practical, on "the intensive culture of arid soils." It is easy to deduce that the prize's funders had in mind the great desert spaces of central

---

[55] Actually, you won't; it's fictitious. It must, however, have been established after 1894, when Alexandra married Tsar Nicholas II, but before 1898, when Alfred Nobel died, his will establishing the prizes named after him. This is consonant with the dating of the earlier scene as 1894.

and northern Asia, which comprise two thirds of the empire of the Tsars, and which might become, if subjected to exploitation, the world's granary and Russia's treasure.

Now this is what Geneviève's idea amounted to, explained in summary. Thanks to an original combination of the transmission of force by telluric currents and electrolysis, the need for chemical fertilizers could be eliminated, and that of their transport, always costly. They would be replaced by the production at a distance of positive ions and negatively-charged electrons, the former in the air and the latter in the ground, by means of which the most arid soil might be fertilized without the great expense of industrial establishments or railways.

Theoretically, the invention was nearly complete. So far as one could reasonably anticipate, from the parts already constructed and the admittedly-hypothetical plan of the remainder, there ought not to be any great difficulties to overcome in giving it a final form. It remained to put it into practice, of course, but the capital for that purpose would certainly not be lacking once the theory was declared viable. In any case, the value of the prize alone represented a sum of which Gasguin had not disdained to dream, on occasion, between his more beautiful dreams of glory.

In the era when the Vaugirard laboratory was entirely occupied with the problem in question, Yvernaux had often said, delving deep into his lyricism:

"When that patent is granted, it's not just the empire of the Tsars that will have found its treasure; it's Geneviève's genius too, for that treasure will be the treasure of the war, no longer of potential but of fact, necessary to become the Napoléon of Science. For in *potential*, as we thinkers mean it, she already is. She would be in *fact*, if she had the means to realize all her dreams. Those means, beyond the most demanding expectations, she will have, thanks to the royalties automatically extracted by the patent from the inexhaustible wealth heaped up in the future granary of the world. I can see them now, those..."

And he launched into veritably epic hymns, in which he soared in hectic flight above a magnificent panorama representing—and with what riches!—the high plateaux of central and northern Asia, once the cradle of the civilization from which ours emerged, becoming the throne of the future civilization to which ours is in the process of giving birth.

To that tableau Aunt Line opened her eyes in ecstasy, as to a fairy tale. And Geneïève too, without any childish cupidity, but hiking about the opulent laboratory she would have, full of innumerable resources, permitting the costliest and most difficult experiments, putting the most chimerical ideas to the proof. As for Gasguin, ever the prudent Thiérachian, even in the wanderings of his most cherished hobby-horses, he invariably finished up saying: "Yes, on condition that the patent is solid and guaranteed, so that no one steals it from us!"

On which Aunt Line intervened, remembering Grandma Hescheboix's tales of invasion, to cry with her arms in the air: "Damn! Does one ever know, with these damned Cossacks always *on the grab*?"

And the suspicion so well expressed thus, in a ludicrous form, was deeply ingrained in all those mistrustful Thiérachian souls, simultaneously peasant and Romany, for whom the worst shame is not to swindle someone else but to be swindled by him. Even Yvernaux, the sincere lyricist, could not help saying: "It's certainly necessary not to let anyone pinch it, even for 65,000 bullets! That would be stupid, wouldn't it, Geneviève?"

He addressed himself to her with a sort of bashfulness that he had, in spite of everything, by virtue of thinking that he might have gone a little too far, but his scruple disappeared on seeing that even Geneviève was thinking along the same lines, for she said: "That's why I'm leaving the idea at the planning stage. I'm like Aunt Line and Grandma Hescheboix, myself—I don't get any odor of sanctity from the Cossacks. If they're ever to be shown a paper on the intensive culture of arid soils, it should be with the patent in hand and guaranteed, as Papa wishes."

"Guaranteed," added Gasguin, "by the French government." Aunt Line nodded approvingly.

And it is necessary to believe, finally, that even that guarantee had not been sufficient for their security, for they had indeed left the idea well and truly at the planning stage, in spite of the near-certainty of success and the lure of the roubles. They had rapidly forgotten it, in fact, a more fecund and more extraordinary idea having surged forth in Geneviève's imagination, overexcited by the very recent discovery of radium.[56]

That new idea astonished Gasguin excessively, in its breadth, and often made him regret having abandoned the previous one, more within his range. So, in spite of his mistrust, he had gone back to it from time to time, insinuating that it might perhaps be appropriate to present his theory of electrical fertilization—the theory along, magisterially enough to carry off the prize, while reserving the explanation of the practical applications subject to the acquisition and sure guarantee of the patent.

But Geneviève had never yielded to these insinuations, absorbed as she now was by the other research projects to which she had, so to speak, fallen prey, so excited was she thereby. Prey, to be sure—and that was why she had been gripped by a kind of terror in their possession. That her secret, ready to be revealed, made her afraid to be the person to reveal it, to the extent of not wanting to be that person, one can easily understand merely by the pronunciation of the name— provisional as yet and rather obscure—by which she, by herself and solely for herself, almost tremulously, designated it: *radioactive aviation.*

Those two words, taken separately, certainly have a sufficiently clear meaning—even the first, in its still almost-embryonic aspect as bicephalous and monstrous new-born. In combination, however, they take on a mysterious, incompre-

---

[56] Radium was discovered by Marie Curie in 1898; again, this is consonant with the internal chronology already suggested.

hensible and menacing air, pregnant with the seed of a progress whose explosion is imminent.

You will have a better understanding in due course of that integral meaning, which is simple enough, without appearing to be at first glance, hidden by the matrix of the coupling that dresses them with absurdity. In that matrix, however, dense as it might be, and unopenable until further notice, the seam of unknown metal, the previously-unknown gem of the secret confided to Geneviève's genius, can doubtless by divined. From the two conjoined words, it seems, even as they are, denuded of all present significance by their illogical amalgamation, mysterious miraculous effluvia already emanate, which explain the terror of the thaumaturge herself.[57]

You can now take the measure of the real ardor, which had nothing feigned about it, that Geneviève must have put into ridding herself of that terrifying anguish, if only temporarily, by thrusting her father away and throwing herself back on to the old track of the Alexandra Prize. It was while clapping her hands, and in a sincere hope of success, with the involuntary autosuggestion of belief, excited by the mere fact of her energetic, imperative and iterative affirmation, that she had said: "Yes, I tell you that I can sense the solution to that problem, as if I already had it."

And everyone's confidence had been captured effortlessly—Aunt Line's blindly, Gasguin's joyfully. Only Yvernaux had baulked at first, when he was told of the abrupt change of direction that evening. He had tried to inveigh against the lamentable intention to "let go" of what he called the "conquest of the gulfs"—"that divine prey"—in favor of "the palpability of roubles, that bourgeois shadow." He had remained alone, however, with his "fanfares of lyricism"—as Geneviève had said to him, not without a certain acidity.

---

[57] Contemplation of what Geneviève might mean by "radioactive aviation," and why she is frightened by the idea, is best postponed to an afterword.

In fact, she slightly resented the expression he had just used: "the conquest of the gulfs." Did he not seem to be seeing clearly, by the light of his metaphor, into the very gloom of that mysterious and as-yet-obscure "radioactive aviation," of which she had never even told him the name, for fear that he might find it a sufficient password? Yes, decidedly, as she had complained to Aunt Line the other day, he had already dreamed too much of it! And that too corroborated the resolution not to give any more thought to her great secret, in order that no one around her should think about it henceforth.

But she knew, too, a continual torture, assiduous, obstinate and furious, nagging, stabbing and corrosive, as if vampiric, so atrocious that Dante had forgotten to put it in his Inferno, doubtless not wanting to remember it by virtue of having been too cruelly tormented by it. It was the torture inflicted on genius by obsession, jealously and exclusively extended in the implacable desire to have its whole due. It was necessary, as a kind of defense against that, also to extend herself in a perpetual effort of reason, incessantly trying, it seemed, to hold herself upright, like the flame of a torch amid gusts of wind, against eddies of folly.

She succeeded even so, but not alone and by her own means. Perhaps, deprived of help, she would finally have succumbed, the flame of her torch going out and her brain blown up like an empty bubble by the wind of dementia. It is only just to let it be known to what she owed the avoidance of catastrophe, which was, to all appearances, the two concomitant treatments administered by those two physicians of absolutely opposed opinion, the positivist Gasguin and the chimerical Yvernaux. At least, they both boasted about it after the fact. You shall see that Aunt Line, who never boasted about anything, also had something to do with it.

At any rate, the story of that cure, as a possible contribution to a psychophysiological study of genius, is doubtless worthy of a momentary pause, however little one can sympathize at present with the patience of either or both of her two doctors, and also with Aunt Line.

XXVIII

You know in what good faith Geneviève had affirmed that she could sense the solution to the problem taken up again, as if she already had it. At the moment when she said that, she did, indeed "almost" have the vision. On the other hand, you will recall—and the explanation is not too difficult to see—that, "theoretically, the invention was very nearly" complete. It turned out, however, as things worked out, that that "almost" and that "very nearly" represented abyssal holes, whose crevasse could not be crossed, nor even its walls discerned.

Geneviève had thrown herself into it, racking her brain, with her most audacious hypothetical thrust and her most powerful calculative motor, but she did not succeed in reaching the other side, nor in sending a sounding-line of light into the depths of its darkness. And those very images by which she involuntarily translated her impotence only provided further proof of the obsession whose victim she was.

Her obsession, in face, which nothing could distract, poisoned all the best mental preoccupations applied to anything else, and tainted them, as it were, with the particular, exclusive and tyrannical appetite of its own preoccupation. In vain, the inventor, the physicist, the mathematician tried to absorb herself in the dogged study of electrical fertilization; she could not do it. Her brain was haunted only by hypotheses, experiments, equations, formulae and—as we have seen—even metaphors inspired by radioactive aviation.

In spite of the prideful reluctance Geneviève had always experienced in admitting to an intellectual infirmity, she suffered so much from this one, and judged it so difficult to cure without help, that she was obliged to confess it—not merely to her old Aunt Line, with whom she abdicated all pride, but to her godfather, whom she feared might treat it as a joke, and even her father, which was particularly hard for her now.

She now disliked humiliating herself before her father, as she had done so frequently as an adolescent. The excess of her discouragement, however, rendered any submission facile, even to the pedantic and meticulous authority of the professor from whom she had freed herself so long before. She even tolerated the pretentiously understanding expression he adopted—without wanting to offend her—in order to say: "I know these hauntings. *All great minds are subject to them.*"

How could she not have endured even that haughty attitude, disparaging her genius by its familiarity? Gasguin was only adopting it in order to give her help, for he immediately added: "Alas, yes, I know the problem—but fortunately, I also know the remedy for it."

And she listened to him devotedly, drinking his words like a calming tisane.

"Here it is—it's very simple. It's sufficient to resubmit one's reason, pitilessly, to a discipulary regime. And that consists of a kind of hard labor, to which one submits the mind by methodical instruction in matters to which one is not accustomed. That exhausts and dislocates the mind, with exercises entirely new it, so that it takes on curvatures that stretch it, put to sleep and relax it. The obsession can no longer find points of support to work upon it. That's always worked for me. Try it—you'll see."

Yvernaux, when consulted, did not think the remedy bad, so it was tried—and not without results, it had to be admitted. Geneviève had already, several times in the distant and near past, purely for love of encyclopedic knowledge, dipped into other sciences than her favorite ones. Biology, in particular, had attracted her. She devoted herself to it again—particularly to medicine. A little relief was procured thereby.

Nevertheless, Yvernaux observed, very delicately, might not the remedy work more forcefully if she had recourse to work antipodean—his own expression—to her customary tasks? In consequence, Geneviève might undertake the studies for which she thought herself least well-endowed—law and judicial procedure for example. Gasguin even conspired with

Yvernaux—and the fantasist thinker thought that admirable—in an appeal to their old shared memories of the seminary in order to compile for their daughter and goddaughter a course in theology and casuistry.

This time, it was a little too much, and, the jester that Geneviève sometimes was—as you have seen—waking up even in the invalid, she said to her godfather one day, slyly and cheerfully: "Oh no, you know! If it's a matter of distraction for distraction's sake, I'd rather recommence the little sessions in which you initiated me into the joys of the 'displaced state.' What do you think? Suppose we get rid of the obsession by drowning it?"

This was only a joke, as you can imagine. Yvernaux, however, had suddenly seized upon it, as a marvelous idea, thanks to an association of ideas of which the following is the incredible but authentic history.

Ordinarily, he would have smiled at his goddaughter's banter. He did not even notice it this time, being in no mood to laugh, but having, on the contrary, a heart and mind full of black anxieties. Aunt Line, in fact, having taken him to one side before he went in, had only just said to him: "Listen, *fieu*—the *ch'tiote* is killing herself with these classes you're forcing her to take again, you and her father. Leave that to Gasguin. You must give her back what she loves—but without her knowing it. Do you know what that is?"

He had replied negatively. She had persisted, talking about the plant to be cared for, and "she who had been a plant in time gone by." The matter remaining obscure to him, he had demanded further explanations. The old woman had gone on: "Well, what? Has she not a soul, in the utmost depths of the other, like mine—and which also thinks, and knows, and remembers as it sleeps? I can't tell you any more, myself, but you know her well, that Geneviève of the underneath, where all the Hescheboix are! You've talked to her about it many times. You give it a funny name, though! That makes me laugh. I think it must resemble your 'displaced state.'"

It was very rare for Aunt Line to say as much as that in one breath. Such a flood of words testified to a profound disturbance. Her gaze, moreover, was unsteady and fluttering. And Yvernaux had abruptly realized that the poor old woman, the perspicacious old woman, the sublime old woman with the atavistic knowledge, wanted to make him understand something.

"I've got it!" he had cried. "You think, don't you, Aunt Line, that I ought to act upon her polygonal self?"

"That's it! That's the word! As for the thing..."

And the seeress, with the instincts of the *Sphex*, the memories dating from the high plateaux of Central Asia, the *merlifiche* for whom the stronger, more intense, more vibrant soul—almost the living soul—had been precisely the thing in question, the "simpleton" who could not explain herself better, had concluded her inexpressible thought with a gaze and a significant gesture as clear as words:

The thing, the soul that I can't name myself, the soul that you call by some more-or-less crazy name, polygonal, subliminal, subconscious, unconscious and other soubriquets, that soul, I have a better sense of what it is than you do; and it is, in Geneviève as in myself, the essential *soul, the soul by means of which it's necessary to cure the other, by drowning it.*

Now, what had been so clearly and so forcefully signified a little while before by Aunt Line, by means of her gaze and gesture, Yvernaux had not "heard" at the moment when it had been "said," without actually being spoken—but in his "polygonal," unconscious memory, it had been perfectly recorded, understood and expressed. And suddenly, his conscious self took possession of the fact thus recorded, understood and expressed. He had a clear notion of it in the abrupt association of ideas that the word "drowning" had released—the penultimate word of Aunt Line's unspoken sentence and of the one spoken in jest by Geneviève.

"Of course!" he exclaimed, as soon as the word had been uttered. "Perhaps you never said a truer word."

"What?" Geneviève replied. "you want me to start drinking again in order to drown..."

"Drinking? No. But I think it's necessary, to cure your conscious mind of its obsession, to drown it—yes, drown it—in the other. In more explicit terms, I'm saying that it's necessary to give the obsession to your polygonal self, as fodder..."

She closed his mouth with a furious: "Oh, no, I beg you! No Grassetian psychology just now! I'm truly suffering. I need consideration."

But he shouted loudly enough to make her ears ring: "That's what Aunt Line thinks!"

"Aunt Line? You're crazy. What has Aunt Line to do with the polygonal self?"

And there was a truly farcical scene between the two of them, one so great, the other so lyrical—until the moment when, with calm heads, with no shouting or misunderstandings, all was explained.

And that farce had, for its very serious and no less original conclusion, the soon-victorious trial of a new treatment, combining Gasguin's discipline applied to the conscious self and Yvernaux's exaltation, reserved for the other, where the obsession continued henceforth. That was how Geneviève avoided the catastrophe. That was the salvation of her genius.

Soon, in fact, only the polygonal self was occupied with the obsession, which ceased to be unhealthy and tormenting, since it was no longer as neglected, seeking to avenge itself by means of an obstinate, corrosive, vampiric haunting. Meanwhile, the conscious self, exhausted by new exercises and reacquiring the notion of obedience therein, no longer had any need to lend itself to foreign matters. It had quickly recovered the free disposition of its faculties for its habitual studies—and thus the problem of electrical fertilization had ceased to conceal its possible solution from Geneviève's patient attention and inventive imagination.

Before the historic conclusion of that strange new cure, from which two gestating discoveries were to emerge one after the other, it is worth making some less important but even more curious observations regarding the employment of propitious means for the favorable excitation of the polygonal self.

If one had the leisure to dwell on it, there would doubtless be material here of keen interest to philosophical physicians like Grasset, and even simple therapists in quest of remedies, not for individuals of genius, but for ordinary neuropaths. We regret being unable to give them ample satisfaction, but once more, we must limit ourselves to a very brief account of facts from which experts, and even amateurs of little-known sciences, might be able to draw fruitful conclusions, perhaps newly informative but, in any case, rich—one hopes—in a certain amusement.

You will not have forgotten that mention has been made—in chapter IV—of "special practices" to which Geneviève had recourse to put herself in a state of fecund but unconscious intellectual labor. She hid them even from Yvernaux himself. It was not therefore, him who had been able to reveal them to her, even partially. We know, nevertheless, and have "the authorization to let it be known" that these practices consisted of a veritable "gymnastics of the polygonal self" and that their principal agent was autosuggestion, after placement in ecstasy—there is no other word more explicit—obtained by an unusual employment of ambient electricity, and the absorption of certain drugs in the form of fumes.

Geneviève knew the power of the electrical bath in which we are always in flotation and which, in stormy weather, represents potentials measurable in thousands of volts. She understood the tenor of these potentials, with respect to the moments and direction of the electrical currents, their variations and the laws controlling those variations, well enough to be able to make use of them in many instances, and did so without the slightest scruple. That was, in many circumstances a pure and simple abdication of what we call free will. She experienced no remorse in consequence.

Even less was she ashamed of a kind of drunkenness, wholly of her own invention, which took the place of the one she had tried in vain with Yvernaux. Her godfather's aperitifs, as he himself complained, could only be dangerous auxiliaries. Opium and hashish are slaves that quickly become abominable tyrants. Geneviève had found the true "motors of the polygonal self"—as she called them, privately—in a powder that she made up, and whose vapors she inhaled, drawing them into the depths of her lungs.

It was by chance that she had first become aware of the principal elements of that powder, a remedy prescribed got certain nervous troubles, whose formula she had found in an ancient pharmacopeia. By trial and error, she had arrived at the exact dosage she required. Dried plants, pulverized and rendered combustible by an adjunction of potassium nitrate, comprising various *Solanaceae*, noxious herbs once dear to witches making philters, such as *Datura stramonium*,[58] poppy, henbane, belladonna, aconite, hyssop and star anise.

Perhaps the demi-revelation of these practical secrets will be considered an admission of voice, and will be injurious, in certain narrow minds, to admiration for Geneviève, but we did not believe, even so, that we ought to leave it out. Let us place the quasi-sacrilege under the safeguard, devoted to the point of adoration, of the mad but simultaneously wise Yvernaux, who seems to have found a definitive formula in a remark quoted above, which may serve as an epigraph for the present study:

"I affirm that true genius consists of exactly that conscious exploitation of one's unconscious."

---

[58] Jimson weed.

XXIX

Novelists of the so-called "psychological genre" have tried too hard, all the same, to dismantle and reassemble the mechanism of the subtle clockwork by which they explain the march of our sentiments and ideas, in order to make our actions mark the hour of their choice. Others, whatever they call themselves, are of the no-less-agreeable party that collects "odd facts" and thread them on to the slightly coarse string of a supposedly-scientific determinism, aiming to render that incoherent Indian file logical. Perhaps the simple story-tellers have the right approach, in wanting to keep to the story and nothing more—but the worst portion of all is that of the conscientious historian, who seeks the humble truth humbly, by no matter what means, and most of the time fails to find it, and must then content himself with guessing it, and giving it at least an air of plausibility.

That is what we have tried to do in this study, and we want to continue to do it, even though the task is becoming increasingly unrealizable, sometimes to the point of impossibility. And is that not exactly the case here, where the truth, such as one believes that one is in certain possession of it, presents itself under the appearance of an implausible fiction, to the point of appearing as aggressive as a defiance of reason? Those interested in Geneviève's genius will judge for themselves.

That Geneviève's thoughts often rested the flight of its dreams on the memory of Joson had been demonstrated, and no one will be surprised by that. That the flight in question had brushed Joson's soul, and had awakened dreams there too, is less easy to imagine. But that, by virtue of that thought and dream-flight, without either of them being conscious of any exchange, a sort of chain was gradually forged between their two beings, is something that many serious minds will probably consider a pure phantasmagoria.

We shall not waste any time trying to convince them of the error of their skeptical neophobia. We only ask them to reflect on the frightful wall of mystery that imprisons us on all sides and to which we never acquire the "Open Sesame." We remind them of the miracle of the vital seed enclosed in an infusorium in a state of desiccation or in a seed placed between the lips of a mummy; merely enclosed, that germ is dormant but not dead, since life revives immediately when the desiccated infusorium rediscovers the fountain of youth of water or when the grain of wheat falls into the maternal bosom of the earth. We shall also mention to them the very recent marvels of wireless telegraphy, of which we know the how but not the why. And finally, we shall ask them whether there is not more of the unimaginable in any one of these thaumaturgies than in the simple telepathic fact—duly established, moreover—of two minds in communion across time and space.

And since the observation of such a fact is frequent and patent, authenticated by indisputable testimony, we shall not risk attempting an explication of it, which is, in any case, unnecessary. We shall accept the fact in itself and henceforth, without any fear of manifest implausibility and without any scruple, we shall give all the details, including the features that that are most strongly stigmatized by the fantastic.

We have sufficiently depicted, we believe—perhaps even overgenerously—the kind of spell, both amorous and mystical, cast upon Geneviève by all her memories of Kairnheûz and the mirages of her imaginary stained-glass windows. Nothing is more natural and more conceivable than that empery over a thirteen-year-old soul, entirely innocent and then subject to the only religious crisis of her life. Nothing is less unexpected, in consequence, than the impulse of that soul continuing to desire to fly toward the other, as if permanently magnetized in the direction of that pole.

What cannot be determined, however—for no one was conscious of the phenomena until long after their production—is how that magnetization had located that pole, and especially, how the pole had been influenced in its turn by the desires for contact extended toward it. It is therefore necessary to limit this reportage to what it was possible to learn, by groping in profound obscurity and without any firm contact, now less than ever, about the why of a mystery, the how of which was so poorly understood.

When Joson had left for his first campaign as a naval officer, he had only a very vague impression of Geneviève in his conscious memory. The two months of his last vacation at Kairnheûz had been occupied, especially sentimentally, by other things than the soul of the little girl catechized by his tutor, about whom the Abbé had not told him anything very interesting. He had only seen her as someone with whom he went for walks, a being mingled with the ambience of those rather fleeting days that he had devoted to his mother, certain that he had devoted to them to her alone, uniquely and willingly.

Nevertheless, as always happens when one is absorbed by an exclusive sentiment, that ambience and the progress of those rapid days had been recalled by the young man's unconscious memory. The photographic images therefore existed, ready for "development," to employ an image that renders these reflexive phenomena more intelligible. Nevertheless, no opportunity arose to "develop" them, or even to suspect that those images existed somewhere, held in reserve and consigned to forgetfulness in a drawer of which Joson did not have the key, or even the knowledge of its existence.

Twice, however, that opportunity could have presented itself, quite naturally, it seems, on the death of the Comtesse and the death of the Abbé. The very violence of his grief in the two cases, however, and the intensity of the memories resuscitated by such deaths, prevented the image of any other individual from being evoked at those tragic moments.

Compared with his mother, whom he had cherished so tenderly and so profoundly—enough to have hated his father, perhaps to the point of thoughts of parricide and perhaps even to the point of the act, as some dared to allege—and with that figure filling all his heart, what significance could there be in the poor pale effigy of the girl whose dull expression had soon been effaced in the mists of the past? Even in his fond remembrance of the Abbé, his tutor for so many years, it had not occurred to him that she had been his catechumen. At the most, and without clearly distinguishing the features of the first communicant, he had seen in fleeting memory the shadow of a white dress pass over the priest's black robe.

And that was all! The drawer with the images remained unopened; only a mist had emerged from it. That mist, that shadow veiling Abbé Denis Gasguin's soutane with a light pale cloud, was all that Joson remembered consciously—and forever, one might have thought—of Geneviève.

All the more so, one can and ought to believe, because his life had been singularly agitated, vehement and adventurous, full of events liable to make one forget many things and many people. Not, of course, facts as capital as the drama with which his childhood had been entangled or the two great occasions for mourning by which his first year of youthful freedom had been so cruelly darkened, but much more so than his insignificant camaraderie of two months with the girl of whom his first thought had been neither more or less, as you might remember, than: "God, what an ugly little thing!"

Joson's life, since his last vacation at Kairnheûz, is an entire other story—and how different!—which it would have been necessary to intercalate with the present story if we had wanted to narrate it, even in summary. Merely compiling the balance-sheet, limiting ourselves to the facts, without seeking any psychological substance or moral reflections, would have involved writing a veritable modern *cape-and-épée* novel.

We shall resist the temptation to amuse ourselves with that as lengthily as the subject-matter would permit. We ought not to be distracted any more than is necessary from the intellectual facts—certainly superior in interest—constituting the history of Geneviève's genius. We shall nevertheless relate that which it is necessary to know for the sake of the history of

that genius, and everything regarding the typical case of telepathy between her and Joson.

The forced amalgamation of the two stories, one of virtually pure philosophy and the other of pure adventure, will, in
any case, prove once more to what petty causes the greatest
effects are often due, and of what hazards the immanent logic
that is claimed to constrain events is sometimes—not to say
always—made.

XXX

Like many calculations "taking the long view" in which an overly complicated politics goes astray by virtue of being too clever, the calculation made over the Abbé's head for or against Josdon's future had been mistaken. Two essential elements, admittedly difficult to foresee, had been omitted therefrom: the death of the Comtesse so soon after her son's departure and the no-less-prompt death of the Abbé after the Comtesse's departure.

If his mother had lived another ten years, and the Abbé likewise, there is every reason to think, in fact, that Joson would have followed the progress desired by *you know who* across the chessboard of existence. Raised in the ideas and sentiments—principles or prejudices—that had earned him the nickname of the Little Chouan on the *Borda*, colliding head-on with the ideas and sentiments—also principles or prejudices—of the modern world, the high-minded gentleman would quickly have become disgusted, first with his career, and then the modern world itself. From that disgust to a desire, and then a need, for the tonic offered by religion, the passage was ready-made. A resignation would have brought him back to Kairnheûz. When his mother died, with the Abbé at her deathbed, having no more than a few decisive words to pronounce, the Company would have counted among its members Comte Elme-Cast-Jagut-Marie-Joseph de Ponhual-Plouër.

That the last descendant of an old and illustrious family was also, by courtesy of his maternal grandfather, a Hugon de La Goëlwec, in line to share in a future inheritance, perhaps considerable if he remained the only heir that it was possible to locate, the exquisite Abbé and the charming Comtesse were absolutely ignorant, but someone knew it in their stead and would have told Joson about it at an opportune and chosen moment—which is to say, in complete detachment from the perishable things of this world.

It so happened that the secret was revealed to the young man at a very different moment. As had been expected, there was then a violent break with an entourage to whom he remained too much the Little Chouan of the *Borda*, but disgust for the world in general had not taken hold of him, nor even for the modern world in particular. Far from it! And it was precisely because of that "far from it" that the revealer of the secret in question had hastened to make him party to it.

A shady businessman, a former chief clerk to the notary of the late Comte Alain-Mathias-Bertrand, that informant had been acquainted with Joson's father during his last years of drunkenness and gambling. He had profited from the situation as a procurer of money-lenders, and even worse, if necessary—notably of dupes. Knowing the father's vices, and foreseeing their emergence in the son, he had remained on the lookout for their possible germination, and had long despaired of seeing them born, but then had recovered confidence following the death of the Comtesse.

There had then been, in fact, a turbulent crisis in the life of the young naval officer, for some two years. Utterly firm in his opinions, but feeble in his conduct, pushing his religious faith to excess and a quasi-ostentatious extremism and scorning the most elementary morality, Joson had established himself as an intransigent Catholic in principle, but only that, and scandalous in his conduct. While awaiting all the vices of all the Ponthual-Plouërs, and even those of the Goëlwecs, to recover in him their splendid blossoming of yore, he allowed to flourish immediately and fully the paternal vices of the more recent past, in particular the two that were characteristic of his race: drunkenness and gambling.

It was that moment that the revealer of the secret of the inheritance had judged opportune and wisely-chosen to offer those vices the aliment that their maintenance lacked—for Joson was not rich, with the small portion of the Comtesse's ill-conserved dowry that had been saved from the demands of the late Comte. That small amount and the price of the estate—yes, alas, Kairnheûz had been sold to the highest bidder!—had soon melted away at the gaming tables and flowed over the counters of drinking dens during so-called convalescent leaves, in which the officer disgusted by his career was already getting a foretaste of his resignation.

The shady businessman had seen this business clearly, with both eyes. So, expecting considerable benefits for himself, he had brought his client a large and unexpected windfall with the revelation of the secret, and what he might get out of it. Guided by him—or rather, letting him act in his name—Hugon de La Goëlwec's heir had one day, as the sole survivor of those having a right of inheritance, come into possession of a veritable fortune, amounting to some two and a half millions.

In spite of the deplorable accounts that valued his opinions—and also, one has to admit, his regrettable way of life—the Comte de Ponthual-Plouër could have taken advantage of these unexpected resources to find his feet again in a profession that he loved in spite of everything. The navy has been, since time immemorial, the refuge of rebels who are able, when the occasion arises, to obtain forgiveness for their so-called "anti-authoritarian" spirit by virtue of loyal service every-ready for heroism. The young officer's name, the new state of his fortune and his professional capacities, unimpeded by his private vices, would have assured him a fine future in the career the two initial phases of which he had already completed.

He made a different decision. Two brief missions on land, in Senegal, had given him a taste for life in Africa, the exploration of savage lands, and the independence from authority that can be exercised therein. He had delighted his adventurous spirit and his appetites for battle therein, sensed his petrel's eyes illuminate with folly and imagined the erne's beak that served as his nose clacking with joy. He therefore handed in his resignation, not in order to enter the Company that had wanted him, but to organize a company of his own to beat a path through the bush, as a conquistador of the modern New World that is Central Africa.

A substantial fraction of his inheritance was rapidly swallowed up by that expedition, with no other result than the vivid joy of a great lord having become a gang leader and a serious attack of cerebral fever from which he nearly died. He gained, by way of compensation the total cure of one of his capital vices, drunkenness, of which the sledgehammer of the tropical sun rid him, striking into his skull with a single blow this morality: "If you feed yourself alcohol here, you'll die or go mad."

He also gained the precious friendship of two men who were to have a considerable influence on his life, as we shall see. One was a younger son of the Irish nobility, Nathaniel O'Deekle, who had had been secretary to the famous Stanley during his last voyage to the Cape.[59] The other was a ruffian from Menilmontant, Jules Guérinet, known as Julot, a former convict liberated from Biribi.[60] Both of them were brave to the point of making Joson himself envious—which was saying a great deal, as you may imagine.

He had lost sight of them at the end of his expedition, one returning to his former employer, who was back at the Cape, the other remaining a *fourbancier*,[61] as he put it, between the various Congos, while waiting for a great scheme to be mounted somewhere else, in Algeria or the Cape—not by himself, of course, since the only capital he had was his bravery and his Parisian cunning, but if his friend the Comte, for example, were to be the leader...

"Oh, in that case, yes! Nice! Now you're talking."

---

[59] The reference is presumably to Henry Morton Stanley's last expedition to the Congo, in 1876.

[60] Biribi is a gambling game, but being "sent to Biribi" was a slang expression used of soldiers consigned to the disciplinary battalion in Algeria, from which Julot has presumably deserted.

[61] A *fourbancier* is a jack-of-all-trades, but the word also carries an implication of sharp practice, suggesting that none of the trades in question is practiced honestly.

And they had, in fact, arranged a rendezvous for a future exploration, as soon as possible: a two-year journey, it appeared, of which Nathaniel had a map, bequeathed to him by Stanley's best guide, a certain Ibn-Aoud-Gadfaia, an Arab-African mulatto, a former slave-trader who knew Africa by virtue of having traversed it at least twenty times from north to south and east to west. According to this map, the ruins of a city anterior to all history existed in the center of one of the monstrous equatorial forests. The map permitted its rediscovery—and fabulous treasures were buried there.

Joson had been obliged to abandon his friends and put off until later the hope of that expedition, the concept of which filled him with enthusiasm. The urgent needs imposed on him by convalescence following his cerebral fever, however, and those of his eroded fortune, recalled him to Paris, from which he would return as soon as possible.

And he had, in fact, returned, but in poorer circumstances than before for attempting with any chance of success the famous expedition of at least two years that the voyage to and from the magical city required.

In the meantime, in Paris, once returned to health, he had been terribly regripped by his second, long-idle vice: gambling. The clubs, then the dens, all the way to the lowest, had seen his elbows leaning on their green baize. He had become one of the heroes of that strange society, where so much virile energy, self-composure and nervous excitement is expended, and so many brains exhausted, in illusory gains and poignant emotions.

The tension of that quotidian battle had preserved him, however, from other combats in which he would have risked losing something much more precious than his money, given the naivety, still pure and childlike, of his heart. Amours, facile or culpable, had been spared him, the former only leaving him with a sentiment of sad pity, the others a sort of horror at the idea of a possible felony. A few minor passions sketched in passing he had escaped advantageously, either by virtue of scorn rapidly felt for his accomplice and himself or, when he had got beyond that, jealousy beginning to bite too hard, and two "jolly duels" in which he had purged his bile by drawing a little blood and having a little drawn.

He had not settled his account with the gambling so easily. His infatuation with the Queen of Spades was not a minor passion but a true, ardent, somber, intense and tenacious passion. How many times he had taken himself in hand, on arriving home in the morning, and sworn not to go back that evening! How many times, on receiving a letter reminding him of his promise regarding the distant expedition, he had said to himself, cursing himself disgustedly: "Joson, my lad, you're the worst of cowards!"

Even so, he continued. And three times his two and a half millions, already significantly eroded by the first expedition to the Congo—but in that instance for a noble adventure worthy of a Ponthual-Plouër—had slipped through his fingers, trickling away with the cards, almost all the way downstream, leaving him virtually dry. Three times his luck had turned and a fraction of the millions had flowed back into his hands—and even so, he continued.

One fine day, however—oh yes, what a fine day! he often said, later—his valor had surged upwards and his courage had remained high. He had just received an almost-insulting letter from Julot. Yes, to him, the Comte de Ponthual-Plouër! Insulting! From Julot, the little ruffian from Ménilmontant, the escapee from Biribi! And rightly insulting, because the Parisian reproached him for two years stupidly and wantonly squandered!

"What's up, then, Monsieur l'Aristo? Going on the spree like any old cretin! Pooh! It's really not worth the trouble of having a long string of names if one doesn't know what to do with them, and fiber in the heart, which is the trump card, and a petrel's eyes, as one boasts, and a nose like…I don't know any more, but something like a sea-eagle, the noisiest of birds after the sparrows of Pantruche...!"[62]

On which Joson, his blood up, and his millions being then reduced to three hundred francs in liquid assets—oh, how few!—had renounced running after his money, realized his disposable capital, practically all of it, packed his bags—which is to say, everything he needed for the famous expedition—and then had cabled news of his arrival to Julot and Nathaniel. He rejoined the former in Dakar, the second at the Cape, and finally set out with them on the great two-year expedition.

It was at this point in particular, by virtue of that journey, that the veritable modern cape-and-épée novel that Joson's life was to become had commenced. A cape-and-épée novel full of extraordinary adventures, as you can imagine, perhaps more extraordinary than old novels of that sort, sometimes going as far as the fantastic feats of chivalric romance. Sometimes too, one ought to recognize, bordering on the exploits of those other knights errant, of industry, who are the heroes of our era, at grips with the new monsters and dragons given birth by the land of "business."

Once again, we do not have the leisure—nor, very probably, the special talent—necessary to the description of those adventures. It would need the authors of *Les Quatre fils d'Aymon, Amadis* and *Esplandian*[63] all rolled into one, and

---

[62] La Pantruche is now a famous Parisian restaurant but Julot is using the term as a slang term for a marionette; the reference is to the house-sparrow, of which 19th-centry Paris was home to several noisy flocks.

[63] The first title is that of a famous Charlemagnian romance; the familiar versions of the two Spanish chivalric romances—whose full titles are *Amadis de Gaula* and *Las Sergas de Esplandian* [The Adventures of Esplandian]—are actually by the same author, Garcia Rodriguez de Montalvo, but the former, to which the latter is a sequel, was apparently based on a lost Portugueuse original of unknown authorship.

some picaresque Cervantes for whom we are still waiting, doubled with a Eugène Sue who would also be a kind of Balzac! Fat chance! For want of that problematic historiographer, we shall be content to summarize, in a few broad strokes, the last fifteen or twenty years of that hectic existence—as they say in *feuilletons*.

We are certain, moreover, of easily receiving credit for these accounts of sometimes-incredible but true facts, which reality offers in such profusion today. We shall reserve the purely psychic facts for a chapter more summary still, since they are much less credible.

XXXI

The urgency that Joson had felt to leave and to act, in order to become conscious of his vanquished laxness and his recovered vitality, had been the cause of the conditions, poorer than before, in which they set forth. The season was wrong, four months too late; the preparations were insufficient, the equipment botched; the recruitment of the troop made haphazardly, almost at random. Such had been the faults of the commencement, several of which were irreparable. Result: a difficult expedition, needlessly costly, which, instead of two years, lasted a full three. And the practical benefit realized? Absolutely none.

It seemed, nevertheless, to hear Joson talk, that he regretted neither the time wasted nor the last remnants of his fortune strewn along the road to nowhere. He was alone, though, with Guérinet, alias Julot, in being of that opinion and thinking that the journey had not been futile. Poor Nathaniel O'Deekle would have been the third to think in that fashion, if he had not died on the very threshold of the Promised Land—as Julot had put it, chancing to remember the Moses of his sacred history.

For those who knew where their pilgrimage was headed had, in fact, found their Promised Land. The others, the brutes serving them as scouts, soldiers or beasts of burden, had not understood why they were marching for so long amid the dark foliage or the miry and sticky marshes of the monstrous equatorial forest, or why they had then halted for such a long time on that chaotic mountain of enormous rocks in the vast desert clearing occupying the center of the forest. But Joson had told Julot why—and they had both laughed and cried with joy.

The story bequeathed to Nathaniel O'Deekle by Ibn-Aoud-Gadfaia was not, then, a tale from the Thousand-and-One Nights due to the imagination of some caravaner drunk on *kif*? It had really existed, that colossal city dating from antediluvian epochs! How could they doubt it, confronted by those enormous ruins covering such a vast area, attesting to gigantic constructions, the extent and mass of which proved the existence of a magnificent, opulent, splendidly-flourishing civilization, whose treasures were doubtless buried there, even more fabulous than Nathaniel had said?

For these stone blocks, which the others took for rocks in chaos, were ruins. And although Joson, like the Irishman, was a Celt inclined to magical dreams, he was also a former cadet of the *Borda*, a naval officer, with a mind sufficiently cultivated to be able to recognize inscriptions, although without being able to decipher their meaning. Now, in these pretended rocks, in many places, signs were traced, not by natural striations but visibly "written" by human hands. Joson had even discovered several depictions of the zodiac, of a capital and manifest importance, of which he had been able to explain to the ill-educated Julot both the character and the significance, which will be explained later.

From all that, Joson concluded, not as a Celt fond of tales, but as a sagacious reasoner, that it was a prehistoric city of an advanced civilization, perhaps as rich or even richer than our own-and, in any case, superior to those that preceded ours. For, by the amplitude and enormity of its vestiges, the city in the desert—Ibn-Aoud-Gadfaia's city, rediscovered by them, Julot and Joson—triumphed effortlessly over the most illustrious and most marvelous of dead cities. Reconstituting it in the imagination—the imagination of a scientist rather than that of a poet—merely according to the testimony of its vestiges, it was manifest that, by comparison, Thebes, Memphis, Ecbatana, Nineveh and Babylon must have been modern and relatively poor cities.

"Yes, Boss poor! As Pantin might be said to be, compared with Paris."

It was thus that Julot, instructed by Joson, had summarized the matter picturesquely. And he and Joson had seen, mirrored in mirages, by the blinding sun that was roasting the

243

ruins, palaces in gold and precious stones, as sumptuous as the chimerical edifices of the clouds at sunset.

It had been necessary, however, to leave those mirages with empty hand—bloodied hands, in fact. A part of the troop had revolted, weary of that halt in the mountainous desert. A battle had started. Joson and Julot had retained their mastery, after the slaughter of half their men, but Joson was wounded and his baggage had been destroyed by the fire. All that remained of his geographical and scientific observations was a single portfolio he had carried on his person, in which, fortunately, were the latest detailed data recorded in order to determine the exact location of the city.

Of the road to reach it—which he had also traced, with carefully-determined reference-point, as befit a naval officer—it was now impossible to have the slightest notion, as it was of the route they needed to follow to return through the equatorial forest. All the instruments—chronometers, sextants, theodolites and compasses—had been smashed, but the essential thing as safe, since Joson had in his portfolio the exact location, fixed by several scrupulous measurements and checked by various verifications, of the discovered "Eldorado."

"Except," Julot had said, "to get back here overland—nothing doing! For in the whole of Africa, it would be like finding a pinhead in a sackful of lead."

"We'll come back by air, then," Joson had replied, "flying."

"As in a dream!" Julot had concluded, adopting a pose from a sentimental romance, raising his eyes to the heavens with his hand on his heart. After which he had warbled, in a whimpering voice that stammered through the tremolos: "All I have in my hour of need, is half of a *hirondelle*."[64]

---

[64] A *hirondelle* is a swallow, but substituting "swallow" in the supposed couplet wrecks the last vestige of its scansion. The citation is metaphorical; Julot's reference to a dream suggests that "half of a *hirondelle*"—a bird possessed of only one wing—is his equivalent of "*l'aile du rêve.*" Unlike Julot, how-

And that while carrying his leader on his back, because Joson had a bullet-hole in his leg and was shivering with fever, and he did not want to confide him to another bearer. For at that moment, as they were returning through the darkness of the forest, they were paddling through a marsh, slipping in the mud, and as there was a danger of falling, of getting stuck therein, the brave Parisian would not rely on any but his own feet—those of a gutter-cat—to protect his boss, who he adored, from a fatal misstep.

The two friends—for the escapee from Biribi and the "little Chouan" had arrived at a complete fraternity—were obliged to separate, however, once they got back to the Cape. Joson still had a few relics of his fortune lodged with a notary in Paris, on which he needed to draw. He had abandoned what remained to him at the Cape to furnish Julot with a small stake, in order to clear the way for an attempt at mining in the Transvaal. He had re-embarked, with his passage paid and three hundred-franc bills in his pocket, promising once again to return.

This time, however, the promise had not been kept, for reasons of *force majeure*. The vague residue of his fortune left in Paris was too vague—just enough to stop him dying of hunger. And again, month after month, and then years, had been used up doing nothing but scraping along, trailing his gaiters through gambling-dens, then taking lamentable jobs for nothing more than food and a bed, sometimes under false names, so ashamed was the descendant of the Ponthual-Ploërs.

A junior teacher in schools devoid of pupils, an overseer industrial labor in dilapidated factories, a clerk in a circulating

---

ever, Richepin would also have been familiar with Sully Prud-homme's poem "*À l'hirondelle*," in which reference is made to the entire bird taking off on "*l'aile du rêve*," so he might have a slightly different equation in mind, in which half of a *hirondelle*/one wing would be equal to *half* a dream—which would make a kind of sense in the context of the subsequent development of his story.

library, a maritime insurance salesman, a recruiter of spade-workers for emigration—those, among other calamitous avatars, some less strange, were endured by the genteel Joson, son of the exquisite Comtesse. Oh, how that noble and delicate creature, so elegant, with the angelic voice, and her expression of smiling pride and distinguished melancholy, would have suffered and silently wept to see her Joson amid the rolling dirty waves of promiscuity, stirred by the eddies of poverty!

More than once, afflicted by incessant bad luck, impotent to raise his head in the swell of relentless blows, he had been tempted to end it al by suicide It was precisely the memory of his mother, the tears that she would have shed over such an end—the tears that she would have shed in Heaven—that had prevented him every time. For, as in the time of his debauchery, today in his time of trials, in despair as in vice, the Breton who was the "Little Chouan" conserved all the integrity of his Catholic faith. And to know that his mother was in Heaven, while he would be damned, was a terror that he had—he, who had never been afraid of anything in the world—and it ensured that he never lost that support.

From the depths of the abyss into which he had sunk, the thrust of that faith had brought him back to the surface, and to land. One day, after many other and worse misfortunes that it would be superfluous to narrate. Joson had recovered his manhood, emerged from the mire and even the quasi-strife, as an employee of a company importing and storing produce from colonies in Ethiopia, something of a colonist himself, and seemed to have achieved a sufficiently tranquil life of honest ease, increasing every day, beneath a sky that pleased him, reminding him of his crazy years of African adventure.

He was then nearly forty years of age, no longer thought about anything but his business and the routines of his existence, and did not even have the idea at the back of his mind that his ease might become wealth and perhaps permit him one day to realize his dream regarding the city in the desert. It seemed to him more curious, and sweeter, to be alone in retaining that dream, and to consider it always and uniquely as a dream.

Not having had, for a long time now, any news of Guérinet, alias Julot, who had replied to his letters at first, he had resigned himself to believing that he was dead—as he surely must have been, the poor devil, to neglect his boss. No one in the world, in consequence, knew anything about the fabulous city. The secret bequeathed by Ian-Aoud-Gadfaia to Nathaniel O'Deekle. having died with the Irishman and then with the Parisian, would not be long delayed in becoming a dead star in the sky, once Joson, in whose mind its last glimmer was mirrored, had died.

And yet, Joson piously conserved, like a relic, the portfolio containing the pages in which he had recorded with so much care, carefully checked by means of reference-points and scrupulous calculations, the exact location of the new "Eldorado." And often, on consulting those yellowed leaves in private, he smiled, without knowing why. And then, always, as if the smile had triggered the memory of Julot, he recalled the ruffian warbling, in a whimpering voice, stammering over the tremolos: "All I have in my hour of need, is half of a *hirondelle*."

After which—in such a way as to encourage the belief that the trigger had also started the mechanism of the memory working, albeit backwards—the reply came back to him that he had made to his companion, who was carrying him through the marsh on his back: "We'll come back by air, then, flying."

And he did, indeed, see himself, transformed into a swallow, returning on beating wings to the Eldorado whose location he knew. But it was no longer a desire for realization; it was purely a dream, a fairy-tale. Only the child-like and poetic Celt enjoyed it, not the man of action any longer. Joson-swallow, Joson the little bird of romance, was the Joson who now set out on the chimerical wing of dream toward that reality, changed henceforth into a dream: toward the desert mountain of rocks in chaos; the so-called rocks covered by inscriptions that were the ruins of the colossal, magnificent antediluvian city full of treasures, older, more civilized, more splendid and more enormous than Thebes, Memphis, Ecbatana, Nineveh and Babylon.

XXXII

What will certainly obtain less credit than such a tissue of adventures—almost banal nowadays, in spite of their copious diversity and curious unlikelihood—is the telepathic thread with which we have said that they were indeed linked, and which will be described in a few brief affidavits without commentary. Hardened skeptics will smile. The conscientious historian, a noter—almost a notary—of gathered facts, has only to record them. Those who have had analogous experiences in their own lives will not smile.

Indubitably, with regard to his conscious memory, Joson only had confused images relating to Genevieve. In the two circumstances in which these images might have had occasion to become more precise—the deaths of the Comtesse and Abbé Denis—they had remained vague. And yet, we have affirmed, between her and Joson a veritable chain had been forged. For the phrase "telepathic thread" employed above, is, in fact, too much of an understatement.

Chain—yes, that is a more expressive word. And a chain forged—another appropriate word—by a communion without communication. For here, as in "wireless" telegraphy, there was no contact!

And in addition, the impressions had been received without conscious perception taking account of them, or the shadow of an advertisement able to serve as a memorandum.

Nevertheless, at a given moment, those received impressions manifested their existence, the dispatched effluvia seeming to cry out: "Here I am! Don't try to comprehend or even to perceive by means of any of your 'usual' senses. Vibrate and forget."

Then, at another unexpected moment, there was the miracle—almost commonplace, in telepathy—of the vibration that reproduces itself, the effluvia that become active, the picture that develops, of the unconscious memory offering its treasures to the exploitation of the "revelator" of conscious reason.

But enough of vain, perhaps erroneous, explanations—which only proceed, moreover, by means of images and which commit the grave sin of appearing to be disguised commentaries. The facts, undeniably, are there, which want to speak, and with what eloquence, even troubling those who will not be convinced.

You will soon learn, in the shock of the final encounter, what riches of magnetism and electricity had "accumulated" over time in Joson and Geneviève. That was the irrefutable proof that it was without their knowledge and complicity that their parts had been prepared. You have seen Geneviève become gradually unaccustomed to thinking about him intensely, and that he had scarcely every thought about her with any consciousness of so doing. And yet, the tension of their occult "accumulators" was such, unconsciously, that certain effluvia had been projected and perceived, manifest harbingers of the prodigious final spark that was to amalgamate them.

Here, narrated without the slightest artifice, without any attempt at literary effect, are those few anticipatory revelations of the magnetic and electric current between the two souls, which united them: testimonies carefully checked, of guaranteed authenticity.

The first time, Joson had, unexpectedly, a vision—clear, this time—of Geneviève. It was not, as usual, the vague drifting apparition of something white passing before Abbé Denis' black robe, which might have reminded Joson in an imprecise fashion of the forgotten communicant. It was, against the wall of the ruined chapel, above the sinister sheen of Kawchmôr, the sad silhouette of a Geneviève seemingly ready to let herself fall into the viscous and avid mire.

Now, comparing the dates, Joson was then completing his first African expedition with his near-fatal attack of cerebral fever, and for her part, Geneviève was in the middle of her famous "black hole," struck by that epileptiform crisis of nerves of which the physicians had no understanding.

The image of Geneviève had, at that moment, been positively resuscitated in Joson's memory. It had not lasted longer than a lightning-flash; then darkness had fallen over the image again, which had become once again the vague fleecy whiteness in front of Abbé Denis' black robe.

Three more times, in a completely different fashion each time, there had been an abrupt establishment of current between their conscious selves, of which he, Joson, became conscious—always with lightning rapidity, after which darkness thickened more blackly, it seemed, since the memory had not been vivified.

At the moment when, after having received the insulting letter from Julot, he had suddenly and bravely resolved to set forth again, leaving Parris, amputated from his laxity, he had heard ringing within him a certain burst of laughter, as of small bells, about which he had said to himself: *Damn it! Where have I heard it before, that particular burst of laughter?*

And immediately, without *seeing* Geneviève's face, he had had the corner of his mother's boudoir before his eyes, where, in response to an anecdote about the *Borda* humorously narrated by Joson, the girl had laughed in that fashion. And he had remembered then, with delight, no longer Geneviève, nor even her laughter, but the soft and musical voice of the Comtesse, his exquisite and adored mother, saying to him that evening: "What a pretty laugh she has, that child! Like tiny silvery bells."

Now, at the moment when Joson decided upon his great voyage to Ibn-Aoud-Gadfaia's city, that was exactly the moment when Geneviève, at eighteen years of age, finally sensed the sun of her genius escaping from the eclipse in which it had nearly been extinguished.

The interval when Joson made his halt in the fabulous city, among the rocks covered with inscriptions affirming a civilization more ancient, more opulent and more advanced than those of Memphis, Thebes, Ecbatana, Nineveh and Babylon, that unique interval in his life, was also the interval, no

251

less unique in Gasguin's life, when Geneviève enabled him to enter the portal of renown on the victorious caravels of the three famous papers. Now, three times in that interval—three distinct times, but by virtue of a manifestation always parallel—Geneviève had "disturbed" Joson, in direct confrontation with those mysterious inscriptions. The third commotion, a sort of strange shock on the back of his neck, had been produced on the discovery of the characteristic zodiac. And Joson had said, each time, to Julot;

"Who is sending me that electric discharge, like the blow of a warm blade?"

And when he said that, the odor of Geneviève had passed through his nostrils: a odor that she had had one evening, after having spent all day collecting gorse on the heath and being, so to speak, clad in it. Her face, beneath the costume of flowers, he had not "seen" at all, but he had smelled it, had breathed in the strong and intoxicating scent through the flared nostrils of his erne's beak, in which was mingled the honey of the heath, the gold of gorse and that of the sun burning it, the iodine of seaweed in the violet of salt-marshes through the fir-trees, and the girl's unripe apricot flesh.

Finally, the supreme telepathic manifestation of Geneviève had taken place at the moment when Joson, with his finger on the trigger of his revolver, was about to put an end to his poverty in all the shameful mire, and had been deflected by the "sight" of the tears that his mother would shed over that death of the damned. Just as the tears had flowed in diamond drops, stabbing him repeatedly in the heart, a breath of fresh air had passed over those burning wounds, sealing them like a furtive kiss. And that breath and that kiss had had a voice, distant and singing, as in a sort of celestial telephone. And Joson had distinctly recognized that voice: it was the one with which he had heard Geneviève recite, in a childish murmur, the entire litany of his names and nicknames, which she repeated like a formula, and which, during that tragic moment, she repeated likewise, distinctly, in the hallucination he believed that he was experiencing.

Now, someone was with Geneviève at that tragic moment, of the crucial nature of which she was absolutely unaware; she was then utterly absorbed in a moment of intense life herself, since she was breathless in confrontation with the last manipulation revealing to her the definitive formula from which her theory of electrical fertilization as to emerge. And while her conscious reason was extended in that work, that birth-process, her unconscious self was doubtless extended recklessly toward the individual in peril, whose peril it "saw." For Aunt Line heard Geneviève then, with the absent-minded expression she often had, and without quitting her work in progress, mechanically murmuring the end of the fairy tale, the end of the fanned-out tail, which she often seemed to recite without attaching any more significance to it than to a nursery rhyme:

"Monsieur le Comte Elme-Cast-Jagut-Marie-Joseph de Ponthual-Plouër, Seigneur des Eihens, des Pierres-Sonnantes, des Treize-Îles and other places, also known as Joson, as so known as the Little Chouan!"

And if Aunt Line had been able to take note of the exact time, to the tenth of a minute, when those chanted words had quit Geneviève's lips, and if someone with Joson had also been able to take note of the instant when he had lifted his finger from the trigger and dropped his revolver, the two notations would have been compounded into one. And similarly, it was with the measured beat of a single metronome that Joson and Geneviève had then, without pronouncing a single word, uttered a long and profound sigh, during which their two beings, without knowing it, fused in the unconscious and were only one from then on.

No one, moreover, except Aunt Line, if she had had the gift of extracting the ultimate consequences of what she "felt" with so much force, would have been capable of perceiving everything that sight would inflate, any more than anyone can divine the series of futures imprisoned in a seed that gestation will liberate.

Even if they had been conscious of their beings fusing in the unconscious, could Joson and Geneviève ever have imagined from what profound depths that sigh came, and toward what distance it was going? Even believing in their telepathic communion, they would have attributed that strange sigh, uttered in unison and toward one another, Joson to the setting aside of idea of suicide, Geneviève to the idea of the "eureka" greeting her discovery—or vice versa, which would have been better still.

And it was even better than that, in truth! And perhaps Aunt Line alone experienced the vague, obscure, unexpressed frisson of it. In sum—she would have said, had she been able to translate it—what was inflated by that long and profound sigh was the occult and absolute certainty, with regard to that tragic moment, that the unique self formed by their two unconscious selves melting into one single entity then acquired. For it sensed, itself, and even "knew"—such a sentiment being the equivalent of the most exact knowledge—that on that moment had depended, not merely the personal fate of each of them, but the fate of the entire world that was about to be born, unforeseen and nevertheless "expected," from their imminent collaboration.

"Expected by whom?" some ironist will be sure to ask.

"Expected," Aunt Line would have replied, "by the flower of the blood of the Hescheboix."

XXXIII

Had there been a slowing down, a cooling, of these telepathic communications between Joson and Geneviève? Or had the established current never had any further need to manifest itself to their conscious self, because of the sufficient satisfactions it found exercising itself in the occult, unknown to conscious accumulation? Who can tell? The patent fact is that the mutual thoughts of the two beings, materially so far apart, had been as if disjointed in the course of the last seven years, during Joson's sojourn in Ethiopia and Geneviève's work at the Vaugirard laboratory.

It was now in a very vague voice, almost without expression, that Geneviève occasionally repeated to Aunt Line: "How we loved one another at first sight!" That, you will remember, in the tone in which she groaned: "To think that it's over—over, alas!" And without even articulating that sad "alas" sincerely, which had become a neutral, empty word now that Geneviève put so little heart into it.

You will recall, on the other hand, with what obstinacy Aunt Line took up arms against that, trying to reignite the love that seemed extinct. She vouched for the fact that it was merely lying dormant beneath the ashes.

And for his part, Joson the commercial representative, Joson the warehouse-manager, Joson the colonist had ended up no longer even nurturing his Celtic reveries of the tale of the fabulous city. His forties turned into a precocious retreat from all action, whether in thought, in imagination, in dreams or in smoking opium, save for his current business affairs, commercial or colonial. He no longer opened the portfolio with the yellow pages containing the location of the Eldorado for years on end. Julot's refrain was obliterated in his memory, no longer humming, even mechanically, on his lips.

Having no Aunt Line with him to watch over the fire lying dormant beneath the ashes, he seemed even more detached than Geneviève from the previous telepathic linkage, not only from her but from his own past. The few English newspapers he read for business purposes did not even cause him to prick up his ears at the announcement of the first attempts at aviation. He had only seen it as a nascent sport, amusing, which he would have liked to try once, but no longer. The whistling of those human flights in the sky had not reminded him of what he had said to Julot in the hope of returning to the magical city: "We'll come back by air, then, flying."

It seemed, therefore, that nothing would henceforth unite those two existences, so far apart, each so devoted to its own evolution, now fixed, closed and sealed off from the other, no longer even having that Hertzian wave which has made the sensitive to one another throughout the past, albeit in an occult and unapprehended fashion. And that was certainly the irrefutable conclusion that anyone inexpert in the subtle psychology of the reflexes and the unconscious would have drawn from their present condition, with the complacency of partiality.

Aunt Line, nevertheless, concluded differently, if not in words, at least in determination. It is true that she was no expert in any psychology, nor in telepathy, nor any science whatsoever, theoretically understood. Does Fabre's wasp follow courses to learn anatomy and the infallible surgical procedure by which it contrives the paralysis of the living prey necessary to its larva, though? In the same way, Aunt Line "knew" that the fire of love persisted, lying dormant beneath the ashes of her dear Cinderella's heart, and that the genius of that pretended, seemingly resigned, old maid needed that love to blossom, and that the supreme prey reserved for that adored larva was that love, and, therefore, that Joson and Geneviève would come together again—or, rather, that they had never been separated, even during that last seven years when it seemed that they had become strangers to one another.

What Aunt Line lacked in the matter of giving reasons and putting forward proofs to clarify these obscure sentiments, stating their results in current terminology instead of burying them in the clay of sibylline words, was a faculty that the women of tomorrow will surely have. Reservoirs of atavistic science, supposedly instinctive but nevertheless intellectual in essence, they can only dispense the profound intuition by means of which they "sense" life in meager measure today. Tomorrow, having doubtless renounced struggling with us in terms of pure reason, giving all that can and ought to be given of their maternal treasure of unanalyzable acquisitions, they will reveal the keys to secrets that we men have never been able to decipher.

Aunt Line was one of those who do not fear, even today, to allow that as-yet-infantile and stuttering language to speak within them and through them. At the risk of being taken for an old madwoman, a failed *merlifiche*, a witch without a broomstick or, at least, a spouter of ridiculous nonsense, she let out—you have seen her in action—all that had might have been severely stifled, and set up the sometimes burlesque or monstrous images of the phantoms she "saw" in the mists of the future.

And that is why, on the day when the telegram from St. Petersburg announced that the Alexandra Prize had been awarded to Monsieur Thibaud Gasguin's paper, while the professor swelled with pride, the worthy Yvernaux clapped his hands and Geneviève started dancing like a little girl, the octogenarian contented herself with mumbling between her gums: "Now the time has finally come for me to repeat it, and for you to hear me, *ch'tiote*."

She had her white eyes, dancing as before, and her pursed lips, whose corners were flecked with light foam—and Geneviève knew, moreover, that those, in the old lady, were the signs of her own "displaced state," similar to the particular state into which Geneviève put herself with her fumigation of herbal philters. So, leaving her father and godfather to congratulate one another, she took Aunt Line into the next room in order to say to her, anxiously and tremulously: "What is it that you have to repeat to me, and what is so necessary for me to hear?"

"How you loved one another at first sight!" muttered the old woman, in a distant tone. Then, drilling her with her sharpest and most penetrative gaze, she added, in an increasingly indistinct murmur; "And now that will be again. Oh, soon! Yes, soon!"

After which she repeated it several times, each time more obscurely, as if, the more secure she became in the occult, the less distinct she became in the visible. Geneviève recognized in that the most profound hypnosis into which Aunt Line's essential, unconscious soul plunged in the fullness of divinatory action. Her anxiety redoubled, oppressively, because of the words, often spoken in the distant and near past, which had lost all suggestive force for her a long time ago, but which, at that moment, recovered an extraordinary vigor, like desiccated infusoria suddenly put in contact with water.

"Will it be again, you ask?" said Aunt Line. "Since I know it! Since I see it!" And the old woman seemed to be litanizing, repeating with a monotonous insistence: "Since I know it! Since I know it! Since I see it! Since I see it!" Litanies that were punctuated by the brusque affirmation, proffered with authority by lips sinuously articulating, firmly and clearly: "*Amon!* You hear me, *ch'tiote*, you hear me."

Then came a gentle flow of honeyed words, as if sung—or, rather, twittered by the chirping of a swallow departing for the lands of the sun: "And we shall be three to tell it, that fairy tale, three, *amon*, three, one a man who will not be your father, but will be, will be, will be..."

And, in a repetitive whisper like that of a little child lulling itself to sleep endlessly singing the chorus of a nursery rhyme—"*il faut, il faut, tirlifaut, tirlifaut, tirlifaut*"—she ruminated, in indistinct soft, dribbling syllables, swallowed with trickles of saliva, the Breton litany of forenames, names, titles and soubriquets of...

To escape the oppression, which had become nightmarish, Geneviève abruptly interrupted Aunt Line, shaking her wrists.

"Come on, then!" she said. "What the devil has *he* to do with the Alexandra Prize? Hear me, in your turn, eh?"

She immediately regretted her brutality, however, on seeing the sudden deathly pallor that covered Aunt Line's face like a shroud, and listening to the hoarse whistle of her respiration, resuming a natural rhythm, and observing in her eyes, ceasing their dance, the vitreous tone that advertised the end of the hypnotic and divinatory crisis—which is to say, the momentary death of the Sibyl Aunt Line.

Indeed, Geneviève could not get any more out of her thereafter, save for vague replied like: "It's over now; I no longer see; I no longer know." Or bleak jokes such as "Was I saying stupid things again, *amon*? About the *young man*?" She pronounced the last phrase in a comical fashion, in order to make Geneviève laugh—but applied to Joson, it was sinister.

"I'm no longer a *ch'tiote*," Geneviève replied, rather bitterly. "And Joson, today, must be nearly forty."

Aunt Line persisted stubbornly in her comical vein, and retorted—mischievously, she thought; stupidly, in Geneviève's opinion: "Do you think he's too old to marry you, *cattelinette* who has coiffed Saint Catherine?"

That image of marriage, with the evocation of herself as an old maid, offended Geneviève, who left the amazed old woman there, behind a slammed door, in order to go rejoin the two men who were still talking excitely about the Alexandra Prize. But Yvernaux was waxing lyrical in a fashion she knew all too well, about Siberia becoming the world's granary, and Gasguin was only taking about the roubles to come. Both of them irritated her. She left them alone too, intemperately.

"What's wrong with her?" Gasguin asked. "One might think that winning the lovely prize doesn't please her."

As Yvernaux continued to wax lyrical, in an epic fashion, Gasguin emphasized: "The patent's been taken out, however, firmly guaranteed. Besides, thanks to my advice and prudent editing, the theory alone is explained in the paper; the practice is carefully reserved." Then, with a grandiose gesture, he added: "What, then? What does she want? The moon?"

And it was, in fact, "the moon," in the coarse terminology of Gasguin, a son of "sod-busters," Gasguins all, in his bones. Yes, the moon, since her anguish came primarily from this: that now that electrical fertilization was resolved, she would finally have to resolve "radioactive aviation." Now, she sensed that it was ready to spring from her unconscious, which was solely occupied by it; but at the same time, Aunt Line had just revealed to her that in the ultimate depths of that unconscious, still subsisting, alive, tenacious, also ready for resolution, with whatever force, toward whatever end and by whatever actions, there was Joson. And was it not wanting the moon, like a spoiled child, to dream of that wing, open in mid-air, with him?

"To dream" is an understatement! To know that something was about to hatch, and to know, too, that *he* would be involved in that hatching: HIM!

In the "accumulators" of profound electricity, of slow magnetism, that had been working within her for some twenty years, which she had thought discharged, she perceived an enormous change, an imminent activity, and she wondered if there was any means of avoiding it—for she was afraid, without knowing why.

She remembered her terror regarding the possible solution of radioactive aviation. She remembered having said to Aunt Line: "I have an urge, with regard to that which it remains for me to know, *no longer to want to be the person who will know it*." And also this statement, heavier still in its menacing prognostication: "I would rather not be the person who will know it, because I'm a coward, because I have an idea that *knowing it will do me harm*."

Now, all of a sudden, a little while ago, while Aunt Line was playing the sibyl, her eyes dancing, the prophetic foam at the corners of her mouth, her voice distant, or authoritarian, or litanizing, or twittering, or falling asleep on the thread of a dream, while she evoked the two months of paradisal vacation and the first communicant's childish love, and the resurrection of that love, during those few moments, Geneviève too had had a kind of aura of prescience—and how cruel and suppliant!

She had had a vision of Joson winged, wanting to fly toward her in order to ask her for the figures and the practical solutions of the paper on electrical fertilization—and she had had great difficulty stopping herself crying out recklessly: "No, no! Don't fly like that! You'll have a horrible fall! Wait! Wait a little longer! Your wings are poor. It only needs one. That wing I shall furnish myself. Wait! Wait!"

And that vision had been succeeded by another, in which she offered him the promised wing, but without being certain that he would be able to make use of it, nor, especially, whether she wanted to let him make use of it—because someone whispered in her ear: "If you are not gods, you will die miserably."

And she ended up alone in her room, saying to herself, while her teeth chattered: "That's what I meant when I said to Aunt Line last year that I didn't want to be the person who would know it, because I had an idea that knowing it would do me harm. And I fear it now. Already, I feel that it's doing me harm."

XXXIV

It is via Yvernaux, on the threshold of the "displaced state," in private, religiously listened to as if he were reciting a poem, that it is necessary to hear the meeting of Geneviève and Joson recounted. Then, and only then, can you grasp the strange scene, the violent color and savor of it, positive and mysterious at the same time, including the most obscure underside, often impossible to clarify in rational terms but also often illuminated, suddenly and fundamentally, by a lyrical tone or gesture, a crazy analogy or a fulgurant image. An approximate translation of that living poem, complete, or rather incomplete, with all the approximations that translation involves—being always insipid and bloodless—will be given here.

It is undoubtedly appropriate first, however, in order that the scene may be put in context, to indicate the place, the time, the surroundings and the state of mind of the participants. Yvernaux, primarily a poet, paid little heed to that. The poem he recited was, however, a kind of dramatic poem, requiring this short expository preface to set the scene.

It was evening, after dinner, in the Rue Malebranche, in the bare tiled room that Geneviève laughingly called her "thinking room." Its furniture comprised a sofa-bed sheathed in faded yellow rep; four rickety mahogany chairs upholstered in the same rep, redolent of an old hotel-room; a little faience stove like those in concierge's lodges in the poor quarters, inactive in the present month of July, on which books and papers were stacked; a blackboard attached to the wall, cluttered with numbers and diagrams traced in chalk; and finally—and most especially, this last item taking up a good third of the room—a large high-topped architect's table in white wood, set on two trestles. The last-named appeared to be for the use, not of a woman, even a scientist, but someone who was indeed an architect, and also an electrician, a manufacturer and an engineer, not to mention an agronomist, and perhaps even a practitioner of astrology or kabbalism, for scattered upon it, pell-mell, were construction-plans on tracing-paper, drawings of buildings and machines, catalogues and ready-reckoners relating to various trades, and a whole heap of sheets of paper that looked like pages torn from a grimoire, so replete were they with calculations mounted on top of one another, drawings and eccentric graphic designs, equations entangling the obscurity of their figures, signs and symbols, encircled, underlined or crucified with multicolored pencil-strokes.

Ordinarily, no one except Aunt Line ever came into the "thinking room"—which the lyrical but sometimes mocking Yvernaux also called, when he was in an irreverent mood, "the 'ladies only' compartment." Geneviève liked to be able, in that corner sealed like an animal's den, to let herself be carried away by thoughts of any kind: the formless abortions of her projects, the most chimerical fetal monsters of her hypotheses. It was her *capharnaüm*—which Aunt Line pronounced, in the Thiérachian fashion "*cafourniau.*"

That evening, Geneviève had not only admitted into it, but invited in her father and her godfather, in order that they might have a serious discussion. It was a matter of deciding whether the 65,000 francs of the Alexandra Prize, available in a few days, in a first practical exercise in fertilization by electricity, or whether to resume the work on aviation that had been suspended. In reality, though—as she admitted later—that was only a pretext.

"What had led me," she said then, "to the unusual idea of gathering around me in my den the only three individuals whose affection for me was assured, was a secret fear of what was about to happen that evening. I didn't know what it would be, but I needed not to be exposed to it on my own."

And Aunt Line corroborated this retrospective testimony in advance, by saying as soon as she came in, as if she had smelled that anxiety— of which Geneviève had given no evidence: "Have no fear, *ch'tiote*. There are three of us to defend you, *amon*!" Against what? She did not know, any more than Geneviève did—in fact, she experienced a short of cheerfulness herself that evening, and found herself, as she put it, "quite well."

The question raised had been formally discussed, Gasguin opining in favor of the practical experimentation that might allow is theory to bear fruit and make money, Yvernaux supporting the opposite opinion, in favor of the risk of pecuniary sacrifice in order to resume the progress—or, rather, the flight—toward the "conquest of the gulfs," and Geneviève seeming only to be concerned with impartially weighing the pros and cons without issuing any personal preference. As for Aunt Line, she was only listening to Geneviève's heartbeat, and that of her own heart, which were in harmony in drumming in their temples—she explained later—a hum of "news *en route*." And she saw and heard clearly that Geneviève, while putting on a show of following the debate between her father and her godfather, was entirely extended inside herself toward that warning noise, which was increasing her anxiety.

The little room was it by two oil-lamps, and, the window being closed on that stormy July evening, there was a heavy and numbing warmth therein. Nevertheless, Gasguin had not succeeded in having it opened. In response to the gesture he had sketched, Geneviève has stopped him with a cry of alarm: "No, no! Don't open it, on any account!"

"Why?" he had asked, not understanding her fear, devoid of any apparent cause.

But Aunt Line had relied, in a peremptory tone, approved by Geneviève's affirmative nod of the head: "Because they'll hear us in the courtyard."

"Bah!" said Yvernaux. "What we're saying here is of no interest to anyone in the house."

"What we're saying at present, no," said Geneviève.

"But," Aunt Line added, mysteriously, "what we'll be saying shortly is."

Gasguin and Yvernaux looked at the two women, and then looked at one another, having observed that, although they themselves still did not understand, the others certainly did. And Gasguin, winking and taping is forehead with his index finger, secretly signaled to Yvernaux that they were in "in one of their funny moods." But Yvernaux, in his turn, felt that their anxiety was also taking hold of him.

"Should we send out for a little beer?" he asked, by way of diversion.

On which Aunt Line went out, in order to give their only maid orders to go and fetch some. "From the tavern in the Rue Soufflot," shouted the beer connoisseur. "Not from the little café next door, which only has hogwash."

"Oh, Godfather!" Geneviève observed. "Such preoccupations at a time like this!"

"What is it about this moment that renders it so solemn, then?" Gasguin wondered.

But Yvernaux had lowered his eyes, in confusion, feeling for the second time that he shared Geneviève's anxiety without knowing its source.

While the maid carried out her mission, Aunt Line stayed in the kitchen, where they could hear her nervously doing odd jobs. There was an embarrassed silence in the "thinking room," the door of which remained open. Before the black hole of the corridor, Geneviève shivered—which Aunt Line apparently perceived at a distance, for she hurried back, picked up one of the lamps and placed it on the sideboard next door in the dining-room, in order that it would brighten the darkness of the corridor.

When the maid came back, Aunt Line was heard telling her to put the liters of beer in the sink, under the tap, in order to keep them cool. Then she added, obligingly: "Now go to bed, my girl. We don't need you any longer. I'll open the door myself if..."

Geneviève coughed, as if she did not want anyone to hear the rest of the sentence, but Aunt Line waited until the pretended cough was complete in order to articulate clearly, in the silence, what she undoubtedly intended to be heard:

"If, by chance, someone comes."

With the maid gone and the entrance door firmly closed, Aunt Line came back at a slow and heavy pace—emphatic, Yvernaux had noted—and said, on the threshold of the "thinking room": "What? Yes, someone."

One might have thought that she was replying to a remark regarding the impossibility of that visit—a remark that no one had made, however. Except that Gasguin had vaguely thought about making it, and then limited himself to formulating it internally, and no more, accompanying it with a furtive shrug of the shoulders.

That was enough for Aunt Line, nailing him down with her stare, to insist: "Who, you ask? Can one every know?"

And on that, Geneviève, trembling from head to toe, her teeth clenched, had begged: "Shut up! Shut up! Don't say anything!"

Then she had abruptly seized the sponge hung up beside the blackboard and effaced, with rapid and feverish gestures, all the numbers and diagrams traced thereon, while she unclenched her teeth to mutter, angrily: "He mustn't! He mustn't! He mustn't!"

With a similar gesture, even more agitated, still punctuated by those voluble and repetitive prohibitions, she had gathered together the pieces of paper scattered on the table into a single pile, which she stacked, folded, rolled up and rapidly stuffed into the fireplace of the little stove. After which, unwinding and going limp, all of her feverish excitement melting into slow tears, she threw herself on to the sofabed, covering her face with her hands, as if ready to go to sleep.

"Are you feeling poorly?" Gasguin asked, affectionately—but an affection that seemed slightly mechanical, accustomed to cruses of this sort.

"Shh! Shh! Let's leave her alone," said Yvernaux, in a whisper, heading for the corridor with a muffled tread.

But as Gasguin prepared to follow him, she recovered from her abasement with a start and, standing up, with her hands together, without a word, imploring pity merely by her attitude, she had made it understood that she did not want to be abandoned and left alone. And Aunt Line, taking her in her arms like a besotted old nurse and sitting her down on her knees like a grandmother expert in coddling babies had sung into her ear, childishly, an old Burgundian nursery rhyme imported to Picardy by the "red-legs" of old, and which, since then, had been gradually rounded off, its conquering words modified into the caressing hisses of Thiérachian endearments:

> *Chés cloch's d'Avallon*
> *N'ony nin d'cotillons.*
> *Ch'est chell' d'Epône*
> *Qu'in ont d'chés longs.*
> *Pain bis, pain blinc, pain d'orche,*
> *Djormiras-tu bintôt, ma ch'tiote?*
> *Djormiras-to bintôt, min ch'tiote?*[65]

Had Yvernaux and Gasguin's hearts been stirred to their most intimate fibers by that cantilena, with words that they had heard when they were in their cradles, to the rocking music into which so many grandmothers had put their loving and consoling souls? Or had Aunt Line brought out, that particular evening, all the souls flourishing collectively in her own? Was there not an entire race, an entire country, expressed therein for Thiérachians? Or, again, had their real and essential worship of Geneviève, for the adored daughter and goddaughter, for the admired genius, which they felt while prey to such a profound and intense disturbance, rendered them more able to identify with her? All of that had truly increased their emotion at that moment, making the tears rolling down their cheeks heavy and inflating he sighs that broke into sobs in their

---

[65] Approximately: "The bells of Avalon/have no skirts./Those of Epone/wear long ones./Brown bread, white bread, any bread/Will you go to sleep soon, my darling?/Will you go to sleep soon, darling mine?"

throats, without their being ashamed of it, sexagenerians re-verted to being "*ch'tiots.*"

It was at that exact moment that the doorbell rang, vio-lently and imperiously—all the more so because it was abso-lutely unprecedented at such an inappropriate hour—ten o'clock in the evening—in the Gasguins' house. Immediately, everyone in the "thinking room," even Gasguin, understood that the "someone" about whom Aunt Line had said "If, by chance, someone comes" was on the landing.

And everyone—even Gasguin—had the sensation that the "someone" in question had not come by chance at all, was awaited anxiously by Geneviève and had virtually been an-nounced by Aunt Line's subliminal and divinatory thought—and that the arrival of the someone had something fateful about it,

That impression of mystery and fatality could not be at-tributed to Yvernaux's lyrical imagination, working retrospec-tively on the incident and enlivening it with involuntary em-broideries. Three facts authenticate the special character of the telepathy concluding in the final combination of the two ele-ments in the supreme spark.

The first fact is the hoarse cry uttered by Geneviève as the bell rang: "HIM!"

That "HIM!" was proffered with a force that inscribed it in hearing in three capital letters, and inscribed in those three letters the entire litany of his names.

The second fact is the word, again spoken by her, in a whisper, while Aunt Line went to open the door: "The wing!"

That word, although spoken very softly, was distinctly head by Yvernaux, who was only to understand it later.

He third fact, finally, is the scientific observation made by Gasguin himself—without any possible suspicion of ampli-ficatory lyricism, and therefore forming palpable evidence—of the electrical and magnetic "commotion" produced in the "thinking room" on all those gathered there, and not just the two active elements, by the meeting of Geneviève and Joson.

XXXV

So, when the bell rang, Geneviève had leapt off Aunt Line's knees and, standing upright, stiff and pale had uttered that stifled, hoarse, extraordinary "HIM!" in which all of her unconscious mind was concentrated, causing something like an explosion. Aunt Line had stood up in her turn, had looked deep into Geneviève's eyes, and had read there the whole of that mind, into which her own sank. Then, with an automatic tread, while the *ch'tiote* pronounced the incomprehensible word that Yvernaux was to understand subsequently, the old *merlifiche* had marched to the door as if she were heading for an irresistibly attractive gulf.

"Evidently," Yvernaux had noted, "she was acting thus under hypnosis, hypnotized by Geneviève, and 'knew' who she 'ought' to find behind the door."

Gasguin had sketched a vague interrogative gesture in his daughter's direction, who had not even replied instructing him to shut up, signifying that much by her statuesque immobility. The poor man's anxious eyes had turned toward Yvernaux, as if to implore: "If you understand, enlighten me."

But Yvernaux did not understand any more than he did, being as completely in the dark. Nevertheless, he was not distressed by that. On the contrary! He enjoyed feeling prey to a sort of magnetic intoxication, to which he abandoned himself delightedly. That, at least, he described the state into which he entered, consisting of being intensely impressed by things, and their immediate effects, without needing to acquire any logical notion of them and trace their causes. Thus, entirely given over to the tragic interest that he scented in the air, he had harshly imposed silence on Gasguin's untimely curiosity with a single glance, impeding the other's in order to satisfy his own, much better adapted to the circumstances.

"For there was," he said, "only one things to do: extend one's entire being to grasp it formally, opening all one's powers of 'receptivity' to the phenomena, inevitably prodigious, that were about to be produced."

Cocking an ear toward the landing, he had then clearly perceived this brief dialogue, whose words, quite simple in themselves, fixed themselves in his memory like arrows, because of the strange character they acquired as they developed, as will soon be evident:

"Excuse me for disturbing you at such an hour..."

"Who, you, disturb us? You, a friend?"

At this point, something was said in a very low voice, almost a whisper, which could not be made out, but which must have been the visitor's name, to judge by the response, which was: "What! You recognize me?"

The rest was clearly audible.

"Yes, *amon*, since we've always seen you."

"Oh! Really?"

"Indeed!"

"Where?"

"Here."

"Then my visit doesn't astonish you?"

"No, since we've been warned."

"By whom?"

"By you."

"Indeed? Explain, I beg you..."

"Come in. All will be explained."

At every phrase spoken by the visitor, Geneviève had been shaken by a great frisson, as if an electrical discharge were running through her. At each of Aunt Line's replies she had given evidence with her head that she was replying internally as the old woman was. And those two manifestations, observed by Yvernaux and Gasguin, led every time to an exchange of increasingly alarmed glances. And how strange a character the words of that dialogue, simple in themselves, were indeed taking on as they developed, when suddenly, after a few rapid and decisive footsteps in the corridor, the visitor arrived on the threshold of the "thinking room" and paused there.

For that visitor, whom Gasguin did not know at all, and nor did Yvernaux, but whom Aunt Line and Geneviève appeared, by contrast, to consider an old, intimate, almost quotidian friend—to judge by the replies of the former and the mute acquiescence of the latter—that extraordinary guest, simultaneously unexpected and more than expected, truly summoned, was the man who had disappeared twenty years before, the man whose effigy in the mystic window had itself paled among Geneviève's conscious memories, but whose soul had never ceased to communicate with, in the unconscious, and to melt into, those of the old digger wasp, Aunt Line, and her adored larva Geneviève.

Neither Gasguin nor even Yvernaux could know that for sure. Perhaps Yvernaux, alerted by a few confidences, had chanced to perceive it to some degree—and he was certainly not without a suspicion of it—but what both of them observed, without the slightest hesitation, Gasguin even better than Yvernaux, for he did so scientifically, out of professional habit, was the coming together of two poles, between which a spark was about to flare up, if not in electrical light, at least in a discharge of effluvia, fusing without lightning. And that the fusion in question, so long latent in the unconscious, was ready to manifest itself consciously, sensible to all those who were present, no one had the slightest doubt.

Yvernaux was enveloped in a kind of aura of fluids, in which he bathed and with which he continued to be intoxicated, was nevertheless paying sharp and perspicacious attention to the state of the others. Even if he had not perceived anything himself, the state the others were in would have been sufficient to reveal the real existence of that special aura. In fact, he saw Gasguin shivering, his hands trembling, the skin of his face grimacing with tics, his eyes bulging, short of breath. In the corridor, behind the visitor framed in the doorway, he divined the presence of Aunt Line, without being able to make her out clearly, by the vibration of the entirety of the octogenarian's old carcass, which seemed to him to be composed of dead leaves dancing in the breeze. And finally, here, close beside him, and there, on the threshold, he was able to examine at his leisure the two poles from which the commotion, supreme in imminence, sprang: Geneviève and the visitor; for it was exactly in the guise of two poles that they appeared to him—and in what relief, and with what unforgettable features!

Geneviève had never confessed the visions of her mystical window to her godfather; otherwise, Yvernaux would immediately have recalled it to mind as he contemplated Joson's head in that frame, thus lit from behind, the light in the corridor forming a kind of nimbus around it. On the other hand, she had mentioned the young Comte to him often enough, at one time, for him to imagine his portrait, and that portrait, Yvernaux had immediately remembered, Nothing had changed of that which was characteristic to it.

Joson still had the bulging forehead of an idealist, his masseters projecting like steel walnuts to clench his carnivorous jaws, his sternly-arched mouth, his erne's nose and petrel's eyes. The black cowl of his hair, in flat strips like those of certain algae, was perhaps a little less thick than before, allowing a clearer view of the gulfs of his temples, and lightly denuding the top of his cranium, where the tonsure of the forties was beginning to appear. A few of those algae, once so gleaming black, had turned to grey lichen, thus announcing the whitening foam of the years. Nevertheless, far from harming the man, age had embellished him.

To begin with, he had gained such precision that he had become an admirable paragon of manhood. The bow of his mouth, sterner than ever, gave evidence of the force that he would have, and could have, exerted to launch words of command like an arrow. His complexion, cooked by the African sun, with the additional patina of the desert, had the warm glow of bronze, reminiscent of those lost alloys in which Corinth amalgamated precious metals like gold, electrum[66] and

---

[66] Electrum is itself an alloy, albeit a natural one, of gold and silver, sometimes known as "white gold."

others whose very names have been lost, with copper. That rich coloration of ardent tones evoked long voyages, adventures, the simoom, the free life, hunts, battles and blood. It made the ridge of the nose, like sea-eagle's beak, stand out more clearly, and brightened the red flame of the petrel's eyes: the petrel intoxicated by peril, whose crazy joy is unleashed by storms.

It was that bird of storms, especially, more than the raptor, in sum, which imposed its vision upon Yvernaux, confronted with Joson framed in the doorway, forming a picture there in the manner of a living portrait. Dressed in an iron-gray suit tailored in the English style, with an ample, loose-hanging jacket and straight trousers slightly taped toward the bottom—a sort of colonial uniform—the man truly had the air of one of those prodigious and beautiful fliers, at rest, with the tips of its wings juxtaposed with its legs and touching the ground, and the stocks of it long curved pinions like raised shoulders, which make such birds resemble upright kites. His costume might have been plumage. His feet gripped the floor like claws. His arms seemed entirely ready to spread out like wings. And the human kite was, one might have thought, only awaiting a taut string to take off.

That string was Geneviève's gaze, which was about to tighten, and that gaze was the famous gaze of Idalie. Yvernaux thought so, as did Gasguin, both picking up the suggestion from a glance of Aunt Line's—who was shouting at them from a distance by means of her mute gaze, but with such eloquence: "Look at those *leumerottes, amon!*"

And in response to the silent summons of the old *merli-fiche*, auditory images sprang from their two memories in unison, singing with the sounds that they could hear—interior sounds but exteriorized by the momentary hyperacuity of their hypnosis—the four cadenced verses in Thiérachian patois that Aunt Line had once improvised when Geneviève had been born, of whose persistence in their inner depths they had been unaware:

Belle! Amon! Chi teu n'crès nin l'vielle,
Woit' à chès leum'rott's, min chtiot fieu.
L'iau veet'dins l'or f'chès gluer d'solel
Qu'étot l'fond d's yux d'min p'tit bon Dieu.

Geneviève had, at that moment, a deathly pallor that accorded with her statuesque rigidity. But that statue, although rigid, had appeared to Yvernaux to be made of mist, so gray, vague and lacking in density was it.

To be sure, even in normal times, the poor creature—especially since the last crises caused by her obsession, her terrors, her discipulary cure, and her two-part overwork—had not had a luxuriant complexion. Thin, frail and weak, her body almost puny, rather boyish in form, it would not have had to fad much to take on the silhouette of an apparition. Now, here—still according to Yvernaux's impressions—she seemed suddenly to have melted, without condensing, if not vaporized, and her effigy had become truly spectral.

But where all of her being remained gathered and concentrated, where the specter proved that it was very much alive, and with an intense, powerful, rich, imperious life, was in the gaze of her "*leumerottes*," like green water running over wisps of sunlight. And Aunt Line had not been mistaken thirty-three years before, when she had "recognized" in that gaze—still enclosed by eyelids but perceptible to her alone—the famous gaze of Idalie...

"My Idalie, my lovely sister, my little God."

She had seen it often enough since, when Geneviève was in the process of intellectual conquest, the gaze of the *cattelinette* in the process of amorous conquest. And Yvernaux, alerted by the old woman, had also feasted upon it, when he surprised is goddaughter, as he put it, in the *flagrante delicto* of her genius. Personally, on the other hand—on several occasions, you will recall—mastered by those eyes intimating an order to his submissive will, he had experienced their authoritarian and seductive fascination directly. After all, he was not like Gasguin, less nervous and less susceptible to influence, who had not been subject to their spell and their power.

At any rate, never—even in front of Aunt Line, with whom she lived as if she were alone, without hiding anything—had Geneviève had that gaze of Idalie's to such an extent as she had it now: that luminous, perverse, profoundly seductive, all-enveloping gaze, of both reckless passion and frenetic tyranny, which "willed" you to come toward it like iron toward a magnet, and more forcefully still, since you knew that in going toward it you were going to burn, as the wisps of sunlight became a blazing fire, and to drown, in the glaucous water in the depths of which that implausible blaze phosphoresced.

That there was all of that in Geneviève's gaze at that moment, the three spectators of the scene, including Gasguin, had the sensation—confused and contused in him, sharp in clear in the other two. And they perceived, too, that the man, prey to the attraction of that gaze, tried at first to resist it Aunt Line held back a cry of anguish or indignation, which she stifled in a grinding of her gums. Yvernaux's beard prickled and he had pins-and-needles in his fingertips. Gasguin, his mouth and eyes hermetically sealed and screwed up, held his breath.

Abruptly—according to Yvernaux's expressive image, not forged subsequently, but born of the fact itself—the string attached to the kite drew taut, and it took off.

"Oh," said the lyricist, his eyes tearful as he recalled it to mind, "what a magnificent tableau, materially and spiritually! For nothing could equal the physical beauty of it, nor reflect even vaguely its intimate splendor. It is necessary to limit oneself modestly to retracing, as best one can, the outline, or rather the diagram, in a line, nothing more, without the shadow of a commentary, leaving everyone the care of reconstituting that visible beauty and that intimate splendor, according to his means, by reference to those he has within himself."

And here, such as it is, from memory, is the approximate tracing of that sketch—or, rather, that diagram—a trifle disordered but sincere.

Joson, after a moment of profound silence and absolute immobility, which appeared to everyone to last an eternity, started walking, taking steps that were both short and heavy.

At the first step he dropped his soft felt hat, which fell limply, like a dead bird into muddy clay. That analogy, suggested to the other two witnesses by Yvernaux, was recognized as accurate. The effect had been lugubrious.

Joson's gait was singular and typical. Holding both hands in front of him, palms open, without any gestures, except to grope the air, he was reminiscent of a somnambulist, and also a bird of the penguin variety, firstly by the heaviness and brevity of his stride, and then—a characteristic detail—by the lack of swaying in his shoulders. They retained a strict horizontal line, his torso progressing in through a series of successive planes instead of following the jerky rhythm, with vertical displacements, of the sideways pressure of his alternately extended limbs.

And it was the opposition between the two rhythms of his gait, by virtue of its anomaly, that gave the impression of the internal struggle resulting from obedience to the tension of the string, everything within him still resisting it. Except that, henceforth, that resistance was the very condition of the tension, and thus of the advancement toward the victorious pole.

These various observations and remarks, due to Gasguin's loyal and severe control of Yvernaux's notations, give them the slightly rebarbative appearance of scientific observations. The strangeness of the subject-matter renders that aspect excusable.

There was, moreover, a veritable torture on both sides. The magnet, it seemed, took no more delight in enslaving the iron than the iron in being enslaved to the magnet. The fixed gleam of the petrel's eyes, with flashes of ruddy fire, was suddenly obscured by a kind of mist of tears, moistening them with imploring pity. The voluptuously imperious gaze of the seductive *cattelinette* sometimes softened into a tenderness that would have consented by asking for forgiveness. And both were suffering, as if they would rather the roles had been the other way around.

That was, in fact, the exact conclusion—momentarily, at least. For, as what followed will make clear, after the unexpected reversal produced at the moment of final combination, there was a complete return to the initial situation, and then a series of oscillations ending in the foreseen and normal fusion. At the exact moment of the discharge when the two electricities and magnetisms in latent communion came into manifest communication, however, it was suddenly Joson, the attracted element, who became the source of attraction, while Geneviève, ceasing to be the pole, behaved as if she were the magnetized needle.

By what seemingly-bizarre phenomenon of induction? By what obscure dynamic mechanism as yet unreduced into laws? Perhaps Geneviève, with her genius, aided by her father's method, will discover that one day. The observed fact, without seeking to know the cause, remains, in what Yvernaux calls so modestly and accurately its "diagrammatic" form—to which we shall return, the last stroke of the pen completing the promised picture.

Only three of the brief steps that Joson was slowly taking still separated him from Geneviève. Once again there was, on his part, a supreme effort of revolt, after a last attempt at supplication.

To his tear-veiled gaze, imbued with humble sadness, expressly meek, dulled by the shame of the imminent and ultimately certain defeat, Geneviève had replied with a gaze more heavily charged than ever with domineering insolence, demanding absolute submission. Under that injunction, as insulting as a whiplash, Joson came to a halt. All of his pride baulked. He stood firm. He was splendid.

His closed fingers digging their nails into his palms, he clenched both fists menacingly. His bulging forehead seemed about to explode. The ridge of his erne's nose, with the outline of a curved blade, was enhanced by the hollows formed near the tip by the harsh breath of a profound inspiration pinching the nostrils. His masseters tightened their steel walnuts as if to break his lupine teeth, which could be heard grinding with ferocious stridency. And his eyes, finally—hard, sharp, crazed, intoxicated by peril and adventure—the ruddy eyes of a petrel, for whom a storm is a celebration, were inflamed by such a blaze of fury that the blaze in Geneviève's eyes was eclipsed by it.

"It seemed to us," said Yvernaux, telling his tale, "that we were seeing the white polar star blown out by red Aldebaran." Thus he expressed the terrible shade of those ruddy eyes in that conflagration, by a purely physical but entirely apt image—he affirmed—and which might have given a painter exactly the right tone to represent "bloodstained water traversed by a flash of lightning."

The gaze by which Geneviève replied to that supreme attempt at resistance was so soft, so graceful, so seductive, so pitying, so sensual, so penetrating and so all-enveloping, all at the same time, that there really was—according to Yvernaux—no means of not yielding to it. It spoke so clearly, that gaze, that not only he and Aunt Line, who were habituated to read Geneviève, but also Gasguin, more obtuse in comprehension, and Joson, the stranger absent from her presence for twenty years, were unable to tolerate the prayer without having the desire to grant it, even if it required instant death.

It said, that gaze, that Geneviève was acting in this manner fatally, that she "needed" to conquer Joson's will, that it was necessary, that all the forces of their two unconscious selves were in accord in that respect, and that she begged pardon for being the pole toward which the magnet was coming, and that soon the two of the would only be one, and that it was atrocious, criminal and sacrilegious to attempt anything that might delay that magnificent, that divine soon, so desirous of coming into being, so long awaited, in which they too had been so keenly avid finally to be born.

Oh, it said all of that, that gaze! What admirable, prestigious, convincing speech Yvernaux credited to it—adding, in good faith: "And we all heard it thus. And that entire scene, moreover, which seemed to us eternal, only lasted two minutes at the most. Yes, two—no more! Scarcely that, in truth, between the first step taken by Joson toward Geneviève and the shock, the explosion, the combination of the two elements, the..."

But letting his lyricism overflow, too verbose when it had reached the "displaced state," would risk never reaching the end of those two minutes, so long and so full. Necessity obliges recourse once again to the modest outline, undoubtedly more expressive in any case, with which he contents himself on days when he consents to remain on the threshold of the displaced state, to complete the depiction of that extraordinary scene.

And the fact is that to that beautiful discourse, spoken wordlessly by Geneviève's gaze, by the *cattelinette* gaze knowing that the triumph of charm is the surest triumph of all, Joson no longer made any reply, save for admitting defeat in the impossible combat. The three small steps that he still had to take were covered in a single stride, as his hands opened again in order to be extended. Supplicant or caressing? Who knows? But vanquished—and, at the same time, invincible.

Aunt Line was still some distance away, all of her poor old octogenarian flesh trembling like a handful of dead leaves. Gasguin had unclosed his mouth and his eyes, and was breathing deeply, Yvernaux weeping exquisite tears that seemed to him to be pearls raining in his beard.

And suddenly, they all saw Geneviève, during the stride taken by Joson, take one too, and let herself fall into those two arms, at the ends of which tender and prayerful hands were extended Her head leaned upon the shoulder of the man whom her childish visions had once apotheosized. She had a blissful, ecstatic expression now, her eyes blank, with no gaze at all except to see inside herself. In a distant, angelic, elect voice she murmured, in a breath:

"Joson!"

Then, utterly pale, and limp and cold—like a melting snowflake, Yvernaux said—she fainted.

XXXVI

To what petty causes the greatest effects are often due is a shamefully banal remark, and it is presumptuous to dare to make it again after Pascal's celebrated fillip regarding Cleopatra's nose. All things considered, however, we cannot help noting here the tiny event by which this entire telepathic drama, with all its force, was triggered and set in motion.

You will recall that Joson, on reading in his English newspaper the first news and then the progress of the airplane, had not been overly excited. An amusing sport, no doubt, which he might once have taken up, if he had had the opportunity—that was all that he had seen. The idea had not even passed furtively through his mind that there might perhaps therein, if not today then some day, a means of reaching the magical city, as he had said jokingly to Julot, by air, flying. In the same way, learning from his mechanically-scanned newspaper about the awarding of the Alexandra Prize to some unknown person, rewarding a work on "the intensive cultivation of arid soils," had not opened the slightest window on the possibility of one day fertilizing the desert in which the ashes of his Eldorado lay dormant. He was very far away from such dreams now!

Suddenly, however, one evening when he was drowsily riffling through that six-page English newspaper, at the end of the three lines summarily reporting the prize, its amount, the title of the paper and the name of the recipient, that name sparked something like a hole of light in his brain, and then a jet of fire. And within his volcanic brain there was an entire eruption, in response to the stone that had fallen into it: Gasguin.

Abbé Denis' brother? Evidently. He remembered a professor of physics, to whom his mother's vague cousin, or foster-sister, the grotesque Mademoiselle Anne-Herminie-Luce de Saint-Ylan, had been married off.

281

Then, with a single bound, his memory had leapt to Geneviève. Thibaud Gasguin's daughter, yes, that little communicant, the companion of his last vacation at Kairnheûz! And he had certainly not forgotten her. Four times, in exceptionally grave circumstances in his life, he had had inexplicable remembrances of her, like signs of some sort.

Those recurrences, like lightning-flashes at the time, immediately extinguished in profound darkness, re-emerged now, all at the same time, melting into one another, becoming a single image of Geneviève, whose silhouette he saw against the wall of the ruined chapel above the sinister sheen of Kawchmoôr, whose laughter he heard like tony silver bells, whose gesture made the hair stand up on the back of his neck, whose odor he breathed in, of gorse, sunlight, seaweed, salt-flats and unripe apricots, and finally, whose distant and singing voice, at the moment when he had almost committed suicide, had repeated to him as in some sort of celestial telephone the litany of his forenames, names, titles and soubriquets:

"Comte Elme-Cast-Jagut-Marie-Joseph de Ponthual Plouĕr, Seigneur des Ebihens, des Pierres-Sonnantes, des Treize-Îles and other places, also known as Joson, also known as the Little Chouan."

At the same time, all the drawers of his unconscious memory offering him their secret treasures, releasing the springs of their hiding-places, a geyser erupted in his consciousness, seething with countless details that he was not aware of having known. Geneviève had been a child prodigy, according to Abbé Denis, her uncle! The Comtesse and the Abbé had often mentioned marvels on that subject. Not during the little girl's sojourn at Kairnheûz, for she had then been taking a cure to "descientificize" her, according to the Jesuit Father's humorous expression, but in other circumstances the Comtesse and the Abbé had talked about the matter between themselves—and Joson had heard without listening, and retained it without knowing it. And now, he was intoxicated by it!

Thibaud Gasguin is doubtless cited in error, Joson thought. *They've put her father's name instead of hers. The prize has surely been won by her!*

That idea planted itself within him with the penetrative force and barbed hook of obsession. And it was her—of that he was absolutely certain—who was the will-power of that obsession, which had cried out to him:

"Joson, abandon everything. You're a coward, going stale here like a dirty bourgeois. Yes, an Ethiopian bourgeois, but a bourgeois all the same. Fie! You, a colonist and a trader—you, a Ponthual-Plouër! You're forty tomorrow. Is that an age for a man to retire? No. The magical city awaits you. The desert that is its tomb is fertilizable, It's possible to sow life there. The civilization of long ago can be reborn there, if you wish, along with the life. It's Providence that has made that child invent this miracle. It's your mother who has dictated it to her, to extract you from your brutalization of satisfaction. The most beautiful of your adventures, O Celt, you shall now undertake. Get up! Go! Abandon everything for that. How you'll get to the magical city isn't important. Flying, if necessary, by air, as you told poor Julot. But since you know where the water is to resuscitate the monstrous infusorium of the fabulous city, you have no right not to go in quest of it, that Fountain of Youth. And if Geneviève was able to invent this 'electrical fertilization,' she might also invent the means of sending you to carry life there. On your way, Joson!"

And he had hastily liquidated all his Ethiopian business interests, as if he were going bankrupt, at a loss, realizing his assets in order to devote them entirely to the crusade to reconquer the African Jerusalem.

He had then embarked, and had arrived in France, and then in Paris, without giving any advance notice, without warning Geneviève, going, as soon as he had leapt out of the railway carriage, in search of the Gasguin domicile, and arriving—as an inappropriate hour: too bad!—dressed as a "globetrotter," as well as a savage and a madman, but in an impulsive surge that had lasted since his departure and would only stop in front of Geneviève, nailing him to the threshold of that room with the gaze of a tyrannical and fascinating serpent.

For he told all that—and how much better, with the natural, imaginative eloquence of a Celt in poetic and adventurous effusion—to Geneviève, recovered from her faint, in front of the stupefied Gasguin, open-mouthed Aunt Line and Yvernaux absolutely drunk with delirious joy, with Geneviève ready to swoon again in incessantly-renewed spasms of ecstatic bliss.

To that fairy tale, what response was possible? None, except that they all believed it, even Gasguin. How could they not believe it? Fantastic and implausible as the embroidery was, the weft was there, palpably, held in their hands. And the embroidery was real too, made of facts, not dreams.

The Alexandra Prize had been well and truly won. The theory of electrical fertilization was in hand and the practical application ready. The fabulous city, the dead civilization to resuscitate, was no less real. Did Joson not possess its exact location, as he had said in the course of his inflamed narrative? And thus, none of it was about to disappear on awakening—for they were not asleep. They were living it, that fairy tale!

And that was what the listeners, dazed with enthusiasm, proclaimed incessantly, Gasguin and Aunt Line by their expressions of happy bewilderment, Geneviève by the gently dewy tears in which her heart—which would otherwise have choked again—gradually relaxed, and the lyrical Yvernaux, finally, in trumpeting cries or the strokes of a gong with his metaphors could not help beating time, so to speak, for the verses of the hymn.

For it was a hymn, in truth! We have not dared to indicate here its movement, its gesture, its accent. Yvernaux himself, when he tried to reproduce it with his imagistic language and his oratorical verve, with his mimes giving body to words and his voice serving as their wing, stopped half way, lost courage and gave up, saying:

"That has to be it. It remains ineffable, irreducible to all translation. Think of that daughter of genius, whose entire soul blossomed in the florescence of her beloved loving her thus! Think of that hero, that modern conquistador, who has dreamed of the chimerical resurrection of a dead world, who is certain to see it alive, able to offer proofs in knowing its exact location, and who possesses, thanks to the chosen one he has finally found—or, rather, found again—the shibboleth of the miracle rendering that resurrection realizable! Think of the state of exaltation in which all..."

And merely by thinking about that state, he was carried away into his displaced state, and with the first hobbyhorse that came along serving as Pegasus bestrode—whether it was the electrical fertilization of the Sahara, to begin with (as the first move in the game) or the fabulous city, a colony, he said, of the famous sunken Atlantis of which Plato speaks in the *Timaeus*, or the radioactive aviation that would supplant (or, rather, according to this ironic expression, "overleap") the airplane, or the prescience of Aunt Line, or his own, relative to that prodigious "romance of the new age" (another of his terms)—and he disappeared from sight amid the whirlwinds of sonorous words, allegories, analogies, parentheses and symbols of which he is (he claims, in the manner of Du Bartas and Ronsard[67] rolled into one) the Zeus, simultaneously the "Nephelegerete" or "assembler of clouds," with regard to ideas, and the "thunderbolt-caster" with regard to images.

At other times, even so, that incorrigible stringer of tintinnabulatory words, was able to emerge from his clouds and explain to you, in a clear fashion, not only ideas but facts—a much more difficult task for a lyricist. It was thus that he had

---

[67] The most celebrated work of the 16th century poet Guillaume Du Bartas is the epic *La Sepmaine* [The Week], also known as *La Création de la monde* [The Creation of the World]. His contemporary Pierre de Ronsard headed a literary school intended to inject new blood into French literature, and is generally credited with having succeeded.

strongly recalled, and that we can repeat after him, the most curious and the most forceful of the proofs given by Joson in favor of the prehistoric antiquity attributable to the fabulous city.

"You're not unaware," he said, summarizing Joson, "that our Zodiac, which is hold in common with all the most ancient peoples, has not been bequeathed to any of them by any known source. Even China, Egypt and Chaldea are too young to have that ancestral honor. The civilization, then very advanced, that invented the signs of that zodiac, and fixed them astronomically, thus marking the calendar, goes back much further. The thing originated in the days when the Sun, at the time of the spring equinox, was in Taurus. We are proud of the calculation the precession of the equinoxes; those ancestors knew it and calculated it before us.

"Of the six thousand and some years necessary for the March Sun to pass from Taurus into Aries, the people of that fabulous city had taken precise account in the zodiac discovered by Joson in the inscriptions he found there.[68] Conclusion: that zodiac brings us testimony of a civilization far anterior to the Chinese, Egyptian and Chaldean civilizations. It evokes for us humans in the midst of scientific observation and cul-

---

[68] In fact, although astrological divination is considerable older, the twelve-part division of the ecliptic into the "Houses of the Zodiac" only seems to go back as far as Ptolemaic Egypt, from which it spread to the omen-obsessed Roman Empire, although the divisions were given the names of constellations established long before by Greek astronomers. Chinese astrology originally used twenty-eight divisions rather than twelve. It actually takes the Sun's apparent equinoctial "location" about 2147 years to traverse a twelfth of the ecliptic, so the astronomy or the arithmetic of the people of the city seems to have been seriously at fault. It is unclear, in any case, how the people of the vanished civilization could have marked and measured the transition in question on any kind of diagram.

ture sixty centuries before the famous forty that we contemplate from the height of the Pyramids..."

When that forced an "Oh!" Yvernaux never failed to add:

"...and would contemplate us, I dare say, with a certain scorn, in thinking about the precession of the equinoxes."

With two or three intimates, furthermore, he never stops talking about that sublime night. Night indeed, for the "thinking room" had, in truth, been a "talking room" until nearly dawn—something, he affirms, approaching three o'clock in the morning. And that night, the calm provincial house in the Rue Malebranche would not have been able to believe the eyes and ears provided by the small panes and lead funnels in the windows of the unexpectedly-illuminated and noisy little courtyard!

It was not only lyrical saliva, a froth of foamy words transformed into multicolored bubbles, that was dispensed there, the worthy Yvernaux said—and he said it not without a certain disgust, which he sometimes had for the excessive verbiage of which he was more often the torturer but sometimes also the victim. Occasionally, therefore, he was keen to savor the taste of a conversation entirely composed of facts, decisions and actions.

Now, that night had been sublime, certainly, not only for the beautiful things said, but also for the council of war held and the plans made to realize all those dreams as soon as possible.

Firstly, it had been resolved that the theory of electrical fertilization would be subjected to immediate trials and put into practice.

"Not on too large a scale!" Gasguin had timidly objected.

"The scale it requires," had been Geneviève's peremptory reply.

"*Amon!*" Aunt Line said, supportively, who had limited herself until then to nodding assent, with sideways glances.

"We shall put the 65,000 francs of the prize into it," Geneviève continued.

"And my Ethiopian capital," Joson added. "A hundred thousand francs, exactly."

"With that," Yvernaux exclaimed, "I dare say there'll be enough to fertilize Arabia Petraea itself!"

"Don't laugh, Godfather," Geneviève said. "But know that I would first like to try it on a soil of exactly that type. At least the proof will be conclusive!"

They sought an appropriate place—not too far away! The gateway to the Sahara did not seem close enough. It was Joson who found what was needed: Arabia Petraea in miniature, the Crau."[69]

"And if the trial goes well…?"

It was Gasguin who insinuated that "if," with an implication of doubt. He had none, however, with regard to electrical fertilization. On the other hand, he sensed the impending corollary—the development of radioactive aviation—of which he was fearful now, since the prize had been won. For that money would be risked on aviation with too little chance of success, he thought surreptitiously, no longer having confidence in the new chimera hat Geneviève was beginning once again to caress."

"The trial will surely be successful," she affirmed. "You're certain of that, aren't you?"

"Yes," he stammered. "And…then…?"

"Then," she replied, with a gesture of faith fit to move mountains, "then we'll set off, as you know full well."

"For the city in the desert?" Joson queried, anxiously.

"Yes, of course," she replied, quite calmly.

"It's just…well…in that case…" He hesitated, seemingly about to stammer, like Gasguin.

She started and blinked, immediately suppressing the reaction and punishing herself for it by biting her lip, drawing blood. "Pardon me," she said. "I thought, for just an instant,

---

[69] The Crau is a stony plain at ancient confluence of the Rhône and the Durance.

that you had the same fear as..." Her glance of disdainful pity was for her father; it was furtive, for Joson was speaking.

"That your father might be a little terrified by the idea of such a journey is understandable, to say the least. But as for me, no—I have no fear of it. If I don't seem to be leaping at the idea, it's only because...well, yes, I'll lay it on the line. It's that our capital is insufficient. To find the place of which I have the location, even if we don't go astray *en route*, by accident or miscalculation, it will take three years and require more than 300,000 francs. That's why I said that, *in that case*..."

She was listening, letting him go on without interruption. That silence seemed to Joson to be discontented. Swiftly, he pounced on the mute reproach, and exclaimed, bravely: "But I'll find what's lacking. I don't know how, but it doesn't matter. I'll find it." And he too, at that moment, made the gesture of the faith that moves mountains.

Geneviève smiled—a smile, Yvernaux said, that opened every paradise—and murmured, very softly, words that, again in his words, had an enormous span in those open paradises.

"The journey there won't cost anything, and will be made, not in three years, but in three weeks, then in three days—and finally, in three hours."

"We were all looking at her," Yvernaux recounted, subsequently, "with eyes ready to pop out of our heads—all of us, including Joson, in spite of his petrel's eyes, and Aunt Line, who can see into her utmost depths. It was just that Geneviève had never, however softly, proffered such prophecies—enormous, I repeat. And we thought, in listening to them and observing her absolute calmness, her paradisal smile, either that we were crazy, or that she was."

Suddenly Joson—who told Yvernaux about it later, when they had become close friends—heard what he had said to Julot as the latter as carrying him through marsh singing inside him once again: "We'll come back by air, then, flying."

And he understood that Geneviève, as he had foreseen in his dream, on quitting Ethiopia, was talking about the inven-

289

tion by means of which she would send him to carry life out there. He seized her hands, kissed them tenderly, and said: "I'll go, then, whenever you like."

"That was said," Yvernaux reported, "with a simplicity, in its grandeur, that caused our eyes to retreat into their orbits and their swelling to diminish in a flood of tears."

"Before accepting, though," Geneviève objected, "at least wait to find out by what means...with what engine..."

"Why do I need to know the means, the engine?" he replied. "You propose it, therefore..."

"Geneviève," Gasguin put in, "isn't yet entirely sure...isn't that so, Geneviève? Come on, speak. Be sincere and honest, as you have always been. Admit that your invention is not at the point of perfect maturity in which you could..."

She was visibly in torment. She kept quiet, even so—and that was a confession that her father was right. That silence weighed upon all of them. An oppression accumulated within it, stifling them.

"Yes, everyone," Yvernaux said. "Everyone—and Aunt Line, this time, more than the others, because she was tortured along with her *ch'tiote*—everyone except *him*, Joson. And that without the shadow of an effort, very naturally, as befit a true son of those Gauls who only fear one thing, which is the sky falling on their heads. Did he even have that fear, since he was smiling at the thought of going to confront it—the sky. For he was smiling in his turn, not a smile like hers, opening all the paradises, but a smile so brave that all the devils in all the hells would have taken flight, their tail between their legs."

And Yvernaux also painted that smile with this little image: "That's how an épée might smile."

Smiling in that fashion, Joson said to Geneviève: "Don't answer your father. Whether your invention is ready or not, since you believe in it, I believe in it."

She gathered in her entire being and said: "Well, yes, I believe in it. I believe in the science that..."

290

He did not let her finish, but exclaimed: "It's you that I believe in, in you alone—and that's enough for me."

She tried again to speak, with an almost-childish stammer. "This is it! The engine...that which will replace the wing...you understand..."

Again he interrupted, violently by the gesture that clenched his fists forcefully, and very tenderly by his voice, which he made very soft, as musical as his mother's, in order to say while looking into her face: "There is only one engine; there is only one wing—and that is Faith."

XXXVII

What remains to be narrated of this story, very real in spite of its underside of strangeness, has nothing much to do with the particular purpose that is proposed herein: a physiological and psychological study—or, at least, a preliminary sketch for such a study—of a feminine genius situated almost entirely in the unconscious. The external manifestations of that genius in the subsequent facts, interesting as those facts might be, lend themselves more henceforth to a sort of chronicle, rich in events and scenes, than to a monograph, perhaps a trifle severe, of the sort desired here.

The strict accuracy and perfect authenticity of those events and sciences, moreover, cannot—it must be confessed, in all honesty—be guaranteed. We only know them by hearsay, some by virtue of having read the accounts—very copious, but quite contradictory—reproduced in the newspapers. Those events happened, in fact, in a secret manner, by design. The scenes were not witnessed by anyone save the people who lived them, who have refused energetically, all attempts to "interview" them. One therefore has the right, and even the duty, to affirm pertinently that all depiction in their regard is contrived, imagined and, in consequence, unworthy of trust.

Only one person in the world, apart from the actors in the drama, has received and retained a few furtive clarifications that might aid in the penetration of the mystery, to the extent that is possible—but for him alone, and the few intimate acquaintances in possession of his confidence and who are worthy of it. Now Yvernaux—you will have guessed that it is him—is a faithful friend, through and through, incapable of treason. The chatterbox knows how to shut up occasionally, especially when there is a duty to fulfill with regard to his adored goddaughter. As for his confidants, the vague enlightenment that he disposes—precious, although vague—and of which he had gladly made them the few gifts permitted, have formally promised him only to use it with his authorization and under his control.

We shall therefore limit ourselves to recording, to conclude this story, the facts certified as real by him—only those, and nothing more. They can only be appreciated, scientifically or artistically, through him. We shall not even attempt to arrange them, or explain them, or add suggestions, in order to increase their "literary" value. We shall retain the bare simplicity that is appropriate to the kind of study to which we are confined.

Certainly, it would be possible to exploit all the elements that are available: material from newspaper articles, reportage, scraps of "interviews" snatched even from refusals, "imaginative" descriptions and supposed photographic snapshots, undeniably convinced of their deceptive quality, in the manner of the majority of "films." With all that, it would not be too difficult to reconstitute the chronicle of events and scenes by virtue of which the present history, whose preoccupations are essentially serious and almost purely scientific, would conclude with a romance almost uniquely picturesque.

That is what we have deliberately not done, and we are proud of it. We do not take any more vanity than is warranted, but we claim a little honor even so, for having resisted the temptation offered by that *desinit in piscem*,[70] evoking the seductions of sirens, perhaps too vulgar to find a place next to the austere Geveniève. We do not doubt the pleasure that some readers would have been bound to find in that second-hand picturesqueness, but besides the fact that we have conceit enough to judge that easy and false picturesqueness slightly repugnant, we also have the pretension of believing that the minds of the new age, even—or, rather, especially—the fe-

---

[70] The Roman poet Horace likened a work of art devoid of unity to a woman *destinit in piscem* [ending in a fish's tail]— hence the subsequent reference to sirens, in the sense equating them with mermaids.

male ones, will henceforth have an appetite for nourishment that is both more refined and more substantial.

XXXVIII

Almost a year has gone by since Joson's arrival. It has needed no less, and no more, to put into execution the entire plan of campaign decided during one final week-long council of war. Geneviève has been able to admire the prodigious faculties of organization what he brings to the work.

"Without him," she often proclaims, "we'd never have got it done, would we, Godfather?"

"Say right away," Yvernaux replies, "that the wing would have remained in the egg."

"Ha ha! Right!" she says, smiling.

Gasguin risks a bitter: "I don't count any more, then?"

And Aunt Line, putting on a show of joking, although knowing full well, deep down, that she is expressing a little-known truth in the mask of whimsy, concludes in Thiérachian: "I've always said that there are men who ought to be doing the housework."

And, in fact, the former ship's officer, explorer, trail-blazer, expedition leader, dealer in merchandise and colonist has, almost single-handedly, put things on a practical basis, the tasks distributed, the capital activated, the preparations pressurized and the business under way. He has proved, in accordance with a remark made by Yvernaux, that, Comte as he was, and Elme-Cast-Jagut-Marie-Joseph etc. of the Treize-Îles and other places, he was a son of the Skylark, one of those Gauls of whom Cato and Caesar had said that two talents were innate in them at birth: *Bellum gerere et arguté loqui*.[71]

"Which," he added, "if the professors had any sense, would be translated into modern argot as *to be on the ball and in the know*."

While Geneviève shut herself up with her father in the Vaugirard laboratory, entirely caught up in the in the final

---

[71] The art of war and fine speech.

experiments, the active, agile and eloquent Joson carried out agronomical trials of electrical fertilization in the Crau. He did that without the government, the Académie des Sciences, the press or anyone else catching wind of it. On a small scale, as Gasguin had desired, at very little expense, he had obtained results sufficient to be certain of future returns, which promised to be a magnificent remuneration. At the same time, Geneviève having talked about finding in the vicinity, by the sea shore and at a given longitude (for reasons of her own) a large area suitable or aviation, he had acquired exactly what was needed, incredibly cheap, still without letting any suspicion leak out of what he was planning. The place was situated in the Camargue, not far from one of the mouths of the Rhône, in the middle of one of the triangles formed by its ancient delta, in the vicinity of the singular little dead city of Saintes-Maries-de-la-Mer.[72]

It is permissible to note in passing for what reasons Geneviève had chosen that particular spot, or one analogous to it, and with what meticulous care Joson had finalized the choice of the terrain. That is, in fact, one of the rare explanations furnished by Yernaux whose transmission is permitted. It opens, positively, a rather luminous horizon to the hypotheses that might be made regarding the as-yet-undivulged theory of radioactive aviation. This is the explanation, which we shall not hide under a bushel—anyone who cares to do so may dream at leisure!

---

[72] Even before the Great War, Saintes-Maries-de-la-Mer, the principal commune in the Camargue, was only "dead" outside the holiday season, when its population increased tenfold. The town's name refers to the apocryphal legend that three Marys allegedly present when Jesus rose from the tomb—Mary Magdalen, Mary Jacobe (also known as Mary of Chopas) and Mary Salome—brought the Holy Grail by sea to the south France (with or without Joseph of Arimathea).

The "right place" determined by Gasguin's caulations in accordance with one of Geneviève's later discoveries had to be "right" in both geometrical and physical terms, so to speak.

"It is the point of intersection of two lines," she affirmed, "giving the direction of two absolutely certain telluric currents. One is marked underground by the fault whose perpetual shocks have for witnesses the eruptions of volcanoes and seismographic readings. The other is manifested in the atmosphere by the mistral."

Now, a location at such a point of intersection, is propitious, not to say necessary, for the activation of the particular engine invented by Geneviève and the liberation of the new force that it employs.

That parenthesis having been closed, and with it the peep-hole that it provides into Geneviève's idea, it is appropriate to return to Joson and his activities of a more down-to-earth variety—which does not prevent their fruits being immediate and precious. And perhaps, in fact, as Yvernaux jokingly said, perhaps, without him, the wing would have remained in the egg.

For not only did he occupy himself miraculously with all the material and financial preparations—the various purchases of metals, chemical products, rubber and silks of special fabrication, and also construction projects, on the basis of plans that were often highly idiosyncratic, disconcerting the architects and technologists, doing the work of a technologist and architect himself, as well as that of an engineer, a manufacturer and a tradesman—but also, and especially, he had the art of raising to white heat Geneviève's enthusiasm for work, courage, hope and faith, in science and herself.

Now, that enthusiasm, that courage, that hope and that faith often had need of that drive to incandescence. In her Vaugirard laboratory, the heroic young woman had, in a manner of speaking, thrown her entire being into the devouring crucible of her research and melted it therein, her heart as well as her brain, and the reserves of her unconscious combined with her father's hectic calculations. It happened occasionally that a tiny error, the substitution of a plus sign for a minus sign, or some almost-imperceptible accident of manipulation, obliged everything to start again-for absolute perfection as required, since it was no longer a matter of a sublime theory, with its near-blanks, but of the final hand to play in practice and reality, with Joson a living card thrown on to the green baize of risk.

At those moments when certainty escaped her, she felt herself change from metal in fusion into, first, a block of stone, and then a block of ice. It was life that escaped her along with certainty. She thought she was on the brink of extinction, going the way of water that runs, boils, evaporates and vanishes. Immediately, she needed Joson. Wherever he was, he had to telephone—sometimes, even, when the crisis of despair was too strong, to come back in haste, before she had ceased to be! For neither her father, nor her godfather, not Aunt Line herself, was capable of warming her up, of restoring the temperature, first and foremost of her existence, and then of her intelligence, both conscious and unconscious, and finally of her genius—the temperature that was indispensable to her, that which Joson alone was able to push to incandescence, that of enthusiasm and faith, red-hot and white-hot.

And Joson came, and he talked (*argute loqui*) and he got to grips with the discouragements of the sublime and childlike soul (*bellum gerere*); and in response to his ardent voice, Geneviève's heart was reignited. And again, in her Vaugirard laboratory, the cavern of a Cyclops forging the lightning, or the summit of the imprisoned Prometheus, she resumed throwing her entire being into the crucible of her research, to melt: all her heat and all her brain, and the unconscious accumulated within her, and her dreams for Joson, and the flower of the blood of the Hescheboix watered by the dew of love in Aunt Line's tears.

And on those days, when Joson had gone back to some distant task, leaving her confident and fervent, with her triumphant gaze, her *cattelinette*'s gaze, which always came back in the end, she said to Yvernaux in an intoxicated voice: "You see, Godfather, that without him, the wing would have remained in the egg."

"I can believe that now," he admitted, to give her pleasure.

But in his conscience, or in private conversation with Aunt Line, he groaned: "Without him! Without him! I should think so—only his name isn't Joson. Who will give him back his true name?"

"What name?" Aunt Line asked, once.

"Why," he declaimed, lyrically, "the great name of the One whose wing has broken the very egg of Being, the sacred name of Eros, Amour, the first-born of Chaos and Night—who remained their only son!"

"*Amon*," replied the old woman, darting out her tongue like a serpent. "Not to mention that that the only son is also the only father of the whole world, damn it!"[73]

Then, after a silence, and as if without comprehension, she added:

"And himself!"

---

[73] It is possible that Richepin is here stretching the meaning of the Thiérachian *Amon* even further, to include the Egyptian god Amon, or Amun—who almost reached the point of absorbing all the others in becoming an all-encompassing Creator, the focal point of a quasi-monotheistic religion—although Yvernaux would be far more likely to indulge in such a flight of fancy than Aunt Aline.

XXXIX

Firm as our intention is not to allow this attempted philosophical study to turn into pure romantic fiction, there is one humble stray fact for whose omission we would reproach ourselves, even though it is only indirectly associated with it. It does so much honor to Joson and heightens the color of his character so beautifully and significantly that we do not have the heart to leave it unmentioned—without, however, extracting any artistic amusement therefrom! By way of documentation, and no more—but truly human, it can be said.

Among all his very various and absorbing occupations, Joson took it into his head—at first unknown to Geneviève, but then with her consent—to learn to fly an airplane. Not, as you shall soon see, that he had to be a pilot aboard the new apparatus, to be guided by someone other than the passenger—but he wanted to familiarize himself to some extent with the sensations of flight, of speed, of altitude and of touching down before the prodigious experience of flight of which he was about to be the extraordinary bird. As he had said since the first moment to Yvernaux, his confidant:

"I don't intend to be surprised, up there, by anything, so that I can be entirely Geneviève's, my entire being in her hands, without any distraction."

Now, at the first aerodrome to which he went in search of a professor of aviation, among the names suggested to him was that of Guérinet.

He is astounded. He seeks further information. It really is his Julot! He races to Levallois-Perret, to the domicile of his lost friend. Instead of the old ruffian, the escapee from Biribi, he finds a gentleman—and yet, it really is his Julot, transfigured by a heroic profession! The Parisian is married! He has a charming wife and a daughter. Not content with going up as a pilot, he has educated himself, and, believing that he has discovered a small improvement in construction, is dreaming about obtaining a patent and becoming a constructor, in order to ensure the future of his wife and child.

Effusion! Mutual joy! The former leader promises his moral and financial support to the brave lad who had become entirely a man. While awaiting the collaboration by which the discovery, truly worthy of a clever man, will be rewarded, Joson advances to his African savior what he needs to construct two models of a monoplane with an automatic stabilizer. It is still the Comte who seems to be obliged to the former ruffian, though, for the master of yore is now the pupil, and the new boss says, swelling to with pride, a rush of argot returning to his lips:

"It's a laugh, all the same! The sea-eagle taking flying-lessons from the Pantruche sparrow!"

It seemed, though, that the sea-eagle had talent. In three lessons, no more. Joson knew, certainly not everything but how to work the controls, to brake, to fly at speed, to climb in a spiral, to descend in a glide, to command the engine and to turn—none of it thoroughly, but he had done everything once or twice, three times at the most.

"To put it bluntly," the professional said, merrily, "everything that an amateur has to know, and nothing that is indispensable to a professional—in sum, just enough for Julot not to be risking his skin too much in supervising him, but not enough not to be almost sure of breaking Monsieur le Comte's head if Monsieur le Comte wanted to take a ride on his own."

We shall be brief, in order to avoid any artistic concern and stick to the strict recording of various facts and to allow to them to operate on sensibility by their own brutal and naïve force. Such as it was reported in the newspapers, it resembles many other tragic incidents, nowadays almost banal, in the already long martyrology of aviation. To the extent that the whole truth can be established, it is out of the ordinary, even among those exploits. We shall therefore establish it, without asking—for once, we have no scruple in doing so—anyone's authorization.

It was the famous day—are they not all famous, these days of aviation?—when, after proofs of altitude, then of gliding, then of landing, various kinds of apparatus presented themselves for examination—or, rather, in competition—seeking the stabilization of the monoplane. A fairly large prize—20,000 francs, plus accessory prizes for certain details—was to be awarded to the victor. The hope was also promised to him, and almost assured, of a patent that might bring in very substantial royalties: in brief, a veritable small fortune in prospect. Guérinet was counting on the prize, not for the sake of vainglory but for his wife and child.

"If I kill myself tomorrow, with what I'd leave them, they'd be safe from hunger—and hunger, oh, if you knew! For women, especially."

He had said these words that very morning, to Joson, tears moistening the habitual mockery of his simian eyes—which then appeared to the poetic Celt to be flowery eyes.

The weather, after having been passable, had become ominous, and then nasty. The wind was blowing in treacherous squalls. Taking off was becoming dangerously risky. Several competitors dropped out. When Julot's turn came, Joson tried to hold him back; he had a kind of sinister presentiment—but the Parisian looked him in the whites of his eyes and said: "It's you who's telling me not to be reckless? Come on! I'll wager that if I listened to you, you'd be scornful. Don't you remember our follies of bravery out in Africa?"

"We were young," said Joson.

"We still are," said the other.

"All the same, we wouldn't do it again..."

"You think that I wouldn't put you on my back to cross the marsh, Boss? You think that! No, you don't, do you?" And he leapt into the cockpit, with a screech like an angry sparrow.

Joson could not help replying to him, making a funnel of his hands: "Bravo, lad!"

Already, the purr of the propeller struggling against the leonine miaowing of the squall, Julot was taking off. Five minutes later, the wings, turned over and torn away, separated from the airplane, which fell, spiraling, as heavy as lead, and crashed into the ground. Julot was pulled out, not dead but condemned to death, almost in his final agony.

"In a quarter of an hour, at the most," the doctor said, "it'll be over."

Joson leaned over Julot, and whispered something in his ear—no one knew what—at which the dying man's face lit up. In his flowery eyes something flourished like an eternal spring—and not in imagination but in reality, for soon, he saw the second model of his monoplane, manned by the Comte, take off into the tempest, turn, rise into the sky, roll, pitch, descend again at a vertiginous angle, and land amid a storm of applause and cheers.

The newspapers said nothing about that incident, not having known the whole truth. For the prize, according to Joson's instructions, was awarded to Guérinet for his automatically-stabilized monoplane, flown "by his pupil and employee, Monsieur Joson."

XL

And now, here is the final act—or, to put it better, the first, Yvernaux prophesied—of the drama of aviation genius that had Geneviève for a poet and Joson for a protagonist, and which will, still according to our prophet, turn the whole word upside-down.

"Of course," he added, "people had little chance of realizing that if they read the critics"—the reportage at the time—"who passed judgment on it. That's the usual fate of masterpieces, to be misunderstood. This one had the destiny, worse still, of not even being understood at all."

And, in fact, the experiment took place last summer, between two "sensational" exhibitions of locomotion by airplane, one in Belgium and one in the Alps, and all the trumpets of renown were busy sounding fanfares to the triumphs or catastrophes. The moment for radioactive aviation had not been very well chosen!

Too well chosen, in fact—for it was in accordance with Geneviève's express desire that it had been thus stifled, far from possible publicity, sheltered from advertisement as if from peril, with all precautions carefully taken to put the finest sleuths of reportage off the track. The place, moreover, was just as cleverly planned, in that sense, as the moment. Could Sextius Costecalde himself, or any of his pupils from "the far south," ever have dreamed that the wing of the new age would be deployed, without anyone alerting them to the fact, in "their" Camargue?

So, none of them was there when the miraculous event transpired. No master of the genre was even able to make a note or take a snapshot, or anything at all permitting any kind of article to be written. Only a few petty local journalists, from sufficiently distant papers, had been vaguely aware of the construction works undertaken in the vicinity of Saintes-Maries-de-la-Mer.

It was in the month of May, the time the bizarre annual pilgrimage of Bohemians to the old church, to pray before the reliquary of, their patroness, Sainte-Sarah-la-Noire.[74] A few young novice reporters, having not yet seen the scene, and desirous of coking up a description, had watched the ceremony—and, on the same occasion, had learned that some kind of hangar for aviation had been built three kilometers away. News of that had reached the dailies in Marseilles and Montpellier—which, uniquely along the entire press, on the day of the experiment, although it was kept secret, reported even so, as best they could (not very well) the fact that it had taken place.

And it was thus, from that angle, that the matter came back—third-hand at least—to the Parisian aviation news; that was the manner in which the capital and miraculous event became known (?) to the public, in something like the following terms:

An attempt to cross the Mediterranean by airplane has almost saddened, by its tragic outcome, the enchanted land of Mireille.[75] A pupil of the late Guérinet, the aviator Joson, was within an inch of death—by virtue of his imprudence, it must be admitted. Firstly, he was reckless enough to set off, in spite of a terrible mistral. Secondly, he dared to confront it in a monoplane of his own creation, it appears, doubtless of an imperfect design. After an excursion of a few hours in the Golfe de Lion, he fell into the water and his life was only

---

[74] In legendary terms, Sarah-la-Noire [Black Sarah] was the black servant of Mary Jacobe, one of the three Marys who brought the Holy Grail to France; she was either adopted as a patron saint, or foisted upon, the Romani who arrived in southern France in the 15th century and consented, or were forced, to convert to Catholicism.

[75] *Mireille* (1859) is a long poem by the Provençal poet Frédéric Mistral, celebrating the popular traditions of the region.

*saved by the habitual heroic devotion of the brave matelots of
Saintes-Maries-de-la-Mer.*

There are no matelots in Saintes-Maries-de-la-Mer—
only a few fishermen. The so-called pupil of the late Guérinet
did not take off in a monoplane of his own creation (!!) but in
Geneviève's new apparatus. His excursion over the sea had
not lasted "a few hours", nor any more-or-less indeterminate
time, but exactly the five hours and twenty minutes that Geneviève had calculated as the time necessary to fly over Mallorca
and return. Joson owed his life, above all, to the insubmersible
gondola with which the apparatus as furnished, expressly in
view of avoiding landing, replacing it with a touchdown at
sea[76]—so much for the apparatus being imperfect! Finally, the
mistral was not blowing when Joson took off; immediately
after his departure, however, a kind of brief and formidable
tornado had swirled turbulently, raised by the departure itself—which Geneviève's calculations had also foreseen.

"Apart from these 'slight' errors," Yvernaux jeered,
"And the complete omission of Geneviève's name, and various other lies and lacunae with regard to this or that, notably
everything, it is a pure masterpiece and a very model of modern historiography, is it not?"

Was that news item not also childish in its absolute ignorance of things? And did it not seem—as little folk say—to
be making a fool of itself? But the same could not be said of
those which, after the fact, taking a vague scrap of half-
glimpsed truth as their canvas, set about embroidering it pretentiously with heir extravagant imaginations.

We have mentioned above, in chapter XX, with regard to
Yvernaux's *Treatise on the Innate Sciences*, the representative
of an American publishing house, a "recordman" of airplanic
information, who has set out to purchase all the documents
regarding the invention of the "Gasguin alerion" (as the appa-

---

[76] The word-play in the substitution the improvised "*amerris-
sage*" [a touchdown on the sea] for *atterissage* [landing] is
unfortunately untranslatable.

306

ratus has been definitively baptized).[77] Now, swollen by his success, that agent has not been able to help blabbing a little—oh, very little, in sum, without betraying any secrets acquired for the excellent reason that he does not have sufficient scientific education to understand them.

That does not alter the fact that he had stuck his nose in, or, on the other hand, as a fine pointer expert in seeking out and flushing out the game of reportage, he had seen something—not very much—of the experiment in the Camargue. It was from some distance away, in Saintes-Maries-de-la-Mer, where he was staying in a hotel on the beach, that he had "seen"—even though it happened by night—the departure of the "alerion." Of that, he had, out of professional pride, released a few trivial details, and it had needed no more to seed the fertile American press, the promised land of "puff" and "humbug."

Thus is explained the efflorescence of bouquets of fireworks that recently threw so much dust in our eyes from that direction, to the glory of what they called "Gasguin's alerion."

To tell the truth, the revelations were so stupefying that few people took them seriously. A few bold thinkers were alone in doing so, and discussing them. The pretended photographs, in particular, encountered no credence; the trickery was manifest. Finally, the near-unanimity of the papers was achieved in the estimation that it was one of the hoaxes so dear to the compatriots of Mark Twain. They are known to have sufficiently poor taste thus to ridicule a scientist as reputable as Gasguin, but the joke lacked tact—and a sense of proportion.

---

[77] I have transcribed the improvisations in this sentence directly, "recordman" being an attempt at English neologism, "aéroplanique" [airplanic] an attempt at French neologism, and "alérion" [alerion] an adaptation of a peculiar heraldic device, representing an eagle devoid of beak and feet, with its wings outspread.

Do you recall certain "illuminations" reproduced as such in our popular illustrated papers, with such headlines as:

THE FIERY WING

THE FLOATING ISLAND

A CYCLONE IN THE CAMARGUE

THE HUMAN SHELL

Oh, those images that would have delighted Épinal![78] One saw there, either a man riding through the clouds in some kind of racing car, like a cylinder with tailfins, or the same man in a seabird's nest on the crest of a foaming wave, or a great expanse of black sky rent be the explosion of a star, or, finally, beneath the funnel of a whirlwind, a herd of the little bulls of the Camargue, harassed by zig-zag lightning-bolts. Brrr!

"And to think," Yvernaux laments, "that all that became fashionable—and yet, that beneath all that nonsense, there was a something real! Oh, if I were permitted to establish the true facts! How much crazier! And more dramatic! And..."

And, when pressed slightly, when he is speaking confidentially, when he knows that what he allows to be deduced will not be abused, this is the light that he consents to cast, furtively, on the mystery, and of which he authorizes, also very furtively but rigorously, the publication—after having prudently revised it and, so to speak, filtered the terminology.

On the apparatus, properly speaking, "in" which Joson took off, no information! Yvernaux affirms that he does not know anything about it, save that it includes a life-saving gondola, hence insubmersible, with a view to the marine touchdown that was to conclude the experiment.

The apparatus was lifted up, at night, by an ordinary aerostat, to a height of 2000 meters. It was in communication

---

[78] *Images d'Épinal* were exceedingly popular cheap prints produced in that town, which featured colored pictures accompanied by captions in verse; they were part of the standard stock of itinerant *colporteurs* [hawkers] in the late 18th and early 19th centuries.

with its launch-station by means of wireless telegraphy. It is also by that method that it was guided, after the fashion of certain torpedoes using a system designed by Branly. Its direction, from the launch-station, was controlled by Geneviève.

When the departure was triggered the aerostat exploded—a phenomenon foreseen and planed. It was at that moment that the new engine came into play.

What had also been foreseen—but in principle, not with regard to the power of the effect produced—was the atmospheric perturbation, perhaps also seismic, that the liberation of the force employed would cause. That resulted in the whirlwind mistaken for an effect of the mistral, the shock described as a tornado or a cyclone, or even as a tidal wave, by various people.

One final, very singular, detail concerned the trajectory followed by the apparatus, which was no less original than the engine. That flight had been made in a time calculated with rigorous exactitude, according to a graphically determined curve—a sort of extremely elongated ellipse, one of whose foci was above Mallorca in the Balearics. Now, the underlying principle of that movement and trajectory was that of the famous "boomerang" of which only the Australian indigenes make use, whose theory Geneviève had discovered.

To these exclusively scientific glimmers of light, Yvernaux adds a few others of a moral character, which no one will deem less interesting. Unfortunately, the godfather only deigns to measure these out in a very parsimonious fashion. It is virtually necessary to worm them out of him, as glimmers reminiscent of vague phosphorescence passing through a fog, when he has surpassed the "displaced state," to the point of only being able to express himself in fragments of phrases whose syllables fade away into the moist undergrowth of his beard. By putting these fragments end-to-end to make sentences of them, it has been possible even so to reconstitute these few facts, whose summary he does not contest.

Before the take-off, in accordance with Joson's expressed desire, he and Geneviève were "religiously" betrothed in the old church of Saintes-Maries-de-la-Mer—but in accordance with another, no less formal, desire of Aunt Line's, after a mass celebrated at the main altar, the vows of betrothal had been pronounced, by special permission, in the crypt where the reliquary of Sainte-Sarah-la-Noire, the patron saint of the Romanies, was contained. The two fiancés had then spent an hour in private, in mutual confession, in the Bohemian fashion.

When they came out, Joson to take his place in the "alerion," Geneviève also to imprison herself in the insulated chair from which she was to put herself in communication with the new force, they were in tears, speaking to one another in the intimate mode.

"They had the faces of saints then," said Aunt Line.

At the moment of the explosion announcing the liberation of the force, the starting of the engine and the departure, Gasguin was in the room next to the one I which Geneviève was stationed, and he heard her sigh profoundly, as if she were exhaling her last sigh: "Joson!" But he was under orders, given by her, not to enter for any reason, and he stayed where he was, continuing—as he did throughout the experiment—to repeat for the twentieth time the formidable calculations of which he was the supreme artisan.

The five hours and twenty minutes of the journey, once completed, had aged the voyager and the pilot by ten years; both had wisps of white hair.

Aunt Line had spent the time in question, which had seemed eternal to her, in prayer, burning candles before the reliquary of Sainte-Sarah-la-Noire, of whom she said, afterwards: "She too was a *cattelinette, amon*!"

XLI

Professor Gasguin has taken his retirement. The most envious of his colleagues think and say that it is a shame, after the grotesque publicity with which his glory—so little merited before—has been tarnished by the story of the "human shell." Some, to complete the ridicule heaped upon him, are spreading the rumor will present himself as a candidate for the next vacant chair in the Institut, and that he is a candidate for the Nobel Prize.

In the meantime, with his daughter and Aunt Line, he has left the small apartment In the Rue Malebranche and the Vaugirard laboratory. All three have taken up residence, in company with Joson, at Kairnheûz, which has been repurchased. The ancient and grim "terrible heap of stones" seems more bristling than before, with its tower threatening the heavens with its fist in front of the large hangars that have been constructed on the Ocean's edge between the heath and the strand—for it is from there, on the next voyage financed by the opulent A.A.A. (Aerian[79] American Alerion) Company, that the definitive conqueror of space will depart.

And this is why. The telluric currents whose point of intersection in the Camargue were insufficient to permit the fabulous city to be reached by the alerion electrically piloted by wireless. It requires two currents with a longer circuit. Geneviève has determined their existence by means of the Gulf Stream and the abyss in which ancient Atlantis lies, the tomb of which is marked by the Sargasso Sea. It is not the point of intersection of two lines of these currents that will be utilized as a departure-point his time, but the apex of the angle made by the two lines. That is located at sea, at one degree of longi-

---

[79] I have transcribed this word directly; it may simply be a misprint for "Aerien" [by air] but is more likely to be yet another improvisation of deliberately murky import.

tude, facing Kairnheûz—and, by a bizarre coincidence, or, where the reference-point was established in prehistoric times of the Pierres-Sonnantes, of which Joson is the Seigneur, serving to indicate, at sea, the direction of the deepest part of Kawchmôr.

The love that unites Joson and Geneviève is strange. It justifies the description Aunt Line gave in emerging from the crypt after their private session with the relics of Sarah-la-Noire: "They had the faces of saints."

With a common accord, in fact, and with the joy of the elect, sure that their ecstasy will have no end, they have resolved only to be married out there in the Jerusalem of the finally-resuscitated desert.

Yvernaux comes and goes between Kairnheûz and Paris. He is avid to contemplate their ecstasy, and avid too for the displaced state in which he immerses himself delightedly at the Brasserie des Temps-Nouveaux. Unable to give up either the mystical intoxication or the other, he does not neglect either, and divides himself equitably between them.

His two apostles, the Comtois mage and the Scandinavia Nietzschean, find an increasing savor of genius in his divagations. They still do not know who Geneviève is. They are still trying to figure it out from the formulae with which Yvernaux salutes her with ejaculatory prayers at the beginning of his *Magnificat*. They have ended up admitting that she is an imaginary being, a chimera, in whom their master incarnates his most transcendental ideas. And that is why they attach a symbolic meaning to his ideas, never seeking to penetrate the simple meaning, and thus missing the extremely curious and significant revelations that the suddenly-clear and highly scientific speech of the poor fellow sometimes let slip, in the bosom of fuliginous claptrap, as they take him home, staggering, muttering and monosyllabilizing, amid hiccups of images, and with the gestures of a madman understood by the stars.

From these rare and illuminating revelations, extracting them from the ambient darkness like gems from their matrix, it has been possible, without them being aware of it themselves and without Yvernaux being able to find fault with it, to compose a kind of diamond key, by means of which a clever mind would not be unable to open a tiny crack in the strong-box in which Geneviève enclose her secret.

Of that key, not cunningly filched but forged with patience and imagination, we shall make a gift here to our patient readers, as a token of our gratitude

That which is called "radioactivity," which Dr. Gustave Le Bon attributes to the dematerialization of matter, that force whose reserves are of an infinite richness, that impulse to diffusion which is the opposite of—which is to say, according to Heraclitus, identical to—the impulse of concentration, is the force that liberates Geneviève's alerion, which is a "miniature comet."

"And there are only two forces, in the All," Yvernaux concludes. "Eros, Eris; Love, Hate; Unconscious, Conscious; Faith, Science; Heart, Reason."

Thus speaks the worthy Yvernaux, when one is able to collect, little by little, every number and letter in his metaphysical equations, like flowers passing by in the eddies of a torrent. And it is not him, in sum, who concludes in that fashion, but it is one for him. Similarly, we shall have the audacity to attribute to him this final summary, in which the thousand scattered facets of his thought have been, as it were, mosaicized, in such a way as to composed a single piece with only one inclusion (not counting, he would say, the exclusions).

"Yes, heart and reason—those two enemies of which Pascal wrote: 'The heart has its reasons of which reason knows nothing.' Except, sometimes, all the same, they understand one another and melt into one another. That's when the unconscious and the conscious kiss one another on the lips. And then, genius is born. And then, creation is born. And then, Being is born."

To which Aunt Line, if she listened to that "nonsense" to the end, would condense their import, in her own fashion, more simply, and without being any more stupid for that:

"Because, you see, a feather is never more than a feather, and it needs at least two, *amon*, to make a Wing."

Afterword

There is a sense in which questions deliberately left un-answered at the end of a text are, by that token, *essentially* unanswered, and thus beyond the grasp, if not the reach, of inquiry—but the temptation to address them remains strong nevertheless. The question of what Geneviève mans by "radioactive aviation" and how her new engine actually works is presumably unanswered because Jean Richepin simply did not know and could not come up with anything that might look like a plausible explanation; the hints given in the text are not only vague and murky but rather inconsistent. There is, how-ever, no harm in trying to cast a little light into that obscurity with the aid of hindsight.

The hints given in the opening sequence of the novel, re-lating to the abolition of weight by using the tangential effects of rapid rotation to neutralize gravitational attraction, are sug-gestive of some kind of antigravity device, but we hear no more of that. Some of the subsequent jargon refers to the po-tential exploitation of "telluric currents," but the meaning of that phrase seems somewhat elastic; initially it seems to refer to induced currents derivative of the Earth's magnetic field, but in the final chapter that meaning seems to broaden out to embrace physical currents at sea and in the air, and seismic "currents"—although it is possible that Richepin is implying an underlying electromagnetic causality to all those phenome-na, just as he does to the psychic phenomena of telepathy and eroticism. What does seem to be clear, however, is that the alerion's engine is triggered and controlled by some kind of radio broadcast sent from a ground-station, and that the engine is enabled by that transmission to draw power from its envi-ronment, in a fashion dependent on ambient conditions.

The term "radioactive" inevitably suggests the unleash-ing of atomic power to the modern eye, and it seems probable, given that Richepin seems to have at least glanced at Gustave le Bon's *L'Évolution de la matière* (1905), that he construes it the same way. It seems likely, therefore, that what the alerion is drawing from its immediate environment is the power of atomic disintegration, activated by means of the radio signals transmitted from the ground. Given the title of Gasguin's second paper, whose specific subject is the wireless transmission of force, and given that the theory has already been tested in one application, it might be the case that the ground-station is actually transmitting the motive power (a notion used in other scientific romances of the period), but nothing in the text suggests a specific link between the alerion and that paper.

However the alerion's power is derived, the question of how that power is then adapted to achieve flight is also unclear. It would be presuming too much to envisage some kind of rocket, but it might be permissible, in spite of the silence of the later text with respect to what was said at the beginning, that some kind of weight-nullification is involved, removing the necessity for lift-providing wings. The general tenor of the text, in addition to its evocations of "telluric currents," suggests that some kind of magnetic, or quasi-magnetic, propulsion might be involved, and nullification of the craft's weight would certainly make it more easily movable by means of energy derived from the Earth's magnetic field or other ambient natural forces.

There is one corollary to this question that is slightly intriguing, and that is the issue of why Geneviève became frightened by the prospect of completing her research on the alerion, only being able resume work on it by courtesy of Joson's moral support. If the internal chronology deduced from the various footnoted hints is correct, then Geneviève is unlikely to have read *L'Évolution de la matière* herself at that stage in the story, and therefore could not have read the wry prediction made by Le Bon—in a passage that made a significant impression on more than one French writer of speculative fiction—that the first person to solve the problem of releasing the energy locked up in atoms more rapidly than the slow natural trickle recently revealed by the discovery of radium would undoubtedly advertize that discovery by blowing himself (or herself) up. She is, however, equipped with psychic powers, and might well have been able to attain a similar prophetic anxiety on her own account.

If the indications of the various psychic powers distributed in the plot are reliable, however—and Richepin does not seem to want us to doubt the destiny implicit in the blood of the Hescheboix—then any such explosions will not prevent the advent of the alerion and its power-source from bringing about the revolution in human affairs whose Messiah (seemingly in a slightly more-than-merely-metaphorical sense) Geneviève-Joson is. Obviously, the New Age in question is dawning in a world parallel to our own deprived history, in which no fateful invasion of Thiérache by nomads from Central Asia ever occurred, and the alerion therefore remained undiscovered (and probably, we ought to admit, undiscoverable).

If the possible direct relevance of the subject-matter of Gasguin's second paper to the alerion remains unclear, there is no doubt at all about that paper's provision of the basis for "electrical fertilization," which is explicitly stated. It is specifically stated, too, that the effects of the broadcast power take effect via some kind of electrolytic process—which is to say, a chemical process triggered by electricity. Logically, that process must produce water, which is, by definition, what arid soils lack. If the water in question were derived from the atmosphere, the technique would be of limited use in real deserts—though not, perhaps, in the Crau—so the likelier contingency is that the reaction takes place within the soil, releasing water from some inorganic source of hydrogen and oxygen. Exactly how that might be achieved is unclear, but given that it can, in the parallel world of the novel, it seems not improbable that some similar kind of electrolysis—perhaps producing hydrogen rather than water—might be involved in the operation of the alerion. Either way, one might expect the general method to have many other transformative applications in addition to electrical fertilization, perhaps of a range greater than the alchemists of old ever dared to dream: the dawn of a New Age in no uncertain terms, and something else that the physics of our own world has forbidden to us.

There are, of course, other questions left unanswered in the text, but they are less interesting in terms of the potential speculations they invite, and there is probably only one that warrants further comment: Did Joson kill his father? Presumably, we need not wonder whether his father really was his father, given his mother's character and the apparent effects of heredity, in spite of what the local story-tellers hinted, so we may take it for granted that, if he had had a hand in Comte Adrian's death, it really would have been a parricidal hand. Given that the devout Joson evidently thinks, however, while contemplating suicide, that he will only be damned if he pulls the trigger, we may surely deduce that he is not carrying any substantial burden of guilt in his conscience. The answer, therefore, is surely no—that Comte Adrian's death really was a bizarre accident, brought about by his own carelessness. It is not obvious why the notional author takes so much trouble to imply otherwise, but he might simply be jealous of Joson's virtue.

We readers should, at any rate, be glad that we can be quite sure, in spite of the notional author's snide hints, of Joson's innocence of murder; otherwise, Geneviève and Joson's joint endeavor, driven by their alloyed soul, would have been tainted with an original sin considerably more serious than taking a bite out of an illicitly-picked apple—and what kind of augury would that be for the dawning New Age? Who among us, after all, could take any pleasure from the suspicion that the world within the text might end up as catastrophically damned as our own shabby Hand-Me-Down Age, in which all we have in our hour of need is half a *hirondelle*?

318

SF & FANTASY

Henri Allorge. *The Great Cataclysm*
Guy d'Armen. *Doc Ardan: The City of Gold and Lepers*
G.-J. Arnaud. *The Ice Company*
Cyprien Bérard. *The Vampire Lord Ruthwen*
Aloysius Bertrand. *Gaspard de la Nuit*
Richard Bessière. *The Gardens of the Apocalypse*
Albert Bleunard. *Ever Smaller*
Félix Bodin. *The Novel of the Future*
Alphonse Brown. *City of Glass*
André Caroff. *The Terror of Madame Atomos; Miss Atomos; The Return of Madame Atomos*
Félicien Champsaur. *The Human Arrow*
Didier de Chousy. *Ignis*
Captain Danrit. *Undersea Odyssey*
C. I. Defontenay. *Star (Psi Cassiopeia)*
Charles Derennes. *The People of the Pole*
Georges Dodds (anthologist). *The Missing Link*
Harry Dickson. *The Heir of Dracula*
Jules Dornay. *Lord Ruthven Begins*
Sâr Dubnotal *vs. Jack the Ripper*
Alexandre Dumas. *The Return of Lord Ruthven*
Renée Dunan. *Baal*
J.-C. Dunyach. *The Night Orchid; The Thieves of Silence*
Henri Duvernois. *The Man Who Found Himself*
Achille Eyraud. *Voyage to Venus*
Henri Falk. *The Age of Lead*
Paul Féval. *Anne of the Isles; Knightshade; Revenants; Vampire City; The Vampire Countess; The Wandering Jew's Daughter*
Paul Féval, *fils. Felifax, the Tiger-Man*
Charles de Fieux. *Lamékis*
Arnould Galopin. *Doctor Omega; Doctor Omega & The Shadowmen*
G.L. Gick. *Harry Dickson and the Werewolf of Rutherford Grange*
Nathalie Henneberg. *The Green Gods*
V. Hugo, P. Foucher & P. Meurice. *The Hunchback of Notre-Dame*
Michel Jeury. *Chronolysis*
Octave Joncquel & Théo Varlet. *The Martian Epic*
Gérard Klein. *The Mote in Time's Eye*
Jean de La Hire. *Enter the Nyctalope; The Nyctalope on Mars; The Nyctalope vs. Lucifer; The Nyctalope Steps In*
Etienne-Léon de Lamothe-Langon. *The Virgin Vampire*

André Laurie. *Spiridon*
Gabriel de Lautrec. *The Vengeance of the Oval Portrait*
Georges Le Faure & Henri de Graffigny. *The Extraordinary Adventures of a Russian Scientist Across the Solar System* (2 vols.)
Gustave Le Rouge. *The Vampires of Mars*
Jules Lermina. *Mysteryville; Panic in Paris; To-Ho and the Gold Destroyers; The Secret of Zippelius*
Jean-Marc & Randy Lofficier. *Edgar Allan Poe on Mars; The Katrina Protocol; Pacifica; Robonocchio; Tales of the Shadowmen 1-7*
Xavier Mauméjean. *The League of Heroes*
José Moselli. *Illa's End*
John-Antoine Nau. *Enemy Force*
Marie Nizet. *Captain Vampire*
C. Nodier, A. Beraud & Toussaint-Merle. *Frankenstein*
Henri de Parville. *An Inhabitant of the Planet Mars*
J. Polidori, C. Nodier, E. Scribe. *Lord Ruthven the Vampire*
P.-A. Ponson du Terrail. *The Vampire and the Devil's Son*
Maurice Renard. *The Blue Peril; Doctor Lerne; The Doctored Man; A Man Among the Microbes; The Master of Light*
Jean Richepin. *The Wing*
Albert Robida. *The Adventures of Saturnin Farandoul; The Clock of the Centuries; Chalet in the Sky*
J.-H. Rosny Aîné. *Helgvor of the Blue River; The Givreuse Enigma; The Mysterious Force; The Navigators of Space; Vamireh; The World of the Variants; The Young Vampire*
Marcel Rouff. *Journey to the Inverted World*
Han Ryner. *The Superhumans*
Brian Stableford. *The New Faust at the Tragicomique; The Empire of the Necromancers (The Shadow of Frankenstein; Frankenstein and the Vampire Countess; Frankenstein in London); Sherlock Holmes & The Vampires of Eternity; The Stones of Camelot; The Wayward Muse.* (anthologist) *The Germans on Venus; News from the Moon; The Supreme Progress; The World Above the World*
Jacques Spitz. *The Eye of Purgatory*
Kurt Steiner. *Ortog*
Eugène Thébault. *Radio-Terror*
C.-F. Tiphaigne de La Roche. *Amilec*
Théo Varlet. *The Xenobiotic Invasion*
Paul Vibert. *The Mysterious Fluid*
Villiers de l'Isle-Adam. *The Scaffold; The Vampire Soul*
Philippe Ward. *Artahe*

Philippe Ward & Sylvie Miller. *The Song of Montségur*

MYSTERIES & THRILLERS
M. Allain & P. Souvestre. *The Daughter of Fantômas*
A. Anicet-Bourgeois, Lucien Dabril. *Rocambole*
A. Bisson & G. Livet. *Nick Carter vs. Fantômas*
V. Darlay & H. de Gorsse. *Lupin vs. Holmes: The Stage Play*
Paul Féval. *Gentlemen of the Night; John Devil; The Black Coats ('Salem Street; The Invisible Weapon; The Parisian Jungle; The Companions of the Treasure; Heart of Steel; The Cadet Gang; The Sword-Swallower)*
Emile Gaboriau. *Monsieur Lecoq*
Steve Leadley. *Sherlock Holmes: The Circle of Blood*
Maurice Leblanc. *Arsène Lupin vs. Countess Cagliostro; Lupin vs. Holmes (The Blonde Phantom; The Hollow Needle)*
Gaston Leroux. *Chéri-Bibi; The Phantom of the Opera; Rouletabille & the Mystery of the Yellow Room*
William Patrick Maynard. *The Terror of Fu Manchu*
Frank J. Morlock. *Sherlock Holmes: The Grand Horizontals; Sherlock Holmes vs Jack the Ripper*
P. de Wattyne & Y. Walter. *Sherlock Holmes vs. Fantômas*
David White. *Fantômas in America*

SCREENPLAYS
Mike Baron. *The Iron Triangle*
Emma Bull & Will Shetterly. *Nightspeeder; War for the Oaks*
Gerry Conway & Roy Thomas. *Doc Dynamo*
Steve Englehart. *Majorca*
James Hudnall. *The Devastator*
Jean-Marc & Randy Lofficier. *Royal Flush*
J.-M. & R. Lofficier & Marc Agapit. *Despair*
Andrew Paquette. *Peripheral Vision*
R. Thomas, J. Hendler & L. Sprague de Camp. *Rivers of Time*

NON-FICTION
Stephen R. Bissette. *Blur 1-5; Green Mountain Cinema 1; Teen Angels & New Mutants*
Win Scott Eckert. *Crossovers* (2 vols.)
Jean-Marc & Randy Lofficier. *Shadowmen* (2 vols.)
Randy Lofficier. *Over Here*

HEXAGON COMICS

Franco Frescura & Luciano Bernasconi. *Wampus*
Franco Frescura & Giorgio Trevisan. *CLASH*
L. Bernasconi, J.-M. Lofficier & Juan Roncagliolo Berger. *Phenix*
Claude Legrand, J.-M. Lofficier & L. Bernasconi. *Kabur*
Franco Oneta. *Zembla*
L. Buffolente, Lofficier & J.-J. Dzialowski. *Strangers: Homicron*
Danilo Grossi. *Strangers: Jaydee*
Claude Legrand & Luciano Bernasconi. *Strangers: Starlock*

ART BOOKS

Jean-Pierre Normand. *Science Fiction Illustrations*
Raven Okeefe. *Raven's L'il Critters*
Randy Lofficier & Raven OKeefe. *If Your Possum Go Daylight...*
Daniele Serra. *Illusions*